COVE

Awakening

– ROBERT OLIVER –

COVENANT Book 1 - Awakening

ISBN 978-1-908374-01-1

First published 2011 by Impressions Print & Publish

Printed and bound in Great Britain by

Impressions Print & Publish
93 High Street Somersham
Cambridgeshire PE28 3EE
Telephone: 01487 843311

'In the sixteenth century there was a French philosopher
by the name of Nostradamus
who prophesised that in the late 20th Century
an Angel of Death shall waste this land'

'A holocaust the likes of which
this planet has never seen
Now I ask you
Do you believe this to be True?'

Philip Parris Lynott
1949 - 1986

Acknowledgements

Covenant is a work of fiction. However it draws on many genuine historical and cultural sources. The author would like to acknowledge that this work is for entertainment, and whilst there is painstaking care paid to historical detail and times, now and then a fact has been stretched or a truth bent for the sake of the story. I have paid particular attention to survivor evidence from the holocaust and testimony from soldiers who fought at Bastogne in the battle of the Bulge. Thanks are due to the many authors of fact and fiction that have fuelled my imagination over the last 20 years. Special thanks are due to Martin Gilbert and Antony Beevor for their magical gift of writing history. Thanks also to Henry Lincoln Richard Leigh and Michael Baigent for awakening my urge to imagine. Thank you Christopher Knight and Robert Lomas for introducing me to Du Mollay. And ultimately to Abbe Saunier and a little village in the Languedoc. I wrote this book on a whim in 1996/7 and it has sat in my den all these years begging to be completed. I'm not sure that I could ever go back to finish because of what it meant at the time and all these years later I've decided to publish it in its unpolished state. Someone once told me that you write your first book for love and wait on the advance for the second! My motivations for telling this story and my belief in fate have never waned. So for the one who knows.....

This book is dedicated to my mother – you gave me the love of reading.

Prologue

Simon who was Peter returned as it had begun to get dark, he had to work quickly, he and his men had only three hours before the dawn of the Sabbath.

He hoped that the Nazarene hadn't suffered, he hoped the mixture of gall and the potion that was concocted had been enough to convince the Sanhedrin and the Romans of his death. He'd been forced to bribe the guard to break the legs of both of the men on the other two crosses to convince the centurion that they were in fact dead. He'd hoped the skewering of the Nazarene didn't spoil everything; Peter hadn't contemplated that a centurion would vent his frustration at his share of the casting of lots by using his spear so savagely.

They carried the Nazarene to the tomb provided by his brother James. Mary of the Magdalene was already there along with the physician,

'Are you sure that the potion will work?' whispered the Magdalene

The physician didn't speak; he was busy swathing the wound in the side of the Nazarene.

'You must hurry, we must get him away from here before light alive or dead!' said Peter

The physician stood back and whispered

'He is alive', take the shroud and cover him, I don't want to know where you are taking him'

Peter removed the body from the tomb.

'If they think he is the one, we will be safe'.

Chapter 1

It was happening again, every time they gathered to worship, the infernal din of noise made by the Hasmonean gentiles pervaded their every sense. Alexander was beside himself with rage but knew that to react was exactly the opportunity the braver of the Hasmoneans were looking for to arrest him. He was a 'Taxo' or leader of his people and the decision that he was being forced to make would he hoped bring salvation to his people and end the earthly suffering at the hands of the gentile.

The Essene believed that the reign of their King would be established through great destruction of men and nations and the final day would bring an end to the reign of the unworthy One. The Holy Habitation that was kept in the inner sanctum of the temple was put in a sepulcher and made ready for the journey.

Their leader, the one called Alexander was an 'Essene' a name derived from the Syriac for 'holy one'. He was born to into the family that swore to protect the inner sanctum of the temple and his people, they were 'his people' born into and pro created from within his holy family. He had reached the decision to leave what he considered to be his rightful place because in his eyes the core of his people's belief had become flawed in the eyes of the great one because of the insistence of the Hasmonean priests in berating and challenging their way, making it impossible for he and his people to honour the days of sacrifice.

He knew that if the Hasmonean found out about his plans to leave him and his people would be in grave danger of being enslaved. Andrew himself had told their chief priest of their destiny.............

'The Heavenly one will arise from His royal throne,
And he will go forth from His Holy Habitation
With Indignation and wrath on account of His sons
For the Most High will arise, the Eternal one alone
And HE will appear to punish the Gentiles.
And he will destroy all idols
And then my children shall be happy.

When it was decided that they were to vacate the temple, 12 men were taken into the sanctum and blessed by Alexander ... they were told that the mission that they had was of divine importance and that the sacrifice that they were about to make would ensure their status in the afterlife. Alexander himself, under pain of death had been told he was never to utter the secret that he carried, he was the only person who knew of the origin, his bloodline had carried the burden for the previous 2000 years and he himself had undergone the seven trials of truth before he accepted the 'way'.

Alexander was about to break the vow, he needed his 12 strongest men to spirit the holy sepulcher away from the temple to a location that only he and the 12 would know... they made ready to leave under cover of darkness... they prayed and then Alexander summoned them one at a time to the anti chamber and ... one by one ...he cut out their tongues ......

Alexander led his people away the next evening, following the path of the chosen, the place he had picked was deep in the wilderness at a place called Qumran, close to the sea of the dead. He had told the 12 exactly what to do, when he arrived, all the preparations were in place. Alexander sealed the Holy Sepulcher in stone.... Never to be uncovered by anyone other than the one who would follow him.

He himself when he was sure that there was no trace of the place went back to the camp, called his people together and told them to make ready for their final journey, they were to place all of their Talmud and scrolls in places that he had identified, he went to the scribes that were had been working for the last two years on his testimony and asked them whether they were ready.... They were confused ... why did he want them to put that work in with the people's accounts.... They were not true, in fact, Gabriel, the youngest of the Essene, could not comprehend the reasoning... Alexander had instructed him to write about his chosen one and how when he had impregnated her, instead of her going with the other women to be cared for until the child was born.... He had been forced into writing that she went and lived in Nazareth with a man called Joseph... he did not know anyone called Joseph and as for Nazareth... Where was this place?

Alexander was adamant, he told him that his fate had been foretold and that one day his writing would protect them.

When all the scrolls were collected, he instructed them to be cut up and put in the caves above the camp, in the spaces that had been made. He went up when this was finished and closed the cave, safe in the knowledge that the Holy Sepulcher was on the other side of the mountain and 'safe'.

He went down the mountain and summonsed his people for prayer, when they were gathered, he blessed them and invited them to break the bread as they had always done. He told them that they would sleep after their long and arduous journey... as they started to feel the effect of the drugged bread and fall into sleep....... Alexander once again summonsed the 12 and instructed them to move amongst the people and kill those who were not already dead. When this was done, a huge funeral pyre was made and the children of the Essene perished.

Alexander and the 12 then went to the top of the mounto n where Alexander took out a piece of scroll and prayed abo the coming of the 'one' who would awaken the 'Essene' an arry on the bloodline.

is the branch

'I shall be the father and he shall be my son er of the law to of my forefather who shall arise with the inte rule in Zion at the end of time'

d wrapped it around

Alexander tore the cloth into five pi send the Essene to the five of the daggers that the 12 had per scrolls, placed in boxes afterlife, all were placed in separ act was to forewarn of the and sunk into the earth ... left that place and walked off power... he and his 12 'di into the desert, Alexander had planned his task with precision and each of the 'disciples' put their hands into the bags that each of them carried and then lay down. The bags that fell to the ground spilled open and the asps moved quickly across the sand, the poison from the bite already working on the disciples. When Alexander completed the coup de grace, he rolled the bodies into the pit that had been prepared and hovered at the lip of it, he was sure the carrion of the desert would make short work of the bodies and taking his sword, he cried out for the forsaken before falling on his sword and tumbling into the pit.

It was dusk; the impending curtain of darkness was chasing away the last protest of the day's sun. One single star, high in the sky, winked mockingly. A light wind rustled the trees away to the left perimeter of the garden, other than that everything was quiet, deathly quiet, expectant. The majesty of the house surrendered its shadow and for a while it was very difficult for him to concentrate his vision on the front door.

He'd lain in the shallow hide that had been prepared for him just the way that he had instructed for almost 24 hours. He eased his body slightly forward and refocused the sighting crosshairs. The Lee Enfield rifle had served him well, this was his 18th or would it be his 19th, not that it mattered now, all that had to be done would be done and he would leave like he had arrived, invisibly. He smiled inwardly to himself; soon it would be over.

Adam Carter sat in the back of his father's car. They had been met at the station by Potter who had driven them out of the hustle and bustle of the city and into the quietness of the Surrey countryside heading for the family home, on the outskirts of the village of Camberly. His father hadn't spoken to him for hours and had sat staring out of the passenger window.

His father, Sir Charles Carter was a serving officer in the British Army; a colonel in the Hussars, Adam didn't really have any interest in the army. His life was in Scotland, a boarding student at Gordonstoun School.

'Make a man of you, it will' said his father 'my father told me the same'.

Adam hated the school and everything about it. He couldn't tell his father about the bullying and the fact that he spent most of his free time on his own. To admit that would be a sign of weakness. When his father had been told of his son's most recent illness, he'd travelled to the school immediately, raising a rumpus upon being told that his son was 'weak' and it was thought he would best recover in more familiar surroundings. Adam was happy enough; there was only

Wakenshaw and his wife in the house to worry about. Potter and his family lived in the gate lodge and he very rarely saw them. Adam liked Wakenshaw and contented himself as they turned off the road and towards the gates of the house, that he might be able to get Wakenshaw to spend some time with him tomorrow when his father returned to London.

The hidden man was completely alert, his breathing had slowed and a sheen of perspiration clung to his forehead. He ventured a glance at his wristwatch. Four minutes past seven. He'd seen the lights go on, lighting up the approach to the house and had watched as a older man had opened the front door of the house sending light cascading out onto the gravel, a natural field of fire.

'Dishonour the oath, die as you deserve' he murmured, his lips curled with irony.

He heard the car before he saw it and watched as the headlights swept an arc across the broad manicured lawns and transfixed the water nymph perched on the top of the fountain in a burst of unexpected light. He readjusted his position and checked the sighting one last time before taking a position to the left of the door, the car had now started its final swing into the space at the front of the house. The old man was standing at the door, ramrod straight and holding a red tartan blanket in his hand. He could hear the tyres crunching through the loose stones as it came to a halt. His breathing quickened as the cross hairs picked out the driver getting out of the seat and scurrying around to the passenger door. He watched as the door opened and Sir Henry got out and stood at the door whilst a boy half stumbled onto the gravel. His finger curled around the trigger, he caressed the well-worn metal and steeled his finger along the shaft of the magazine and fired.

Sir Charles Carter fell forward and hit the ground, Wakenshaw ran around the car and pushed Adam to the ground. Adam reached out and touched his father's outstretched hand.

'They must not succeed' whispered Sir Charles 'they m not...

Charles Carter breathed his last.

The funeral of Sir Charles Carter was a typically military affair. It passed Adam in a daze of misgivings; he was oblivious to all of the chastened looks and attempts to comfort him by telling him to 'stiffen up' and 'be a man'. Unsure of what was going to happen next, all he knew was that provision has been made for him to return to school until the will and testament of his father had been read. He'd stayed with his father's body at the front of the house until the Police had arrived; He'd remained in his rooms as faceless men came and went, Wakenshaw comforted him when he asked questions

'It'll be all right, you'll see' Wakenshaw reassured him.

'I'm not going back, Wakenshaw' cried Adam.

'You'll make yourself sick again, we'll see what happens'. Wakenshaw pondered the quandary that a boy of eleven found himself in, he had no parents now and his only blood relative lived in Europe somewhere. Of course he, Wakenshaw would do anything he could do to help but looking at Adam; all he felt was pity.

He returned home to the house after the funeral. As he wandered through the hall, he noticed that the door of his father's private study was open. He'd never been in there before, never allowed. He glanced furtively across to at the door where Wakenshaw had his quarters and seeing no one, darted into the room and closed over the door. He stood with his back to the door and quickly swept his eyes around the room. There was a large portrait of a woman on one of the walls, she was dressed in black and Adam could have sworn that her eyes were boring into him. A large bookcase ran the length of the far wall and facing him were framed photographs of soldiers and officers. His father's gun straddled the fireplace and his desk and chair faced towards the French windows that commanded a magnificent view of the well-manicured gardens.

Adam went over towards the desk and walked around it once. He then sat down in the chair and looked at the pictures on the desk. There was a photograph of his father standing beside a woman, Adam picked up the photograph and looked at it. The woman was the same as the one in the portrait, could it be his mother? Adam wondered as he replaced the frame, his eye catching a glimpse of an old style-firing pistol that was sitting on the desk. He lifted it and marveling at the intricate markings and magnificent inlaid handle, aimed the gun at the windows. All at once, the sight of his father falling back onto the ground, a pool of blood spreading like a red carpet made Adam stifle a cry as he dropped the gun, it hit the desk and a drawer shot out from the bridge of the desk.

Adam jumped back in horror and for a few heart-rending minutes, he held his breath, half-expecting Wakenshaw to come thundering into the room and discover his disobedience. When no-body came he went back towards the desk and saw a funny shaped casket lying in the concealed drawer

He opened it again and peered inside, there was a funny looking object, like an upside down sundial and a smaller package. There was also a very old long bladed knife in the box as well. He lifted the smaller package out on to the desk. There was a letter with his name on it. He put the package back and closed the box and put the letter into his trouser pocket and closed the desk, crept out of the room and went back up to his own room. He sat down on the bed, and took out the letter. He held it in his hand as thoughts of his father came flooding back into his head. He looked at the handwriting and turned the letter over in his hands before finally carefully opening the flap and taking the page out of the envelope.

Dear Adam
If you're reading this letter then something has happened and Wakenshaw has followed my instructions

Wakenshaw! ,

He was downstairs in the kitchen. Adam rushed over to the door and opened it and listened for any sign of Wakenshaw. He saw him come out of his father's room and as he stepped back, Wakenshaw called out just as Adam hastily closed his bedroom door

'Master Adam!'

Wakenshaw walked up the stairs and into Adam's room. He saw the letter on the bed and said

'You've been in your father's room!'

Adam shrank back; he had never seen Wakenshaw so angry.

'How did you find it?'

Adam relayed the story of his discovery and pointed at the letter.

'I'll leave you in peace to read your father's wishes' said a more mellowed Wakenshaw 'I'll be downstairs if you need me but I must warn you that I cannot answer any of your questions about your discovery, that is MY legacy to your father's memory'

Wakenshaw got up and left the room.

Adam reopened the page

There are things that I have done in my life that I am not proud off and the main one was not telling you that I loved you very much. I cannot dictate what will happen now, Wakenshaw has instructions with regard to your welfare and schooling and provision has been made for him and his wife to retain the house and stay in it until you decide what you wish to do with it.
When you reach the age of 21, your life may change. If it does then I apologise for any hurt I've caused you. Believe me when I tell you that whatever your destiny, you must always ensure that 'They do not succeed'
Your Father
Charles Carter

17 January 1912

Adam sat staring at the letter: it had been written well over a year ago, what did it mean? His destiny and those words again, he'd heard them the night his father had died,

Who must not succeed? What is it all about?

Adam put the letter back in the envelope; he put the letter in a box in his room that he kept trading cards and locked it. He carried the box down the stairs and met Wakenshaw coming from the dining room.

'Can you tell me anything? Asked Adam

'Only that your father suggested that I take care of your letter until you come of age. I will place it and the box from your father's room in safe keeping at the bank' said Wakenshaw

'They must not succeed', that's why my father was killed, wasn't it?

Wakenshaw stiffened, just for a minute

'Your father was one of the most honourable men that I know and he died in protecting honour, some day you will understand'

'Who is the lady in the painting?' asked Adam

'That' said Wakenshaw 'is your mother.'

Adam handed the letter to Wakenshaw and they both walked to the front door; Wakenshaw opened it as Adam glanced over at the spot where his father had lain. He stifled a sob as Wakenshaw put his hand on Adam's shoulder and guided him out of the house and down the path towards the gate.

Chapter 2

For 40 days he moved among them, telling them of his fate, how could this be so? They had all seen him die on the cross, ridiculed by the Romans and shunned by 'his' people.

'Save yourself if you are the one' screamed the crowd and went away laughing as he called for his father. When it was over, Joseph of Arimathea and two other disciples took him down and removed him to the place where he was to be laid. When the Magdalene summonsed them the next morning, their incredulity was stifled by their panic. Suppose they were blamed for hiding the body in order for the prophecy to appear to be true. Was the Nazarene indeed the 'chosen one' as foretold in the scripture, if so why did he leave them so soon, if not, where was the one that could help them now.

Peter was angry; he had still not come to terms with his denial and was committed to protecting out the truth. He had questioned the woman from Magdalene but was suspicious that she knew more than she was telling. His anger had stemmed from the fact that he had done all that was asked him and had even arranged for the physician to be silenced. He was even prepared to deliver the 'gospel' as he had been instructed but he needed more in order for him to perjure himself on the scale that he was about to undertake.

He had yet to 'see' him but James and John had talked about walking in the light and Iesus, talking to them. He wasn't there when Thomas claimed to have felt his wounds but he knew enough to know that they were doomed if they tried to distance themselves from his teaching. They couldn't just go back to being fishermen and tax collectors, no, the Nazarene had put them on a path and

Peter knew he had to follow, to see if the time had indeed come for the kingdom of Israel to be restored.

There was also the question of the messages he was receiving as he slept in his bed at night compelling him to praise the Nazarene as the true son of God, that was what he was told to believe, why was he doubted so, the conflict of the agreement that he had made with the Nazarene and the other man, a man Peter did not know, a man who kept his face covered when he spoke.

He was so sure of his following initially, hadn't he been on the Mount of Olives and seen the light from heaven, he had been given the message to go forth and spread the good news. He returned from that place to Jerusalem along with the other 10. He was sure that the role that Judas had been given would become clear even though he couldn't understand why the Nazarene had to be 'betrayed' by one of his own, everybody knew who he was, as for what he was, that was a different story. Peter didn't know that the forces at hand had conveniently announced that Judas couldn't live with his act of betrayal and had committed suicide, whatever Peter's search for the truth, he knew that he'd be dead as quickly as Judas was if he failed to fulfill his role. Judas had been buried outside the walls of the city, he had hanged himself earlier in the day of the death, people said that he kept talking about what was to come, the message had been lost and that they would not succeed.

Peter had been told that the ministry must continue so he sent the 10 off on their way to spread the gospel of the Nazarene and tell the people of the happenings in the city and then baptise them in the name of the Nazarene. He didn't question the granting of tongues to the 10 nor did he question Thomas when he claimed to have removed his doubt, he was the leader now and was expected to deliver the message as agreed.

The crowd was growing restless as Peter came to the front of them; some of them were shouting blasphemies and were encouraged by the Pharisees in the crowd to abuse Peter. He stood, with his hands raised and prayed to his God

'Brothers, no one can deny that the Patriarch David himself is dead and buried, his tomb is still with us. But since he was a

prophet and knew that God had sworn him an oath to make one of his descendants succeed him on the throne, that man is the Nazarene'.

Hearing this the crowd asked what they must do

'You must repent and every one of you must be baptised in his name'.

Many of the crowd rushed forward to comply; this same scene was taking place all over Palestine. Pilate sent for the Sadducees of the temple and said to them

'I crucified this man on your say so as a blasphemer, I released the scoundrel Barrabbas to attack and scourge my patrols and now I am faced with this new problem, just who do these Christians think they are?'

The Sadducees warned Pilate that if he did not persecute these apostles then he would have riots and unrest on his hands. They themselves had warned the apostles never to speak of this so-called 'miracle' again but the one called Peter did not take any notice. They hired brigands to attack gatherings of these Christians but when they were brought before the courts, there was no way to punish them, the Sadducees were losing control and Pilate appeared to be their only chance.

They knew that the apostles all used to meet by common consent in the Portico of Solomon and whilst no one ever joined them, the people were loud in their praise. People had come crowding into the city from all the surrounding towns asking for favours of every kind and claiming miracles as they left.

The high Priest arrived to the place with all of his followers and had all of the apostles arrested. They were taken in front of the Sanhedrin the following morning; the high Priest demanded an explanation. He warned them that they had already received a warning not to preach.

'You have filled Jerusalem with his teaching and seem determined to blame us for the death of the Nazarene.'

Peter stood up and addressed the gathering

'Obedience to God comes before obedience to men'

At that, a Pharisee called Gamaliel stood up and asked that the men be removed. When this was done, he addressed the Sanhedrin and warned them not to take these people lightly. He suggested that if they were left alone they would disperse in the way that some of the other rabble-rousers had dispersed.

'If this movement is of human origin it will break up of its own accord'.

The High Priest, mindful of Gamaleil's status as a doctor of the law, relented but agreed with his priests that attacks and assaults should be organised to assist with the task. He then summonsed the apostles, ordered that they be flogged and warned to desist in their preaching.

The word spread right across the country, the Romans were now crucifying any Christian that was found worshipping their God in public. The Emperor himself had brought Christians to the coliseum and watched them die for their God. There were rumours however that officers in his own army was converts to this God and in some cases were protecting these 'Christians' on pain of their own death, one of the praetorian generals had recently caused a furore in the coliseum by claiming he was wearing the robe of the Nazarene as the lions savaged all around him, he claimed protection from the beasts and they did not touch him, he was crucified and burnt as a challenge to this 'God' and for the pleasure of Caesar.

Despite all of this pain and suffering, people in Cyrene and Alexandria, in Cilicia and Asia were converting to this God despite their apostles and messengers being stoned to death. As quickly as one was killed, another took his or in some cases her place.

There was bitter persecution started against the church, a man known only as Saul led this persecution with great zeal, he wanted the total destruction of the church and went from house to house arresting men and women and committing them to prison. Saul was a very embittered man, at first he had embraced this new cult, he was impressed with the way in which they spread their word and he went forward asking what he must do to join them, he was told to relinquish all of his worldly goods and take the word to the people.

He asked what the word was and was told that it would course through his veins and he would be saved. Saul didn't like being told this and decided to test their belief, he persecuted them at every opportunity, even threatening to slaughter the original apostles and had gone to the high Priest and sworn allegiance to him. The high Priest cultivated his hatred and very soon Saul was as feared by the Christians as Peter was revered.

One day, the high Priest sent for Saul and told him that he was to go to Damascus and purge the city of Christians, he was to bring any that he found back to Jerusalem, if they resisted, he was to slaughter them. Saul arose early the next morning inspected his cadre and set out for the long journey to Damascus. On the second day of the journey, the group had made camp for the evening and Saul was in his tent when he heard a disturbance outside. One of his men came forward; he had with him a woman.

'She claims to be the Magdalene' said the guard. Saul dismissed him and led the woman into the tent.

'Who are you' he commanded.

'My name' replied the woman 'is Mary and I am of Magdalene'

'You were with the Nazarene' exclaimed Saul

'Yes' replied Mary 'and he has to know why you persecute him so?

Just as Saul was about to strike her for her insolence, he became aware of a bright and shining blue like light radiating from the woman, he looked at her and she spoke in a voice like no other voice he had ever heard

'Do you know what I am'

Saul fell to the floor as the message of the one was relayed to him, he could not see nor speak at that moment. The light disappeared and when he opened his eyes, there was no trace of the light, the woman stood in front of him.

'What must I do?' said Saul

'Go into Damascus and restore your belief by proclaiming the good news of the Nazarene in the house of the disciple called Ananias, he will tell you what to do. You must praise the Nazarene as the true messiah, be filled with the spirit and go forth to the masses and baptise them in the true faith'.

'But' said Saul 'from your own lips you have told me that he is not the one, he is of the Essene but is dead and buried'

'Do not doubt' replied Mary

'You are the instrument chosen to protect the Holy Sepulcher and you must not question your destiny' Go before pagan Kings and tell them of the miracle of the Nazarene, tell of him as the Son of God.

Saul reached Damascus and did as the voice as said. He had allowed the Magdalene to go on her way, before she went she told him of the actual happenings in Jerusalem and why he must fulfill his destiny. Saul approached the house of Ananias and proclaimed the words as he had been told.

The gathered crowd, aware that he was the man who organised the attack in Jerusalem, they expected to see summary justice delivered to these 'Christians'. They saw, instead, a tall strong man with a head and beard of pure white hair stand in their midst and preach

'The Nazarene is the Son of God, repent and be baptised in his name'.

At this, large crowds flocked forward and repented and Saul became a powerful man.

The Chief Priest was furious, he immediately requested a meeting with Pilate to advise him of the treachery of Saul and request that he be hunted down and killed as a danger to Pilate and Rome. The Jewish community in Damascus had already been thrown into confusion by his preaching, so forcefully was he able to demonstrate that the Nazarene was indeed the 'one'. Pilate relented and sent a messenger to Damascus to tell the leader of the garrison to arrest and crucify Saul as a lesson to all the rest of these 'Christians'. He was coming under increasing pressure from Rome to deal with them, whole households in Rome were flocking to secret 'masses' conducted by the one known as Peter and all Rome hunted him.

Saul was in the house of Ananias when the message came that he must leave immediately, a slave in the household of Julius Gauss had overheard the plan to arrest him. Saul was taken to the city walls and was lowered to the ground in a basket, thus making his escape. He headed for Jerusalem and tried to find any of the 10, they would not believe him, they were too afraid. Saul himself was also deeply troubled, he could see the increasing numbers of people turning to his word and believing him. It had got to the stage now, where to denounce the word of the Nazarene would condemn thousands of people to death, he could not understand why he did not tell the truth, he knew that the Nazarene was a messenger, like he was. He knew of a great and noble power to come and rule Zion as the scriptures had foretold.

Would it not be better to greet this redeemer now? Saul struggled with these things as he preached, he preached of the love that the Nazarene had for all men, he went to the Helense and told them of his 'conversion' on the road to Damascus. He begged them to turn away from their denial of time and their foolish attempts to control the calendar, they argued and when Saul returned to the house of James, he was told that his life was in danger and that he would have to go to Caesurae and from there to Tarsus.

There began the ministry of Paul, his chosen name, he spent the next 30 years preaching the false word as he knew it with spectacular results.

He was eventually imprisoned in Rome and was executed in 67 AD. He had succeeded in spreading his message right across the civilised world of the time through his letters and in the reports of the Acts of the Apostles. There was however one letter that was never published, never spoken of, one letter that had been hidden deep in the catacombs of the temple by Paul himself before he left for Rome for the last time, the letter of Paul's testimony of the meeting with the Magdalene and the truth as he had been told.

For now all was safe.

The rain had been falling steadily for nearly two days; an umbrella of grey unyielding cloud covered the whole of the city. Adam Carter had been living in Berlin off and on since 1924, working as a foreign correspondent for the Times in London; he had got the placement more by luck than talent. The only topic on everyone lips in Berlin at the moment was the NSDAP or Nazis and their dynamic leader, a veteran of the Great War who was claiming to be the saviour of Germany.

His name is Adolf Hitler.

At the beginning of World War I he volunteered for service in the Bavarian army. There he proved to be a brave soldier, but was never promoted beyond the rank of a "Gefreiter", because his superior officers didn't believe he would have any qualities in leadership. Shortly before the end of the war in 1918, he was injured by an English gas attack. He lost his eye sight temporally and spent several months in hospital. At the end of war he returned to Munich. He joined the National Socialist German Workers' Party in 1919 and from April of the following year he worked for them on a full time basis. In 1921 he was elected as party chairman, or "Fuehrer ".

Adam had become aware of him in the early days when he first visited Germany, he and some of his friends had spent a few months in Munich as part of their training. One afternoon, returning from another long sitting of the state parliament, Adam had been cajoled into wandering into one of the bierkellars in a salubrious part of the city; it was here that he first heard of Hitler. Adam listened for a while with the rest of the small crowd who had gathered to listen. Adam had a good grasp of the language and was taken by the power of his oratory even if his message was somewhat lost on him. Four or five jugs of beer later, Adam was incapable of speaking let alone remembering anything that Hitler had said.

Hitler however, soon became a key figure in Bavarian politics and he spread his ideas about racial hate and objections to democracy. In November 1923 he led a coup de tat in Munich against the post-war Weimar Republic, proclaiming himself chancellor of a new authoritarian regime. However this putsch failed. He was captured and sentenced to five years imprisonment in Landsberg. During this time he dictated his autobiography "Mein Kampf". Due to a general political amnesty he already was released nine months later and he immediately began rebuilding the Nazi party. Adam had been trying for nearly two months to try and get access to him, as no foreign press had been able to access the man directly. Adam was determined to get his man, he'd already succeeded in getting interviews with party officials Goebbels and Hess and was determined that he would land the biggest scoop of his career to date. He'd learned very quickly that it wasn't what you knew it was who and the 'who' sometimes depended on how you could spread some money around. Adam had plenty of money and wasn't afraid to use it and never let it get in the way of him getting access to supposedly 'closed' party events, hell, he'd even started referring to Berlin as 'home', he hadn't seen Wakenshaw from he'd left his house and the sad memories that it held for him.

After his father's funeral and the discovery of the letter he'd become very unsettled at home. Wakenshaw had convinced him to return and finish his studies and a deal was struck whereby summers would be spent with them in the family house in Camberly. It was here that he stayed, protected and cocooned from the ravages of the First World War.

Both Toby and Jeremiah Wakenshaw had both gone off to fight, Adam recalled the day that the message came to say that Jeremiah had been killed at a place that Adam couldn't pronounce, it was called Ypres or something like that. Toby Wakenshaw was the younger of the two and he left in 1916 when he was a day over his sixteenth birthday, he lied about his age and joined the same regiment that his brother had been in, The Foresters. Toby wrote to Adam as best he could, he wasn't the cleverest boy but Adam liked him because he had befriended him when he was lonely and had shown him all the hides in the house that even his father didn't even know about. He'd even taught him how to shoot a gun like the one that was in his father's study. The first time that Adam fired the gun, he ended up nursing a bruised shoulder for nearly two weeks after it. Toby had left for the war three days after that.

Before he left he'd told Adam

'You'll soon be seventeen, you'll be able to join up and get over to France for the grand finale'. They say the war will be over by Christmas'. It was April 1916.

'Somehow I think your father and school will have something to say about that, exclaimed Adam

After Adam's father's funeral, Wakenshaw had called some of his father's friends and it was arranged that Adam would be able to transfer to the London Oratory and it was there that he met Frederick or rather Freddie Bradshaw.

Freddie Bradshaw had been in and out of three different schools in London, his unruly behaviour and lack of discipline had been his undoing. His father, a publisher, had moved heaven and earth to get Freddie accepted into the Oratory and he started on the same day that Adam Carter arrived to begin his studies. They became firm friends and went through school and university together. Freddie had introduced Adam to his father who subsequently gave him his first job on the newspaper when he graduated. Freddie was working in an accountancy practice in the City. Adam knew that Freddie was only doing this so as to please his father. Freddie had confided to Adam that he wanted to be a pilot and he was taking secret flying lessons at an airfield out at Wembley.

'One day Adam, I am going to take you up in the sky to see what you are missing! It's a damned pity I missed the chance to fly in the War; I'd have showed those Huns a thing or two.

'Freddie, old boy, not on your life' replied Adam 'if God had intended us to fly, he'd have given us wings'

'I've got my sports car, that's the only thing 'I'll be going fast in!

Adam had got the car as a 21st birthday present, well that wasn't actually true, he'd bought himself the car as a 21st birthday present. It transpired that when Adam came of age, he inherited a substantial estate from his father, making him a very wealthy young man. He'd been asked to attend the office of the family solicitor on the day of his birthday and had insisted that Wakenshaw come with him. The solicitor, Mr. Curbishly, outlined the conditions of the inheritance and instructed Adam to sign a series of documents. At the finish of the meeting, Curbishly produced a letter from his safe and handed it to Adam saying

'This is the last wish of your father; I was to give you this on the day of your 21st birthday'

Adam looked at Wakenshaw, hoping for a clue as to what he should do. Adam knew that this letter would refer to his father's death and the one and only conversation that he and Wakenshaw had, on the day that Adam discovered the box. He stood, transfixed, staring at his name written in his father's handwriting, what was inside? What would he find out? Adam was conscious of being watched by both Curbishly and Wakenshaw

'Do any of you know what is written in this letter? Adam asked

Wakenshaw spoke

'That is your father's testimony to you, it is only for you and neither I nor Mr. Curbishly has any idea as to its content'

'In that case' said Adam, ripping the envelope open and gazing at the letter, 'It has a series of letters and numbers and reference to what I think is a safety deposit box'

'Anything else?' asked Wakenshaw

'A note from my father' exclaimed Adam 'marked private and confidential'.

Adam stopped at this point, fondled the letter in his hand and then walked over to Mr Curbishly's desk and lifted the letter opener and carefully slit the letter open. Adam removed the single folded page and opened it and read

'They must not succeed'

Adam shuddered involuntarily in reading the last words of his father to him, he continued reading

21 34 55 43 61 17 95

Mr. Pesotti, Banco Aambrosi ... The letters faded away.

Adam couldn't make out the second word and had no idea what the numbers referred to, he suspected that the bank was his father's private bank, he'd been there a few times in the car with Wakenshaw, they'd know what the numbers would mean. Adam resolved to call them tomorrow and folding the letter he put it back in the envelope and shoved it into the inside pocket of his jacket.

'I'll read it in my own time'. With that, Adam rose and quickly proceeded to the door

'I shan't be home this evening, Wakenshaw, I'll be with Mr. Bradshaw'

'Very well sir, when should we....

The door slammed as Adam bounded down the stairs in search of a telephone to tell Freddie of his good fortune.

'We'll go out and celebrate!' shouted Freddie

'Where will we go?' asked Adam

'It's about time you were introduced to the delights of the West End! exclaimed Freddie

'Meet me at the Savoy at 5.00'

Adam went and got his hair cut and was walking down the Strand towards the hotel when he spotted Freddie and two girls coming walking towards him

‘Adam old boy exclaimed Freddie ‘I want you to meet two of my friends’ Freddie stepped forward and with a most outrageous wink said

‘May I Present Lucy and Megan, ‘I’ve asked them to join us for the evening’.

Adam felt himself blushing as he nodded at the two girls. It was very obvious by the way that she was hanging on to him that Lucy was very interested in Freddie. They walked on ahead towards the hotel as Adam stood, unsure what to do

‘Shouldn’t we go with them?’ asked Megan

‘Of course!’ stammered Adam, by now even more embarrassed as Megan slipped her arm into his.

‘Freddie tells me you work for the Times’ said Megan ‘What sort of a reporter are you?’

Adam stammered again ‘I’ve just started with the paper and well, to tell the truth, I haven’t really written anything yet!

Megan smiled and Adam felt himself warming to this girl, she was different, she didn’t seem that worried that he was a cub reporter. He felt slightly more at ease with her than with any of the others from the usual cadre of women that Freddie seem to have ‘on tap’.

She had black hair, that she wore in a bob was nearly as tall as Adam and was very slim and carried herself well, she had the most magnificent eyes that seemed to have a life of their own and sparkled as she talked. Adam found himself stealing glances at her, foolishly thinking that she didn’t notice.

‘What do you do?’ said Adam

‘I’m studying to be a doctor, I’m currently studying over at Guys at the moment, it’s my first year, it’s really very exciting at the moment. Yesterday I saw my first baby being delivered and the day before I saw my first dead body, I cannot wait to attend an autopsy’ exclaimed Megan

Adam quickly changed the subject and hurried after Freddie into the hotel.

The night was long, by the end of the meal all four of them were very drunk and were attracting disapproving stares from some of the other guests in the restaurant

'Lets get out of here' said Freddie 'I know a great club we can go to

'I can't' said Megan 'I'm on duty early tomorrow' I'll have to go'

Megan stood up and Freddie nudged Adam and eyed him to go.

Adam cleared his throat and said

'I'll see you home if you like?' to Megan

Megan smiled and nodded her head, minutes later they were standing at the door, it was raining heavily and Adam immediately took his coat off and draped it around Megan's shoulders, he walked out onto the street and hailed a cab. They both got in and Megan snuggled into Adam's shoulder and closed her eyes. Megan lived in an apartment in Chelsea and when the cab arrived at the door, Adam jumped out, told the driver to wait and opened Megan's door. She got out and he walked with her to the door

'I'd invite you in' said Megan 'but I really have to rest, perhaps another time?'

'I'd like that' said Adam.

Megan reached up and stroked Adam's face

'I'm really glad to have met you Adam 'she said before kissing him lightly on the lips, she then turned, put the key in the door and went inside.

Adam stood for a moment, transfixed as he touched his face where she had put her hand. He only came to his senses when the Taxi driver sounded his horn. Adam awoke the next morning with the mother of all headaches and Freddie knocking his door. He jumped out of bed and pulled on his robe

'Come in Freddie' called Adam

Freddie entered the room and plonked himself down on the bed

'Well?'

'Well what?' replied Adam

Freddie smirked, 'I didn't hear you come in last night, you must have been late'.

'O.K Adam, she's a very nice girl and we had a wonderful evening

'And you'll see her again?' asked Freddie

'I hope so' mused Adam 'I do hope so'

Freddie rolled off the bed and slapped him on the back. 'Onwards to breakfast, dear chap, let's see what the world throws at us today'

'Wait' said Adam 'I've nothing dry to wear, we, uuuuh I mean I was soaked to the skin last night'

Let's gets these clothes down to my man, he'll have them laundered, I'm sure I have something that will fit you said Freddie. 'Where did you throw your jacket?

Adam stopped

'My jacket?'

Of course, He'd put it around Megan's shoulders when they'd come out of the hotel and she was still wearing it when they got out of the taxi, he ran back down to the taxi when he'd heard the horn, jacket less.

Adam cursed

'Damn, my father's letter was in the jacket!

'Damn'

'Cancel breakfast, Freddie and call me a cab' said Adam 'I've got to get that jacket!

He'd remembered that Megan said that she was working in Guys Hospital; he took the taxi to the front of the hospital, spotted a reception and went over intent in enquiring as to the whereabouts of Dr. Megan? Adam slapped his head, Christ he didn't even know her second name. He found a telephone and placed a call to Freddie

'May I speak with Mr. Bradshaw please?' said Adam

'Hello' answered Freddie

'It's me, said Adam, listen Freddie, what is Megan's surname?

There was a raucous laugh down the phone

'You took a girl home and you didn't find out what her name was! You must have had some have fun, chuckled Freddie.

'It's not like that!' said Adam 'Dammit, Freddie, what's her name?'

'Relax old chap. Her name is Robertson, Megan Robertson, where are you?

'I'm at the hospital, I'll explain later' said Adam and put the telephone down

'Can I speak to Megan Robertson please? Adam asked the receptionist.

'May I say who wishes to speak to her?

'My name is Adam Carter'

Megan came walking across the concourse about five minutes later, she had a quizzical look on her face but when Adam turned around to face her, she gave him a wonderful smile

'Adam, what are you doing here?'

‘I’m sorry to bother you’ stammered Adam. It’s just that I left my jacket with you last evening and there is a letter in it that I need

Don’t worry’ said Megan, I brought it with me this morning, It’s down in the laundry being cleaned…

Megan didn’t get a chance to finish the sentence.

‘Where’s the laundry?

‘It is in the basement, why…

Adam raced towards the stairs with Megan following behind him in total amazement at his behaviour. She’s asked the laundry man to dry the jacket for her intent on calling Adam later on in the day to return it to him.

When she reached the laundry, Adam was standing in the middle of the floor with an absolutely crestfallen look on his face. The laundry man on seeing Megan exclaimed

‘Dr. Robertson! The jacket you asked me to clean this morning, I think it’s been stolen, I’ve called the police and…

Adam’s face paled as he spoke

‘When? How? I must have my jacket; there is something of absolute import…’ Adam’s voice trailed off

The laundry’s man heart skipped a beat. Usually the lost clothing scam netted him and his associate a few pounds and this man’s reaction sounded like there was something really valuable in the coat.

‘I’ve organised a search around the hospital, it was a black jacket sir, wasn’t it?

Adam nodded and stared forlornly at the door of the laundry

‘I’m very sorry ‘said Megan ‘is there anything I can do?’

Adam replied, struggling to hide his panic ‘no, no it will be all right’.

‘The least I can do it get us some tea, we’ll go up to the staff canteen’ smiled Megan

'That would be very nice' said Adam,' he tried to put the business of the letter to the back of his mind by saying to himself

'It'll be alright, Wakenshaw would know what to do'.

When Adam eventually arrived back at his own house, he went straight down to Wakenshaw's quarters and told him what had happened. Wakenshaw paled when Adam told him about the loss of the letter. He rushed over to the telephone and rang Curbishly, to find out if there was a copy but he already knew that he was ringing in vain and he struggled to hide his emotions, the look on his face betraying the shock of the news.

'What's wrong?' whispered Adam.

'There isn't a copy. That was your father's explicit instruction' said Wakenshaw.

'I suspect the contents of that letter would have revealed information that your father wanted you to know. You'll recall that he mentioned it in his letter to you when you opened the box when you were younger.

'Of course! Of course!' exclaimed Adam 'at aged 21, my life may change'

'You'll have found out for yourself now whether it will or not for yourself' said Wakenshaw.

The laundry assistant and his associate met up later that evening in their local pub.

'How much did we get?' asked the laundry man

'The usual' grumbled his associate 'two pounds in change and ten shillings from the rag and bone man'

'What!

The laundry man grabbed his associate by the lapels of his jacket 'I told you about the black jacket... what was inside it?

'I dunno what all your fuss is about' squealed the associate, acutely aware of bad breath turning his stomach, all there was in the pockets were two and sixpence and a tie and a couple of pages in a letter...

'What was in the letter?

The laundry man relaxed his grip.

'How do I know? You know I can't read the best, there was no money or anything like that, I threw it in the fire like I usually do before I went to the rag and bone man'

The laundry man scratched his head and then guffawed...

'It was probably a love letter that he didn't want his girl to find, get me a pint, it's been a long day.'

Chapter 3

'Put my statue in their temple' roared Caligula 'then they'll know who their true God is!

They said Hell was coming, they didn't tell them it would be in the shape of a Roman legion. Barrabas stole down to the gate at the far side of the Western Wall, it was at dusk and there weren't that many people about. He waited for three movements of the dial and then struck the flint on the side of the rock, the lintle flared and he cupped his hand over it, to protect the light, he watched as each of the pre built bonfires spat their flame up into the sky. When it was his turn, he walked over and watched, as his own sparked to life.

He sprang back against the wall, his heart wildly beating in his chest, as he waited for Siomon Ben Gorias, the Zealot leader to come out of the desert and take command of them. By now, those Jews who didn't believe would have had their doors marked with the blood. For it was written

'And then his Kingdom shall appear throughout all his creation
And then Satan shall be no more
And Sorrow shall depart with him…
For the heavenly one shall arise from his Royal throne
And he will go forth from his HOLY SELPULCHRE
And with indignation and wrath on accounts of his sons
The most high will arise, the eternal one
And HE will punish the gentiles
And he will destroy all idols
And thou, children of Andrew, shall be happy

Cestius Gallus had entered Palestine with a strong force of legion and auxiliary troops, he encountered little or no opposition. Now as he watched the fires light up the walls of the city, he called to his Legion commanders and ordered them to make ready.

He retreated to his tent to don his battle colours. He pushed through the flap, dismissed his slave and took a drink from the goblet sitting on the table, he heard a noise and when he spun around to see who had disturbed him, he became conscious of a strange blue light enveloping the space in front of his eyes.

Gallus called his troop commanders and ordered them to make ready to withdraw, they formed up their massed legions and retreated northwards.

Barrabbas watched all of this through disbelieving eyes, at first he thought it was a trick within the Roman battle strategy. Hell was coming and the One would rise to protect them, it said so in the scripture. The Romans simply marched away. The 'taxo' called them all to arms back in the city and then stood them down; they were free to celebrate the victory. They had rebuffed Hell.

'We will pursue Satan and kill him in the desert' said the Taxo the next morning. Barrabas and his men fought in the front of the army and when the battle was done they had killed 6000 Romans. The One prevailed, his people were safe.

Adam started work with the Times in earnest and was proving to be quite a useful cub reporter and everyone at the paper seemed to be very happy with his progress. He'd been rostered to working on the German desk, initially because of the severe lack of manpower and the fact that Germany was not coping very well with the loss of the war and seemed to be spiralling into chaos, something that the Times took great satisfaction in reporting. Adam had filed his first report on the 3 February 1919 and a copy of it was now cut and stuck on the wall beside his desk.

NEW PARTY ENTERS THE GERMAN POLITICAL SCENE.

A new party made its appearance on the already crowded and confused political scene in Munich, the capital city of the young Bavarian republic. The establishment of the German Workers' Party, as the new group called itself, went virtually unnoticed. The formation of new political groupings was hardly unusual in revolutionary Bavaria. A few contemporary observers predict that this party, which lacks a program, an organisational structure, and financial resources, will in the years to come develop into a decisive political force among the Bavarian opponent of the Weimar Republic.

The German Workers' Party claims it will rise above its unprepossessing beginnings because its leader, Adolf Hitler chooses to associate his propagandistic and Organisational talents with the new party. The party is the joint creation of two men, a toolmaker, Anton Drexler, and a journalist, Karl Harrer. Since initially Harrer is the more dominant partner, the earliest political activity of the two men has been organised along lines suggested by him. Harrer seems to prefer a seem-conspiratorial discussion group to a public party as an organizational format. At his insistence membership in the group, the "political working circle," has been restricted to seven.

Adam Carter

Adam continued to see quite a bit of Megan but only when her training permitted. He resisted Freddie's many temptations to stray from the path and sample some of the other women from his 'harem'

'I don't know how you could be bothered, Freddie, what's the point of keeping these women in tow when you've no intention of...

Freddie cut across him 'variety's the spice of life my boy', I'm not like you Adam, its plainly obvious you and Megan are 'together'

Adam felt his face warming as Freddie playfully teased him that she had her eyes on him and would catch him for good.

Freddie qualified as a junior `accountant later that same year but against his father's wishes had joined the Royal Flying Core and was away every weekend training on new aircraft. In late 1919, he flew his first non-stop flight from London up to Glasgow; he telephoned Adam from Glasgow and told him to have the champagne on ice for his return. Adam called Megan and told her of Freddie's flight and the plans to celebrate. Adam admired Freddie; he had a lot to thank him for. His job for one, he was improving in work and had been confirmed as after his probation period was up he would be offered a contracted staff position at the Times. Adam had shown great promise and had been tenaciously following the story that he had first broken earlier that year ... the rise of the new NSDAP party in Germany.

The situation in Germany was becoming increasingly worse; the country as a whole had suffered immensely from the Great War and as a result, political turmoil was the order of the day. It soon became clear to Adam that changes were afoot in the party that he'd been reporting on.

Drexler, the joint founder of the NSDAP, realized that the type of activity and organization that his party had been engaged in did not serve much purpose. Drexler proposed that the Society should establish a political party to publicise the group's political views, and win new members for its cause. Harrer, another founder member, then yielded to the wishes of the majority and on January 5, 1920, the NSDAP was organised initially in Munich but with plans to go nationwide as soon as possible. Adam had gone to his editor and requested that he be allowed to go to Berlin to follow the story first hand as opposed to relying on the wire from the Europe correspondent who was based in Paris.

'I'll pay for my own accommodation' said Adam 'I want to follow this Party story myself'. The editor liked Adam's directness

'You can go out there for a month' he said 'we'll review it then'.

Adam thanked him and rushed out to call Megan and tell her of his news.

Adam's intuition was right to a point, there was something going on in the party circles.

For some time the NSDAP existed largely on paper, while the "political working circle" continued its regular meetings and thus remained the real focal point of early Nazi activities. The NSDAP still had not found the courage to schedule public rallies, both Drexler and his friends invited ever-increasing numbers of potential sympathisers. By August the party was already moderately well known among rightist groups in Munich. It was now able to attract as speakers at its meetings such prominent men as Gottfried Feder, the opponent of "interest slavery," and Dietrich Eckart, at that time publisher of the violently anti-Semitic journal 'Auf gut Deutsch'. Adam maintained and updated a daily log of the happenings in Germany but he was frustrated that he still had no direct firsthand knowledge of the situation and was counting the days to when he would arrive in Berlin on his first 'foreign assignment' He had, however, some personal matters on his mind that he had to resolve before he left for Berlin.

Adam had Freddie to thank for introducing him to Megan in the first place. He was his best friend and Adam was determined to celebrate his friend's flying success with gusto. He'd booked a table at the Savoy, he thought that would be apt and had roped Lucy, Freddie's fiancée, into the celebration plan.

On the night in question, Adam arrived with Lucy, they'd got a big banner made and Adam wanted to make sure that all the plans he had made were in place. They checked everything and Adam called for a drink, the waiter came over and took the order and headed off to the bar. Some other friends had arrived and Adam was talking to one of Freddie's accountant friends when he heard a call from the concierge for him to go to the main reception.

Adam excused himself, set his drink on the table and went out towards the reception area that was located across the hall. He went up to the desk and gave his name; the receptionist gave him a severe look and asked him to step into the manager's office

'Is there something wrong?' asked Adam

Please take a seat in the office Sir' said the receptionist. 'The manager will be with you shortly'

Adam went in and had just sat when the door at the far side of the room opened and the manager walked in, followed by Megan. It was obvious that she had been crying and when she saw Adam she burst into tears again

'Megan! What has happened to you? What is wrong?' shouted Adam

'You'd better sit down, Sir' said the manager 'There's been a terrible accident

'Megan!' said Adam 'Megan!

'He's dead' blurted Megan.

'Dead?' shouted Adam 'Who's dead?

Megan blurted out

'Freddie's dead, he's been killed in a plane crash'

Adam fell back down into the chair, a numbing sensation crashing over him like a wave.

'Freddie dead! How?'

'I was at the hospital when the call came through' said Megan'. 'Apparently there were two planes involved, Freddie was coming into land and a plane taxied right across his runway, he swerved to avoid a collision but in doing so, his plane somersaulted and burst into flames, the rescue services was not able to get near him'

'It can't be Freddie' cried Adam, 'he's being flying now for nearly three years, he's a great pilot' are you sure?' Adam's eyes pleaded with Megan to tell him that there had been a mistake.

'I'm sorry' said Megan 'I'm so sorry'.

Adam sat motionless in the chair and began to weep to himself, Megan came across and tried to comfort him but he pushed her away, he wanted to be on his own. All he saw at the forefront of his mind was his father's body lying on the floor of the house, a crimson stain spreading out on the carpet and then an explosion, a fireball that caused Adam to wince. He composed himself and spoke to the manager.

'The party, I don't...'

'Your lady friend has told them and they've dispersed, she told me to tell you that she had gone back to the hospital to see if she could learn anything, she would call you later. I'm very sorry for your loss and if there is anything I can do' said the manager

'That's very kind of you' said Adam 'perhaps you would arrange a cab for me. I wish to go home now'.

'Of course' said the manager.

Adam didn't see Megan again until the day of the funeral

'I've decided to go Berlin tomorrow' said Adam

'I'd an idea you might do that' said Megan 'It won't be that bad, I've still got four years of internship left to do, we'll still be able to see each other at holidays and other times'

I'd like that very much' replied Adam 'Megan, there is something you should know'

Adam had agonised about what he had to say, he knew he loved Megan but he knew that he had to get away and he knew that pushing Megan away would break his heart. He was somewhat reduced to more tears when he spoke

'You're all I've got now' said Adam 'and one day I hope we'll be together but if you want to do other things or…'

Adam stopped as Megan put her arms around him and whispered in his ear

'You take care for me, I'll be here and ready when you are'.

Adam left for Berlin the next day.

For the next three years Adam threw himself into his work in his new city. Things were beginning to happen at a rapid pace and the undercurrents of unrest and dissatisfaction amongst the people of Berlin and the other major cities in Germany were palpable. Adam presumed that he'd heard the last of the NSDAP, they'd tried to overthrow the regional government of Bavaria in a coup de tat in 1923 that had failed miserably and their leader Adolf Hitler was in jail. He couldn't have known the changes he was about to witness in his new home in the early months of 1924. Adam having his home in Berlin was a celebrated member of the party scene in the city. Megan regularly joined him in Berlin and they had wonderful times together as Adam showed off the city and its nightlife. Adam's editor had confirmed him, as the German correspondent for the paper such was the quality of his work over the previous four years and his celebrated chronicle on Adolf Hitler.

Hitler had joined the then named DAP in September 1919. With his extra-ordinary talents as a public speaker he rose quickly in the party's organizational hierarchy, and by the end of the year he was both chief of propaganda and a member of the executive committee. But Hitler was not content with his rapid promotion. On the contrary, he continued to find a great deal to criticise in the DAP. He was appalled at the inefficient and un-bureaucratic business procedures in the party and he severely attacked the system of intra-party democracy that characterised the internal administration of the DAP. Like most of the groups on the far right, the party took an ambiguous stand on the question of democracy and parliamentarism. While it vehemently opposed the national parliamentary system of the Weimar Republic, the DAP's internal decision-making processes were subject to very elaborate democratic rules.

In December Hitler proposed a thorough reform of the party's organisation. At present, he claimed, the DAP resembled a 'club' more than a political party. As immediate measures to tighten the party's organisational structure, Hitler demanded the dissolution of the organisational bonds between the DAP and the "political working circle" and an increase in the independent decision-making authority of the executive committee.

The DAP's old-line leadership rejected Hitler's ideas at this time, but the proposals indicated a considerable level of political shrewdness on Hitler's part, even at this early date. Unlike his more timid partners in the leadership corps of the party, Hitler had recognised that the DAP as presently constituted had no real political future. Like so many other groups, the DAP understood the "evils" that had led to the collapse of the empire and the establishment of the Republic. The party had even gone one step further and decided to impart its newly acquired knowledge to the public at large, but neither of these activities in any way singled out the DAP from the dozens of extreme rightist groups. The present leadership was content with the status of one among many. It was at this stage that Adam had begun to follow the fortunes of the world war one veteran and he began to build up a file on who exactly this Hitler was.

When Hitler joined the party, the DAP's leadership regarded propaganda activities as ends in themselves. Only Hitler looked upon public rallies as the means to achieve a far

›reater end: the overthrow of the Republic and the seizure of power by the far right. The differing concepts of the party's future were reflected in the divergent organisational paths of Hitler and the old leadership. An organisational structure administered along democratic lines would be able to plan impressive rallies but would be an ineffective conspiratorial instrument. At that moment, however, the gulf that separated the political concepts of Hitler and the old guard was still bridged by their agreement that the party's immediate task was the improvement and expansion of its propaganda activities. They began to actively court the attention of the local press and it was Joseph Goebbels who brought to the attention of Hitler, the fact that the famous Times from England was beginning to take an interest in him and the party. Hitler read the article with interest but disagreed with Goebbels that he should speak with the reporter to wrote it

'I will give him an interview when I have done something that warrants it'

Although the DAP was evolving into a more efficient and bureaucratised organisation, the old leadership continued to reject Hitler's more basic organisational reform proposals. By late spring Hitler became convinced that the DAP would not become a centralised, bureaucratised political party while the old leadership retained its positions of power. The only real change he was able to effect was the change of the name of the party from DAP to NSDAP. If Hitler were to further transform the party into a power-centred instrument of political activity, he would have to go outside the confines of the executive committee.

Two courses of action were open to him. He could attempt to win the approval of the present membership for his ideas and thus force the committee to adopt his scheme. This approach, however, held little promise of success. The newly named NSDAP's still relatively small membership was socially and economically, a very homogeneous body. For the most part the members came from the same social milieu.

Adam loved Berlin; he loved the people and the culture. He continued to send reports back to London on a weekly basis and had been publicly acknowledged for the first time in late 1923 by the managing editor for a piece that he had done, telling the story of the Munich uprising or 'Beer Hall Putsch' as the now newly named NSDAP or Nazis referred to it. He'd gotten the story from one of his party sources and although he still had not spoken to Hitler, he was very aware of what Hitler had achieved in ousting both Harrer and Drexler as party leaders and was in 'de-facto' control of the party. Adam had in fact planned to go to the bier keller in Munich to see for himself what was going to happen but he'd been given the wrong date by his informant and arrived the day after the event and filed the following piece.

A large patriotic gathering met in the Bürgerbräukeller on the evening of 8 November to hear Kahr speak. The Bavarian Prime Minister, the police chief, Colonel von Seisser and other members of the government and officials were present. In the middle of the proceedings Hitler, whose storm-troops had surrounded the hall, burst in, brandishing a revolver. Mounting the rostrum, he fired shots at the ceiling and announced that the governments in Munich and Berlin had been overthrown and that a new 'National Republic' was being formed.

In Bavaria he himself would lead the new regime, with Kahr as Regent and Pöhner as Prime Minister. At Reich level Ludendorff was to be given command of the army with Lossow as Minister of Defence and Seisser as Minister of Police. Temporarily stunned by this irruption, Kahr, Lossow and Seisser retired to a backroom where they agreed, at pistol point, to Hitler's plans.

In the meantime Ludendorff, still a legendary figure, arrived on the scene and, overcoming his surprise, gave Hitler his backing. News of the Putsch was flashed to all wireless stations and appeared in the early morning edition of the Munich newspapers.

But in the course of the night the 'triumvirate', having returned to their offices and learnt that their colleagues were opposed to the whole enterprise, decided not to take any further part in it. News that Seeckt had been given plenary powers by the Reich government influenced their decision. Though Röhm occupied Army Headquarters in Munich, most public buildings remained in the hands of the government. By midday the press carried the news that the Putsch had failed. Ludendorff, apparently unaware of this, and convinced that the army would not oppose a march on Berlin, persuaded Hitler to hold a demonstration in Munich to rally support.

On its way to the Ministry of War in the centre of Munich the procession of 2,000-3,000 Nazis found the way blocked by police. A shot was fired, followed by a hail of bullets, and altogether 19 people (15 Nazis and 3 policemen) lost their lives. Ludendorff, marching at the head of the column, was not fired on, but was taken prisoner. Hitler dragged to the ground when the man next to him was killed, fell and broke a bone in his shoulder. He fled and was captured two days later. Among the other wounded was Göring, the former air ace who had commanded the S.A. since March 1923. He escaped to Austria. Röhm at Army H.Q. capitulated.

Although the two men were not involved in the charge of high treason that faced Hitler, they were both discredited. They had failed to stop Hitler's obvious preparations for the Putsch, and the assertion that their temporary assent to Hitler's plans was only the result of duress was widely disbelieved. Kahr resigned, and Lossow, who had disobeyed his military superiors before the Putsch, was dismissed. Kahr's belief that he could make use of Hitler without destroying his own position was typical of the approach of many conservatives

Adam concluded his report.

The trial of the accused Nazis took place in February and March 1924. Hitler accepted responsibility for what had happened, thus attracting the limelight to himself, but he also drew attention to the share of Kahr, Lossow and Seisser, t embarrassing the judges and influencing them in favour ot leniency. In defending himself he seized the opportunity to make political speeches which were listened to respectfully by a court whose members were openly biased in his favour. His rousing oratory, defiant, not apologetic, was addressed to a wider audience. Adam sat in the court, mesmerised by the power of his oratory. Hitler raised himself up, gripping the dock hand rail so tightly that Adam could see that his fingers were white, he was also conscious of his eyes, staring, penetrative and at one time they locked with Adam's for a fleeting moment causing Adam to involuntary shudder before turning away. Hitler spoke

'The army we have formed is growing from day to day.. I nurse the proud hope that one day the hour will come when these rough companies will grow to battalions, the battalions to regiments' the regiments to divisions, when the old cockade will be taken from the mud, when the old flags will wave again. When there will be reconciliation at that last great divine judgment which we are prepared to face. . . For it is not you, gentlemen, who will pass judgment on us. The eternal court of history speaks that judgement. You may pronounce us guilty a thousand times over, but the goddess of the eternal court of history will smile and tear to shreds the brief of the State Prosecutor and the sentence of this court. For she acquits us'.

Though Hitler was not acquitted by the court that gave him such a sympathetic hearing, its sentence of five years, detention was in the circumstances mild enough; and in the event he served only nine months of it. Even the Bayerischer Kurier complained of the one-sidedness of the trial and described the day on which sentence was passed as a black day for Bavarian justice. In prison Hitler was treated almost as an honoured guest, and given every facility for writing his memoirs. In the nine months in Landsberg fortress, Hitler produced the document that was to prove decisive in dictating the future fate of Germany ....Mein Kampf.

Adam continued to attend the party rallies in Berlin; he was drawn to them like a moth to the flame and like the swelling numbers of ordinary Germans was in many way inebriated by the pomp and in some ways pageantry of these torchlight rallies. Adam had noticed that Hitler had changed the whole tact of his speech making and was now bringing his considerable oratorical power to bear on specific subjects. A more sinister element was the growing claims that the problems that Germany suffered was being caused by international Jewry and that the Jews must be brought to account in the new 'Fatherland'. Adam knew for example that when Hitler talked about the Jews, invariably a Jewish business had its windows broken. In some cases an increasing number of them were being burned. Tonight, as Adam huddled for warmth in the cold of the evening, the topic was the reversal of the treaty of Versailles. This subject brought the manic best out of Hitler as he ranted and raved about its injustice and urged all Germans of the need to rearm and reclaim the position that they enjoyed prior to the First World War.

Amid the swirling mess in Berlin of political intrigue, rumours, and disorder, the SA, the Nazi storm troopers, Hitler's private army stood out as an ominous presence. By the spring, many in the German democratic government came to believe the Brownshirts were about to take over the country by force. Adam's writing reflected this and his filings which up until now had been complimentary to all that the NSDAP had been doing began to reflect the mood of the other political entities as Hitler continued to tale massive liberties with the rule of law.

There were now over 400,000 storm troopers under the leadership of SA Chief Ernst Röhm. Many members of the SA considered that they were to be a true revolutionary army and were anxious to live up to that idea.

Adolf Hitler had to reign them in from time to time so they wouldn't upset his own carefully laid plans to undermine the republic. He'd listened to both Hess and Goring who sensing the mood of the people and the negative press reporting h urged caution.

'We are not yet ready to assume our destiny' cautioned Hess.

Hitler knew he could not succeed as Fuehrer of Germany without the support of existing institutions such as the German Army and the powerful German industrialists, both of whom kept a wary eye on the revolutionary SA.

In April, Heinrich Bruening, Chancellor of Germany, invoked Article 48 of the constitution and issued a decree banning the SA and SS all across Germany. The Nazis were outraged and wanted Hitler to fight the ban. But Hitler, always a step ahead of them all, knew better. He agreed, knowing the republic was on its last legs and that opportunity would soon come along for him. That opportunity came in the form of Kurt von Schleicher, a scheming, ambitious Army officer who had ideas of leading Germany himself. But he made the mistake that would prove fatal, of underestimating Hitler. Schleicher was acquainted with Hitler and had been the one who arraigned for Hitler to meet Hindenburg, a meeting that went poorly for Hitler. Schleicher was also; unbeknown to Hitler, the source of most of Adam Carter's information and the reason why Carter was now the most widely read foreign correspondent and the doyen of the Nazi hierarchy.

On May 8, Schleicher held a secret meeting with Hitler and offered a proposal. The ban on the SA and SS would be lifted, the Reichstag dissolved and new elections called, and Chancellor Bruening would be dumped, if Hitler would support him in a conservative nationalist government.

Hitler agreed.

Schleicher's skilful treachery behind the scenes in Berlin first resulted in the humiliation and ousting of General Wilhelm Groener, a long-time trusted aide to President Hindenburg and friend of the republic. In the Reichstag, Groener, who supported the ban on the SA, took a severe public tongue lashing from Hermann Göring and was hooted and booed by Goebbels and the rest of the Nazis. Adam did his bit as well by giving prominent coverage of the exchange in a filing, including a verbatim quote from Goering.

“We covered him with such catcalls that the whole house began to tremble and shake with laughter. In the end one could only have pity for him.’

Groener was pressured by Schleicher to resign. He appealed without success to Hindenburg and wound up resigning on May 13. Schleicher’s next target was Chancellor Bruening. Heinrich Bruening was one of the last men in Germany who was capable of standing up to Hitler with the best interest of the people at heart. He was responsible for getting Hindenburg re-elected as president to keep out Hitler and preserve the republic. He was also hard at work on the international scene to help the German economy by seeking an end to war reparations. But his economic policies at home brought dismal results. As Germany’s economic situation got worse, with nearly six million unemployed, Bruening was labelled “The Hunger Chancellor.”

Bruening had also continued the dangerous precedent of ruling by decree. He invoked Article 48 of the German constitution several times to break the political stalemate in Berlin.

As far as Adam was concerned, it appeared to him that he was simply in the way and had to go. This became more apparent as news began to leak that Schleicher was undermining the support of Hindenburg. Bruening was already in trouble with Hindenburg, who blamed him for the political turmoil that had made it necessary to run for re-election at age 85 against his nemesis ‘the Bohemian Corporal’ Adolf Hitler.

Bruening also made an error in proposing that the huge estates of bankrupt aristocrats are divided up and given to peasants, sounding like a Marxist. Those same aristocrats, along with big industrialists, had scraped together the money to buy Hindenburg an estate of his own. When Hinden took his Easter vacation there in mid-May, he had to listen to their complaints about Bruening. All the while, Schleicher was busy in Berlin speaking to all that would listen and claiming that Bruening had to go.

On May 29, Hindenburg called in Bruening and told him to resign. The next day, Heinrich Bruening handed in his resignation, effectively ending democracy in Germany.

By this stage Adam had started to get visits from Brownshirts, who didn't like what he was writing, telling him

'Go home Englisher if you know what is good for you!

Adam wasn't daunted by this but he had become increasingly aware of the way that some of the smaller, mostly Jewish run, newspapers were effectively ceasing to exist. He'd also realised that his information or inside track was also starting to dry up and his editor was putting him under increasing pressure to deliver the Hitler interview. Adam by this stage had decided to seek a personal hearing with Hitler and called his office where he spoke with Herr Dr. Goebbels as Joseph was now fond of calling himself.

'Herr Dr, began Andrew 'The British people would like to know about the Mr. Hitler, he is big news there and I...

Herr Carter' smoozed Goebbels ' be patient, I will see what I can do, you must understand' he said in a whined voice 'The Fuerhur is a busy man'

'Fuehrer?

'The Fuehrer will speak with you presently, I will be in touch, Good day Herr Carter.

Adam replaced the buzzing telephone back into its cradle.

Adam telephoned Schleicher and asked him if he could do anything

'I will be able to do more than that, soon I will be able to tell him what to do, and then I promise you, you will get your story'.

Schleicher was now in control. He chose as his puppet chancellor, an unknown socialite named Franz von Papen who had grave doubts about his own ability to function in such a high office. Hindenburg, however, took a liking to Papen and encouraged him to take the job. The aristocratic Papen assembled a cabinet of men like himself. This ineffective cabinet of aristocrats and industrialists presided over a nation that would soon be on the verge of anarchy.

When President Hindenburg asked Adolf Hitler if he would support Papen as chancellor, he said yes. On June 4, the Reichstag was dissolved and new elections were called for the end of July. On June 15, the ban on the SA and SS was lifted. The secret promises made to the Nazis by Schleicher had been fulfilled.

Adam's correspondence became more and more graphic in its detail as he described the turnaround in how power was being wrested away by the Nazis. Since Schleicher had assumed control, he'd effectively blocked all access to Adam and when Adam tried to ring him he was threatened and harangued by Schleicher's officers.

A new wave of indiscriminate murder and violence soon erupted on a scale never before seen on the streets of towns and cities in Germany. Roaming groups of Nazi Brownshirts walked the streets singing Nazi songs and looking for fights. What began as broken windows and the odd burning of Jewish property had now erupted into a state where Jews did not dare to venture out onto the streets after dark.

"Blut muss fliessen, Blut muss fliessen! Blut muss fliessen Knuppelhageldick! Haut'se doch zusammen, haut'se doch zusammen! Diese gotverdammte Juden Republik!", the Nazi storm troopers sang.

"Blood must flow, blood must flow! Blood must flow as cudgel thick as hail! Let's smash it up; let's smash it up! That goddamned Jewish republic!"

Megan was suppose to come over for a visit but Adam called her and told her to stay at home. As far as Adam was concerned, the most disturbing part of the whole change was the absolute devotion of the teenager to this new cause. It was obvious to him that the ultimate object for any German youth was to own his own Hitler Youth shirt and eventually graduate to wearing the near mystical black shirt with runes of the SS, a secret police organisation under the control of Heinrich Himmler. Adam hadn't heard of this man but had seen the sinister black shirted men accompany Hitler everywhere that he went now and he'd heard that in some cases they had had fights with brown shirts in different towns and cities. As he awoke each morning, it was now common for four or five people to have died the previous night as gangs of Nazis fought running battles through the streets.

The Nazis found many Communists in the streets wanting a fight and they began regularly shooting at each other. Hundreds of gun battles took place. In July, the Nazis under police escort brazenly marched into a Communist area near Hamburg in the state of Prussia. A big shoot-out occurred in which 19 people were killed and nearly 300 wounded. It came to be known as "Bloody Sunday." Papen invoked Article 48 and proclaimed martial law in Berlin and also took over the government of the German State of Prussia.

By this stage it was clear to Adam that Germany had taken a big step closer to authoritarian rule and he concluded that things were about to change for the worse as he suspected that Hitler had now decided that Papen was simply in the way and had to go. Adam had spent the last seven years watching and reporting on the Nazis growth from a rag tag collection of zealots to become the most powerful force in Germany and in that short time Adam was aware that Hitler had gone on record as saying to Van Papen

'I regard your cabinet only as a temporary solution and will continue my efforts to make my party the strongest in the country. The chancellorship will then devolve on 'Me'.

The July elections of 1932 provided that opportunity. The Nazis, sensing total victory, campaigned with fanatical energy. Adam reported that Hitler was now speaking to adoring German audiences of up to 100,000 at a time. The phenomenon of large scale 'Fuehrer worship' had begun. On July 31, the people voted and gave the Nazis 13,745,000 votes, 37% of the total, granting them 230 seats in the Reichstag. The Nazi party was now the largest and most powerful in Germany.

On August 5, Hitler presented his list of demands to Schleicher - the chancellorship, passage of an enabling act giving him control to rule by decree, three cabinet posts for Nazis, the creation of a propaganda ministry, control over the Ministry of the Interior, and control of Prussia. As for Schleicher, he would get the Ministry of Defence as a reward.

Schleicher listened, didn't say yes or no, but would let him know later.

With gleeful anticipation, Hitler awaited Schleicher's response and even ordered that a memorial tablet be made to mark the place where the historic meeting with Schleicher had occurred.

Meanwhile, the SA began massing in Berlin anticipating a take-over of power. But old President Hindenburg soon put an end to Hitler's dreams. Hindenburg by now distrusted Hitler and would not have him as chancellor, especially after the behaviour of the SA.

On August 13, Schleicher and Papen met with Hitler and gave him the bad news. The best they could offer was a compromise - vice chancellorship and the Prussian Ministry of the Interior.

Hitler became hysterical. In a display of wild rage that stunned Schleicher and Papen, he spewed out threats of violence and murder, saying he would let loose the SA for three days of mayhem all across Germany.

Later that same day, President Hindenburg summonsed Hitler. The former Austrian Corporal got a tongue lashing from the former Field Marshal after once again demanding the chancellorship and refusing to co-operate with Papen and Schleicher. In the presence of the steely-eyed Prussian, Hitler backed down. The gamble for total victory had failed. He put the SA on a two-week furlough and went to Berchtesgaden to lick his wounds. They would all have to wait, he told them. Just a little longer. On September 12, the Reichstag under the new chairmanship of Hermann Göring gave a vote of no confidence to Papen and his government. But just before that vote was taken, Papen had slapped an order on Göring's desk dissolving the Reichstag and calling yet again for new elections.

This was a problem. Everyone was getting tired of elections by now. Goebbels had a hard time getting the Nazi effort up to the same level of a few months earlier. In the middle of the campaign, Hitler's girlfriend Eva Braun was reported to have shot herself in the neck during a suicide attempt. Hitler was still haunted by the suicide of his beloved niece a few years earlier. Eva Braun was deeply in love with Hitler but didn't get the attention she craved. Hitler rushed to the hospital and resolved to look after her from that moment on.

This distraction served to slow down the already sluggish Nazi campaign. More problems came after Goebbels and a number of Nazis went along with the Communists in a wildcat strike of transport workers in Berlin, thus alienating a lot of middle class voters.

Bad publicity from siding with the Reds plus the bad publicity Hitler got after his meeting with Hindenburg combined to lose them votes.

Adding to all this was the wild antics of the SA. On November 6, the Nazis lost two million votes and thirty-four seats in the Reichstag. It seemed the Nazis were losing momentum. Hitler became depressed whilst his opposition danced in the street.

But, as Adam reported from the wings with dismay, there was still no workable government in Berlin. Papen's position

› chancellor was badly weakened. And Schleicher was now at work behind the scenes to further undermine him. On November 17, Papen went to Hindenburg and told him he was unable to form any kind of working coalition, then resigned.

Two days later, Hitler requested a meeting with Hindenburg. Once again Hitler demanded to be made chancellor. Once again he was turned down. This time however, Hindenburg took a friendlier tone, asking Hitler, soldier to soldier, to meet him half way and cooperage with the other parties to form a working majority, in other words, a coalition government. Hitler said no

On November 21, Hitler saw Hindenburg again and tried a different approach. He read a prepared statement claiming that parliamentary government had failed and those only the Nazis could be counted on to stop the spread of Communism. He asked Hindenburg to make him the leader of a presidential cabinet. Hindenburg said no, and only repeated his own previous requests.

The Government of Germany had ground to a halt.

Meanwhile, a group of the country's most influential industrialists, bankers, and business leaders sent a petition to Hindenburg asking him to appoint Hitler as chancellor. This group had set up a small secret society called the Thule or 'The Spear' and had committed themselves to supporting some strange notions about the Germanic people being antecedents of the famous lost city of Atlantis. They had spent significant amounts of money propagating their theory on the 'master race'. They believed Hitler would be worthy of their support as they believed he was malleable and would easily buy into their 'master race' theory in return for their support. Hess had been at the forefront of this group as far back as 1922 when Hitler was first beginning to make a name for himself.

Hindenburg was in a terrible bind. He called in Papen and Schleicher and asked them what to do. Papen came up with a wild idea. He would be chancellor again and rule only by decree, eliminate the Reichstag altogether, use the Army and police to suppress all political parties and forcibly amend the constitution. It would be a return to the days of Empire, with the conservative, aristocratic classes ruling.

Schleicher objected, much to Papen's surprise. Schleicher said that he, not Papen, should head the government and promised Hindenburg he could get a working majority in the Reichstag by causing a rift among the Nazis. Schleicher said he could get Gregor Strasser and as many as 60 Nazi deputies to break from Hitler.

Hindenburg was dumbfounded and finally turned to Papen and asked him to go ahead and form his government. After Hindenburg left the room, Papen and Schleicher got into a huge shouting match. At a cabinet meeting the next day, Schleicher told Papen that any attempt by him to form a new government would bring the country to chaos. He insisted that the Army would not go along and then produced a Major Ott who backed up his claims. Schleicher had been at work behind the scenes to sway the Army to his point of view. Papen was in big trouble.

He went running to Hindenburg, who, with tears rolling down his cheeks, told Papen there was no alternative at this point except to name Schleicher as the new chancellor.

"My dear Papen, you will not think much of me if I change my mind. But I am too old and have been through too much to accept the responsibility for a civil war. Our only hope is to let Schleicher try his luck." President Hindenburg told Papen.

Kurt von Schleicher became Chancellor of Germany on December 2, 1932.

He sent for Adam

'Take a message to your people, tell them that I wish to be friends, tell them that I want their help to defeat this upstart Hitler, tell them that he is a threat to the peace...

Adam sat and listened, he hadn't spoken directly to Schleicher in nearly a year and had been threatened by his men.

'What are you going to do about the attacks on the Jewish people in Berlin? How are you going to control the Nazis?

Adam flipped open his notebook and pen at the ready began to scribble down a response when the door knocked

'Herr Strasser is here ...

Adam stalled 'Strasser! What was he doing there?

'We'll finish this later' said Schleicher 'You can wait if you like.'

Adam stood up as Strasser, dressed in his black uniform walked into the room

'You know where to contact me' Adam turned and walked directly to the door.

Schleicher was trying to make good on his promise to try to split the Nazis. Gregor Strasser, a Nazi who had been with Hitler from the start, was offered the vice-chancellorship and control of Prussia. To Strasser, the offer was quite appealing. The Nazi party's recent decline, losing millions of votes and now experiencing terrible financial problems, seemed to indicate that Hitler's rigid tactics might not be the best thing for long-term success. Strasser had also acquired distaste for the brutal men who now made up Hitler's inner circle. Unfortunately for Strasser and Schleicher, Hitler found out what was going on.

On December 5, Strasser and his infuriated Fuehrer met, along with other Nazi leaders, in a Berlin hotel. Strasser insisted that Hitler and the Nazis co-operate or at least tolerate the Schleicher government. Göring and Goebbels opposed him. Hitler sided with them against Strasser.

Two days later, Strasser and Hitler met again and wound up getting into a huge shouting match. Strasser accused Hitler of leading the party to ruin. Hitler accused Strasser of stabbing him in the back.

The following day, Strasser wrote a letter to Hitler, resigning all of his duties as a member of the Nazi party.

Hitler and the Nazi leaders were stunned. One of the founding members and most influential leaders had abandoned them. The Nazi Party seemed to be unravelling. Hitler became depressed, even threatening to shoot himself with a pistol.

Strasser headed for a vacation in Italy. Before he went, he sent a quote to the Times desk which Adam printed verbatim in the next day's issue.

"Whatever happens, mark what I say. From now on Germany is in the hands of an Austrian, who is a congenital liar (Hitler), a former officer who is a pervert (Röhm), and a clubfoot (Goebbels). And I tell you the last is the worst of them all. This is Satan in human form."

As for Hermann Göring...

"Göring is a brutal egotist who cares nothing for Germany as long as he becomes something."

Hitler assigned his trusted aid, Rudolph Hess, to take over Strasser's duties. Over the Christmas season, Hitler became quite depressed over the failing fortunes of his party. And it seemed to many political observers that the danger of a Hitler dictatorship had passed. Adam had reported that Hitler was under increasing pressure and that in his opinion, he would not last as a force in German politics much past the New Year.

But the New Year brought new intrigue. The big bankers and industrialists who had petitioned Hindenburg on behalf of Hitler still liked the idea of Hitler in power. And Papen was now out to bring down Schleicher. On January 4, 1933, Hitler went to a meeting with Papen at the house of banker Kurt von Schroeder. Papen surprised Hitler by offering to oust Schleicher and install a Papen-Hitler government with himself and Hitler, both equal partners. Hitler liked the idea of ousting Schleicher but insisted that he would have to be the real head of government. He would, however, be willing to work with Papen and his ministers. Papen gave in and agreed.

When Schleicher found out, he went running to Hindenburg, charging Papen with treachery. But Hindenburg had a soft spot for Papen and would not go along. Schleicher's position was already badly weakened. He was unable to get the government moving because nobody trusted him enough to join him in a working coalition. The German government remained at a standstill with the people and Hindenburg getting more impatient by the day. Something had to be done. Hindenburg authorised Papen to continue negotiating with Hitler, but to keep it secret from Schleicher.

Adam went to the small German State of Lippe, to cover local elections that were scheduled for January 15. Hitler and the Nazis took this opportunity to make a big impression. They saturated the place with propaganda and campaigned heavily, hoping to win big and prove they had regained momentum. Adam was amazed at their strength and more importantly, how much they were feared by the local people.

They received a small increase in votes over their previous election total. But they used their own widely circulated Nazi newspapers to exaggerate the significance and to once again lay claim that Hitler and the Nazis were the wave of the future. It worked well and even impressed President Hindenburg. On Sunday, January 22, 1933, a secret meeting was held at the home of Joachim von Ribbentrop. Papen, Hindenburg's son Oskar, along with Hitler and Göring, attended it.

Hitler grabbed Oskar and brought him into a private room and worked on him for an hour to convince him that the Nazis had to be taken into the government on his terms. Oskar emerged from the meeting convinced it was inevitable. The Nazis were to be taken in. Papen then pledged his loyalty to Hitler. Next, Schleicher went to Hindenburg with a proposal, He should declare a state of emergency to control the Nazis, dissolve the Reichstag, and suspend elections. Hindenburg said no.

But word of this proposal leaked out, bringing Schleicher the wrath of the liberal and centrist parties. Schleicher then backed down, bringing him the wrath of anti-Nazi conservatives. His position was hopeless.

In January, he went to Hindenburg and asked him once again to dissolve the Reichstag. Hindenburg said no. Schleicher resigned.

Papen and the president's son, Oskar, moved in on the old gentleman to convince him to appoint a Hitler-Papen government. Hindenburg was now a tired old man weary of all the intrigue. He seemed ready to give in. Hitler sensed his weakness and issued an additional demand that four important cabinet posts be given to Nazis.

This did not set well with the old man and he started having doubts about Hitler as chancellor. He was reassured when Hitler promised that Papen would get one of those four posts. Presently a false rumour circulated that Schleicher was about to arrest Hindenburg and stage a military take-over of the government. When Hindenburg heard of this, it ended his hesitation. He decided to appoint Adolf Hitler as the next Chancellor of Germany.

However, a last minute objection by conservative leader, Alfred Hugenberg, nearly ruined everything. While President Hindenburg waited in the other room to give Hitler the chancellorship, Hugenberg held up everything by arguing with the Nazis over Hitler's demand for new elections. He was persuaded by Hitler to back down or at least let Hindenburg decide. With that settled they all headed into the president's office.

Around noon on January 30, 1933, a new chapter in German history began as a teary-eyed Adolf Hitler emerged from the presidential palace as Chancellor of the German Nation. Surrounded by admirers, he got into his car and was driven down the street lined with cheering citizens. Adam watched with an impending sense of doom as a jubilant Adolf Hitler exclaimed

"We've done it! We've done it!" -.

Chapter 4

Simon ben Gorias had never seen an Army like it. There were at least four Legions and as many auxiliaries and they were preparing to siege. The son of Satan was camped at the gates. Titus had brought with him a mighty army. Gallantly Simon and his men fought hand to hand, street by street. ON the fortieth day he called Barrabas

'Take your men and protect the temple and when you cannot protect any longer, you are to burn it to the ground'. Satan must never enter the sanctuary'.

Barrabas responded

The One will save us, it is written; listen as I tell you...

And they will all mix together; the blast of the fire; the flaming breath and the great tempest; and fell with violence upon the multitude who were prepared to fight and burned them up everyone, so that upon a sudden of an innumerable multitude, nothing was perceived but only dust and the smell of smoke: when I saw I was afraid.

'Hear ye,O my beloved, behold the days of trouble are at hand but I will deliver you from the same'.

Simon ben Gorias on hearing Barrabas knew that the intervention of Yahweh was near, His great secret would be saved by His unveiling as He rose to smite his enemies at the twin pillared entrance.

But no one came

After a battle of one hundred and thirty nine days, the temple fell. Barrabas and some of his men escaped through the maze of tunnels that lay under the temple. Barrabas fearing the worst, hid the words that they held so dear in the deepest recess of the darkest room. He then put on his white rope and tied it with his red cloth and joined the rest of the Nazarenes in the final hours.

When it was over, they ceased to exist.

Adam was staggered by the treatment of opposition to Hitler; he has heard stories of 'camps' that have been set up for 'corrective retraining'. There was also a torrent of abuse and isolation being propagated against anything Jewish who seemed to be getting the blame for all of the misfortune that has ever befallen Germany. The vitriol that was being spat out by Joseph Goebbels and another particularly nasty piece of work called Julius Streicher were inflaming youths to attack Jewish property.

Another frightening development in the last few weeks was taking place at the processions where there would be orchestrated book burning sessions. Adam was sickened as he saw limited first editions and works of great literary value being defaced and burned by people who claimed that the books were part of the grand conspiracy and was not fit to be read by any pure 'Aryan' German. Books by Mann, Remarque, Alfred Kerr, Hugo Pruess, Jakob Wassermann, H.G Wells, Havelock Ellis, Frued, Gide and Proust were condemned to the flames. The Nazis were rewriting German history and the new Ministry of Culture with Goebbels at its head was claiming that

'In order to pursue a policy of German culture, it is necessary to gather together all of the creative artists in all spheres into a unified organisation under the control of the Reich. The Reich must not only determine the lines of progress, mental and spiritual, but also lead and organise the professions.'

All of this rhetoric left Adam feeling decidedly ill at ease; he wasn't the only reporter in Berlin who had serious misgivings about the direction that politics was taking in the new 'Reich. Across the city lived another reporter who was living in fear.

Maria Tannenbaum worked for 'Vossishe Zeitung' a paper that was comparable with the Times in both London and New York, as a reporter. Adam had known her for a while as their paths often crossed and he had read some of her work with professional interest, he didn't know that she was a member of the Socialists and more importantly a Jew. They'd spoken on a few occasions and Maria had continually stressed the need for Adam to tell it how it was and what was really happening inside Germany at that moment. She wanted him to tell how every morning the editors of the Berlin daily newspapers and the correspondents of those published elsewhere in the Reich gathered at the Propaganda ministry. There they were told by Dr. Goebbels or one of his aides what news to print and suppress how to write the news and headline it, what campaigns to call off or institute and what editorials were desired for the day.

Adam had heard these stories and didn't believe them, his relationship with the Propaganda Ministry was managed from London and whilst he sometimes didn't agree with his editor, he was happy to follow the lead he was given. This was primarily because of the rapid revolution in German industry and the British Government's continuing attempts to curry favour with the new regime.

Adam met Maria at one of the foreign press conferences

'Ah, the mercurial Adam Carter' said Maria 'Apologist in chief for the Nazis'

Adam smiled at Maria 'I'm glad to see that your spirit isn't just in your writing' said Adam

'I'd be a wee bit more careful as to who I offend, however. Germany is changing fast and I don't know how much longer your kind of radicalism is going to be tolerated'

'No thanks to you' flared Maria.

We'll talk about that over dinner, care to join me? said Adam

It was Maria's turn to be taken aback

'After what I've just said to you '

'I never let professional opinion stand in the way of an empty tummy' said Adam as he escorted Maria out of the room and down the steps to a waiting taxi.

Over dinner Maria started 'When are you English going to realise that Hitler is the biggest threat to World Peace since 1914! Have you heard the latest edit to come from them?

Adam smiled at her, she was very animated and in her anger she betrayed a zest and passion that Adam liked, she reminded him in some ways of Megan. They'd had sort of consummated their relationship on Adam's first visit home and the past five years had seen Megan in her last year as a intern doctor, she'd be finished soon and then what? Adam had been avoiding this and suspected that Megan was doing the same but he put her out of his mind and concentrated on Maria

'This new Reich Press Law, what have you heard about it? said Maria

'Not much really, replied Adam, Doesn't affect me does it?

'Sometimes I really do think you are impossible! Don't you see what they are doing to free press' flared Maria 'Journalism is now deemed to be a public vocation. Regulated by law it says that all editors must possess German citizenship, be of Aryan descent and NOT married to a Jew!

Adam stopped 'They can't do that ...Can they?

Hah! said Maria,' not only can they do it, they've done it, as from today it is law! Listen to this; Adam sat still as Maria read from the edit.

'Editors must keep out of the papers anything that is misleading to the public, tends to weaken the strength of the German Reich outwardly or inwardly, the common will of the German people, the defence of Germany'

'Need I go on? hissed Maria, when are you going to open your eyes and start telling your people the truth?

Adam spread his hands as if to calm her down. It proved to be a fruitless exercise, the rest of the people having heard her outburst were staring at their table, Maria glared at them as she pushed back from the table saying

'If you won't do something I'll have to find somebody who will' said Maria and lifting her coat stormed out of the restaurant. Adam got up and followed her, catching her at the end of the street

'Let's go for a drink. I promise to listen to what you have to say'

Adam got very drunk that night and buoyed by her company, they exchanged life stories; everything was very cordial until Adam told her about his father and how he died. When he told her about the fatal night and ' you will not succeed' he was conscious of her going very quiet, in fact she looked at him as if she's was terrified of him and what he might say next.

She got up to leave and Adam misreading her intentions caused a scene that was being watched by another man who got up and left when she did. Adam woke up the next morning, severely hung over and struggled to recollect, he tried to reach Maria at her office but was told she hadn't appeared in. He confirmed his identity and asked for her address, with the intention of going round that he did.

He didn't see the black sedan sitting across the street, nor did he pay any attention to the man standing at the corner as he passed. He reached the address and he knocked the door which was opened by an elderly gentle man who invited him in on hearing his name and inquired as to his business with Maria. Adam was aware of the old man being scared, he couldn't comprehend why. The elderly gentleman's name was Solomon Tannenbaum, he said he was Maria's father. He explained that Maria didn't return home last evening and he was becoming increasingly worried because of her behaviour of late. Adam asked him what he meant and Mr. Tannenbaum explained that in the last 3 months Maria had become pre occupied with 'missing people' she scours the newspapers and wires for evidence of their 'disappearance'. As Adam rose to go, Mr. Tannenbaum caught his arm and looking him in the eye, told him to take care, promising Adam that he would tell Maria that he had called.

Maria did not go home, she headed across the city, through the Brandenburg Gate and into the Wedding district.

She kept to the back streets, as she'd known for weeks that she was being watched. She took comfort of the fact that she was still classified 'German' but realised that it was only a matter of time before her editor discovered her origins and in keeping with the race edit would have to restrict her news gathering. She didn't know that the SS had already being told of her interests in the 'camps' and whilst they were unsure as to who she was and what her interest was, they were nevertheless trailing her. She reached the house and knocked the door and stepped inside, she stumbled and was caught by the old man. He lifted her and asked her what was wrong, 'Yahweh is here' she stuttered. The old man slapped her hard across the face, he grabbed her by the shoulders

'What did you say child?' he demanded, Maria repeated, the old man fell back against the wall 'Could it be? How? He asked out loud before staggering as he reached for the chair that was against the wall. In his anger, his glasses had fallen and Maria saw that a sweat had broken out on his scant brow. He wasn't a tall man but he'd managed grab Maria and was now mouthing an apology.

'I'm sorry child, pleased forgive me, I did not mean to hit you'

It's alright' said Maria, very much taken aback by his actions

'Is he the one? asked Maria in a hushed tone

'Time will tell' soothed the old man

Maria looked at him in total mystery, she knew something of the secret that he possessed because he made her promise that she would safeguard a package if anything ever happened to him. He said it was vital that she never speaks about their conversation. The old man had never told her of the origin of the secret, as he knew it, and the way that it impacted on her, he kept back the information he deemed she didn't need or want to know. All she knew was that he protected a box that contained vital information. The old man put his glasses back on and smoothed his shirt

'I think it is time to move the box' said the old man 'several people were picked up in a sweep last evening and those damned Brownshirts are continually haranguing the orthodox'. Only this morning, I heard that they were cutting the yarmulke off victims and then giving them terrible beatings.

Streicher! This was his fault' said Maria 'He's been encouraging rabble rousing Jew baiting and spouting to the uniformed thugs that were roaming the streets and then handing them a licence to do what they liked'. You're right' she said 'Go and get the box and I will take it with me to my own house'

No! said the old man 'it's not safe their either, you'll have to find somewhere else, somewhere that is safe enough for me to collect it from tomorrow'

'Why tomorrow? Maria had a hesitant look on her face.

The old man walked across and patted the top of her head before cupping her face lovingly in his wrinkled hands 'Maria, my beautiful child, it is time for us to get away from this place. You must go to your home and tell your father to be ready for us when we come for him'. We have to leave now while we still can'

She started to form words of argument to throw back in the face of her old but looking around the living room of the house, it's wall paper peeling away and the smell of old leather and parchment and candles burning.

'But what about your work, your parchments, you cannot take them with you'

'Mrs Rubenstein's son. you know him, the tall skinny boy, he'll look after the house and will make sure that nothing happens, I'll take what I need with me, now hurry.

Maria left the house by the back door, and walked down through the alley like she had done a thousand times before. She slipped out on to the street and began to make the circuitous journey back to her own house. She reached the corner of her bloc and held the package ever so tightly as she moved down the street, oblivious of the fact that she was being followed. The man who was following her had signalled to the car at the other corner of the street to stay where it was.

Adam was coming down the steps from her house and he saw Maria coming towards him, he stood, awaiting her, she rushed up and pressed a wrapped package into his hand and said something like

'Yemon' or 'Yamon' and 'they must not succeed'

Adam turned around, but Maria has gone past him, just as she got to the corner, a black sedan pulled across the street in front of her, two men got out and grabbed at her, Adam ran towards them as they pushed her into the back of the car. One of them alighted and punched him hard in the face. He fell back and as he lifted his head, he saw Maria staring back at him through the back window of the car that rapidly gathered speed and hurtled off down the street

Adam got back up on to his feet and looked around, what should he do, He looked around and was conscious of a woman peering from behind a curtain and another quickly slamming a door for fear that he would ask for help. Adam stood up and gingerly felt across his scalp before stretching his 6foot 2inch frame and checking that he wasn't hurt, that wasn't true, and he'd been hit with some sort of cosh and could feel the welt at the side of his head, causing him to stagger slightly. He looked back up the street before bending down to lift up the package that had been thrust into his hand by the girl. He did think about calling the police until he remembered that it was a black sedan that had spirited Maria away, as far as Andrew was concerned, calling the police was a waste of time as most of them craved after the power that was behind the wheel of the car, the Nazis could also claim to have an informant network that was unrivalled throughout the country, hell Andrew had used it to his own advantage in his work with the party from time to time, he of all people knew the significance of a sleek black sedan lifting people off the street in broad daylight in downtown Berlin. He chose to follow his own nose on this one, it shouldn't take him that long to find out what had happened to the girl and depending who he was able to talk to, he might even discover why she had been lifted. Stuffing the package in his pocket, he headed for his office and telephoned the paper that Maria worked for.

Can I speak to the editor bitte?

Adam recounted what he had saw to the editor of the paper, he swore and told Adam that she had probably been taken to Prinz Albertstrasse, it wasn't the first time that it had happened to her.

'What do you mean?' said Adam

The editor paused, 'Do you read our paper Herr Carter? If you did you'd know that the state would very much like to sensor what we have to say. We have been in business since 1704 and we have served the country through good times and bad, nothing has ever been as bad as this' If you'd read our paper you'd know that we do not acquiesce to the ramblings of that idiot Goebbels. Oh yes, you do of course know who own the paper don't you?

Adam felt stupid, 'actually no,' he mumbled 'I don't'

'It's hardly important' said the editor in a resigned fate, 'enough to say that they are one of the most famous Jewish families in the whole of Germany'

'I see' said Adam 'and Maria?

'She'll be alright, they usually let her out after a day or two, they do this to intimate us, do not worry about her Herr Carter, if you want to help, use your influence to get your paper to tell the world the truth, shout it from the rooftops, Germany is changing into a dangerous animal, one that is getting ready to strike...

Adam put down the telephone receiver and pondered his options. It was then that he remembered the package that Maria had pushed into him. It was wrapped in newspaper but it felt strangely familiar. Feeling the need for a 'stiff' coffee, he made his way across to the café and called for a drink.

The next 3 or 4 minutes completely numbed Adam Carter, he had never been a religious man and had no sense of faith, he used to mock his classmates about saying their prayers and ablutions every day and religious education was an excuse to sleep at the back of the class but as he opened the wrapping to uncover a small wooden box and a thing that looked like a small upturned sundial, a sense of great foreboding and coldness overcame him.

There was a note

If you are the one... You will have the key ... Maria.

He reached to his neck and touched the key he had worn all those years. The box, his box was in his bank in London, he took the key from around his neck and put it into the lock turned it and the box clicked open. He lifted the lid and there it was the same piece of cloth as he kept all these years, no wait! This one was different but he still didn't understand what was going on. He sat back and thought of what Maria had said to him as she ran past him, 'they must not succeed' like a bolt of lightning it struck him, up the stairs in his father's house, his house ..... 'You will not succeed'.... Adam shuddered

'What was going on?

He gulped at the brandy-laced coffee and decided that he would go to Maria's father and confront him, maybe he knew something. Tightening his resolve he headed for the house of Solomon Tannenbaum.

It was dusk when Adam reached the house and as he walked up the steps he realised that the front door was open, he pushed it but couldn't see, he called out to 'anyone home' no answer, he went through the door but the house was in darkness. There was light coming from under a door at the bottom of the hall, he approached it and rapped the door

The sight that greeted Adam Carter would stay with him until his death. He had never seen so much blood in all his life. There was a man slumped in the corner in a chair, he wasn't sitting, more lying. His head was lying back and his throat had been cut from ear to ear, his blood had spurted and cascaded to the point where the wall to his right was splattered the man's chest area was red.

Adam retched, he was transfixed to the spot, he turned his head, and someone had daubed 'Jude' on the wall in blood. Adam turned and headed for the door, blindly he wrenched the handle and stifled a scream as an older man put his hand over Adam's mouth and hit him hard on the back of the head, the old man caught Adam under the arms and pulled him across to the door, he propped him against the wall and opened the door whereby two younger men came up the steps and carried an unconscious Adam down the steps and put him into the back of a car.

It was dark when Adam came round, he woke with a start and was conscious of sitting in a chair, and he couldn't move his arms or legs and upon inspection realised that he had been tied up. Adam didn't know where he was or how long he had been there. He looked around; he appeared to be in a sort of study. There were mountains of books and dust everywhere. There was a large map on the wall but he couldn't figure out where it was. One wall was shelved and weighed down with what appeared to be scripts of some sort. There was a lit fire on the other wall and Adam as he got his bearings became aware of a snoring behind him...

'Who's there' Adam shouted...

Ah, so you're awake are you?

'Who are you? Why am I tied up? I demand... I am a British...

Quiet! snapped the old man ... 'You do not know how lucky you are to be alive

At that, Adam fell silent and gaped blankly at the old man.

'My name is Isaac Tauber and you my young friend ... do not know who you are'

He made a pot of strong tea and began to question Adam about his father, about things Adam knew nothing about ... he asked as to whether he had received anything from Maria.

Adam said nothing ... until the man relaxed and started to tell him about a British Expedition Force in Palestine in 1885 and the discovery that five friends made at a campsite on the top of a hill near the Dead Sea...

Hours, it seemed like days later ... Adam stopped the old man

What did the cloth mean? Why did they divide it in five? What is 'Yahweh'

Isaac Tauber sat and looked at Adam, he was sure now that Adam knew nothing and was unaware of his importance. He also knew that he had to get himself and Adam as far away from Germany as possible. He knew what was going to happen, he'd seen it in his homeland in Russia in 1917 when the white then Red army slaughtered his people in pogroms of bestiality....Babies on pitchforks, women raped, men killed, hung, crucified. He looked up...

'We must go to London' he bluffed... I know Maria gave you her 'piece' because I translated it for her ... It said

'Shall be my son, he is the branch'

I know that you too possess a piece and I also know that your life will be in grave danger if you remain here. You must find a way of getting me out of Germany'.

Adam looked at him, after what he had seen in the room at Maria's, he could see the sense of getting the old man away, Adam was beginning to realise what Hitler and the rest of the Nazis were capable of and that Mr. Tannenbaum's death was only the tip of the iceberg.

.... He wondered about Maria

'Wait a minute' said Adam 'who are you? What do you want from me? Do you think I can just go into my office in Berlin and say?

'I'm just off to England with an old man I've never met in my life before, oh yeah and by the way, a man has been murdered and his daughter was taken away in front of my eyes, what do you think my editor will say?

'Young man' rasped the old man 'I am probably the only man who can keep you live long enough to return to England, I suggest you use whatever influence you have to make travel arrangements...I will say only one more thing to you now ....

Adam waited

'They must not succeed' hissed Isaac 'words I believe you are familiar with!

The next twenty seconds shook Adam to his core as a maelstrom of images flashed across his brain, memories of a pool of blood and his father whispering those very words, Maria pushed into a car, she said the words as well, no she reacted when she heard Adam speak them, and then what of the man in the flat, his throat cut ..... blood everywhere

'All right old man, I'll see what I can do'

To more pressing problems, how was he going to explain to his desk editor that he had to return to London on urgent business. It was then that he remembered that he'd promised to drive to Paris to meet his friend at the weekend.

Simple!

He'd take Isaac in the car to Paris, put him on an overnight boat train to London, drop the car off and follow him home once he had cleared it with his boss. Adam recited his plan to the old man and told him to be ready, they would leave that evening

Adam agreed that he would return and left the house, it was mid afternoon and he decided to go to his office and try and find out what he could about Maria. It was a very warm day and the street shimmered in the quivering heat of the afternoon. Adam's clothes were sticking to him as he walked, hot and sweating the remainder of the way to his office. He was about to cross the road when he stopped dead in his tracks and stared across at the entrance to the office, the same black sedan that had taken Maria was sitting at the kerb.

Its engine idling, the two men that had been in the car were manhandling Frau Beier, the housekeeper down the steps towards the car. Adam quickly retraced his steps, hailed a taxi and directed the driver to his apartment. He got out at the bottom of the street and stood in the shade of an alley for two or three minutes as he watched the front of his house. He was just about to run across the road when he heard the squeal of brakes and looking up the street saw the sedan careering towards him, he fell back into the alley, his heart pounding and sweat pouring down his forehead and into his eyes, he half expected hands to reach in and pull him out. He heard a shout and peering around the corner, he watched as the second man got out of the car and went up the steps to the door of Adam's apartment, the sound of splintering wood told him it wasn't a social call as he gathered himself and headed off down the alley, he got to the other side, hailed a taxi and returned to the house of the old man.

'Gather what you need, we're leaving now!

'Maria! stammered the old man 'Is it Maria?

'The men who took her are looking for me, I don't know what is going on here but I do know that I don't want to find out from them. Collect whatever papers that you need and be ready to go, if they found out my address and they have Maria, it will only be a matter of time before they reach you.'

'Hurry up' said Adam.

A voice snapped into his ear 'Did you get him?

'Nein Herr Hauptmann' He hasn't been seen at his house this last couple of days. I .....

'Fool' screamed the voice 'Stay where you are until he appears!

By the time the two men returned to their base, Adam and the old man were out of Berlin and heading towards the border in a stranger's car.

Threadneedle Street in London is famous for housing the Bank of England headquarters, it is also home to a host of other, less well-known banking institutions. It was to one of these 'Banco Marceli' that Adam and Isaac headed. Once inside the vault room ... Adam went to his box and took out the key.... Isaac marveled at this.... The boy did not know! He'd had to validate who he was and the manager remembered the correspondence from his solicitor all those years ago and confirmed that they could access the lock but not what was inside the box and the person named had to have the key.

Adam lifted the piece out and laid it flat on the table, it was bigger than the piece that Maria had given him and Isaac had gone deathly quiet as he pored over the lines and writing with a magnifying glass and wrote down words

'Show me the dial', he commanded

After a period Isaac said....'We must go to the British Museum'.

Adam found himself sitting at the reader's desk in the West Wing of the Museum. Isaac was coming towards him with a huge voluminous book. He slapped it down on the table and opened it, greedily switching through until he came across what appeared to be a scribble......

'I think I know what the piece says' he exclaimed triumphantly. Let us go to your apartment and I will explain

Adam was becoming increasingly perplexed with the behavior of Isaac, he had lost all sense of what the old man was saying and needed some answers.

'Kaballah' explained Isaac, ' is the study of ancient Jewish texts. I have been studying the bloodline of the Essene for the last 30 years of my life and have come to the conclusion that they hold the key to the mystery of the scripture.

Isaac was lying back at his ease in Adam's flat, his shoes kicked off, his necktie loosened. He'd benefited from a good night's sleep, Adam was still trying to waken, and Isaac had stirred as the first shafts of daylight bludgeoned into the darkness of his bedroom.

'Coffee' thought Adam 'and then I'll be o.k.'

Isaac continued

'There has, however, been so much conflicting evidence produced over the centuries about their existence, making it near impossible to get at the truth'.

'The who' asked Adam, who by this stage was completely confused by the whole situation and could not follow Isaac's reasoning. He had never been a religious man, as far as he was concerned, Allah, Buddha and all the rest of the world's deity's had every right to compete for the affections of faith as much as Jesus Christ did. The Bible, he presumed was a method of validating the faith, he'd never really considered its relativity up until now.

'So, these Essene's were special people? What happened to them?

Isaac explained what he could or rather what he knew. He told Adam of the flight into the desert as a result, that had been recorded in the Hellenic documents found at the end of the first crusade. There was speculation that they became or were the lost tribe of Israel and had wandered the desert for 40 years, eventually becoming assimilated with a Taureg people. No one really knew what happened to them or their leader who was called Alexander.

Adam responded 'Why are they important? What have they got to do with us?

'Ah' said Isaac 'this is where it gets difficult'...

Adam looked at Isaac inviting him to go on, after all he was a journalist, a listener and therefore should be able to comprehend what was being told, the kettle whistled and as Adam rose to go into the kitchen, Isaac spoke

'Do you believe in God?

Adam stopped, scratching the two day growth on his face replied 'I suppose I've never thought of it as a belief, more a comfort zone.'

Isaac pondered what Adam said for what seemed like a long time. Adam went out into the kitchen and returned with two steaming hot cups of coffee, the aroma pungent in the room and the steam rising from the cups. He handed a cup to Isaac, who clasped it in both of his hands, blew on the liquid and tested a sip on his lips before speaking again

'What if I were to tell you that all Christianity as you know it is based on a falsehood of proportions so great that public knowledge of it would devastate mankind' said Isaac.

What do you mean? Said Adam ' Who has created this so-called falsehood?

'I know them as literalist Christians, you'd probably recognise them as followers of the Roman Catholic Church. From the beginning of its history up to the present day, Christianity has been a religion of schism and conflict. There is not a single document in the New Testament that does not warn of false teachers or attack other Christians, I have spent the best part of my life uncovering their mistruths. They have forged letters created gospels, eradicated and prosecuted those who did not comply with their point of view'.

'Which was?' asked a non- pluses Adam

'That the Jesus story as bizarre and mythical as it sounds was in fact a true account of miraculous events which had Jesus as the epicenter of a cult who steadfastly believed that he was born of a virgin, was crucified and resurrected during the governorship of Pontius Pilate. What if I told you that Jesus had a brother called James who was more important than him?'

'Why do you think that on every crucifix scene, you see Jesus wearing a loin- cloth?

Decency? mused Adam

'I don't think so, artists were instructed to paint decency!

Why? said Adam

'Simple really, grinned Isaac, 'had the scene be shown in its true light, evidence would be there for all to see that the supposed son of man was a Jew!

How? Adam blanched, his interest quickening in what Isaac was saying only because he'd never seen a nude Christ on a cross! He started to snigger but quickly suppressed it when he saw the look on Isaac's face.

Isaac said ' All Jewish men were circumcised' Rather obvious actually, how would the great and good explain that one. Jews have the blood of Christ on their hands? The only thing the Jews were guilty of was killing another Jew!' We all know that the Christian churches have made great dogma on the fact that the Jews killed the Son of Man who came to save all mankind, The Jews killed one of their own, another Jew. The Christian Church has perpetrated a 'cover-up' if you'll excuse the pun, of monumental proportions by garnering him with a son of god deity identity.

Adam mooted out loud 'if that could be proved, the outcome would be...

'Their worst nightmare', Isaac stared hard into Adam 's face before continuing

Furthermore, what if I was to tell you that Jesus Christ was not the Son of God and was

buried in a secret tomb in the South of France. What if I was able to back it up by proving

that the New Testament is nothing more than a fabrication of mistruth and legends that

started with letters written by Paul in 50 ad'.

'But' stammered Adam, the gospels ....

Isaac raised his hand and spoke

'Were written, or should I say fabricated between 70 and 220 ad to help the new

literalism reign supreme in the quest for the control of religious practice.'

Isaac warming to his theme went on, a look of absolute conviction on his face that held

Adam spellbound as he continued.

'It is my considered opinion that the New Testament as you know it is nothing more than a fanciful collection of stories put together to support the theory that the Nazarene was truly the 'the messiah'. The earliest gospel, that of Mark, never even mentioned the resurrected Jesus, it stops with the women finding the empty tomb, it was then that the

Christians through the add on of stories by Matthew and Luke and eventually John propagated the notion of the resurrection. As for the letters of the Apostles, they appeared between 177 and 220 ad, 150 years after the 'messiah' died.'

Adam sat enthralled as Isaac spun out a tale that was so fantastic, it beggared belief, yet he, Adam Carter had heard some pretty unbelievable things in the last few weeks and his journalistic mind was discounting nothing. Adam didn't even notice that he still holding an ever cooling cup of coffee in his lap as Isaac spun a storyteller's spell upon him.

Isaac was enraptured as he pieced together the fruits of his life's research for Adam.

'What if I said that a group of Templar Crusaders discovered evidence of the Yahweh and in return for the untold wealth of the Essene was sworn to secrecy. Furthermore what if you discovered that the whole of the Inquisition was no more than a smokescreen thought up to mask the fact that Rome had decided to act swiftly in the protection of the lie'

Adam stared hard at Isaac .... 'You are hypothesising ...... aren't you?

Isaac continued ... When Martin Luther nailed his 96 articles of faith to the door of the chapel in Germany all those years ago, he effectively split the Catholic Church straight down the middle, why?, because he also came to discover part of the reason why the church acted so arbitrarily in dealing with dissension. '

Think about it, Adam ... the traditional history of Christianity is potentially the greatest cover up of all time with the truth being ruthlessly suppressed by the mass destruction of the evidence and the creation of a false history to suit the political purposes of the Roman Church. All those who questioned the official history were simply persecuted out of existence until there was nobody left to dispute it. They did it then and they are doing it now'.

Adam's mind whirled, he didn't know his religion but he'd majored in Medieval History at Balliol College and was completely aware of that particular historical time line.

More importantly the fact that he couldn't find any doctrine or timeline to disagree with the hypothesis that Isaac was so eloquently putting in front of him. .

He looked blankly at Isaac .... 'So this means ...... he trailed off

Isaac looked at him, got up and walked around the table and put his hand on his shoulder.

'If I am right, then we are two parts into discovering the greatest secret of the all, the evolution of life as we know it and the reason why it has been protected for 7000 years and longer'.

'We, my young friend are about to embark on a very perilous journey, one that we may not see the end of and one that we do not know what the outcome will be'

Adam nodded his head as Isaac said 'be scared Adam ...... be very scared indeed.

Chapter 5

800 years after the 'death' of the Nazarene, the Roman Empire had been re-invented by Charlemange as the Holy Roman Empire. Its churches used a Latin liturgy and the Holy Roman Emperors saw themselves as the protector of the Pope in Rome ... the same Pope who purported to be a direct descendant of Peter, the rock on whom the church was built, or so scripture said. The Holy Roman Empire had its base in Constantinople and whilst they were constantly repelling Arabs and retaking lost ground, the city was proving to be an impregnable fortress. This however was not the case in Europe as Norman armies led by Tancred De Hautville took control of most of Italy whilst from the East came the Seljuk Turks who attacked Constantinople and took control.

Meanwhile there was total anarchy in the relationship between the Pope and the Holy Roman Emperor, each set off on a course of action that led to The Pope's armies, supported by the Norman brigade, smashing the combined might of the Holy Roman Emperor, Henry.

After consolidation Pope Gregory's successor, Urban, began to look at the gains of the Turks. He cleverly manipulated the situation to engineer a 'holy' element to the forthcoming bloodshed in that he was protecting the church from Moslems In a field in Clermont in 1095 , Pope Urban made an announcement that would change the world.

He summonsed all Christian warriors to go and rescue their brothers in the East and in doing so committed Europe to the fighting of the first Crusade.

Their goals were simple, fighting under the cross of the redeemer, they would seek to extend the rule of the church over all Christendom, there was to be one solitary overarching church with one ruler. Urban decreed that Jerusalem, the holy City had to be rescued as it was the spiritual and therefore physical centre of the universe.

He hoped Jerusalem would be ruled directly by Rome i.e. him, Pope Urban. In order to raise an Army, Urban decreed that all those who fought wearing the mark of the cross would as well as pay receive the ultimate bounty.

'Whoever for devotion alone, not to gain honour or money, goes to Jerusalem to liberate the Church of God can substitute this journey for all penance'.

Urban with this edit offered paradise to believers, anyone who went had their sins forgiven. Fighting the Pope's cause was not only an obligation, it made you righteous. With this one idea, ideology was born and the Crusade was set in motion. Urban did not appreciate the ramifications of what he had done.

His words touched a chord amongst common people and hundreds of thousands of ordinary peasants flocked to the sign of the cross, to do their bit for Pope and God. This resulted in what is commonly referred to as the first Holocaust, it wasn't the Turks or Arabs that suffered, it was the Jews of Germany. They were perceived as enemies of the true God, if it was pardonable to kill enemies in the East, then why not at home? The Jews were killed simply because they had killed the Christ, the fact that he himself was a Jew was forgotten in the bloodlust.

A simple hermit called Peter called on the people to form a peasant crusade, when they eventually reached the Holy Land, it wasn't God that was waiting for them, the Seljuk Turks were and duly dispatched them to their God.

Finally, fully 4 years after the speech in Clermont, Tancred and his Crusaders attacked the city of Jerusalem. As they swept down from the North Wall, they rampaged through the city, killing all in their path. The Moslems fell back to the Dome of The Rock and then the al Aqsa mosque but it was all in vain as Tancred and his men pursued them, desecrating the Dome of the Rock and when they entered the mosque, they butchered every man, woman and child.

The Jews did not escape either, the synagogues they sought shelter in were locked and burned to the ground. This wasn't pillaging, it was ritual slaughter, spurred on by the fact that the Crusaders were securing their place in heaven.

A group of Crusaders had broken away from the main party and sought out the Church of the Holy Sepulchre as they had been told that this was the place where they would find the true cross, the one that the saviour carried to his death. They were intent on returning To Rome to present it to Pope Urban, he would have no comment to make, having died a few days before the news of the capture of Jerusalem reached Rome.

The remains of a dinner had been pushed to the side of the table, Adam had lit the fire which was now roaring up the chimney. He'd poured two large whiskies, Isaac's sat untouched beside him as he re arranged his papers for the umpteenth time that day.

'What has all of this got to do with us? asked Adam. 'I cannot understand why you are telling me all of this'.

Isaac chided him

'Patience, my young friend, you must have patience, all will become clear in time' replied Isaac, 'now where was I .... ah yes .... do you remember Saladin the Magnificent?

Yes, replied Adam 'as I recall Jerusalem was in control of one and then the other side over the next 150 years, wasn't Saladin the chap who led an Army from Damascus to repel the Crusaders and throw them out of the Holy Land for good?

I'm impressed', replied Isaac, his eyes ravaging the text in front of him 'Saladin entered the city on the anniversary of Mohammed's journey to heaven from the Foundation Stone. It had taken the Moslems 88 years to recapture the city.

'He threw the Templars from the Dome of the Rock, reopened the Mosque and although advised to destroy the Church of the Holy Sepulchre, closed it for three days only and then reopened it to Pilgrims'

'I'm sorry' said Adam 'I fail to see the relevance of this story'

'Right' said Isaac, somewhat bemused

'It is unfair of me to expect you to know anything of the Grail'.

'The Holy Grail? said Adam

'The very one' Isaac, once again looked at Adam and said 'it was discovered in the catacombs beneath the Church of the Holy Sepulchre along with some other interesting artifacts including a testimony which though part destroyed was said to have been written by a man named Saul'

Adam blinked and swallowed hard ' Our Saul?' he whispered

'Saul who became Paul' beamed Isaac. ' Are you ready to go on?

Adam nodded his head before taking another sip of his whiskey.

'There were a further three crusades including the one led by Richard the Lion Heart'.

Isaac began searching his notes looking for his time chart as he referred to it. He told Adam of the Saladin V Richard battles, the sacking of Constantinople by the fourth Crusade, it did absolutely nothing to harm the Moslems. They destroyed the Eastern Church and imposed the Latin one and the riches of Byzantium began to fill the churches of Europe purloined under the guise of them being '*furta sacra*' or 'sacred thefts'

The knights who had gone into the cave were Templar Knights and were based in southern France in the Languedoc region. When they returned home from the Crusade, they boasted an incredible wealth, Dagobert, their leader commissioned a series of splendid churches and forts in the Rennes le Chateau region and the Templars enjoyed a power unrivalled in all of Europe. Their bloodline became sacred and their power immense.

'Did they find the Grail?' Adam looked at Isaac, willing his answer

'That was the rumour at the time' It was said that they assumed the riches of God for discovering the grail, remember that the Grail has been a almost revered artifact of which there has never been any proof that it actually existed'. Isaac went on, ' Consider the tales of your Arthur and the knights of the Round table and their quest or the Grail' If the Templars did find it, then it would go some way to explaining their power'.

'You don't believe that, do you? Adam asked as Isaac furrowed his brow.

'Correct, my young friend, I think they discovered a treasure much more valuable, I think they found the last will and testament of Paul and in whatever they discovered therein lies the secret of their wealth and power'. I, unlike many others have not bought into the grail story, I have a much different interpretation.

'What is it' asked Adam

'Later' mumbled Isaac

'You mean this Yahweh? don't you? said Adam

'The power of the Templars lasted for about two hundred years until they were betrayed in the most savage fashion. It was purported that they had links with the Cathari or ' Pure Ones'. These Cathars were a poor simple people who believed they were the true followers of the Nazarene, they developed a church and their doctrine spread. They were pacifists who broke bread to signify a sacrament that cut them from the physical world'.

'By 1208, Pope Innocent was so inflamed that he invoked the reward in heaven clause offered to the Crusaders to anyone who waged a holy war against these poor people. Rome had to be seen to be all-powerful and the Crusaders were the Pope's assassins'

'A war against heresy was a war against difference, Consider for a moment who I am and where I have come from' said Isaac

'I am a Russian Jew who left my country as the Russian Revolution was starting. A small number of communists took power, yet within a few years' huge numbers of people, including many of the civil servants that had administered the previous regime had joined the Communist Party. Why? Because if you wanted to get on, you had to be a party member and if you associated yourself in any way with the past regime. You were branded a subversive, an enemy of the state and hunted down. Sound familiar?

Adam at this stage was gripping the arm of the chair so as not to show Isaac that his hand was shaking.

'You see now' said Isaac. 'Once Christianity became the religion of the Roman Empire, its numbers swelled enormously. The priests were not required to pay taxes, if you wanted to conform in Rome you became a Christian, if not you ran the risk of being branded a pagan, an enemy of God. There had been enough Christian bloodletting in the Coliseum before it was fashionable to be one for them to ruthlessly adopt the same practices and worse against those who they thought were a threat to the new found popularity of Christianity. Like Communism, Christianity began with a message of freedom and equality but ended up creating an authoritarian and despotic regime. The Church in Rome has imposed it's creed with threats and violence'.

Adam stopped Isaac 'Isn't that what Hitler is trying to instigate against your people?'

'He isn't trying, said Isaac ' he's doing'. Look at what's happening, it's Russia all over again with the only difference being that they're marching to a different tune.

Isaac paused then, he lifted his glasses onto his head and looked away. Adam thought that he could see tears in the old man's eyes and suggested they had done enough for one day. He helped the old man to his feet and packed his books away. Adam took him back to his room and put him to bed. He wandered back into the front room and stood at the window looking out over the city. His mind was a whirl with thoughts of conquest and pillage, he still was no closer to discovering the secret of his Father. He did not know what this Yahweh was, he did know that whatever it was, it was imperative that he discover it's secret, if only for the sake of his father and the only other person that he knew it had affected

…………….. Maria.

Maria had been taken to Wilhemstrasse in the sedan, she knew where she was going and who had taken her, she had heard about the basement of the building and what went on. This building was the first stop on the way to 'corrective re-education' in one of the new camps at Dachau or Mauthausen.

The car slewed to a halt and she was manhandled into a room, it was very well furnished and she sat down in front of a large desk. There was a bust of 'Der Fuehrer's' head on the desk, a light and a blotter. A leather chair was at the other side and the room was very tastefully decorated. She sat quietly for some 10 minutes, unaware that her every move was being watched through a two-way mirror on the far wall. She fingered her press card, nervously, it said her name was Maria Shultz and that she worked for 'Vossische Zeitung'. She had been very careful not to give any indication as to her true identity on the insistence of her father, he kept saying that it was better that way. She didn't really understand at the time, given what she now knew, it was probably the only thing she had got going for her.

'Good morning, Frau Tannenbaum'

Maria froze, how did they know? She sat, rigid in the chair as a tall, well groomed man came around to the leather chair and sat down.

'You are surprised? he said

Maria didn't speak

'Come, Come, Frau Tannenbaum, you didn't really think that a false identity card would protect you'.

The man smiled, Maria became aware of him looking at her, he ran his eyes up and down her body, she flared and was aware of her face reddening.

'You have nothing to fear so long as we talk to each other' said the man. He was wearing a well-cut suit, a white shirt and tie and had a small swastika badge in his lapel. His hands were well manicured and Maria smelled the hint of cologne from him.

'My name is Alfred Rosenberg and I am an advisor to the Fuehrer on, let us say, special affairs. I believe you can assist me in solving a little puzzle'. He smiled.

'I don't know what you are talking about, My name is Maria Schultz and I am a reporter. I demand to know why I was arrested and why I am being held.

Rosenberg's nostrils flared, he dropped his voice and hissed at Maria

'Listen, you little Jewish Bitch, with a click of my fingers I can condemn you to a death you will not enjoy. You have been poking your nose where it does not belong and you will end up the same way as your father if you do not co-operate'

My Father! Maria stifled a shout, 'what about my Father?'

Ah, said Rosenberg, regaining his calm, 'It would appear he cut himself shaving ....

Maria stared at the man, her eyes filled with tears and she started to shudder.

'It makes little difference to me, Jew, You will tell me what I want to know, one way or the other'.

Maria looked at him, this evil in front of her, 'What is it you think I know?

'That's better' said Rosenberg ' Where is Isaac Tauber?

Maria stammered 'Who'

'Ah' said Rosenberg, 'Isaac Tauber, you know him, he is the Jew that was helping you decipher your piece of cloth. What did he think that it said?'

Maria's mind was in a twirl of confusion, what did they know?? She struggled to regain her composure and think, think!! . The room started to spin as Rosenberg smiled at her again

'Before you speak, think very carefully, if you tell me what you know, I will ensure you are kept alive, if you do not'..... he shrugged his shoulders.

Maria said 'I don't have it, I gave it to Tauber. I don't know what it meant, all I knew was what my mother told me when she gave it to me ......

Rosenberg's head jerked up ' What was that'

Maria replied 'They will not succeed '

Rosenberg could not contain his excitement, he knew it! The Jew, Tauber must be found at once, he must have the piece in his possession, this would ensure his destiny, to think that he Alfred Rosenberg had the power to deliver the Third Reich its most potent weapon!!

He lifted the telephone and summonsed a guard ' Take Miss Shultz to the 'salon', ensure she is comfortable, she is not permitted to leave and is under my direct control'.

Maria got up and turned towards the door

'Stop, a moment Fraulein, you said your mother gave you the package, what else was in it?

Maria told him about the upturned sundial like instrument.

'One last question please' Rosenberg stood up and walked around the desk to face her.

'Your Father, what did he do?

'My father was a baker, sobbed Maria, what have you done to him, why was he killed?

That is of no importance to me now' snapped Rosenberg 'Did he have a brother?'

Maria looked at him, puzzled. 'His brother died when I was very young, I think he was a soldier in the British Army and was killed in Palestine.

Rosenberg beamed and slammed his hand down on his desk, he knew one of the five!

That morning, Isaac Tauber had gone with Adam to the British Library at St Pancras, a landscaped square off Euston Road. He had slept well and whilst he was happy at being in

England, he was troubled at the knowledge or rather the lack of it that he possessed. He still did not know what Yahweh meant, he was sure the boy didn't either. He also knew that Adam did not know where his father had acquired the contents of the box. Adam had shown him the letter that his father had written for him, the letter he had taken from the box., he had read and re-read it over the years but he still couldn't understand the references. As he and Adam made their way through the plaza and past the large bronze statue of Sir Isaac Newton, Isaac pondered on what to say to the boy. He asked Adam where the 21 letter was, Adam told him that he never found out what was in the letter and found himself telling Isaac all about Megan.

When they finally got inside the library, they'd gone up a broad set of steps and directly into the reading room and on through the discreet paneled door that led to the carrels. Isaac settled down in the double carrel that he'd had Adam reserve for them the day before and sent Adam off to get some coffee.

He had seen the same letter written to Maria's mother and passed on to Maria. He knew of the platoon that had made a discovery on a hill near the Dead Sea. He didn't know what they had discovered, and wasn't convinced that they themselves did. He knew that each of them had a richly jeweled dagger in their possession and that the 'funny sundial' was some form of measuring instrument. He didn't know why they had kept their secret for so long and why it had been important to pass it on. This uncertainty was heightened because despite his reading and investigating, he still could not comprehend who must not succeed. At least now he had two parts of the scroll to work on.

He was sure that Adam was innocent to all of these things but like Maria possessed a tenacity that was likeable ... Maria?, he wondered what had happened to her? He hoped she was safe, it was fortuitous that she had given the package to Adam when she did and that it was safe. He wondered about the path he was on, for 30 years he had been convinced, through his interpretation of the scripture that the Nazarene was not the Messiah and that the world awaited the coming of the one.

From his earliest days in Leningrad in 1860, he had been attracted to the written word and study. It was dangerous to acknowledge your birthright in those days for fear of the ghetto, like Maria, he had been known as Isaac Slovinsky in those days and he preached the Russian Orthodox faith. He was a good student and promised much. He became a teacher to the children of the rich sea merchants and spent his free days in the Hermitage and the other places of learning. For 20 years he taught like this, until he got an opportunity through one of his sponsors to travel to Moscow and teach at the Great University. Isaac was elated, as far as his peers were aware, he was a studious and well liked man who was diligent in his work. He traveled to Moscow in 1905 to take up a position in the department of Religious Works on the University campus.

One day, whilst researching an old Jewish manuscript, he found a reference to the children of the Essene. From that moment on, he became engrossed in his search for these people. He trawled through the scriptures and manuscripts of the testimonies of the library, looking for clues as to their existence and the secrets that they held. In 1917 when the Aurora was firing blank shells to start the Russian Revolution, he headed back to Leningrad and then on to Germany where he settled in Berlin using his proper name of Tauber and teaching in the Great Synagogue School in Freidrichstrasse. It was here that he met Mrs. Tannenbaum and her daughter Maria and through the friendship, learned with increasing excitement of the fate of her husband, Maria's father.

On the day in question, he was sitting at home when Maria appeared. she was distressed, saying that her mother was unwell and that she (Maria) was to fetch 'nice Mr. Tauber' . He went round and realising that she was dying, sent for a doctor and tried to make her as comfortable as he could.

'Look after Maria for me, Mr. Tauber ... 'Please'

'None of that talk' soothed Isaac ' you'll be all right, try to rest now'

'Mr. Tauber, she said' here is a box under the bed, it is Maria's legacy from her father, I trust you will know what to do'

'I don't understand, Mrs. Tannenbaum, surely Solomon is Maria's father'. Isaac watched as the old woman's eyes clouded over 'Solomon is my dear husband David's brother. When David died, Maria was but a baby, it was decided that Solomon would live with us, he has been like a father to Maria to the fact that she refers to him as her father'.

Isaac was stunned and when Solomon came into the room, Isaac asked him if that was indeed the case, Solomon Tannenbaum began to weep and admitted that he was indeed the brother of David Tannenbaum. He admitted that when David died, Eva and the child were in danger of being forced into the ghetto. He assumed his brother's identity and it has been their secret all of these years. He had tried to be a good father to Maria, she thought that her uncle had died in Palestine, it seemed like the easiest way at the time.

Isaac nodded and agreed to keep their secret. He was much more interested in the box and when it was opened he could see the parchment cloth with the hieroglyphics. He held it in his hand and looked at it. He was speechless, there before his eyes in the bottom corner of the tear was a mark that he had waited to see all his life... The mark of the Essene

Maria's mother died a week later and Maria continued to live with her 'father' oblivious that she now held the word of the Essene in her possession. She was oblivious of its importance until the day that she had been arrested. Isaac had not told her everything, she was not strong enough to know who her real father was and the importance of the legacy, thankfully she didn't know what the translation referred to and was not aware of Yahweh.

Adam returned with two cups of coffee and was amazed to see that Isaac had even more heavy large volumes of reference material spread across the green leather topped desk, Isaac was busy scribbling away on a writing pad, oblivious to his return.

Do we continue? he smiled brightly at Isaac

'Yes 'said Isaac 'but first there is something you should know. You recall I told you about your father and the four other people making their 'find' on that hill in Palestine?

Adam nodded

'Maria's real father was along with him', Isaac then proceeded to tell Adam the story of David and Solomon Tannenbaum.

There was silence for a long time until finally Adam spoke, ' you said yesterday that you thought you knew what my inscription meant, tell me what you think'.

Isaac looked at him over his glasses and sighed ....

'When we finished yesterday I was telling you about the slaughter of the Cathars on the Pope's command'.

Chapter 6

Jaques du Mollay was the Grand Templar Master at the time of the Inquisition. He was a very powerful man with command of riches beyond the wildest dreams of every other leader at the time, including the King of France. Philip IV was essentially bankrupt and knew that the riches of the templar's would solve his worries in one fell swoop. Shortly before daybreak on Friday 13 of October 1307, he made his move.

He fabricated a charge of heresy against the Templar order and had all of their members including their Grand Master arrested.

William Imbert was appointed the chief inquisitor of France and was deeply versed in all inquisitorial arts and practices and was charged by Philip to get a confession by whatever means necessary from the leader of the Templars, Jacques Du Mollay.

Imbert, having being wrongly convinced that the Templars had defiled the cross, decided on the torture he would use on Mollay.

He stood awaiting the leader of the Templars to be brought before him.

'Strip him' commanded Imbert

Mollay was tied by two ropes and then having been whipped and bloodies was dragged across to the large wooden door in the centre of the room.

'Stand him on a footstool' commanded Imbert, 'You are about to learn the folly of mocking the true cross'

Imbert's chief assistant slapped Mollay hard in the face and forced a thorn crown onto his head. He then pulled Mollay's right arm almost vertical above his head and drove a nail between the radius and ulna bones, carefully making sure that he did not cut into any veins. HE then pulled Mollay's left arm sideways and upwards but at a lower level and nailed to the door. Imbert then approached Mollay and pulled his left foot across his right one and drove a third nail in, securing both feet to the door.

Mollay screamed in pain, the force of the first nail had dislocated his right shoulder. Imbert began to chant and then question Mollay about heretical practices in the Paris temple. In order to inflict as much pain as possible. Imbert opened the door and when Mollay did not respond, he simply opened the door and swung it to and fro. Mollay began to sweat profusely and his heart was pounding wildly. Just as he believed he was about to die, Imbert stopped the torture and placed his body in a shroud, Mollay's supposed mocking of the use of a shroud had not gone un-noticed..

Philip had warned Imbert that he had to get a confession, if he did, Mollay was his to kill. If he didn't, Mollay was to live.

They did not succeed.

7 years later, they tried again…

On the 19 March 1314, Jacques du Mollay was taken to a small Island in the river Seine called Ile des Javiaux where he was slowly roasted to death over a hot smokeless fire. The heat was applied with great care, first to his feet and genitals, to ensure that the suffering lasted as long as possible. Before he died, Jacques de Mollay, his body black in death, screamed in his pain

'Let evil swiftly befall all those who have wrongly condemned us – Yahweh will avenge our deaths'

Twenty years later the World was ravaged by bubonic plague, commonly known as

'THE BLACK DEATH'

They were in the main reading room of the British Museum, Isaac involuntarily lapsed into periods of silence as he drank in the magnificence of the building, the books, the reverence with which the students conversed in miniscule language at their desks. He beckoned to Adam to come closer to him and he began...

'It was feared that the Cathars claim to be the true followers of the Nazarene was embarrassing the church. The papacy in the middle ages was a cesspool of every kind of calumny that man could inflict on man. First we had the Borgia Popes and for the next 250 years, holy was the last thing you needed to be to wear the mantle of Peter'. Isaac settled into his monologue again succeeding in capturing Adam's attention until he was in an almost trance like state.

'In 1232, Gregory 1X, then 80 years of age published a 'bull' establishing the Inquisition. Between 1232 and 1573, a series of Papal laws did away with every shade of difference in belief' Isaac went on 'The Jews were not the only ones to suffer the imposition of pogroms against their faith. The Pope appointed the Dominicans as papal inquisitors and believe me Adam, these people had a license to do and go where they wanted and no matter the falsehood, if they found you guilty, you perished. Do you see what is happening?

'But why?' said Adam

'O, there have been many reasons put forward for this bestiality, you have to remember that these people acted in secret and completely arbitrarily. There were no guidelines for guilt, in many cases, if they thought you were guilty, they tortured you until you admitted what they wanted. Consider this scenario ' An inquisitor had absolute decree of life or death and in the name of the Pope could murder anybody. Suppose you or any of your family cross him or any of his 'friends', no debate, torture until you confess, man, wife, children, nothing was sacred. They were explicitly forbidden to have mercy.

'Now, suppose Rome had discovered the truth behind the testimony of Paul or even had an inkling that the Faith that they were preaching was false? . Consider the church's ownership of the crucifixion, in those years, artists had to show Jesus fully dressed on the cross in a glorious celebration of martyrdom. When pain was described, his Jewish origin had to be protected, after all The Jews had killed God'.

'The same church that professed toleration and the 'turning of the other cheek' exterminated them because they feared that the Templars or Cathars would spread the truth'.

'In the Inquisition, guilt was presumed, the victim never knew what the charges were and was forbidden to ask. At no stage was he allowed to ask a question. He soon learned that every semblance of justice was to be denied him. His prosecution produced the most implausible of witnesses in secret, he could not question them or produce witnesses of his own for rebuttal'.

'Can you think of a better way to suppress the testimony of Paul, given that he was revered for his role in the establishment of the whole 'Christian' institution in the first place. Do you think anybody would dare to utter that Jesus was not the messiah let alone think that he was buried in the south of France.'

'So' said Adam 'they knew about Yahweh?

'Not necessarily' said Isaac 'I'm pretty sure that they feared the truth and in their own testimonies knew that The Nazarene had a brother called James. In their own bible he is referred to as the 'favourite' and 'most loved' of the 12 . When Jesus died, there was no reaction by the population. When James was murdered, the Jews started a war with the Romans that lasted for 30 years and ended in the sacking of the temple in Jerusalem. The seat of the church was in Rome, it is totally implausible to consider that they did not know part of the truth and so long as it was buried, they didn't care. The Inquisition was enacted to ensure the truth stayed buried.'

There were few left in the library, another day had passed but Adam wasn't ready to leave just yet, he pressed Isaac

'Isaac, you must tell me about Yahweh, tell me what you know, what does my cloth say?

'Why does the church go so far to Protect its identity?

'How is my father involved?

'What has happened To Maria?

'Why did those men take her?

Adam stopped, his eyes were wet and there was so much he did not understand, what he did know was that he would have to follow this to the end. He was a journalist, he should be unemotional, but this was different because it was personal. Adam had to find out about his Father, he had to put the jigsaw together and at the moment the only person who could help him was Isaac.

'I shall be the father and he shall be my son' is the rough translation of your piece' said Isaac ' and when you put it together with the piece that Maria gave you, you have

'I shall be the father and he shall be my son' ' he is the branch'

Adam looked at the translation, It's obviously a reference to a resurrection'

'I agree', said Isaac, 'there is only one problem ... this was written nearly 2000 years before the birth of the Nazarene. All of my research would indicate that the Yahweh has yet to happen. There are clues, Saul, the Crusades, Templars, Kaballah, Cathars, the Inquisition as well as all of the testaments discovered over the centuries. There is the mark of the Essene on your cloth as well. I have also studied the writings of a 16th century called Michal Nostradamus....

Adam stopped,

'Coincidence? I mean, the name?'

Isaac smiled, listen to what I have to say about him, you can make your own mind up.'

Isaac recited the story like he had written the words himself

'In 1555, Nostradamus produced a series of writings or prophecies about things that were going to happen in the future. He foretold of man being able to fly, he predicted the First World War. His foretelling also speak of a greater threat that will come from the East and will result in the deaths of many. He makes reference to the blood of the broken cross and the wrath of a knight called Hister. More importantly, Nostradamus foretold of a new era where 'time would not be time as we know it and that the one who was the father and the son would come to take his rightful place. I think he was a messenger, like all the rest who had been empowered by the Yahweh to let generations know of the great lie by telling them the truth. At the time he was castigated as a mad man that should not surprise you when you consider the treatment meted out to such luminarii as Galileo.' Isaac paused for a breath before continuing

'Here was a man who was professor of mathematics in Pisa by the time he was 25, twenty years later he was hailed as the greatest philosopher of his generation and as the inventor of the scientific revolution. He turned his invention, the telescope to the night sky and concluded that the heavens were not celestial, the truth had been 'missed' for 2000 years, the earth was not static, it moved around the sun. In another case, the monk, Copernicus had suggested this as a mathematical hypothesis and had been forced upon pain of death to withdraw it. Can you imagine the reaction an already paranoid church was going to have with this revelation. Once again the precious argument about the revolution of time and the meaning of the stars was under investigation. Galileo begged disciples of Aristotle, (Aristotelians) to look at his findings, they refused saying

'How could a tube with glass at the end disprove Aristotle and an interpretation of scripture that was centuries old?'

'The ones that did look were convinced that what they saw was in the glass and not the sky! Galileo contented himself by saying that when they died, what he saw they, too would see on their way to heaven'.

Isaac paused again for breath, the effort of the past few days were starting to tell on him

'Do you understand? Adam ..... The pope decreed in March 1616 that to suggest that the sun was an immovable object in the centre of a universe is ' foolish and absurd, philosophically false and formally heretical, This edit remained in place until 1822! The list goes on as Newton, Darwin and Freud all suffered the same fate as Galileo. You should now begin to understand why it was so easy for Luther to question the wisdom of these people. It wasn't for lack of evidence to prove that they were completely immoral, false and most of all had created the greatest holocaust of all time by following their ridiculous beliefs. Now consider what you have witnessed in Berlin, the book burning, the Nazification, the indoctrination, the ruthless stamping out of all opposition, a ministry of propaganda?'

'What does that tell you?'

Isaac paused and looked over to where Adam was sitting mesmerised at what Isaac was telling him. There was a force or entity existing, a new truth, one that would bring the world to the brink, its very existence questioned and challenged. what a power it would be to understand the truth, then he stopped and considered the awful reality of what he was thinking, Yahweh had to stay hidden and his Father knew this, he and his four colleagues had to ensure this. That meant that there was someone out there who knew of the Yahweh and wanted to control it and was prepared to kill as many as was necessary to discover its secrets. It all made so much sense, after all his father had been murdered, Solomon dead, probably Maria as well and but for the grace of God .... He stopped.... Grace of whom?

He had got Isaac out of Germany in time. He did not yet know the full story but he was convinced of one thing ... for as long as he breathed... they, whoever they were would not succeed.

Isaac broke the silence 'Your father, Adam, he was a soldier, yes? He fought in Crimea and was then garrisoned in Jerusalem around 1885 or so as part of a British Expedition Force, what do you know about him?

'Not a lot really', said Adam recounting the times he'd spoken about his father. 'I asked Wakenshaw to tell me about him and my mother, I also asked Mrs. Govan, she was my governess. They told me that he was a very proud man who loved my mother very deeply, she traveled with him on his journeys and they were very happy. I found a few old diaries of my mother in the house when it was being closed up and I kept them ...... they gave me a good understanding of my parents although interestingly enough, my mother noted in her diary about a change that came over my father around about the time that he supposed to have made his discovery.

Isaac asked him to explain

Adam continued ' She said he became very withdrawn and would not speak to her about what was wrong, she knew there was something because the wives of two of the other soldiers were complaining of the same thing, Adam paused ....

Mrs. Reid and Mrs. Johannsen ...... that means we now have 4 names!! I can go to regimental headquarters and pull their records!!

'Lets Go' ....said Isaac

Chapter 7

Alfred Rosenberg was convinced that Adolf Hitler was the 'one' described by Nostradamus as 'Hister'. He and Rudolf Hess had encouraged him from the day that he joined what was then the German Workers Party. They engineered him to the leadership of the party and enthralled by his vision and rhetoric, devoted their life to the delivery of his vision. His vision was enshrined in Mein Kamfp (My Struggle) and in it, he laid the foundation of a 1000-year Reich based on the principles of Aryanism and Blood sacrifice.

Secretly, Rosenberg and Hess belonged to a grouping called 'Thule'. They were a group of very rich German business and professional people who bankrolled what became the NSDAP to further their beliefs. They were convinced that the astrological studies they had carried out had foretold Hitler as being the one and everything they had heard had furthered this belief.

Rosenberg himself had committed his thinking to print, in 'The myth of the 20th Century' he talked about 'the religion of the blood being the blood of the people being the soul of the race and the vehicle of the spirit'. He challenged the Biblical account of evolution and spoke about a master race of Teutonic Supermen from the mystical world of Atlantis. When this world was destroyed, the survivors came ashore in India and eventually settled in Tibet. Rosenberg was convinced that these people were the forefathers of the German race, they worshipped the broken cross or swastika and practised in a hidden world.

The Thule had already sponsored anthropological expeditions to the region to validate their theory, hundreds of physiological experiments had been carried out to determine heritage traits and it was during these that they stumbled, quite by accident on the mystery of the lost tribe of the Essene.

At first, Rosenberg dismissed the claim, the hatred of the impure, the Jew had already been festering in Germany since the end of the first World War. The 'friecorps' had their regular blood swathes through the ghettos of most German cities during the depression, killing and maiming Jews in blame for their country's situation. Hitler had focused on developing blame and with the help of people such as Goebbels and Rosenberg had whipped up an anti - Semite atmosphere that suited their purpose. They used pamphlets and magazines such as 'Ostara' to spout their hatred. There were plans in place for Blood laws when Hitler eventually came to power whereby Jews would be denied citizenry, it would be forbidden to consort with Jews, inter relationships were banned and there was mysterious talk about a 'final solution'.

Rosenberg knew that he had to understand the Jew in order to control them, he undertook to research their culture and had a full department working on 'deciphering' their 'torah'. It was here that his interest in the Essene was awakened. The Eastern churches had suggested the existence of this 'holy tribe' who were revered by the masses and as he started to delve into their mystery, he found references right through the early church of a forbidden secret.

Rosenberg had gained another stoke of luck, by chance he was in the press room one day and spotted an article condemning the lack of information on corrective training, scouring it he saw that it was written by a Maria Schultz. He lifted it and called Heinrich Mueller at the Geheime Statzpolitzi headquarters and asked him to do a check on the girl. What came back staggered him, she was a Jew, who has succeeded in hiding her race and acting as a German. His first inclination was to have her arrested but he changed his mind and coerced the editor of her paper on pain of his own and his family's death to give her access to confidential information and interviews with some of her 'missing' people.

He wanted to see where it would lead him and when he discovered the identity of the reporter she was meeting with, he was convinced that he was on to something. He wondered who the older man that she visited was, it didn't seem important until, running out of patience, he decided to act. He sent that fool, Mueller, instructions to interrogate her, they went to the house and when she wasn't there, they roughed up the old man, discovered he was a Jew and murdered him.

Their report told of him shouting about the 'demon or yamon', telling the goons that they would not 'succeed'. They had brought back the old diary that they had found as well, it was written in Yiddish, when Rosenberg had it translated, he sat, stunned, at what was in front of him, the story of 5 men and a discovery of such proportions that it led to the death of one and the disappearance of 4 others ...... A cloth, some funny shaped dials and a sign...The sign of the Essene

The next day, it took Adam and Isaac a good two hours to get to Sandringham. Adam had phoned ahead and had managed to get speaking to a captain in his father's regiment, he told him what he wanted and was told that he would be expected and to get directions to the Officers Mess from the Gate sentry. As Adam and Isaac approached the Mess, an officer approached them.

'You must be Adam Carter' boomed the officer, my father served with the General, damned fine soldier, My name is Reid, Captain Harold Reid.

Isaac stopped, Adam gaped....... 'Is there something wrong gentlemen?'

'Can we go somewhere to talk, Captain? said Adam, 'this is my friend, Isaac Tauber.

Isaac and the captain shook hands.

‘Lets go to my office’, Captain Reid led the way and they were escorted into his office. There was a picture on the wall, Adam recognised his father, ‘when was that taken? asked Adam

‘Middle East somewhere, that’s my Father to the left of yours

‘Is there a Johannse?’... Isaac’s eyes were riveted to the frame.

‘Ah yes’ Sergeant Johannsen is at the end of the line, he’s the one with the French Kepi on.

Now, what can I do for you?

Adam sat down and explained the story of the find that his and Captain’s Reid Father made, he started to describe the cloth when Captain Reid stopped him

‘Was this in an old wooden box, like ammunition casing only inlaid with some markings?

Isaac looked at Adam.... ‘Yes’ said Adam

Captain Reid got up and walked over to the bookcase and took out... an old wooden box!

‘I’ve kept this for sentimental value, my mother gave it to me when My Father died, she said that it was his dying wish that I was to have it and that I must always keep in on my person. I’ve been carrying the damned thing around for the last 14 years and have no idea what is in it.

It was Captain Reid’s turn to be amazed as Adam pulled a key from under his shirt and put it into the lock, it opened and Isaac lifted a piece of cloth, a dagger and a funny shaped article that looked like an upturned sundial.

‘You’d better sit down, Captain, what we have to say will take a while’.

Adam looked over at Isaac and almost agreed without speaking that they would only tell Captain Reid what they needed to. They explained the presence of the cloth and the objects and Isaac’s flight from Germany. They also told him about Maria, Adam, as a journalist, wanted to investigate this as it may give clues as to why his father was murdered. Captain Reid listened to their account, he confirmed that the last he heard, Johannsen was living in Denmark or Germany, he wasn't sure. It had started to rain and Isaac was keen to return to London before nightfall, Adam had agreed to meet the Captain the next day at the Museum to try and translate his piece of cloth. He didn't close the box again and the Captain was enthralled by the dagger. He took it out of the sheath, there appeared to be an inscription on the blade...

How stupid they had been!

Isaac berated himself for not looking, he copied the inscription and promised to check Adam and Maria's dagger's when he got back. They got up to make their leave but just as the Captain opened the door, Isaac paused...

'Tell me Captain, have you any idea why General Carter and your father would have gone to such great lengths to protect what they had discovered?

'No, I'm sorry' said Captain Reid ' Maybe it was something to do with the photograph'

'The what' said Adam and Isaac together

'The photograph on the wall there' said the Captain 'there are only 4 officers in the picture'.

'Yes' said Adam 'we know that, what was the photograph of?'

'Lets see' said Captain Reid. He went over and took the frame down from the wall and looked at the inscription 'The sons of Zadok 1885'

'Ah yes 'said the captain 'a famous chapter'

'What do you mean?' asked Isaac

'Oh. I am sorry, not something one talks about I suppose...

'What?' they both said simultaneously

The captain looked at both them, 'You obviously didn't know, the sons of Zadok was the name of their lodge'

'Lodge?' Adam looked at the captain

'Freemasons, Adam, four of the men belonged to The sons of Zadok Lodge.' They were all freemasons.

The colour drained from Isaac's face and he went to sit down again, he could feel his heart pounding in his chest and his head, he was aware of a sweat breaking out all over his body and his breathing became very shallow. He tried to focus but the room started to spin, the last thing he remembered was the picture on the desk before he collapsed.

Chapter 8

At that very moment, Major Erich Nuemann was painfully aware that his boss, Sturbann Fuhrer Alfred Rosenberg was not very happy. Nuemann and his men had searched Berlin long and hard looking for Isaac Tauber. They'd wreaked his house, looking for, what?

They'd discovered the visit of a younger man and discovered Adam's name and address.

They'd gone round and his landlady had told them that he was a reporter. Further questioning uncovered the fact that him and the old man had left in a car for Paris four days previously, the day after the Jew Bitch had been arrested. Nuemann went back to headquarters to report this and witnessed one of his boss's famous temper bouts. He longed for 'salon' duty, to start later on that night, at least he would be pleasured by that part of his duty.

Rosenberg was raging!

'Think' he commanded himself. 'Who was this reporter, Johnson? And what was his connection to the Jew. Where were they? With a four-day start they could be anywhere! Damn, Damn! He sat down, wait a minute! The men who arrested the Jew girl said they had punched someone, they also said they thought she had given him something, they were not sure. It was time to have another talk with the Jew bitch.

'Ah, Fraulien Shultz, come in, so glad to see you again, I trust you are comfortable?

'When can I go? asked Maria 'I've told you all I know?

'I think I'll be the judge of that, please sit down.

Rosenberg had the translation of the diary in front of him. 'Tell me, do you know anything about your 'Uncle' and how he was killed.

'I'm sorry 'said Maria 'I've told you all I know'.

'Very well' said Rosenberg 'let me tell you some things about your family!'

Maria felt the water on her face, she came round to find herself sitting in the same chair, she was panicking, how could they know? Rosenberg watched her with interest, he had told her about his idea that her Uncle was in fact her father and that he along with 4 other men had discovered a secret so great that he may have been killed to keep him silent.

He told her about family detail that he could not have possibly known unless, had they captured Tauber?

What about Adam?

Rosenberg spoke ' Why did you give your package to the Englisher?

Maria looked at him, what to do? She gathered her thoughts, if they had captured any of them, then they would have the cloth by now, of course, they couldn't have it, Maria laughed to herself... they escaped!

Looking at Rosenberg she said 'You will never succeed' by now the pieces are in a safe place. Immediately she spoke, she realised what she'd said, stupid.

Now it was Rosenberg's turn to smile, he knew the identity of two of the five!

Isaac awoke to find himself in a bed in the camp hospital, Adam had fallen asleep across the bottom of the bed. Isaac looked at him and wondered whether they were wise in going on with their journey, so much of the unknown elements of his life's work had been brought out into the open in the last few weeks. He was delirious with discovery, now however he was starting to question the price that had to be paid.

Of course! , Captain Reid's assertion put a vital part of the jigsaw in place, Maria's father, David could actually have been killed to ensure his silence, stop him talking about the discovery, what discovery? A discovery serious enough to kill for, why, how?

By then, the other 4 would have known the significance of their find and how easy it would have been for David to have been given a dangerous duty when he returned from his leave, the others would have been familiar with the history of freemasonry. Furthermore though Isaac was sure that the cloth was in fact the last testimony of the Essene, given the history of the Templars and their close association with the establishment of Freemasonry in the Middle ages. He could not discount the possibility that the five officers were covering up some freemasonry secret and had been posted to the Middle East, immediately he thought of this however, he discounted it, where did the cloths and the boxes come from? No, whatever discovery that was made had been made in Palestine, wait a minute, Of course!!! Isaac berated himself, the five had discovered something in the cradle of Judaism and Christianity, something so powerful that it had killed and would keep killing to stay protected.

Isaac also knew of the degrees of Freemasonry, he knew of their secret beliefs and their nearly tandem worship of a quasi religion that could be traced right to, not Jesus but James!

Isaac mind raced, suppose James was a messenger who instructed Saul through Magdalene to preach the false doctrine, this would be a perfect way to protect Yahweh, no one other than a handful of people would know the truth, Yahweh would be safe. Was freemasonry the modern day guardians of Yahweh!. Isaac sat up and at that Adam awoke with a start...

'You are all right? asked Adam

'Yes' said Isaac ' what happened to me? Where is Captain Reid?

'You passed out as Reid was telling us of the origin of the picture. We had you checked and put you to bed. Reid and I went back to the mess.

'Did he say anything to you?

'Well, Yes he did actually, he seemed surprised at your reaction to the fact that his father and mine were freemasons, he told me that all his family had their lodge membership

'Is he a mason? breathed Isaac

'Yes' said Adam, that's what he was talking about, he wanted to know about what we were doing, what your interest was and where we had come from. I told him about Maria'

Adam jumped at Isaac's response

'You what! Quick, we must get out of here, I'll tell you as we go. Isaac got up and he and Adam went across the parade ground to the car, they were going through the gate as Captain Reid was coming towards them in a jeep, as they drew level, Reid waved them to stop, Isaac shouted at Adam...' Keep going, keep going'. Adam drove on and when they were clear of the base, he pulled the car into the side of the road...

'Right' said Adam. 'I need some explanations!' Isaac looked at him, was this too much for them ... he shook his head, 'Adam' he said 'Your father may have had something to do with the death of Maria's father!

'That is the most preposterous thing ...

'Wait ' barked Isaac 'I know these things' Your father and his friends had no choice, in discovering what they did, they had no choice, they had to protect their find because for the first time in 4000 years, they had found evidence of the truth of something so terrible it had to be kept secret '.

He went on to explain the Freemason connection and promised that all would become clearer when they translated the copy of Reid's cloth

'But we are seeing him tomorrow' ...... Adam's voice trailed off

'Somehow or other, I don't think so' replied Isaac.

Captain Reid didn't know what to do, he knew that the old Jew stumbled onto something and that he had inadvertently confirmed his suspicions. He wasn't worried about young Carter, he seemed oblivious to the whole thing. Reid pondered his options, He could do nothing, not really an option he thought. He could call his brother, a civil servant in London or he could speak to his worshipful master. Lifting the telephone, he called over to Regimental and asked to be put through to the Colonel.

Reid recited the events of the previous few hours to a silent Colonel Maxwell, when he'd finished, the colonel asked him what had happened as the young man took ill. Reid repeated that as he fell he kept muttering what he thought was ' must not succeed 'or something to that effect. The colonel froze, he hadn't heard those words in over 20 years, he'd had to kill the last time he'd heard them and now the son of the man he had killed and some old Jew were coming back to haunt him. He told Reid to say nothing to anybody, he'd speak to him later. He then got up and went over to a cabinet where he pushed a bookend, a secreted door opened and he took a booklet from the compartment.

Returning to his desk, he stared at the cover, a set of dividers and the words Rex Deus inscribed beneath them, he opened the book read off three telephone numbers and dialed them, telling each recipient what had transpired in detail. When he had finished, he put the book into a wastepaper bin and set it on fire, making sure that it had been completely destroyed, he poured himself a large whiskey and sat back in his chair.

'You know what you must do' rang in his ears, he put the glass down and opened the top drawer of his desk and took out his service revolver, he checked the chamber, put the barrel of the revolver in his mouth and fired one shot...

Isaac and Adam were now in Adam's apartment. Adam had gone and fetched all of the material from the museum and Isaac had already translated the piece from Reid. It said

'In Zion at the end of time'

Isaac spoke in a low voice

'The 11 Templar Knights that discovered the secrets of the temple were from the most important families of the time. They assumed the role of 'Kings of God' and used the tarot cards to worship and communicate. As these families assimilated into a Christian culture they protected their identity as an evolving alternative to the Catholic cum Christian telling of the messianic story. When their last leader was murdered in the Inquisition, the families went underground under the guise of ancient freemasonry, not the 17th century English nonsense, no, direct bloodline assumption from the original Jewish organisation. The families ensured the bloodline as the eldest son of each of the families reached 21 and were told of the history of their destiny and their responsibility to the truth'.

Adam had never seen Isaac so animated and intense

'They possessed the secret of the Essene, the scrolls discovered gave knowledge of the testimony of Saul and the presence of the deity! ' Your father's lodge, Adam is one of the oldest lodge's in existence tracing its history to the time of the crusades and I think that the discovery that those men made in Palestine confirmed the truth of the testimony of Saul and the whereabouts of the holy habitation!

Adam looked at Isaac 'so that means that I am...

Isaac continued, 'there was a group here in London, called the Bloomsbury Group, they were a collection of intellectuals and prominent thinkers, the group included people such as

Virginia Woolf, the economist John Maynard Keynes and the essayist E.M Forster. Another member of the group was a Dimitri Mitrinovic, he was a Balkan scholar and had written extensively on The sons of Zadok lodge and had built up a considerable library on the Templar/Masonic link'.

It was in his research that I discovered absolute proof of the link between the Templars and the Masons. It was hidden in three undiscovered 'degrees' they were

The knights of the west and East

The knights of the Holy Sepulchre

The knight of the Sun.

Mitinovinic was convinced that ' Masonry had been the expression of Christianity for the last 2000 years.'

Isaac sat back, he was exhausted and borne down by the weight of knowledge he had, sitting not ten feet from him was a direct link to a secret that had plagued mankind for 2000 years. This secret was so great that men would kill to protect or uncover it not knowing the hell that they were unleashing on the world.

Adam spoke

'Isaac, you'll have to slow down, tell me the secret that the masons protect, what did my father do, was he killed because of this 'secret'. Why don't we go to the Police?'

Isaac snapped ' My God boy, have you not been listening? Your very existence is in danger at this moment, you have in your possession three parts of a secret that has lain dormant for nearly 7000 years and I've told you what happened when there was a danger that it may have been uncovered even then. We must protect you and your information and make it so you are not a threat, that way they'll leave you alone, they wouldn't harm a 'chosen one'. One thing is for certain, you cannot return to Germany'

Adam flared.... 'Fuck them'

Rosenberg stormed into his office and lifted the phone

'I must talk with the Reich Fuehrer immediately.

'Jahowl Mein SturbannFuehrer'

Himmler's voice whispered down the telephone line

'My dear Rosenberg what can I do for you?'

Rosenberg cringed as he heard Himmler's voice, he hated the man and could not understand why the Fuehrer tolerated him. Rosenberg thought that Heydrich was much more suited to head up the SS, he currently headed up the SD and was the reason why Rosenberg needed to speak to Himmler.

'I need Heydrich's department to head up an investigation for me' Rosenberg waited

'Aaaaah, the mercurial Reinhard Corps ' sighed Himmler 'may I ask what you require his group's special talents for?

'It is a matter of national state security'

'Are not all of their project's matters of national state security?'

Rosenberg grimaced, he was not going to tell Himmler more than he needed to know, this was a not an official SS sanctioned operation yet and if anybody could discover the whereabouts of the Jew, Tauber, Heydrich's people could. Rosenberg could always have turned to Heinrich 'Gestapo' Mueller but given the mess that Nuemann had made on his first 'investigation' made him pause.

'I'm waiting, Alfred' hissed Himmler

'I need him to find a Jew that may have some clues that would help with my work with Eichmann. He was in Berlin some days ago but now seems to have disappeared and I need to find him.

'And would this Jew's name be Tauber ...Isaac Tauber?

Rosenberg stammered.... 'Why yes it would. Why do you ask?

'Isaac Tauber is in London, he is staying with a journalist called Adam Carter and they are researching an old manuscript, I believe they have discovered some interesting facts about 'The Sons of The East', a military freemason lodge and a manuscript that was discovered in Palestine'

Rosenberg baulked, 'but how did you....

Himmler responded ' My dear Rosenberg, when you arrest someone you should question them correctly. I had the Jew bitch questioned, let us say 'persuaded 'to volunteer any information that she had. Now I suggest that we stop playing silly games and get to the bottom of this or shall we go to the Fuehrer together and explain your lack of success?'

'Very Well' said Rosenberg 'have you heard of such a thing as the Yahweh?

Himmler clenched his fist and slammed the desk, he was right! He knew that Rosenberg had wanted to uncover the secret of the Temple and bring it forward as his 'discovery', did he not know that I, Heinrich Himmler have made it my life's work. The destiny of the 1000-year Reich lies in the palm of the hand of the person who wields such power.

Himmler composed himself 'Come over to my office now, there is someone I would like you to meet.

Rosenberg took his car across to Himmler's headquarters, he was raging at being out thought by Himmler, he had to admit however, that in underestimating the ReichFuehrer SS he had made a grave mistake. He was ushered into Himmler's private study

'Ah Rosenberg, Would you like some water?

Nein, danke' replied Rosenberg

In that case, to our little 'problem'. You have information from the Jew Bitch's journals, yes?

Rosenberg nodded

You know the identity of two of the men on the dig? They are Tannenbaum and a Major Carter?

Again Rosenberg nodded

Himmler rose and lifted the telephone, a moment later the door knocked and in entered one of Himmler's 'praetorian' guard, blond, blue eyed, 6.2' straight back. He walked over to the table and delivered the perfect salute

'Heil Hitler'

Himmler nodded and told him stand easy

'SturbannFuehrer Rosenberg, may I introduce UnterscharFuehrer Matteus Netzer. I believe you may be interested in what he has to say. Himmler nodded at Netzer who began to speak, he told of his background and being brought to Germany when he was a little boy by his mother after his father had died.

'My mother was a German, my father a Dane' said Netzer.

'Tell him what you father did? urged Himmler

'He was a sergeant in the British Army in Palestine'. His name was Johannsen

Rosenberg stared at him.

'What do you know of his time there? asked Himmler

'Nothing' said Netzer 'other than what he left my mother and I'.

'And what was that? said Rosenberg

'An old wooden box with a piece of cloth and a funny looking object and an old piece of cloth in it'

Rosenberg could not peel his eyes away from Himmler, he struggled to regain his composure, where, how, why.

Himmler removed his glasses after dismissing Netzer.

'He will be sent out on detail tomorrow' said Himmler.' His mother is on her way to Dachau as we speak and I have the box here.'

'Perhaps it is time for us to discuss our next move, Alfred, is it not?'

Himmler got up and walked around to the front of the desk.

'Have you read the report that has come from Frank yet with regard to the Jewish problem yet?

'I've had it forwarded to me by Eichmann; I'll read it on my return'

'Be sure that you do, Rosenberg, Be sure that you do' beamed Himmler

Chapter 9

Adam spoke to Isaac ' Now take it easy Isaac, I can follow the history lesson so far and I know that I could be someone who has the responsibility of this Yahweh knowledge as a result of what my father discovered. I am not a freemason, I do not know what they do, and I don't even know if I believe in a God. All I want to find out is who killed my father and why?'

Isaac looked into the fire before turning to face Adam.

'The why is easy, Adam. Your father stumbled upon the greatest treasure of all and in discovering what it was realised that all he had done was bring absolute secrecy and subterfuge on all that he done from that date on'. ' You see, Adam, Your father was a Rex Deus freemason. He was probably third or fourth degree. His lodge, the sons of Zadok used the wording of the three lost degrees of ancient freemasonry in its title and he would have been aware of that'

'How?' asked Adam

'Easy' said Isaac 'your father served with a Scottish Regiment, Yes?

'Yes', confirmed Adam.

'Their Regimental Chapel was in Rosslyn, outside Edinburgh, Yes?'

Adam nodded again, he'd visited the old chapel on several occasions with his father on the way back up to boarding school in Gordonstoun.

Isaac pressed on 'The lost degrees that I refer to date from a Scottish rite of Freemasonry and suggests that the original degrees were suppressed in the early 18th century by such people as the Duke of Sussex. This was done for various reasons, the only people who would have had knowledge would have been the original 'Sons of the East', and your father was the oldest in his family, Yes?

Again, Adam nodded

'Like the Templar bloodline, when your father reached 21, he would have been told of the true belief, when he discovered the find, he became a very important man. He would very quickly have known the importance of his find and sworn the other three to secrecy that is why I think Tannenbaum had to die...

'My father would never murder anyone' shouted Adam defiantly

'Your father probably did not even know, by that stage he would have returned to England to your mother, remember that Maria's father was killed after he returned to the regiment, he had left his 'box' behind him. Adam fell silent, slowly it was dawning upon him, the magnitude of his predicament.

'There is only one thing for it, he said ' whatever this thing is, we must continue to make sure that it stays hidden and that they, whoever they may be do not succeed.

Isaac felt his eyes moisten, how could he tell the boy of his destiny now. At that moment, he, Isaac Tauber decided what they must do. He told Adam that they would have to place all of the original material in a safe place, it would be better if he did it himself, Isaac would not know where to go to get it if anything happened and at least it would be safe. They would then try and find any trace of Sergeant Johannsen and find out if he knew who the fourth man was.

Adam spoke 'I'm still not clear on the link Isaac, what is this great secret that people are killing for

Isaac sat back, pushed his glasses onto the top of his head and sighed 'The Templars found evidence of the Yahweh under the temple of Herod in Jerusalem, this knowledge made them the richest and most influential grouping in all of Europe. They built countless churches and cathedrals, the most impressive being the Cathedral at Notre Dame in Chartres. All of this was done to assimilate their knowledge, they were doing what Saul had done all those years before, protecting the truth. No one knew what they knew and as the whole cult of Freemasonry could trace its lineage back to the days of the temple, it was easy for them to create their own brand. Modern Freemasonry, the Catholic Church, if fact Christianity in general were oblivious to what they were doing, so complete was the assimilation'

'Why Isaac, Why?' Adam groaned.

'Because my young friend, they knew that the Nazarene was a man of God and they asked their members to focus their love upon God rather than the false idolatry of the cross. They also considered themselves to have the true apostolic succession, the Roman Pope being a respected but entirely secondary figure!'

'When you say God, you mean this Yahweh, don't you ' whispered Adam 'That's the great secret, isn't it?'

'Yes' Isaac again looked at Adam, he felt so sorry for him because not only did he now know the great secret, he was one of only five people who could claim to have access to the deity. Isaac knew that Reid was unaware of his heritage. Maria was in prison, Adam was with him... did Johannsen have a son and who was the fourth man?

All of these things troubled Isaac as they settled down for the evening, He went on to bed leaving Adam alone with his thoughts.

Meanwhile, certain other interested parties were trying to unravel the puzzle...

'Have you had the piece translated ReichFuehrer?

'Have you read the report? Rosenberg, I have yet to receive your comments'

Rosenberg had regained his calm and was now furiously trying to establish in his mind what he needed to do.

'The cloth is useless, Rosenberg, it only refers to a sign and someone called Alexander.'

'He didn't know, Mein Gott, he didn't know who Alexander was!' Rosenberg asked Himmler if he could have the cloth and was granted his wish with a disdainful swipe of the hand. Rosenberg was dismissed and realised when he got back into his car that he was perspiring heavily, Alexander! The leader referred to in the original scroll that had started him on his 'crusade'. This proved that there was indeed a 'lost tribe', their leader was Alexander and they had committed the ultimate blood sacrifice. Rosenberg had the Jew's inscription and Johannsen's testimony, it was imperative that Heydrich find that damned Tauber!

If Rosenberg was correct in his assumptions, then Tauber knew more than Rosenberg and might be able to shed some light on the whereabouts of the treasure of the Sepulchre. Rosenberg's belief was rooted in the notion that Alexander and his people were direct descendents of a tribe of 'supermen' who hailed from the mystical city of Atlantis and came ashore in the Middle East 10,000 years ago. He was convinced through his astrological and occultist studies that these 'supermen' were the forefathers of an Aryan brotherhood that he, Alfred Rosenberg was going to recreate in the establishment of a 1000-year Reich. One only had to relate to Richard Wagner's opera's of Tuetonic struggles and in Parcival, mystical Grail quests to understand the Germanic association with this truth. Rosenberg was convinced that whoever held the key to the past ruled the future, an old Jew named Tauber and some Englander journalist were not going to be permitted to interfere in his destiny.

He got back to his office and related the whole afternoon's events to Hess who immediately decided that he must inform the Fuehrer. When he returned he told Rosenberg that friends in high places in England would ensure that if the Jew was in England he would be located....

'What is the name of the journalist? asked Hess

'Carter, Adam Carter' replied Rosenberg

Oswald Mosley headed up Britain's fascists, He was glad to be of service to his German 'brothers'. He'd been asked to discover the whereabouts of a journalist called Adam Carter. Twenty minutes after the call, he had spoken to SturbannFuehrer Rosenberg himself, given him the information he required and agreed to have the house watched by one of 'his' people until necessary arrangements could be made for someone to take over. A watch was put on Adam's apartment...

Captain Reid was a very worried man, he'd heard the gunshot from across the parade ground and had rushed over to the Colonel's quarters where upon bursting into the room had discovered the Colonel, slumped to the side, very dead. Captain Reid didn't get to where he was by being stupid, he knew it had something to do with his conversation and by logical deduction made him an accessory to the event. He'd gone to the British Museum the next day, they hadn't turned up. Now he was really puzzled, how could they have known about the Colonel.

Reid gathered his thoughts ' what paper did young Carter says he worked for? Ah yes, it was The Times' He rang their office purporting to be an old college friend and had gotten his address. Reid decided to go round and confront the two of them and headed off across Fleet Street on foot, he never saw the car that hit him and was dead before he hit the ground.

Isaac, meanwhile had risen early and was downstairs working on the timeline of his hypothesis, he thought it would be useful for Adam if anything happened to him. He had a premonition in the past few days that as history started to unravel before his very eyes, each discovery that they made was bringing him a step closer to his nemesis. He knew that Maria was probably dead by now, certainly silenced. He didn't know where to begin to look for Johannsen and could not go back to Reid at Sandringham to ask, as for the fourth man, where to start. He was alone with his thoughts when he heard the door bell, he got up and shuffled out to the door, ah, the daily paper. He lifted it and was walking back to the room when he heard Adam shout from the kitchen

'Morning Isaac, would you like some tea? shouted Adam

'Yes, thank you ...... he wandered on into the room and put the paper on the table, he was sweating profusely and felt a tightening in his chest, and he sat down and breathed heavily. Another attack, it would pass, but they were happening with more frequency now. The doorbell sounded again and Adam shouted

'Get that Isaac. I'm burning the toast ' cried Adam.

Isaac struggled to his feet and went and opened the door to a tall stranger who said

'Good Morning, I wonder if you could help me, I'm looking for a Mr. Richardson. I believe he lives at this address '. Isaac looked at the man, well dressed, blond, but for his accent he could double as one of those Nazi morons back in Berlin.

'I'm sorry' said Isaac 'there is no one of that name lives here'

'Oh, I do beg your pardon, I apologise for disturbing you'

The man turned and walked back down the steps.

'That's him. I'm sure of it' exclaimed the man sitting in the car across the street, call Oswald and tell him to call our friends and tell him that the Jew is here!

Isaac closed the door, again there was another shooting pain up his arm, his chest again tightened and he felt very dizzy. He managed to bluff Adam at the camp about his 'faint' but this was serious, he was unwell, sick and he knew he couldn't carry on the way he was much longer. He needed a rest, a long slow recovery under a warm sun, somewhere far away from all of this madness.

Composing himself, he walked back into the room and covered up the timeline, he'd go back to it later. He heard Adam whistling in the kitchen and lifting the paper, he spread it flat on the table...

Adam was in the kitchen, whistling. He'd had a good night's sleep and woke to the new day with a fresh determination to unravel his 'missing bits'. He'd taken the brew from the stove and put it on the tray when he heard the crash and his name shouted in anguish

'Adddddaaaaammmmmmm'

Adam dropped the teapot on the floor and rushed up to find Isaac on the floor, he was panting in small breaths and in a bad way, Adam lifted a cushion and placed it under his head .... 'You've fallen, I'll telephone for the Doctor, Adam went to move but Isaac grabbed his arm and pulled him down close

'The paper, Adam, they must not succeed' Isaac whispered

'What paper, what are you saying? What is wrong with you? shouted Adam panic-stricken

'Take care Adam, no matter what, they must not succe...... and at that Isaac Tauber's head fell back and his grip on Adam's arm relaxed until his arm hit the floor with a dull thud. Adam shouted at him

'Hold on Isaac, don't leave me, we've so much still to do, I cannot finish this without you'

Adam wailed and cried out loud ' Why now? Why did you take him now?

Adam held him for a long time, 'what am I going to do now? He decided to telephone Charing Cross, Megan would know what to do.

He got up to go and use the telephone. As he freed laid Isaac down on the carpet, he noticed the paper on the floor, lifting it, Isaac had said something about paper...... he spread it out and looked at the Headline

'ARMY CAPTAIN KILLED IN HIT AND RUN: POLICE APPEAL FOR WITNESSES'

Adam read with a sense of impending horror

'A 37-year-old Army captain was killed yesterday in Fleet Street by a hit and run driver. The soldier has been named as Captain Harold Reid of the Scottish Borderers Regiment. He was a staff captain stationed at Sandringham. Police are treating his death as a murder inquiry and are appealing for witnesses who were in the Fleet Street area at approx 4.00 yesterday to come forward.

Fleet Street thought Adam 'He was looking for me! 'If he was followed then whoever killed him knows about me!

'Think Adam Think!

He went to the telephone and called Charing Cross Hospital and asked to be put through to Dr Robertson.

'Adam?

'Yes, Megan, it's me. I need to see you, to talk to you.

'O.K, 'Adam is there anything wrong?

'Megan, I'll tell you when I see you... Adam paused

'Megan, I need you'.

It was Megan's turn to shiver, Adam would never say that unless he was in dire trouble. They had agreed after their last 'love' attempt that if either of them needed help or were in any kind of trouble they would make contact with the words that Adam had just used. 'I'll come around' Megan stuttered

'NO' shouted Adam, I'm sorry Megan, I'll see you at our usual place at 6.00 tonight.

The men who were watching the house saw the ambulance and the doctor arrive almost together. Some time passed and they watched as a body was carried out and put in the back of the ambulance. They retreated into the alley as Adam and the doctor exchanged words at the top of the step before the pair shook hands and the doctor descended the steps and got into his car.

The information was relayed to Rosenberg. He telephoned Hess

'The old Jew is dead, a heart attack' The journalist is on his own and we are probably safe to assume that he knows what the Jew knew'.

Rosenberg paused ... ... 'Shall we take him?

'No' said Hess ' Put your people in to watch him, give him no inkling of our interest, lets see where he leads us or rather what he leads us to'

'Very Well' said Rosenberg and replaced the receiver. He instructed a message to go to Mosley asking him to continue tacit surveillance until his 'package' arrived.

Chapter 10

At the very moment that Adam's future was being discussed in Germany, three men entered a room deep within the headquarters of the United Grand Lodge of England in Great Queen Street, London.

The three men were all very senior Freemasons, General Sir John Smythe, Chief Justice Richard Hemmindale and Professor Henry Mollayan They gathered together to discuss the affairs of the last days and take some decisions.

'That Reid fellow' had to have an accident, I suppose, questioned Mollayan

Smythe snorted ' Don't see we'd any choice old chap, it would not have taken him long to work out the connection, not like his father at all, more's the pity, may have saved his life.

'I agree' said Hemmindale 'He would have contacted that infernal Carter boy again, first chance he got, that boy knows far too much for his own good, damn him.

Mollayan spoke up ' He's a first born, albeit he does not know of his heritage, we are bound to watch him at all costs until we discover what he does know.

Smythe stood up 'I don't agree, lets just 'remove' him, what he doesn't know is of no consequence now, he has three of those infernal pieces of cloth....

'Three?' the other two spoke simultaneously

'I'm afraid so,' Smythe continued ruefully 'some of my chaps intercepted a message to Mosley's headquarters, the pattern fits with those earlier communiqués that that fool Rahn was sending back to Germany from his wild goose chase in Africa. Apparently young Carter ran into Tannenbaum's niece or something and the old fellow that died in his apartment apparently translated the scroll for him.'

Hemingdale spoke next 'Adam Carter knows three parts of the scroll, we know that the Germans have one part because of that Netzer woman, we should have killed her the same time we killed that fool Johannson'. We haven't had any trouble since and it certainly taught the others not to get greedy'.

Johannson had had a particularly gruesome death, he had been 'suicided' in his own home, a letter that Hemmindale wrote would have convinced anyone of his intentions, the false doctor's notes confirming that he had contracted a debilitating depressive disorder were slightly more difficult but in the end, his wife had been handsomely compensated and moved back to Germany, pity about the box not being found.

Hemmindale was sure it would not resurface, he did not count on the widow being wooed by an Unterscharfurerhrer in Himmler's SS and her son graduating from the Hitler Youth as a fully-fledged member of the new Aryan fighting force.

Smythe mused 'You are of course sure that this 'fourth man cannot be traced?'

'Yes' they both replied,

Mollayan sighed and reached for the bottle of port on the tray, 'Anyone care for a top up?' He poured each of them a drink and then sitting down, said

'Gentlemen, the issue at hand, if you please?

'Remove him' Smythe said 'all complications ended, no loss to us' Have you considered what would happen if the Nazi's got their hands on him

‘I agree about the Nazi’s’ said Hemmindale, if they get their hands on his information, our life’s work is at an end and all that we have striven to protect, the true path of the Great Architect will be at an end.

Mollayan nodded ‘ so we are agreed then’ Who will do it?

‘Leave that to me’ said Smythe ‘do we need to know what he knows?

It would be nice to disprove the Templar nonsense once and for all, uncover the great lie? mused Hemmindale

Mollayan was now standing at the window looking out over Covent Garden. Hemmindale spoke ‘If we ‘remove’ young Carter, the only link that is left to Palestine is the fourth man, we have done enough with our misinformation to discredit that ‘ sons of Zadok lodge’ once and for all. ‘In fact all of the Scottish regiments have signed up with lodges that do not recognise those outdated Jacobean degrees as a result of our work’.

Hemingdale was particularly pleased with his part, the trial of the alleged homosexuals in the Borderers had ruined the reputation of that infernal lodge. It was very distasteful at the time and he’d had to ensure that he was quite removed from the complainants, four orphans who swore to being taken from their orphanage and subjected to the most heinous assaults on their young bodies by men that they pointed out in court.

They followed the description they had been given to the letter about the inside of the lodge building and the faces of the men who ‘abused’ them. By the time the trial was over, the last remaining leaders had had their reputations ruined and their lodge sworn to infamy.

The three men agreed on a course of action and left separately, Smythe returned to his car and went directly home, Hemmindale went to a gentleman’s club he liked to frequent.

Mollayan walked towards Trafalgar Square and on towards the river, he had to move quickly if he was to protect the truth…

The first thing that Adam did after Isaac's body was removed was to ensure that his instructions to his bank had been carried out. He was assured that the courier had placed the package at the banks disposal and his written instruction had been followed, immediately he could visit the bank, the 'valuables would be transferred unopened to his own safety deposit box.

He then arranged for Isaac to be claimed by the Synagogue, Isaac would have wanted someone to say Kaddish for him. He went up the stairs and lay down, falling into a fitful sleep, unaware of what was going on outside his very door. In dreaming, he thought of Megan, dear sweet Megan, what was he going to tell her? The truth he supposed as he drifted off to a troubled sleep…

When he woke, it was with a start, shit! He was late, he changed and rushed out the door, hailed a cab and was away before the man across the street could react.

'He's gone Sir'

'Where to? demanded Mosley

'I don't know Sir, he moved too quickly Sir, In a cab, Sir

'Fool! said Mosley 'Stay at your post and call me the moment he returned. Mosley himself, had no idea why this journalist was so important, if, however, it was important for the Reich, then he would take the opportunity to show that British Fascism could be as effective as its German counterpart in information gathering and subversive activity.

Mosley longed for the day when his flag would fly alongside the swastika in London and all would know the 'master race' for what it was.

Adam headed for Richmond, he stopped at the top of the main street, paid the taxi and walked back towards the river, and he arrived at the boat club first and asked for a drink to be brought to the table.

He had not seen Megan in nearly six months or so, it had been their longest time apart and although they kept in touch by telephone and the odd letter, that was it. So fortified by his first whiskey, recalled their last meeting...

They'd been on the train at the end of a quite magnificent day together, they had gone back to his apartment. He'd turned on the wireless and smiled in memory at her words

'Switch it off and come over here'

And taking off her necklace, removing her shoe, aaaaaaaah the zip fastener

'How calm your hands are' she purred

'Be careful that you don't tear my stockings, I don't have any other ones with me'

'Oh, did you not say something about going to sleep.

One waits for so many superfluous things, Adam thought, and because they are superfluous he was impatient and restless, even urgent ending up more confused than normal. But that night was different...

To look up into a pair of eyes in which a wave comes and goes, to unite body and soul, bigger waves crash, come of themselves, washed across their faces, shaken to their depths, felled, the two of them...

Adam was sitting over beside the fire when Megan entered the club, he stood up and she waved and walked over, Adam took her in his arms and kissed her on the side of the cheek, she smiles and squeezed his hand

'you look fabulous as always Megan'

'I wish I could say the same for you, you look dreadful, what's wrong?

Adam sat down, he thanked Megan for making the arrangements for Isaac's removal and subsequent questions at the hospital. She dismissed him,

'What trouble are you in Adam?

Adam looked up, Megan could see that he was upset and seemed to be struggling with himself, 'I know, said Megan. 'I have the car outside, lets get out of here, we'll go over to Daddy's apartment in Chelsea, he's away on some infernal government business at the moment, I've been using it... we'll be alone'

Adam nodded, helped Megan with her coat, and went outside to her car. They got in and Megan started the engine, as she did so, Adam leant across and squeezed her hand. She felt a shudder go through her, a shudder only Adam could engineer, she looked at him and they smiled as she put the car into gear and headed for Chelsea.

Adam told Megan as much as he could about his experience in the last two weeks, she was silent for the whole of the time and when Adam finished, they had reached Chelsea. It had started to rain as the ran from the car up to the apartment, got inside and went into the lounge.

'You're soaking wet 'said Megan 'Go upstairs and see if one of daddy's shirts will fit you, I want to get out of these wet clothes. Adam went upstairs, found a shirt and changed, he came out of the room and was going past where Megan was changing, as she called out '

'Fix us a drink, I'll be down in a minute.'

Adam stopped and looked to where the voice had come from, he could see Megan drying herself in the mirror and Adam found himself gazing at her beauty, her magnificent breasts with fiery nipples, her flat stomach which contoured away towards her ....

He went downstairs and was fixing drinks when Megan arrived. She had put her hair up and was wearing what looked like a silk kimono or sari. She glided across the floor, lifted the drink and stretched out on the chaise long that was in front of the fire.

'I think you have to get away from here for a while, you cannot go back to Germany and if what you say is right, then even England is dangerous for you. What about a foreign assignment for the paper?'

'I'm on sick leave, remember? They have no one to cover the German desk, 'If I go back then that's where I will have to go' said Adam. He had moved over in front of the fire and was now sitting on the floor with his back against the chaise, looking towards the fire. Megan swung her legs across and plumped down beside him. He could breathe in her aroma and sense her touch as he tingled with excitement as their arms brushed.

'Go to the Embassy and tell them what you know ' offered Megan

'I don't think so, what am I going to tell them?' Oh excuse me, I've got this cloth that says all that we believe in is false and the Germans are looking for it, if they find it they'll rule the world!'

Megan laughed, the way she always did, she stretched across and tousled Adam's hair, he put his head down and lifted his hands to tickle her .... they stopped and looked at each other .... no more words were spoken as Adam reached up and undid the clasp at the neck of Megan's sari, it fell away from her shoulders to reveal her naked beauty, Adam began to greedily kiss her neck and shoulders ...... he stopped again and looked

...Megan smiled and watched as Adam struggled out of his clothes. She reached across and fondled his face, drawing him towards her, they kissed, lightly at first, Adam stirred and placed his hand at the nape of her neck and began to caress her breast as his tongue greedily searched her mouth, she sighed and Adam could feel her back arching, he cradled her and kissed her lips, chin and neck. Her eyes were closed as she moaned 'Adameeeeee'

Adam felt her nipple harden between his fingers, at the same time he felt her hands tracing shapes on his back, he got up onto his knees and began to kiss her stomach, he moved down began to flick his tongue towards her passion. Her hands on his back were kneading on his shoulders, the patterns being traced were becoming much more forceful.

Adam flicked with his tongue, Megan moaned and brought his head towards her, Adam was becoming excited, conscious of her words to him, his swell was overpowering and as Megan began to gyrate her hips on the floor, he became overcome with urge… He lifted Megan over, lifting her up unto the chaise long, she gripped the top of it with her hands, as Adam entered her, , she gasped as Adam's hand came around to find her nipple, he then began to move within her, the warmth of the fire rebounding off them … Adam was now kissing Megan's neck. She snaked her hand around his neck and held on. Adam began to tense, he could feel a surge as he drove forward, Megan breathing hard 'Yesssssss Yessssssss, their sweat mingling as they collapsed in an eternal caress to the floor.

How long they lay there didn't seem to matter, it was the same as all the other times. Adam would get up, make his excuses and leave with promises to call, to see. He never thought about anyone else the way that he thought about Megan, he knew she felt the same, why else would she put up with him. As he lay there, thinking, Megan's head on his chest, she stirred, he tousled her hair and heard her purr with contentment. She really was something special and he was very lucky, a smile formed as he slipped off in to a very contented sleep.

He woke the next morning on his own, he panicked initially and then relaxed as the previous night's events came flooding back. He heard the shower and called out 'Megan', he heard the shower being turned off and Megan walked back into the room, there was a towel wrapped around her body and she'd put her hair up. She smiled and pounced back onto the bed.

Adam started to say something but Megan put her finger to his lips and silenced him...

'Adam' she said ' What I am about to say may or may not come as a surprise to you .....but .... 'I love you' I've always loved you

Adam was conscious of a strange feeling washing over him. Megan continued

'I need to know how you feel, we cannot continue like this...

Adam looked at her and said 'Megan, you are right in what you say, I think of you like I think of no one else and if that is love, well......' Megan wiped away a tear and smiled

'I also think I can solve all of your problems Adam'

Now it was Adam's turn to look bemused. She continued ' Some evil people are looking for you, there have been bad things happening so listen to me. I have accepted a two-year sabbatical in Harvard. I am scheduled to leave the day after tomorrow. Come with me, let us see where this takes us. Even if we don't work out, you'll be out of the present situation and will be able to take some time out to think about your next move'.

Her words tailed of and she trembled involuntarily at the magnitude of what she had just said, of course she loved him, she'd always loved him, from the first day she had laid eyes on him and now she could do something to protect him.

Adam gazed at Megan and realised that in her he had a very special person. He knew that his options were few, he couldn't go back to Germany, he had no leads to develop, the information from Isaac was safely in the bank, and a quick visit would put it in his box.

The apartment could be closed up again, he didn't really fancy going back after what had happened to Isaac. The events of the last few days had frightened him, he didn't have to worry about money and time in America would allow him to catch up on some research on his new found notoriety. He made up his mind ... ' When do we leave?

Megan stopped, stunned

'Did you say 'we' Adam?

'Yes' said Adam 'I've been a blind fool and could have lost you that would have been a tragedy because I do love you'.

The tears welled up again in Megan's eyes 'look at the state of me' as Adam reached out to embrace, the towel happened to fall away as they fell down onto the bed again ...

It was afternoon when they rose, Megan buzzed about, fixing some food. Adam was the shower, he came out wearing her father' dressing gown.

'Where to we leave from?

'Southampton, midday on Thursday' said Megan

'Do you need the car today' asked Adam 'I'll need to get some stuff and make a few arrangements.

'Do it tomorrow' said Megan, for the rest of the evening we can work out ours plans, you take tomorrow out to tie up your loose ends, we can meet here late tomorrow night or first thing on Thursday morning, Daddy said he would drive me down, I'll have to tell him of our news!

'You're Father? Adam looked at Megan in trepidation. Megan teased him ' Daddy's little girl is all grown up and blissfully happy, he'll be happy to and anyway he always liked you.'

'If you say so' said Adam reluctantly, he wasn't looking forward to his meeting with Sir Henry even if it was in a car on the road to Southampton.

Rudolf Hess was alone in his study when the door knocked, opened and in walked the Fuehrer, Adolf Hitler. He was wearing a black shirt and tie and had SS runes in his shirt collar, the Iron cross was pinned to his breast. Hess stood up and saluted

'Mein Fuehrer'

Hitler waved at him and invited him to sit down, Hess sat behind the desk, Hitler strolled over to the window and looking out over the Wannsee said

'I have decided what to with the Poles'

'I have instructed Frank to recruit a team to deal with the 'problem', he should be ready to move soon.

'Gut' replied Hitler. ' Another issue has been brought to my attention, what is being done to regain these infernal Jew messages'. Hess looked Hitler

'Fuehrer?'

'The cloths for Himmler', he had that fool Rahn travelling all over France looking for religious artifacts. Rosenberg tells me that we are close to a breakthrough and know where these 'cloths' are. Hess again relaxed ' Mein Fuehrer, men from our friend in England are following the Jew, I have sent two of our best men to link up with them'.

'We will not fail, Hess...Do I make myself clear?

'Mein Fuehrer.

Hitler left the room, Hess lifted the telephone and called Rosenberg 'Have you any news?

Rosenberg swallowed, 'He has vanished, hasn't been seen but don't worry, Berger and Maier will be in London tonight, they'll find him'

'I hope so' whispered Hess 'I hope so'.

Adam got up early on the Wednesday morning, he had slept well and hadn't heard Megan leave, the note on the table with the keys of her car told him that she see him at whatever time that night ... her father was collecting them at 7.00 am the next morning. She had gone to tell him her news and then over to her own apartment to have her luggage sent ahead.

She'd laughed when suggesting Adam did the same, any stuff he had was still in Frau Morring's boarding house in Berlin.... He needed some new clothes anyway, Adam smiled as he remembered her laugh.

He was happy, in fact the pressures of the past few days seemed to lift as he made plans in his head ...... go to America, try and take in what had happened, do some research .... He had a busy morning, the bank, his office, the apartment, at least he had the car. He lifted the keys went down and drove over to his Bank and effected the transfer of the artifacts to his own box, he then arranged for the translations and Isaac's papers to be forwarded to Megan's address at the University. He spoke to the Bank Manager and told him he would be out of the country for the foreseeable future, could the manager possibly arrange something with a bank in Boston that would allow him access and facilities. The manager drafted a letter of introduction and credit and Adam thanked him and then headed for Fleet Street and the chat that he wasn't looking forward too.

Megan walked unannounced into her Father's office, oblivious of his company 'Oh Daddy, I'm so happy.... Adam has agreed to come with me to America' Megan beamed. .

'Adam? Adam who asked Sir Henry... 'Megan, can't you see I have company dear girl?

A tall man stood up ' Oh' he said ' don't let me come between a man and his daughter'

Megan stopped and blushed, she stammered 'I'm sorry' Her father spoke 'Megan, I'd like you to meet Henry Mollayan, he is an old friend of mine. Mollayan took Megan's hand and pressed it lightly 'I'm pleased to meet you, Megan.

Megan smiled 'I apologise for interrupting your meeting, I had news that couldn't wait.

Sir Henry spoke ‘ Now Megan, this wouldn’t be young Adam Carter would it?

Yes, Daddy, Yes, cooed Megan, he’s coming with me to America tomorrow, I can’t wait to tell you all about it.

Mollayan stood, ‘Sir Henry.... Lunch as promised, Your club?

‘Of course’ said Sir Henry ‘I apologise for my daughter’s behaviour.

We’ll speak at lunch’

Mollayan rose and walked out of the office.

Having left the bank, Adam headed round to Fleet Street to talk to his boss, John Roper foreign Affairs editor with the Times. He hadn’t spoken to John directly since the dash from Berlin and although he was aware that Adam had come home, he didn’t know why.

How was he going to take being asked for an unconditional sabbatical to allow Adam to go to America. Adam was pondering this question as Roper’s door opened and he was called in

‘Good Morning John’ ventured Adam

‘What is fucking good about this morning, pray tell? And where the fuck have you been? Close the door behind you!’

It was blatantly obvious that small talk and niceties were out of the question. ‘I need to go to America......... Tomorrow............ John...........

Adam watched as first the coffee cup which was in Roper’s hand fall gracelessly to the floor, shattering on impact, followed by a hand lifting the telephone to mouth out that they were not to be disturbed.

‘You ‘d better start at the beginning, Adam and I warn you, I’m in no mood for crap!

Adam told him a story of how he had met Maria and how she had asked him to get her poor sick Uncle out of Berlin because of the Nazis. He went on to tell him about Maria's apparent arrest and the fear he felt in smuggling the old man out. That was why he felt that he could not go back. Roper sat and listened and when Adam stopped talking, he said '

'That is the biggest load of rubbish I have heard in a while, however you are right about one thing, you cannot return to Berlin, no matter for what reason, you've assisted the escape of one of their 'citizens', what's this about America?

Adam told him of the opportunity he had to get access to Harvard and how it might be useful if he could begin to start filing an American perspective on Europe, he got to mid sentence when Roper raised his hand

'I should boot you out of here for what you've done but today is your lucky day, Bob Collins been badgering me for a cub reporter for the last three months. You'll be based in Boston but you will have to go to New York and Chicago, maybe Washington, Philadelphia on the odd occasion.'

Adam was staggered, this was working out better than he'd ever expected, 'I don't know how to thank you, I won't let you down' beamed Adam

'Oh, don't worry about me', grimaced Roper ' save your groveling for when you meet Collins. Now get out of my sight, I've a paper to run!'Adam stood, shook Roper's hand and smiled 'I won't forget this'

'Go on, get out before I change my mind' smiled Roper.

Adam popped out of the office and headed down the stairs, he couldn't wait to tell Megan of their luck! He had one more call to do, round to the apartment and make arrangements to have it closed and then back to Megan at the apartment. He got into the car and headed for his house.

At that same moment Megan had finished telling her father what Adam had told her about his situation, leaving Sir Henry deeply troubled. Of course his first loyalty lay with his only child and he could see she was deeply in love with Adam. He had known his father very well and had always considered him to be a fine upstanding man, young Adam always seemed to be mannerly and he was aware of meetings that he and Megan had had before this. Megan had assured him that all was fine and that he shouldn't worry, there was however, something troubling him, something that Megan had said and an impending lunch meeting that he had with an earlier guest.

Megan had left her father, gone over to the hospital to say her goodbye and went up onto Regent Street for some last minute shopping in Liberty. She planned to be back at the apartment in good time to make them evening dinner.

Adam, meanwhile had gone over to the property company and given instruction for the house to be let whilst he was away. It was foolish of him not to get and income from the house whilst he was away. He sat in the manager's office and agreed terms plus a % for the servicing of the lease and then got the keys... 'damn' he exclaimed ' the keys are round at the apartment' .

'Don't worry' said the manager 'I'll send the office boy round, where are they?'

Adam countered 'I've got to go around their myself to pick up some things' I'll take him with me and send him back with the keys'

They stood, shook hands and the manager opened his door and asked for Mr. Carson to accompany Mr. Johnson to his apartment. A young man, no more than 16 or 17 came bounding up the stairs, listened to the manager and then followed Adam out into the car. They went round to the front of the apartment and both got out of the car

'That's him, That's him, call headquarters now'. One of the men went around the corner to telephone whilst the other man noted the make and model of the car and a description of the boy. Adam remained in the house only for as long as it took to pack some sentimental things into his case, retrieved the spare keys and was back out in the car within 10 minutes.

‘They’re on their way’ said the watcher who had gone to the telephone, two of our people from Germany.

‘They’d better hurry up, look those two are leaving now’.

Adam got back into the car and Carson started back towards the office with a ten-shilling note in his pocket for his trouble. One of the watchers started to follow him and the other jumped on a bicycle to try and keep within distance of the car. He failed and had returned to his point as a large black Mercedes pulled up and the two strangers got out, the watcher relayed what had happened and the two strangers jumped back into the car, armed with the description of the car and Adam’s description.

Sir Henry arrived at the Constitution Club at 1.00 p.m. He had made final arrangements with Megan for the journey in the morning and by the time he had reached his table, Mollayan was already at it. They ordered drinks and Mollayan complimented Sir Henry on his daughter, ‘ she’s going away? asked Mollayan.

‘Yes said Sir Henry, ‘She and her young man are going away to America for a couple of years, or rather she is away for two years, I’m not so sure about him’

‘Oh’ said Mollayan .... Sir Henry went on, ‘knew his father, sound chap, terrible death, shot as I remember’.

The boy... His son? asked Mollayan

Yes, said Sir Henry ‘ Adam is a nice fellow, Megan has known him for years and I think they have had feelings for each other’ I think however that he has some problems that he needs to sort out. Megan told me some things that I don’t understand and I’m concerned for both of them.

‘What do you mean?’ asked Mollayan

‘It seems like the boy is troubled by something from his father’s past and that he has some information that somebody in Germany is looking for, Megan said something about him having to leave rather quickly’

Mollayan relaxed, if Adam got out as quick as he had intended with Sir Henry's daughter to America, he couldn't be traced by anyone. It would be easy for Mollayan to pick up his trail through Sir Henry and give the boy whatever protection he needed. Mollayan knew that Adam didn't understand his legacy as his father had died before he was 21, he would never have found out if, had he not met the Tannenbaum girl and subsequently the old Jew. Mollayan was pretty certain that as long as Adam caught the boat tomorrow...

Yahweh would be safe for now.

Rosenberg raged at Mueller ' Where is he, how could you lose him, you promised me your best men' The Fuehrer will not be happy'

'He was using a car that we had never seen and we......

'Never mind your excuses' thundered Rosenberg ' Get inside that damned house and see if we can find anything'

Mueller spoke ' There was an estate agent around this morning, as we speak both Albertz and Maier are 'viewing' the house.

Keep me informed' Rosenberg dismissed Mueller.

As Mueller closed the door, Rosenberg's telephone rang, he lifted the receiver, listened and then replaced the telephone.

He went over to the picture of the Fuehrer on the wall, pulled it back to reveal a wall safe, he spun the combination and opened the safe, removing a buff coloured folder. He returned to his desk and placed the folder in front of him. The front of the folder had an eagle and standard clasping a swastika on the front and ' Geheime Statzpolizia' stamped across it. He opened the folder and started to read the contents, the report from Rahn about his activities in the South of France, the information that Eichmann had provided about the Essene, the translation of the diary brought back by Nuemann from the old Jews house. He also had been sent over a transcript of the Netzer testimony that he'd heard in

Himmler's office. He took the translation out and began to read ... just at that the door knocked and Hess walked in...

'Mueller called me, his boys found a diagram in the Englander's house, we should have it tomorrow'

'Gut' mumbled Rosenberg 'I have done as you asked, 'what are we going to do now?

Hess sat down ' We have to consider that the Englander has gone to ground, if we cannot find him, we will have to continue our quest without him. Let us examine the facts as we have them at the moment'.

Rosenberg listened as Hess went on. 'By the end of the year, we will be ready and the Fuehrer will assume complete and absolute power. We will get rid of that damned Treaty of Versailles and claim the Sudetenland back as our own. Austria and Czechoslovakia will soon be ours and then we will deal with those damned Poles!

That will give us the capacity to increase our manufacturing activity, we will never be dictated to again. We will deal with the Jews once and for all and lay the foundation for the 1000-year Reich'

Rosenberg was used to hearing this rhetoric from the Fuehrer but when Hess spoke, he delivered it with such a belief that it was their destiny that he, Alfred Rosenberg was inspired.

History would remember him as one of the architects of the greatest ever dynasty to grace the world. If they could find the artifacts that they required, their power and control would be limitless......... To focus on the problem at hand meant that he and Hess would have to determine a course of action that would fulfill their destiny, they have to control this secret, to control it they have to find it. They settled down to a long night's work.

Adam and Megan were breakfasting the next morning when Sir Henry called.

'Daddy, you remember Adam Carter? Megan beamed.

'Sir Henry, said Adam putting out his hand 'It's been a long time, I remember you when you used to call with my father'.

Sir Henry shook Adam's hand ' so you are going to America with my daughter?

Adam reddened 'I... Sir Henry.... I ... We are in love and I

Sir Henry stopped him ' She is my pride and joy, treat her well and look after her for me'.

'You can be sure of that, Sir Henry' affirmed Adam

Megan came in and seen both men shaking hands ' Oh Daddy, I'm so happy'.

'Lets get underway, We don't want you missing your boat'.

Hemingdale telephoned Mollayan 'I've had Smythe crawling all over me this morning,

he 's disappeared!

'Who's disappeared' asked Mollayan

'The boy, of course! Who else? Hemmindale was shouting, 'If we don't find him, we'll lose the sanction!!

'I don't know where he is, I left you and Smythe to make details' said Mollayan.

We'd better meet this evening .... 7.00 at Great Queen Street.

The journey down to Southampton was uneventful and Sir Henry watched as Megan and Adam went up the gang -plank and left down towards the viewing area. Sir Henry smiled as he spotted Adam and Megan waving at him, it seemed like minutes and then the ship's horn sounded departure, by the time Sir Henry was back at his car, the ship had cleared its mooring and was steaming towards the mouth of the channel, the Atlantic and America.

Adam and Megan went to their cabin and embraced, Adam thought about the past few weeks and wondered what trials and tribulations lay ahead, he'd taken Isaac's papers with him to read, they may give him more information or a better understanding of his 'destiny' . He also had Bob Collins to look forward too, for now he had Megan to cherish and as they stood in the cabin, he wondered at his good fortune and realisation of how he felt for her.

'Megan' he said.

She stopped unpacking and stood to face him ....

'I made a trip to the bank today to deposit the papers ....

'Yes? said Megan.

'When I was there, I collected something for you .....

Megan stared as Adam walked over to her, he kissed her lightly on the forehead and lifting her left hand, he slipped a ring on her third finger saying ' Megan, I love you and want you by my side for the rest of my life'

Megan started to cry ' There's nothing wrong? panicked Adam ....

'No my darling .....cried Megan 'If that is a proposal, then the answer is Yes, Yes, Yes.

Mollayan, Smythe and Hemmindale sat around the table in the back room of the lodge. No-one spoke until Smythe cleared his throat and said ' He's gone and no one knows where he is, I checked with our people within Mosley's operation, they said he drove off in an unmarked car towards Chelsea, after that ....poof ...... nothing.

'All we can do' said Mollayan ' is to continue doing what we always do, we protect.' he continued ' if and when he surfaces, we'll be ready.

Hemingdale agreed ' Maybe he doesn't know anything, we'll have to wait and see'. There is one thing for sure however, he cannot go back to Germany or he'll die, if he's in England, we'll find him eventually. Mollayan nodded in agreement, he knew exactly where Adam was but as a direct line descendent of Jacques de Mollay, the last of the Rex Deux leaders. He had carried his family's secret with him, he knew what Adam didn't know and for now they had not succeeded.

Yahweh was safe for now.

Chapter 11

The only other man alive who could possibly know anything was the son of Nicholas Lassiter, the last of the five and he was somewhere in Australia, probably in the footsteps of his father as a sheep rancher in the territories and oblivious to the furore in Europe. Mollayan had devoted his life to protecting his forefather's legacy from within the very organisation that sought to destroy or discredit it. When the time was right Yahweh would be unveiled in all its glory as the true path to eternal salvation and all the efforts of the Jews, Catholics and Freemasons would not stop Yahweh from destiny.

It was morning when Hess and Rosenberg finished their work. They sat, drinking coffee and debating their discovery…

'Let us see what we have' said Hess

The 'Five'

1. The leader, Major Carter
2. The Jew, Tannenbaum
3. The Dane, Johannsen
4. ?
5. ?

'We know that they were testing some explosive substance on a hill in Palestine near the Dead Sea, the discovered artifacts and information that was of such significance that they killed the Jew. They all belonged to a freemason lodge and the leader Carter seems to have enjoyed wealth and rank up until his death / murder. The Jew diary gives us an idea of the location of the find, it tells us about the death of the Jew and the legacy that he left. From that we can assume that they divided the booty on the spot and only realised the significance of their find when they returned from their last leave. They 'arranged' the Jew's death but did not count on him hiding his share'.

Hess paused and took a sip from a glass of water before continuing

'We know from Eichmann, that there is this mystery tribe called the Essene and that they worshipped a great God/Idol. Their mark is on the Johannsen piece of Cyrillic and that proves the authenticity of the find. We know that the old Jew Tauber passed on all of his information and assistance to the Carter boy. We can only assume that he has at least three pieces or four pieces of the cloth, he'll possibly know the significance of his find and may possibly know the location of what we are looking for'.

Rosenberg added what he knew

'We have all that mumbo jumbo from Rahn about the Nazarene and what he believes. When you consider our own destiny and the results of the experiments in Tibet, I am convinced that we are the chosen people and that this great mystery is ours by birthright. We are destined to rule the world and no one will prevent us from succeeding. It would appear that the term 'they will not succeed' keeps cropping up that may suggest the protection of a secret or a knowledge that other people possess. We must redouble our efforts to locate the Carter boy and discover the identity of the fifth man'

Just as that the door knocked, Nuemann entered and passed a sealed envelope to Rosenberg saying ' This was found in the Englander's house, it seemed to be the only thing out of place'. Rosenberg ripped open the seal and placed a single sheet on the table, it appeared to be a timeline, similar to the one that Isaac had been working on before he died. It was in fact a copy of Isaac's work up until but not including the information that Captain Reid had given both Adam and him.

'Wunderbar' exclaimed Hess ' we can build our own information into this paper, it should help Eichmann in his research. Hess read the sheet and was increasingly silent as he followed the 'Yahweh' information along the strands as portrayed by Isaac Tauber. He could not follow the Templar link, he didn't understand the relevance of it but he stopped and looked up at Rosenberg suddenly ' What do you know about the Holy Grail?' he demanded. Rosenberg informed him that Rahn and his team was on the checklist searching for it and the supposed Arc of the Covenant.

'Contact him and tell him to redouble his efforts, if we find that we may find the key to unlocking this mystery of time'. With that, Hess lifted the page and left the office, he went back to his apartment, informed his staff he was not to be disturbed, went into his study and made two telephone calls ... one was to Oswald Mosely, asking him to redouble his efforts in the search for the Carter boy, the second call was placed through a scrambler to an address in Scotland and Hess remained on the call for 35 minutes. By the time Mueller had received the report of the call, Hess had asked for an audience with the Fuehrer.

Adam and Megan set sail for America on the 28 September 1933, Germany formally withdrew from the League of Nations Disarmament Conference on October 15. Famous Jews including Albert Einstein and Ernst Chain had already been displaced out of Germany as refugees. Hitler had already called for *Anschluss* and the Nazis in Austria were promoting union with Germany as an immediate priority. All this was far away from Adam and Megan as they sailed across the Atlantic. Adam had decided that he would chronicle all that had happened to him and attempt to understand the scale of what he'd been exposed to, all of his waking hours. He thought about Isaac and at night as he lay beside Megan, Isaac and Maria and his father and Freddie visited him in his dreams bringing on nightmares from which he often awoke, sweating and shivering.

'It's O.K, darling, you were dreaming again'

Adam was sitting up in the bed and Megan had got up and brought him a glass of water.

'We'll soon be in Boston and we can start to make plans for the future, what was the name of your new boss? Asked Megan

'Bob' Adam replied 'Bob Collins'

Bob Collins was living up to his reputation at that very moment.

'Whaddya mean, I can't come in, dammit woman it's my house as well!'

'You shouda thought about that before you drank the bar dry' Do what you like Bob Collins you ain't getting in here tonite'

And with that the window slammed and the light went out, Bob shrugged his shoulders,

'Women!' Bob turned away to walk back up the block towards the park where hopefully he'd get a taxi to the office, another early start.

Adam reported to Bob three weeks later, he'd arrived early and was sitting in the reception of the Park Plaza when he heard a commotion at the door.

'I haven't got a tie to put on!'

'Hotel policy sir' If you stay here I will get one for you'

Adam watched as the concierge returned with a tie and handed it to the man, he was in his late 50's, about 6.0 tall with a shock of red ginger hair that was growing wild off his head. He was wearing a pin stripe jacket and non-matching trousers, he had a pencil stuck behind one ear and the remains of a cigarette butt behind the other. He walked over to the reception and to Adam's horror, turned and began to walk towards him, this couldn't be Bob Collins.... Could it?

'So you are Roper's boy wonder?

Adam stood up and stammered

'Mr. Collins, I'm pleased to...

'Less of the Mr. bit, O.K, name's Bob plain Bob.

'Sso Bob', stammered Adam nervously

'I'm told you were in Germany boy... ' What did you say your name was again?'

My name's Adam Carter

'Can't have that' mused Bob. 'I know, we'll call you Ade, that should do'

'But my name is Ada....

'Ade it is then'.

At that Bob turned on his heel and headed for the door, simultaneously removing the tie and throwing it in the general direction of the concierge and quipping

'This joint needs more than a tie for it to be swell'

Bob took Adam on a whirlwind tour of the city and found out all there was to know about England at the same time.

'Huh, glad I never went there, much too quiet for my liking, tell me, are you limeys all the same?

Adam returned home that evening, Megan had arranged quarters in the University for them and they'd been able to negotiate with the previous tenants for the contents of the flat.

'He is impossible' ranted Adam ' uncouth, loud, insists on calling me 'ADE' and to top it all, I don't think he has showered in a week!'

Megan giggled at him

‘That’s the first time I’ve seen you angry’ she said ‘ You really are quite adorable when you’re shouting

Adam stopped and looked over at Megan and burst out laughing

O.K, I’m sounding like an American already, I know, when In Rome and all that...

Adam and Bob formed a formidable partnership and through most of 1934 and into 1935 they were responsible for breaking and reporting some of the biggest stories in the city. In March, Adam met Dorothy Thompson, she was an American reporter who being thrown out of Germany on the orders of Hitler. She had started to publish a weekly column and was doing Radio broadcasts denouncing the Nazi regime. She told him of what was happening in the streets, Jews had been castigated as vermin and were being openly attacked in the street, there were more and more unexplained disappearances as opposition to Hitler was all but eradicated.

In June of that year, Adam watched as the wires reported on the death of Ernst Roehm and the dissolution of the SA. Adam called Dorothy and together they made an impassioned plea for America to put pressure on Britain to step up its protest at what Hitler was doing. All was in vain however, as in accordance with his mastery of the diplomacy of deception, Hitler continued in public to make considerable efforts to express peace-loving sentiments and continued to re-assure those who might fear that Germany intended to use its armaments for war. In Britain the only voice of dissension seemed to be coming from an M.P who had fought in the First World War, Winston Churchill.

Adam at this time however has more pressing problems, he and Megan had married four months after they had arrived in Boston, primarily as a result of Megan falling pregnant. Adam’s son had been born the following June and he now had to contend with a second arrival. Of course, he was deliriously happy, he had happiness in his home life and Megan had continued to work right up to when the child was due. He’d even begun to have a little bit of influence on Bob who made an effort to at least be cordial. His idyllic world was about to change in ways that Adam, given all that he had been through would struggle to come to terms with.

The Anschluss finally took place on 11 March 1938 and still Britain and France cried an appeasement that was trumpeted through the national press. Churchill had managed to garner some support but was constantly undermined by Neville Chamberlain's policy of appeasing Hitler and in many ways giving indirect succor to his actions by not taking a stand. Adam was so incensed that he, in a fit of pique protested to his old editor, John Sugden.

'The Americans are laughing at us, Dorothy Thompson is all but calling us collaborators! The paper has to take a stand!' raged Adam.

Sugden responded

'We will take our lead from the Government, there will not be a war and anyway what is Austria to you? You didn't even know that there was a Sudetenland when you worked in Germany, so a few Jews have gone missing, hardly worth starting a war for now is it?

Adam resigned the next day.

He was sitting with Megan in the house that they had purchased in Framingham, some way out of the city. He had gotten a job with the Boston Globe and he and Bob had managed to remain friends throughout. He watched with a sense of impending horror as Europe slipped closer and closer to War.

'I have to go to England' said Adam

Megan's face crumpled in a vale of tears, she pleaded, threatened, begged him not to go. She tried to be rational with him until eventually she told him that he had a duty to her and the children and he could not put himself in jeopardy on some quest that he wasn't even sure about anymore. When she's calmed down, Adam spoke

'I love you and the children, don't you see that is why I must return. We have a son like I was my father's son, he was able to tell me what I was, what would happen, we lost the letter remember? How can I protect our son if I don't find out what I am supposed to 'be'? I owe it to him and to his children to at least discover what he will inherit. I promise you, I will stay in England, I will not go to Germany and I will stay with your father, in his house and immediately I discover anything, I will return.

Megan sniffled ' Where? How? What will you do?

'I suspect' said Adam 'that I will not have long to wait before someone contacts me, I'm supposed to be special after all'.

Adam also knew that to complete the circle and be able to continue to protect the Yahweh through his son, he still had to find vital pieces of information that were missing and he had no one to talk to. What Adam didn't know was that both the German Abwher and the Grand Lodge of Freemasons knew where he was in America through his reports. He has had a few lucky escapes and seemed to be enjoying the protection of person's unknown or unseen and more importantly was blissfully unaware and has remained oblivious to the danger that surrounded him.

When the lodge discovered where Adam has gone, they initially decided to leave him where he was, he could not harm them in America other than by publicising something that Mollayan had succeeded in convincing the other two he was sworn by his birthright to protect. Smythe was called up to go to Ireland as part of a garrison command. Mollayan was given the job of monitoring the wires to see the type of copy that Carter was filing. He also knew of his resignation from the Times and suspected from conversations that he had with Megan's father that Adam was thinking of returning to England.

Mollayan prepared for that eventuality.

The telephone call that Rudolf Hess made on the night that he had the audience with Hitler about the Yahweh cloths was to an emissary of Edward V11 of England. Hess had been in contact with this emissary since his fledgling days in the party. The emissary knew of his power and influence and cultivated the relationship whilst at the same time keeping the King informed of developments in Germany.

As part of Hitler's bluff strategy with regard to his ultimate intentions he negotiated a concordat with the Pope in 1933, the terms included the Catholic Church agreeing not to carry out any political activities and in return Hitler promised not to interfere with catholic life inside the Reich, this concordat was signed on the 20 July, Five days after the signing of the concordat, the Nazis proclaimed that there would be compulsory sterilization for all individuals who were blind, deaf, deformed or suffering from mental disorders in direct conflict with an earlier papal encyclical which declared that 'public magistrates have no direct powers over the bodies of their subjects, they can never harm nor tamper with the integrity of the body either for the reason of eugenics or any other reason.

Worse was to come, on July 29 Baldur von Schirach, the leader of the German Youth in the Reich announced that all members of Nazi youth organisations were forbidden to hold membership of church youth groups. As most jobs had membership of the Hitler Youth as a pre requisite, the order was particular harsh on the Catholic Youth which was by far the most populated by youth. As Catholic priests protested, they were arrested and sent to the camps. Protestants suffered as well, Hitler was urging the church to adopt an ordinance whereby only those of Aryan descent could be ordained ministers, and any ministers married to non -Aryans were to be dismissed.

Two months later, Hess had met the Representative of the Holy See in Berlin and shown him the evidence that they had collated on Yahweh.

Perhaps we have a common interest in this defamation, your Excellency? mused Hess.

The papal nuncio tried his best to remain calm, of course he had heard all of the stories that came from even the lowest seminarian in Rome about the hidden archives in the Library of the Lost in the Vatican. Everyone knew about the third secret of Fatima, the so- called 'Armageddon' truth, whereby the end of the world was predicted by an apparition to three children on a hillside in Portugal.

He spoke directly to Hess,

'I will inform the Holy Father of your findings.'

'I trust we understand each other' murmured Hess' It would be unfortunate if these 'lies' were to be made public'.

'Is there anything that you wish me to ask of the Holy Father?

Hess's lips curled back to reveal perfectly formed gleaming white teeth. He sat in the ante- chamber of the apostolic chaplaincy in Berlin surrounded by statues of the forgotten and great works of art. He was wearing a plain black suit and could have been taken for a priest other than for the presence of a small, round badge with his own type of cross in the lapel of his jacket.

'You can tell the Holy Father that Germany remains committed to a peaceful negotiation of the wrongs that were imposed on the Fatherland by the Versailles treaty. We wish to make Germany great and wish him to know of our intentions.'

'Very well' said the nuncio.

Hess stood up, clicked his heels together and walked out of the room wearing a large smile. By fait accompli, The church in Rome's hand had been forced. They thought they had the measure of Fascism in Italy through the controlling of secret funds being channeled to Mussolini and his Blackshirts and thought that it would be easy to manipulate the German equivalent in the same way. They were wrong and were yet to realise how catastrophically wrong they had been.

The Pope had his own agenda for the proposed attack on Abysinnia by Mussolini, he wanted certain artifacts returned to Rome for 'safe keeping'. He was not unaware of the Nazi interest in historical artifacts, he was shocked when he saw the evidence and was forced into ignoring the blatant contempt with which Hitler dismissed the terms of the concordat.

In one swift move Hess had effectively wiped out the power of the center right in Germany, the traditional power base of Catholicism in Germany. The Holy See didn't really have a choice as Hess threatened to leak the Yahweh information, calling into question the divinity of the church's doctrine, the pope did not want another possible reformation on his hands.

Rosenberg and Hess through the Thule organisation planned the autocratic plunder of Europe and once they had annexed the Sudetenland, Austria and Slovakia, they fought a phony war with Macmillan. The annexations all followed the same formula in that Nazi agitators would infiltrate the various state legislatures and create trouble. They'd bring their people out onto the street and at the same time would initiate attacks against Jews. In the case of Czechoslovakia, Germany had succeeded in surrounding it on three sides as a result of the nefarious activity of the Anschluss policy. The German speaking Sudetenland contained all of the Czech armaments factories. The Czech's knew after the annexation of Austria that they would be next and Prime Minister Hodza had promised that they would defend themselves 'to the very last'. The Sudeten German leader, handpicked by Hitler of course was a man called Konrad Henlein who promised his people 'Victory is certain'.

In England, Churchill continued to voice loud opposition to Hitler. He asked what was to become of Britain by 1940 when the German Army will be much larger than the French Army and all the small nations would have abandoned the

League of Nations. He insisted that there had to be collective defense and even Chamberlain's attempts to appease him with a re-armament strategy for Britain failed to stop him.

Chamberlain was convinced that Germany and Hitler could be accommodated. Even when France issued a strong statement of support for the stand that Czechoslovakia was taking, he and Halifax were ruminating as to whether 'it would be not be possible to make some arrangement which would prove more acceptable to Germany'. As a result of this conversation Chamberlain and his cabinet agreed that pressure should be put on Czechoslovakia to make concessions to its Sudeten minority.

Adam raged when he read this, had they not learned anything about Hitler and his policies. Could they not see that he was preparing to play a much bigger game with much higher stakes? He raged in his column at the paper until he day he announced that he was flying to London to act as the foreign correspondent for the Globe. He promised his readers a firsthand account of the appeasement policy propagated by Chamberlain.

Adam Johnson's first copy reported on the Sudeten Germans demanding reparations for the 'injustices' committed against the region since 1918. The Czech's threw out the so-called 'Karlsbad Programme' which the Germans had put forward. Adam's column reflected the absolute disaster of Chamberlain's policy when Britain coerced support from France and both of them applied pressure to Czechoslovakia to acquiesce.

His old boss at *The Times* responded to Adam's scathing attacks by filing copy stating that

'It might be worthwhile for the Czechoslovak Government to consider whether they should exclude all together the project which has found favour in some quarters, of making Czechoslovakia a more homogeneous state by the cession of that fringe of alien populations who are contiguous to the nation to which they are united to by race'

In this single paragraph, *The Times* gave its support to the most extreme of the German demands, the complete cession of the Sudetenland. Britain was making it very clear that it was not prepared to go to War in order to prevent Hitler acquiring the Sudetenland. Churchill commented that the failure of Britain to take action in the last five years against the German problem meant that;

'We seem to be very near the bleak choice between War and Shame, my feeling is that we will choose shame with War thrown in a little bit later, on even more adverse terms than at present.

Germany annexed Sudetenland after Chamberlain flew to Munich and worked out the details of the transfer, there was no place at the negotiating table for the Czechs. Prime Minister Benes was presented with a fait accompli and told to accept it as there was no point in arguing as all had been decided. The Shame was complete.

As far as Adam was concerned this was the straw that finally broke the camel's back. He wrote his most vitriolic piece of copy ever and warned his editor that any dilution or change of copy would result in his immediate resignation, 24 hours later he began receiving telegrams of congratulations from all over the United States, America had finally woken up to what was going on in Europe.

Heinrich Himmler had set about creating the most fearful fighting army and police state that the world had ever seen. He kept a close watch on developments with Rosenberg but he was unaware of the significance of Thule and was tolerated because of his unswerving allegiance to Hitler.

After all he had played his part in wiping out Ernst Rohm, in that one night remembered by the faithful as 'The night of the Long Knives' the SS murdered practically all of the leadership of the SA including Rohm himself. This cleared the way for the SS to be the dominant force in the country. The Wehrmacht did not feature in Himmler's plans as he set up Deaths Head brigades recruited from pure Aryan stock. He also set up the Lebensborn project to ensure that racially acceptable children were born from pure Aryan stock, German women with the proper racial purity offered themselves a swilling mates for SS racially pure German men, the belief being that the resultant offspring's would be pure Aryan blood 'supermen' in keeping with the blood sacrifice of the occult.

Himmler also implemented the camp network, at the end of 1937, there were over 100,00 Germans in custody in Himmler's camps... lots more were to frequent them in the next 11 years.

The most sinister development was the initiation of a 'special department' within the Gestapo, The Institute for Jewish Affairs was run by Adolf Eichmann, who like Heinrich Himmler, was a lapsed Catholic and occultist who had been put in place by Rosenberg and Hess to discover the comprehension of Judaism. Eichmann believed in re-incarnation, in keeping with his master's philosophy, hadn't Himmler created a 'Grail Chapel' in the basement of his castle at Wewelsburg, 12 places in the round for his chosen 'knights' adorned by a mystic sun wheel carved into the middle of the floor. Himmler had appointed Otto Rahn to head up an expedition to find the grail, he believed it to be somewhere in the South of France. In finding the Grail, Himmler believed he would unlock the its secret and use it to prove that the German/ Nazi culture was bloodlines from the 'chosen ' race, the 'lost tribe' of supermen.

He saw the Jews and strangely Freemasons as a huge obstruction to his cause. Eichmann had been assessing all of the information that had begaun to filter down to his department. Eichmann could comprehend the anti Semite stance, Freemasons? He was at a complete loss until he started to delve into their history and began to consider their origins, he discovered their inception. He discovered their link to fundamental Christianity, he discovered their protection of a secret, what it was he didn't know but his 'boss' was sure to be pleased with his report on what was planned for the Jews, so what if a few freemasons went the same way, he didn't care, he only did what he was ordered to do.

Eichmann opened and reread the first few pages of the latest report that had come from Himmler.

"As far as the Jews are concerned, I want to tell you quite frankly that they must be done away with in one way or another.

The Fuehrer said once:

'Should united Jewry again succeed in provoking a world-war, the blood of not only the nations which have been forced into the war by them, will be shed, but the Jew will have found his end in Europe'. I know that many of the measures carried out against the Jews in the Reich at present are being criticised. It is being tried intentionally, as is obvious from the reports on the morale, to talk about cruelty, harshness, etc. Before I continue, I want to beg you to agree with me on the following formula:

'We will principally have pity on the German people only and nobody else in the whole world. The others, too, had no pity on us. As an old National-Socialist, I must say: This war would only be a partial success if the whole lot of Jewry would survive it, while we would have shed our best blood in order to save Europe. My attitude towards the Jews will, therefore, be based only on the expectation that they must disappear? We can do nothing with them either in the 'Ostland' nor in the 'Reich kommissariat'. So liquidate them.

"Gentlemen, I must ask you to rid yourself of all feeling of pity. We must annihilate the Jews, wherever we find them and wherever it is possible, in order to maintain there the structure of the Reich as a whole. This will, naturally, be achieved by other methods than those pointed out by Bureau Chief Dr. Hummel. Nor can the judges of the Special Courts be made responsible for it, because of the limitations of the framework of the legal procedure. Such outdated views cannot be applied to such gigantic and unique events. We must find at any rate a way which leads to the goal, and my thoughts are working in that direction.

"The Jews represent for us-also extraordinarily malignant gluttons. We have now approximately 2,500,000 of them in the Reich, perhaps with the Jewish mixtures and everything that goes with it, 3,500,000 Jews. We cannot shoot or poison those 3,500,000 Jews, but we shall nevertheless be able to take measures, which will lead, somehow, to their annihilation, and this in connection with the gigantic measures to be determined in discussions from the Reich. The Reich must become free of Jews, the same as the Reich. Where and how this is to be achieved is a matter for the offices that we must appoint and create here. Their activities will be brought to your attention in due course."

Jews should be removed from the area of the Reich as quickly as possible, because it is here that the Jew represents a serious danger as a carrier of epidemics. In addition his incessant black marketeering constantly upsets the country's economic structure. Of the approximately 2.5 million Jews in question, the majority is anyway unfit for work

Eichmann had been given free rein to pick from the cream of the SS finishing school at Sennelager to assist him with his task. One of his first appointments was a young German of Danish extraction. UnterscharFuehrer Matteus Netzer who quickly showed great promise and was immediately sent to join Heydrich in the SD. Heydrich, noticed him and in 1938 he was one of Heydrich's fencing partners as well as being one of his most trusted officers

Chapter 12

Nicholas Lassiter was court-martialed by the British Army for insubordination in 1901. His commanding officer and friend, General Charles Carter interceded for him and as a result, the court sentenced him to be demoted and put in charge of a battalion of conscripts in Australia. He resigned his commission 4 months after he arrived and headed off into the outback with an Irish girl, the daughter of a businessman in Sydney. He worked hard on the various sheep stations and got together enough money to buy a holding near Alice Springs. He and Emily D'arcy married in the winter of 1903 and nine months later Emily gave him a daughter Mary. There then followed two miscarriages and then in the spring of 1907, Emily produced a son, he was called Andrew after Nicholas's father.

Tragically there were consequences in that Emily lapsed into unconsciousness whilst giving birth, she died 4 days after Andrew was born. Nicholas Lassiter was a broken man when this happened but he returned to his holding and with the help of an aborigine woman, the wife of his chief farmhand, Mary and Andrew were raised as best as could be expected. Nicholas always made sure that they were raised as Emily would have expected and he allowed them to spend time in Sydney with their mother's family.

Emily's father made arrangements for them to come to Sydney as much as possible and it was whilst they were there on one occasion, they received news that their father had been badly injured in a farm accident. He was too ill to continue so he was moved to a convalescence home in Sydney in the hope that he would recuperate enough to go back to the farm.

Years passed, the farm continued to be managed by Muxola, the chief hand. Mary and Andrew visited as much as possible and were happy enough to allow that to continue until the day that their father returned. He did so in 1916 and was able to take a passing interest in the farm. Mary at that stage had gone to boarding school in Sydney and Andrew had expressed an interest in going into a seminary, he'd gone to a school run by Christian Brothers and they'd been impressed by his scholastic ability, so much so that he'd been awarded a scholarship to the seminary in Melbourne.

Andrew quite liked the idea of study as he was a very shy child and had learned to be comfortable with his own company. He loved his father and sister and was captivated by his grandfather's tales of Ireland long ago. As he studied he became increasingly aware of his desire to accumulate knowledge, at 16 he was fluent in native aborigine, French, Irish and Latin through his teaching at the seminary and had a thirsting quest for history. On passing his finals he followed his calling and entered the seminary in Melbourne. He studied well and showed a great aptitude for the classics, so much so, that in 1929, he travelled to Rome with the intention of enrolling in the Irish College, his Grandfather had interceded on his behalf with the Apostolic Nuncio in Sydney and as a result of that and two papers that Andrew had written, he was recognised as a very successful student and was ordained in Rome in February 1931 as a priest. His sister Mary travelled there with her new husband and though she was happy for her brother, she had bad news, their father's condition had worsened as they were leaving to come to Rome and the news that they brought was not good in that Nicholas Lassiter wasn't expected to live much longer.

Andrew, naturally enough thought that he was to return to Australia in a pastoral capacity and comforted Mary by saying that he would seek dispensation to travel to Sydney and on to the farm with them before he took up his new position in the outback. Shortly after his ordination he went to his college to find out where he was to be stationed. He was met on the steps by the Dean of the college and invited to walk with him

'Your father is unwell, I believe' said the Dean 'I shall pray for him tonight'

Andrew bowed his head 'Thank you Eminence that is very thoughtful of you'

They continued to walk towards the gardens in silence until Andrew noticed another priest walking towards them and very quickly fell into step with them.

'Father Lassiter, may I introduce Giovanni Batista Santini
'

Andrew was stunned and stammered a hello and a very weak handshake. Santini! Every one of the seminarians knew of him and the work that he was doing, why some were saying that even now he was considered to be a future 'papa bile' a future 'papa'. He was the national chaplain of the 'Federazione degli Universitaria Cattolici Italiani, the only serious opposition to fascists in Italian Universities as well as having important duties in the Secretariat of State. He spoke in a very low voice to Andrew, all the time staring at him through the circular glasses that he always wore.

'It has been decided that you stay in Rome for a while, Father Lassiter and assist me with my work'

Andrew's mind whirled, to work and live in Rome! to have access to the history of where it all started was too good an opportunity. Then the thought of his father made Andrew express a wish that he knew may mean him having to question the decision.

'May I be permitted to return to Australia? My father is dying and I would like to see him and tell him of my position'.

Santini relented and told Andrew that he must return to Rome by May of 1931 to begin work.

Andrew travelled home and was at his father's side as the doctor declared that they could do no more other than make him comfortable. His father seemed to strengthen slightly upon the sight of his son and asked to be left alone to talk. Andrew presumed that he wanted to receive confession from his son; it was something that they had joked about in his early years in the seminary. He nodded at Muxola and when he left the room, Andrew prepared the sacrament and put on his vestments and turned to his father.

'Il nombre de padre y du...' started Andrew only to be stopped by his father.

'Save your words my son, you have been well raised but there is so much that you do not know and now as I am dying, there are things that you have to know'.

'But father' said Andrew 'I am here to help you prepare for your...

'Stop it boy' commanded his father with all the strength he could muster, ' what I am about to tell you will shake your belief so much, I have dreaded this day but my obligation to you is only superseded by my obligation to a greater power'

Andrew was staggered, he'd expected his father to be dying and had prepared himself for the worst, but delusional, that was something else. He stopped and invited his father to continue.

Nicholas Lassiter started by telling his son about his life before Australia and about a discovery that he and four friends made on a hill in Palestine, a find that changed his life. He gave him instructions as to where to search for the proof of what he was saying, there was a box buried outside the house near the grave of his mother, Muxola would show him where it was.

Andrew sat on the edge of the bed, listening to his father's story and in his mind he could not determine what significance this 'find' had for him or why his father was so adamant that he allow him to finish.

His father had fallen back, he was sweating profusely and as Andrew started to mop his brow, he thought that his father would sleep, he didn't. In a much lower voice, Andrew heard him say 'They must not succeed' he bent down to listen to his father and heard him repeat 'they must not succeed' Andrew asked 'Who must not succeed? His father became wide awake 'read the testimony in the box and you will understand, I'm tired now and I can see your mother, she is calling me'

'Let me hear your confession Father, let me do this for you, pleaded Andrew

His father looked at Andrew 'I have committed the most grave sin of all my son, I murdered my friend to protect our secret, I took the life of a man in order to protect'.

Andrew was white with shock 'protect what' he whispered

'Yahweh' said his father, I cannot receive your absolution, I have carried my guilt for years, and your absolution is no use to me now'. His breaths were becoming quicker and shallower, he grabbed Andrew by the arm, 'promise me they will not succeed, promise me Andrew!'

Andrew gazed at his father, what was this madness that had overcome him, what was he talking about, who was this man he had killed, what was he part of, who must not succeed, what was Yahweh?

These questions swirled in Andrew's mind as he felt the grip on his arm relax, he re focussed on his father as his eyes closed for the last time ' Go to my mother' Andrew whispered.

Nicholas Lassiter passed away peacefully.

Andrew presided over the burial of his father two days later; he was, as per his wishes, buried beside his wife on the plot overlooking the homestead. He had left a will and both Mary and Andrew decided that they dispose of the holding to Muxola, as a thank you for his long years of service. Muxola had four sons of his own and there was the proviso that he nor his sons could sell the holding, they would pay an nominal rent and the house would be closed up, only to be opened if Mary or Andrew desired.

Andrew then began to make plans for his long return to Rome. He was saddened by his father's death and troubled by his last words. These sensations however were nullified as he wondered what experience lay ahead of him within the Vatican. Here he was a 24-year-old priest about to enter the secular world of the Roman Curia.

He was sitting out on the porch late at night when he heard a noise, he turned round to find Muxola standing beside him, he was sweating and filthy, it looked as if he had been digging. In his hands was what looked like an old tin box, it was tightly sealed and quite heavy.

'What is this, Muxola? questioned Andrew

'Your father asked me to make sure you got this, he said you would understand and told me to tell you that 'they must not succeed'

At the sound of those words, Andrew froze. He was alone with his father when those words were spoken, how did Muxola know to speak those words to him? He turned, angrily towards Muxola who appeared very calm ' Your father told me to tell you that it is your destiny and that you must open this box and read the contents, then all will become clear'.

'Do you know what is here? asked Andrew

'No' said Muxola 'but your father was the brother that I never had and it was his last request that I bring this to you if he died. You are going away in a couple of days; perhaps you should find out what you father has left for you'

At that, Muxola turned away, leaving Andrew alone with his thoughts of his last conversation and an old rusted box. He sat for a long time on the porch just looking at the box and wondering what the implications would be if he opened it, given what his father had said to him as he lay dying. Eventually he shrugged his shoulders against the cold in the air and walked into his bedroom, sat down at his old study desk and prised open the lid of the box.

There was a funny shaped object, like an upturned sundial, a piece of what appeared to be cloth of some form with an inscription on it, protected by a cover of some sort, a dagger of some kind, it looked very expensive and what appeared to be a recently put it letter in an envelope with addressed to Andrew in his father's handwriting.

He lifted the envelope and held it in his hands, he shook involuntarily and held back a sob as he placed the letter on his desk and picked up the object, the lettering was most certainly Greek or Yiddish of some sort.

Andrew passed it between his hands and then put it down. He spread the cloth out in front of him but could make neither head nor tail of the scribble and sign on it. Finally he lifted the letter and opened it...

To My Dearest Son Andrew

Andrew

If you are reading this letter, then I have gone to join your mother in a better place. I wish there had been an easier way to tell you of this burden that I must place on you. I should have told you when you passed your 21st birthday, I didn't because I know you are committed to your choice and what I have to tell you will not be easy.

Before you were born, I killed a man. I killed him because of what I have left for you. It was found by 5 of us on a hill near the Dead Sea in Palestine when I was a soldier in the British Army...

Andrew re-read, his father a soldier in the British Army? He bristled given the stories that he had been told about Ireland by his Grandfather, the glorious insurrection in 1916, suppression by the same British Army, an army his father had been a member of! He read on...

Two of us were members of a secret society modelled on a Freemason's lodge. Our discovery proved the existence of the deity that we worshipped; the deity was Yahweh, an all seeing all-powerful entity. I don't expect you to understand all this at the moment, When we realised what we discovered, a decision was taken to bury our knowledge because we were fearful that our find would lead unbelievers to the Holy Sepulchre.

We do not know where it lies but one of us wanted to go off and try and discover its whereabouts, we could not allow that to happen, despite every form of reasoning, he was determined to follow his course of action, we all returned home to our families and we hoped that he would change his mind when we returned. I pleaded with him to desist but he was not one of us so it was decided that he could not be allowed to continue. I drew the short straw and he had to be 'accidented'. We went out on a patrol and I pushed him over a cliff.

I have lived with his death on my conscience every day since and consider myself to be beyond your salvation. I intended to disappear in Australia and would have done my secret would have died with me. I met your mother however and the rest you know. I am so sorry that I have to burden you but no one must be permitted to succeed in discovering the Yahweh.

I know you have so many questions, questions that I cannot answer. I can tell you this, Yahweh is the balance of time action threat and counter threat and we all exist oblivious of its role, existence and impact on all that we are... Yahweh is what is, has been and will be and is enshrined in the fundamental presence of our being.. It will come again to claim its rightful place, until then we protect it and must lay down our lives to do so. I realise, son that you may not accept what I am saying... if so destroy this letter and the other things in the box and on my honour never breathe a word of the content of this letter to a soul... as my confessor you will do that.

I am truly sorry for the hurt I may have caused you, please forgive me and pray for your mother and me.

Your Father

Nicholas Lassiter.

Andrew was shaking and crying and shouting, so much so that Muxola opened the door

'Get out now! Leave me alone' he screamed.

It was morning when Muxola eventually ventured back into the bedroom, the previous night was a night he would not forget for a very long time as Andrew roared and shouted at his father and then roared through cries of apology for him. When he went in the next morning he found Andrew deep in prayer at the side of his bed. Andrew motioned that he stay, he blessed himself and ended his ablutions

'Muxola, I apologise profoundly for any grief or insult I may have brought you last night'

'Andu' said Muxola 'I loved your father like my brother and will do whatever you tell me to do for you, I promise him that I will also look after you and sisa Mary.

Andrew's eyes shone, he was genuinely touched at the piety of this old man, loyal companion of his father and affectionate friend of his.

'I want you to forget all about last night, I do not ever wish to discuss last night's events again'.

'That ok Andu' Muxola grinned ' just as papa Nick say'

Andrew smiled but he was deeply troubled, this thing that he had, his father had killed for, he had asked Andrew on his deathbed to protect this Yahweh thing... They must not succeed. Perhaps things would become clearer to him.

He went over to the dresser, having dismissed Muxola and reread his father letter. There was a second page attached to the letter and it said

Major Adam Carter...Piece 1

Sergeant Erich Johannson...Piece 4

Corporal John Reid...Piece 2

Private David Tannenbaum...Piece 3

Sergeant Nicholas Lassiter...Piece 5

Each of us was given a guider, that's the dial like object you have. There is a stone plate in the 'sacred place' and when all of the guider's are installed, the sun will catch the angles and pinpoint the whereabouts of the Holy Sepulchre. Be warned however that the full translation must be known because hidden in the words of the translation is the location of the 'sacred place'. Do this and you will discover the Holy Sepulchre, discover this and all that you know will be proved as a falsehood of unimaginable horror.

May your God have mercy on your soul.

Nicholas Lassiter.

Andrew lifted his own prayer book as gifted to him by his Grandfather, he lifted a knife and slit the binding at the top, folded the letter and then stitched the tear himself. He put the object and scroll, the lettering of which he had copied, back in the box and called Muxola, he told him to rebury the box in the spot that it had come out of and to tell no one of what he had done. Andrew then put the copy in the fly-leaf of his bible, closed it and started to make arrangements for his long journey back to Rome.

Giovanni Santini welcomed Andrew back with open arms

'You are in my prayers Father, Your own father has gone to a better place and will intercede on all our behalf in these difficult times. We have much work ahead of us and we need for you to come to terms with the workings of the Secretariat of State and the curial procedures. Events in Italy and Germany are to the forefront of all of our minds'.

'I am your humble servant' Andrew was still on his knees when Santini bade him to sit beside him a while.

'You have come through a difficult time, do you need to rest before we begin?

'No, monsignor, I am happy to commence, I would however beg you to hear my confession.

'Of course my son, this evening, after Vespers. Now let us see about getting you some quarters....

'I have rooms in the Irish College Monsignor' said Andrew.

'Bravo',

Santini smiled, he had high hopes for this young man and prayed that he would be up to the delicate nature of the work that he, Santini was undertaking. He was convinced that the would be charismatic demagogues in Italy and Germany would not last long and he was actively involved in promoting a 'leadership in waiting' amongst the intelligentsia from both countries. He had a network of special envoys that were working to undermine the current trends and the principles of a post fascist leadership were being developed. They were based on the notion that the common good would be the norm and that genuine democracy would be the means.

Andrew retired to his old rooms, elated at his welcome, he had a free three or four hours before Vespers and decided to go over to the Sistine Chapel to pray and consider his confession. He liked Santini and even though he was unsure as to the work that he was going to be asked to do, so long as it was with Santini, he did not mind. He always marveled at the sights of the Chapel and became so engrossed in his reverie that he almost was late back for Vespers. When Vespers was over, Santini approached him and said

'Father Lassiter, I was to do something for you this evening, something has come up and I would appreciate your assistance in helping me address it.'

'But of course Monsignor' beamed Andrew, he had well and truly arrived in Rome.

'Father Lassiter, may I introduce Father Chenu, he is the librarian and collates most of the work here. Andrew was in a large sparse room, there were three desks pulled together and wall to wall on the far side were books and rolled manuscripts of every shape and form.

'Welcome to the Sacred Congregation for the Propagation of the Faith' said Santini. This will be your work space for the foreseeable future. You may read everything, you are not permitted to remove anything on any account. You will act as my research assistant and will along with Father Chenu provide me with what I require, is that clear?

Andrew nodded

'Very well' said Santini, I wish for you to do some specific research for me, until I return, I will leave you two to get acquainted' and with that he swept out through the door.

Andrew walked over to the older priest, 'It is indeed an honour to meet you Father Chenu'

'Call me Bernard please, I will call you Andrew...... Santini is a hard taskmaster, I will show you the system and the sooner you can get started the better for us all'.

For the next two weeks Bernard Chenu took Andrew on a whirlwind tour of the most fantastic library he had ever seen. The trial notes from Galileo's trial, all of the Dominican Inquisition Papers, a complete history of the Roman Catholic Church, the Papal bulls of over 70 Popes, a veritable treasure trove. Andrew wondered as he worked in this place whether it could possibly hold any answers to the questions that arose as a result of his father's revelations, if there was any truth to be found in his father's ramblings, he might find it here, he had plenty of time and comforted himself that he was to play so important a role so early in his career. Bernard was a good friend and after 2 weeks of constant cataloguing and training had grown to like the young Lassiter.

Andrew saw Santini for his confession and held back his trouble with his father, it seemed trivial and if he himself could disprove his father or get to the bottom of something that drove his father to murder another man then the secret could remain amongst him and his father as he was sure that Mary knew nothing and Muxola was sworn to secrecy, Andrew made sure of this by invoking an old Aboriginal 'jinju' on him, it had hurt Muxola at the time, he thought Andrew would have trusted him but in the end he understood why Andrew did what he did after Andrew told him that it was done to protect the honour of his family.

Andrew set out with the best intentions, three years passed and he had still not addressed any of his own issues. During that time he had accompanied the Monsignor all over Italy, most of France, three trips to Germany and two to Spain. The Holy See was concerned at the absolute upsurge of Fascism in Italy, Spain and Germany and Santini 's department had been tasked with keeping tabs on developments. These developments did not make for happy comprehension by the church, the church was being abused and forced to fight a rear guard action and make pacts with the 'devil incarnate ' as Santini described Hitler.

They were also concerned about the Duce, Mussolini, who wanted to invade Abyssinia. There was also a new threat in Spain, fascists led by General Franco were hell bent on subjecting Spain to bloody Civil War and international brigades were being formed all over Europe and America to fight against him. It seemed that the Europe was heading straight for a conflict of global proportions and nothing could prevent it. The Vatican, declaring neutrality, was doing everything in its power to broker but was in many cases failing to plug even the smallest hole as the men of war seemed hell bent on destruction.

On the 10 February, Pope Pius X11 died at 4am in the morning. The first person to be summonsed to his bed was the now Cardinal Giovanni Santini, Pius's death had made Santini 's future more problematical and in doing so had also thrown into confusion the future of his most trusted confidant and now private Secretary ... Andrew Lassiter

One evening Andrew was in the library reading when Father Chenu walked in

'Good Evening Monsignor Lassiter' smiled Chenu

'Even after all these years Bernard' grinned Andrew, they laughed.

'Any luck with the Rahn papers yet? asked Andrew.

The Cardinal was most anxious to try and find out why the Germans were hunting Europe and the Middle East for religious artifacts. He suspected it had something to do with proving Aryanism or discrediting the Jews but he had tasked Bernard and Andrew to try and use their network to discover what was going on.

There was a rumour that Himmler was behind it all, Santini seemed convinced that this operation had all the hallmarks of Rudolf Hess and he was the one Nazi that Santini was fearful of him and the power that he possessed. Oh yes, everyone feared the Fuehrer and Heydrich and Himmler, they were obvious in their megalomaniac demagogue stance, Hess, however was the brains behind the whole rise of the Nazis. Santini had met him once and had been amazed by the presence and power he commanded. Their debates about anti – Semitism left him chilled to the core. This was important. It was March 1939 and Europe stood on the brink of War.

Bernard had discovered that Rahn had died in mysterious circumstances in 1938, about a year earlier, he gotten a report from the brother of one of his co workers 'It appears, Andrew, that our friend Rahn outlived his usefulness to the Nazis, he had been given every available resource to find the mystical 'cup of Christ' the Holy Grail, but to no avail. It appears someone took objection to a piece he wrote in 'Volkisher Beobachter' a Nazi newspaper and that sealed his fate.

Andrew stopped what he was doing 'Oh ' he said ' what did he write?

Bernard quickly skimmed the report, 'that's an old story, we knew about that in 1930!

'What was that asked Andrew

'They shall not succeed' said Bernard.... It's the story of the Essene again'. There was a silence and Bernard stopped and turned to look over at Andrew who was sitting rigid in the chair '

'What did you say? whispered Andrew to Bernard

'The story of the Essene, they shall not succeed, what's wrong Andrew?'

Andrew was not listening, he never thought he'd ever hear those words again. His father's words invaded every particle of the room 'they must not succeed, promise me Andrew, they must not succeed' Andrew reeled back in the chair, he was conscious of Bernard speaking but he didn't hear the words other than 'The Essene, 'that's an old story, we knew about that in 1930!'. When he finally regained his sense of where he was he felt Bernard shaking him

'Are you all right Andrew?

'Yes, Yes' said Andrew, 'Bernard, this is very important, you must tell me all that you know about this 'Essene' and bring me all the references that you have on the subject, there is something I must do'.

With that Andrew arose and left the room, he had to go and reopen some old wounds. He didn't even have to retrieve his father's letter, he knew what it said, and those words were burned into his soul. As he walked back to his private rooms, he struggled to recall the order in which his father had spoke on the deathbed, he recalled the word Yahweh, what was it his father had said, a great deity, yes that was it a deity that would come again. In the privacy of his room Andrew removed his father's letter

'Yahweh is what is, has been and will be and is enshrined in the fundamental presence of our being. It will come again to claim its rightful place.

Andrew had made a promise to his father, the least that he could do was find out what it was that had caused his father to kill.

The conclave was called for 1 March 1939, 63 cardinals went inside and elected Pope Pius X11 to the throne of Peter. There was a certain consternation however that the cardinals had erred in their choice. Eugenio Pacelli was a quiet shy timid man, he most certainly was not a fighter and tried to please everybody all of the time, he was said to be 'handicapped by a caution that was a result of anxiety and also a lack of drive' This did not appear to be the qualities required of the spiritual leader of the largest congregation in the world, especially at so dangerous a time. There was certainly work for Cardinal Santini to do in Rome.

Andrew Lassiter had been busy also and had changed almost overnight, most people put this down to the crazy hours he was putting in along side Santini, Europe was going to War and even in 1939, Rome had heard rumours of a 'final solution' for the Jews.

Santini certainly was not one who believed that this involved forced repatriation to Palestine. Andrew had withdrawn into himself and any free time that he got was spent in the Faith Library. Father Chenu went to Santini and expressed his concerns, Santini agreed to speak privately with Andrew over dinner that evening.

There had indeed been a fundamental change in Andrew Lassiter. He had begun to read the 'legend' as Bernard called the Essene and was astounded at his findings. He tracked the Yahweh from the Jewish inscriptions, he discovered the presence of James, the brother of Jesus. As he read, he started to comprehend the scale and significance of the perpetration of the sin by the medieval church, his church! He read and reread Galileo's testimony, he went back and cross-referenced the Essene bloodlines. He poured over the Crusader accounts and the plot against the Templars. His father had discovered the truth, he didn't know what form it took but he was only guilty of killing one man. Andrew's church had killed millions through the century, 'They must not succeed' took on a different meaning with the Catholic Church, Yahweh was a threat, a rival that had to be suppressed at all costs. All of the messengers had to be vilified or silenced and as Andrew read more and more, he began to experience a guilt that he felt sure he could identify with, he had seen it before in mannerisms, temper tantrums, sleepless nights, he used to think it was because his father was a sad man or drank too much, he now knew that the reason his father behaved the way that he did was down to a burden that no man could be expected to bear. Andrew looked at the parallels in what was happening now and what happened in the 15th century, books were burned, authors barred, the very things that were happening in Germany had been perpetrated there 500 years earlier by the church.

When Andrew uncovered Martin Luther's original 96 articles, he was amazed to see that some of the articles referred to the 'one to come '. His mind was in a whirl but deeply troubled as he was, he understood enough to know that he was destined to fulfill his destiny, he would protect this Yahweh and from what better place than inside the organisation that had done the most over the years to suppress it.

He could trust no one and if he could unravel the puzzle then he may be able to assist those burdened with the same destiny. What was he saying? This was a betrayal of his God, his church, and his life's work. He had to try and resolve the Yahweh on his own, only by doing so would he be true to the memory of his father. He went to dinner that evening with the Cardinal; they passed pleasantries and then ate in silence until Santini spoke

You are not yourself Andrew, Is there something troubling you?'

Andrew looked across the table, his Cardinal, Could he confide? A confession maybe? He answered 'I worry about the world, eminence, We are reaping what we sow'

'You have been my secretary for 6 years now Andrew and I have relied heavily on you, I fear that we are at the edge of the abyss and the die has already been cast, the Holy Father is incapable of leading the way to the Lord. We tried to prevent Italy joining this war on the German side, we need days of reflection and contemplation as we are to pursue our task of keeping the Holy See safe and protecting the flock'.

'Bernard tells me that you have become interested in the history of our Church?

'Yes, eminence, I wish to understand the mother as a child should do and avail of the opportunity to satisfy my thirst. I study in my spare time, it does not affect my work'

'On the contrary' mused Santini 'Your knowledge will be valuable as we formulate our policy, we cannot let them succeed now can we?

Andrew stopped, just for a moment, enough for Santini to detect his uncertainty in what he had said ' No Your eminence, they must not succeed.

'Good' said Santini 'I will retire now, we have busy times ahead Andrew'. Santini stood up and Andrew went over and kissed his ring

'Remember this Andrew, sometimes the truth can be hidden so well that to suggest telling it would condemn the teller '.

With that Santini left the room and Andrew sat, convinced of what he had to do. He rose and went back to the library and continued where he had left off, he had been drawn to one of the original accounts from one of the children who had witnessed the supposed apparition of Mary, the Mother of Christ at Fatima in 1917 . The account spoke of a bright and shining light and a voice telling the children not to be afraid, no matter what was said to them, there were things that had to be told. The child then spoke of being told of three great secrets, when it was over the light lessened.

Andrew's interest was sparked by the words of the boy ' before the voice stopped, it asked us be good and told us it had come because of ' one to come no matter what happened.'

The third secret of Fatima was deemed to be so serious that it was effectively buried and the only person who was allowed to access it was the current Pope. It was said that it foretold the Second Coming or the end of the world.

What Andrew knew was that when Pius V11 read the secret, he had to take to his bed for two days and aged visibly. He could and did not bear witness to anyone about it but no one could be in any doubt that the legacy of the secret and the effect that knowledge of it had on anybody who had access to it. Two of the three children had been sequestered into a holy life, the boy had been branded 'stupid' and the two girls had been convinced that they should devote their lives to the service of Mary, they were both in enclosed orders, many miles apart. Two of the children were now dead, supposedly taken to the side of the 'apparition'. As Andrew read the testimonies he kept thinking of his father's words and the words that Santini had spoken to him about 'not succeeding'.

Was he referring to this Yahweh? Andrew vowed to continue his quest, he would discover the truth. He realised that he had to understand the Essene, all of his research and his reading showed that the church feared them, no, they were denied by the church. He began to concentrate on Jesus and began to comprehend the historical uncertainties within the timeline of the testament, he began to recognise why articles of faith were so essential to the very fundamentals of the teaching of the church, he himself had never stopped to question anything of this nature but then he had been exposed all through his academia to the one story. He had no doubts as any misnomer was explained as an article of faith. What if another slant was placed upon the teachings, what if the bedrock of the church was tested, if a fundamental lie was propagated as a truth.

Andrew stopped himself, what was he saying! These thoughts were heretical in the least and not in keeping with his status as a trusted Monsignor in the church with access to the most delicate of secrets within the seat of Peter. He had to rationalise his thoughts, do his research and look for a sign, a signal that would show him the way of the truth. Unknown to him at that time, he wouldn't have too long to wait

Chapter 13

'Without Hitler, there would never be war. He acts with a cynicism, brutality and decisiveness and clarity of mind that the continent has not experienced since the days of Napoleon. He has reunified Germany, he rearmed it, he has smashed through and annexed his neighbours with the sole purpose of making the Third Reich the most terrifying war machine that the world has ever seen.'

Adam finished off his leader

'What do you think Bob? I've been telling anyone and everyone that would listen that this man is only fulfilling his destiny, he's been talking about this since 1931. How long did that fool Chamberlain think he could pander to a man like that, on the day that Chamberlain went back to London with ' the promises of the German Chancellor' Hitler and his henchmen were saluting the next stage of their strategy with a new toast ' Sterben Juden'

'Do you know what that means Bob?

Bob shook his head

I'll tell you' said Adam 'it means ' May the Jews die'

'He has attacked Poland with this 'blitzreig' of power, what chance do horses and cavalry have against dive bombers and tanks, Poland will fall, Britain will declare war and where are we then?'

Bob sat impassively and watched Adam Carter tear himself to pieces, he'd no doubt as to his passion and as he'd got to know him over the last number of years had come to the conclusion that Adam was driven by something that wasn't obvious to everyone. His lovely wife Megan and his son and daughter were the focus of his life, he idolised them, that didn't stop him championing any cause celebre. Bob had come over to London with the first wave of American reporters and Adam insisted that he stay in the apartment.

'Adam' called Bob, ' Roosevelt is proclaiming that America will remain neutral at the moment even though Britain have declared war and mobilised an Expedition Force to go to Europe'.

Adam shouted back at him

'There are people being murdered as we speak for no other reason than the fact that they are Jewish or Polish'.

'The Fuehrer has proclaimed that 'Germany will destroy and exterminate the Polish nation'

'He had already awarded Theodore Eicke for 'outstanding valour' despite every General from the Model group describing his actions as nothing but 'wanton butchery'.

'Eicke himself has gone on record, as saying the SS would have to 'incarcerate or annihilate every enemy of Nazism'.

'Tell that to Roosevelt!'

For the rest of that year, the rest of the world watched as Germany effectively annexed all of Europe. Unknown to the rest of the world however, the Nazis has already decided the fate of the Jews in Europe. The greatest killing machine that mankind had ever witnessed was slowly being put in place. As the blitzreig steamrollered through Europe, SS Deaths Head brigades butchered Jews, Romany Gypsies and Slavs in staggering numbers. A special 'Camp' section had been established within the SS and concentration camps were springing up all over the Eastern territories to compliment those in Germany. The SS had a rail network in place and as the Wehrmacht charged forward, Jews were 'encouraged' to 'resettle in the East' by SS police units sweeping up the rear.

In Poland alone extermination camps were built and capable of murdering 100,000 people a day. Names like Belzec, Sobibor, Majdanek, Chelmno, Treblinka and Belsen meant nothing to the masses outside, they meant death to the vast majority of those that entered through their gates. This 'resettlement' of European Jewry effectively meant death. As early as summer of 1940 and on into 1942, Jews were being gassed by the thousands, their bodies were incinerated, their hair used for mattresses, their bones for animal feed, they had in death become a 'war commodity' .

British Intelligence learned of this mass murder in 1940 as a result of them successfully beginning to receive reports from Polish underground, the problem was that they would not act without corroboration and would not consider the scale that the Germans were killing people as being possible. The accounts were marked Top Secret and filed for the discretion of very few people indeed. The first report that came into their possession detailed the personnel that were to be used in the mass murder in Poland

The Jewish question in this region must be solved as quickly as possible. Dr. Buhler's request was given a positive response. The General Government consisted of the districts of Warsaw, Cracow, Lublin, Radom, and Lvov. According to the estimate of the German authorities, hey were inhabited by approximately 2,284,000 Jews. A special organization was set up in Lublin to prepare for their extermination. The actual killing will be carried out in three death camps -- Belzec, Sobibor and Treblinka, at the eastern border of the General Government. The geographical location of the extermination sites also served as a pretext for the claim that the Jews were to be deported to ghettos in the East. Their disappearance could thus be explained in terms of their transportation to labour camps

Brigadefu"hrer Otto Globocnik was entrusted with conducting Operation Reinhard -- In this office he was Himmler's immediate subordinate; as the commandant of SS and Police in the Lublin district he was subordinate to the Supreme SS- and Polizeifu"hrer of the Buhler General Government, Obergruppenfu"hrer Friedrich

Kruger the principal tasks of Globocnik and his staff was the overall planning of the deportations and of the extermination operations; the construction of extermination camps; to coordinate the deportation of Jews from the different administrative districts to the extermination camps; the killing of the Jews in the camps; to secure their belongings and valuables and transfer them to the appropriate German authority.

Headquarters was responsible for co-coordinating the timing of the transports with the absorption capacity of the camps. The organization and supervision of the respective transports from the entire area of the General Government and later on also from other European countries was the task of the RSHA and its departments as well as of the supreme commandant of the SS and Police and his subordinate departments. To date no written orders by Himmler to Globocnik concerning Operation Reinhard have been discovered. A reason for this may be that either Himmler issued no written statement on this subject, or that any orders and directives were destroyed.

The man at the centre of this information was a man who had previously held a Professorship at the London School of Economics, Professor Henry Mollayan. He had worked diligently with his two research teams and with the assistance of some considerable work done in the field of mathematics by some learned Polish scholars nearly a decade earlier had developed the system by which the underground could get messages out. . It was through this work that Mollayan discovered evidence of this 'Final Solution' against the Jews. He uncovered the actions of The Gestapo and the SS within Hans Frank's so called protectorate and the development of the death camps. He was able to follow train journeys from France and Belgium to locations within Poland, the trains always returned empty.

He forwarded the report straight through to Downing Street and waited and waited, no response was forthcoming, it was if the British didn't want to know. He decided to resubmit the report and was able to bring first hand information as one of his operatives had managed to get inside one of the outer work camps. He brought out a story of unbelievable horror, crematoria, mass open graves, shower blocks where the people went in alive and were carried or rather shoveled out by prisoners and brought to be burned.

Mollayan was livid with anger, he was sure that something had to be done, even if it were Jews that were suffering, he didn't know that at that very moment that he was pondering the situation, the son of a person who he thought was 'safe' was asking the same question.

Mollayan decided that he would have to initiate action himself and sent a coded message to a press bureau in Boston, marked for the attention of their London correspondent concerning unsubstantiated reports about mass murder in occupied Poland of Jews. All of Mollayan's skill and ingenuity were used in smuggling stories to the free world, using daring and cover, he had risked his life and the lives of his network. All he wanted was for someone, anyone to cry out to tell the world, who better than a writer with the Boston Globe. But this was different, he recollected the words in the report

'saw them make women stand one behind the other and the first woman was shot, they gambled to see how many more could be killed with the same bullet.'

And then there was the bragging, the Jew baiting, the giving of false hope, the wanton murdering of babies.

Rome also knew what was happening to the Jews in Poland, they'd known there was something terrible happening as early as September 18 1940. The primate to all Poland had fled directly to Rome with stories of unmitigated brutality and wanton murder only to be castigated by Pius as being been fainthearted. The leadership of the church in Poland was taken over by Archbishop Adam Sapieha of Krakow, in whose diocese was the small town of Oswiecim or as the Germans called it, Auschwitz.

Archbishop Sapieha had direct contact with the Holy Father through Cardinal Santini and as the first reports began to come through, Sapieha begged the Vatican to tell the world what was happening. He told them about the building work and sent a report that had been given to him by an Ulany captain who had managed to infiltrate the camp.

Report NO.1

I was able to enter into the main body of a camp disguised as a polish laborer, I entered the outer compound at approximately 8.00 in the morning through a set of steel gates. There was a sign hung over them that read Arbeit macht frie, (work brings freedom) We were working on the construction of a barrack bloc roughly 50 meters from the inner camp.

I managed to secret myself into the roof of the building and removed a pair of field glasses to observe the goings on in the inner camp. The first thing that I have to report is the smell, it is all invading and clings to your nostrils and clothes like some sort of invisible dust. The inner camp in surrounded by two high fences; one of them I suspect is electrified. Between the two fences there is a continued presence of Ukrainians with Alsatian dogs. There are also four high guard towers, each of them were manned by German troops in all black uniforms. Looking across from my vantage point I could see a train pull in and there seemed to be a lot of activity there, I noticed a number of men in white coats sitting at tables as the people who had come off the trains approached them. I could see that women and children and men were being separated, the women and children were being herded towards what I could clearly identify as warehouses, there was an orchestra playing outside one of these and the sign above the door said 'Sanitation Centre'.

I watched as the women and children were ushered into the sanitation room, approximately ten minutes later my ears were assaulted by a burst hideous screaming, I had never heard the like of it, even on a battlefield. I watched as male prisoners (I later found out that they were called 'sonderkommandos') went in and brought all of the people who had gone in out on trolleys. It was then that I noticed the four large chimneys away towards the back of the camp. I stayed in my place for over two hours and by my calculations there were 300 or so going in every 20 minutes or so.

As I watched more closely. I noticed three people on the top of the flat roof of the sanitation centre, they were dropping something into the building, it must have been what killed the people because they were all wearing gas masks.

Before I left I witnessed two large hills of bones some two stories high.

Archbishop Sapieha had held his head between his legs and vomited, he vomited until his guts screamed with pain. Page after page it went, he cried aloud and the puke and the tears and the pain crushed in on him until he fell to the floor of his room in a dead faint, When he awoke, he was alone, he got up, washed and went over to his desk and wrote a letter to his superior in the Holy See, he attached the copy of the report and summonsed the courier. He then waited for his instruction. He didn't have long to wait.

Three days later he received a communiqué in the usual way. He prayed that he would have the strength to protest, to tell the world from his pulpit of the inhumanity that was being perpetrated in his country.

The Holy See advised him that to take that course of action at this time may 'give rise to further persecutions'

He was to maintain contact and do... Nothing.

He had worked in the secretariat of state in the Vatican during the WW1 and knew the machinations of the Vatican very well. He was told that he was to use his own network to keep the Holy See informed, any information was to be directed through to the Secretariat directly, to the desk of Monsignor Andrew Lassiter.

Rudolf Hess stormed into his office, he lifted the telephone....

'Rosenberg? Is that you?

'Da '

'Get over here right away'

Hess slammed the telephone down. He was furious, he could see his life's work dissipate in front of his very eyes, 20 years of careful planning was in danger of being destroyed if the Fuehrer listened to Himmler and Bormann and went ahead with the madness of attacking Russia in the summer. Even Heydrich could see the folly of such a measure, he knew that they could not count on the Italians if the going got tough, he however was completely involved in instigating his own particular brand of terror in Moravia. The reports from Rommel in North Africa suggested that if he had the resources he could completely wipe out the Allies. He'd already won a famous victory at Tobruk. Hess had begged Hitler to land ground troops in England after Dunkirk, that fat fool Goering had argued that his Luftwaffe would win the day, how wrong and potentially damaging could his inability to deliver on conquering England prove to be.

Ever since the early days of the Thule, it had been agreed that the Reich would hit hard and fast and be merciless, not stopping until the only thing between them and America was the Atlantic, the U boats would look after the rest. America would seek peace and eventually an alliance that would permit the Reich to attack and defeat Russia. The world would belong to the Reich and the Aryan legacy would be in place for 1000 years.

In order to achieve the this objective, the Thule's plan had been to exterminate the Jewish race, undermine the might of the Christian, Catholic Church and coerce the remaining strains of Protestantism under a united banner as a 'chosen race'. Hess, as the architect of the strategy, had to have the artifacts of the Roman Faith and believed that he would find the evidence of the lost tribe, the Essene eventually. This would permit him to proclaim a Germanic 'Thule' religion that would control the destiny of mankind.

To attack Russia was madness and a folly. He'd already structured a deal with Stalin over the division of Poland, he knew that Germany, the Reich was not ready. Russia would fall on his terms, a religious war that would destroy

Communism as the orthodox Russian Church took their place as the head of Rodina, with the assistance of America but all under Hess's control of course.

He had cultivated the Duke of Windsor to his cause when he had introduced him to Hitler in 1938 and undertaken to put him on the throne of England as a King within the new Thule inspired master race. Joseph P. Kennedy was American Ambassador in Berlin in 1938 and had expressed complete agreement with Hess's philosophy in dealing with Russia and communism. He also was impressed with Hess's thinking on race and believed that he could be well positioned if Hess's brand of statehood reached the United States. Kennedy knew that there was going to be a problem with communism, he reasoned that if the Germans dealt with it, America would benefit, his first mistake was to underestimate and think he could control Rudolf Hess.

The office door was knocked

'Come in, Rosenberg, we have work to do. We must find the missing pieces of the scroll if we are to convince the Fuehrer of his folly over attacking Russia. Himmler is convinced he is the reincarnation of an ancient king and he had persuaded Bormann that the Fuehrer cannot be defeated by anyone. We have yet to establish the parameters of the Western Front, an attack in the East will stretch us to the limit and if America enters the war, we will be in serious trouble.' The Fuehrer has codenamed the operation 'Barbarossa' and is adamant that it will take place in June, he expects to be in Moscow before the winter.

'But surely the Fuehrer knows what is best', said Rosenberg

Hess grimaced

'I fear the little Austrian Sticklegruber has already outlived his usefulness, he is starting to believe his own rhetoric and is forgetting who put him where he is'

Rosenberg was staggered, he suspected that Hess was the real power within Thule for years, he'd never heard him criticise the Fuehrer before, Rosenberg began to think that it was Hess that was losing the plot, he told himself he would have to be careful from now on.

Where is the Englander?' demanded Hess

'He is still in London, we cannot get at him, he enjoys a profile as one of their most informed correspondents and has been urging America to enter the war on the allied side.

'We should just kill him and his family' said Rosenberg

'And lose our only link to the Yahweh? Hess scorned at Rosenberg.

'No, I have a much better plan'. Hess pondered as to whether he should tell Rosenberg of his plan to fly to Scotland to seek the secret of the Rosslyn church but decided against it, the information being provided to him came from an impeccable source within the British establishment that had been cultivated by Mosley in London.

'What about Carter? asked Rosenberg

'He'll eventually come here if America enters the war, we'll get him then... Hold on, what happened to that Tannenbaum bitch?

Rosenberg smiled ' Last I heard she was in Belzec or Birkenau'

'Take her back to Germany, put her in Buchenwald, we'll keep her alive and see if we can tempt the Englander here with a few selective quotes to our sympathetic press in America.'

Unbeknown to Hess, the information that was being fed to him from his group of 'friends' in London was in fact being controlled by the same man who had discovered evidence of the camps in Poland, Professor Henry Mollayan. He had long since traced and nullified Mosley's network of spies and had succeeded in turning three 'sleeper' agents to feed information that he fed them. A listening post in Paris intercepted messages including 'they must not succeed' as it was being relayed. Hess was convinced that the message was genuine, he read and reread the first communiqué

'Rosslyn has been breached stop imperative you respond stop line in danger stop they must not succeed stop'

The listener had identified who had sent the communiqué in the usual way and Hess was convinced it was genuine... just as Henry Mollayan hoped he would

Chapter 14

By the start of 1941, Andrew Lassiter's disenchantment with the Vatican was complete, he had been disciplined and removed from his position as a result of his incessant demands that the Holy See take a position on this 'Jewish Question'. Santini no longer invited him to his table and Andrew knew that Santini himself had received a report from Count Malvezzi that corroborated everything that Sapieha had told him, he'd seen it with his own eyes! Andrew only ever challenged Santini once about the report and Santini reacted angrily saying

'I cannot check the accuracy of these reports!'

Andrew retorted, 'That is feeble, Auschwitz is only 40 miles from Krakow, the church's problem lies in imagining it as death has never before been industrialised.'

As he left the secretariat that night, he decided to walk to the Piazza. He came down through the courtyard of St. Damascus. Even after all this time in Rome, Andrew was bewildered by the cruel tensions that were housed in the building he had just left and confused by the thought of the trials and tribulations that lay ahead of him. He walked through the gate and smiled to himself and beside it the peaked red roofed Sistine chapel. Slowly the magnificence of the piazza exploded into view, the sweep of Bernini's colonnade around the piazza, the massive Portoni di Bronzo, how many times had he marveled at their beauty and the mystery and history that the long staircase beyond them held.

From where he was standing he could see most of the museums and right up there, on the top of the Janiculum Hill, the American College. He hailed a taxi at the top of the Via della Conciliazione and got out to walk across the Victor Emmanuel Bridge. He was going to walk as far as the Circo Massimo but something stopped him and he turned and headed back towards the Irish College and his private rooms. He was walking for about 10 minutes when a car drew up beside him, a door opened and a voice boomed

'Get in I'm going your way'

Andrew ducked into the passenger seat as Bernard steered the car away from the pavement.

Andrew at that moment wanted to tell Bernard of his quandary but he decided to return to his room. He sat down at his desk and removing the bunch of keys from under his cassock, unlocked the bottom drawer of his desk. He lifted the buff coloured folder up onto the desk in front of him and started to work through the collection of papers, every single report that had ever come across his desk from Poland had been carefully Photostatted and he had removed it from the Secretariat. He'd also been careful not to alert Bernard to the copies that he had taken of the evidence of the Essene that was contained in the apostolic library. The new directives and organisational work kept Andrew busy until late each night, it was also a perfect cover for him to do his own work. For the first time since he had read of the happenings in Poland, Andrew Lassiter was at peace. He removed his clerical collar, rolled up the sleeves of his black shirt and leaned back in the chair, locking his hands behind his head. and thought of the course of action he was about to commence. He stared at the picture of his father that was sitting to the left of the desk and he said out loud

'What should I do father?'

It was as if his father was smiling at him, he quickly took the manila envelope and taking the pen in his left hand wrote that address on the front of the envelope

Mr. Carter
26 Harberton Mews
Kensington
London
England

He opened the envelope and placed the copies of the report that he had copied 23 pages of copy that made up the report of Count Malvezzi. He attached a hand written note to the report that established his bonafide and sealed the envelope

Andrew rose early the next morning, he prayed in the college chapel on his own, showered, had breakfast and went back to his room where he prepared to send Adam the testimony that had been smuggled out of Birkenau by the Ulany captain and sent to Rome. He also sent a report that had been corroborated by Malvezzi and was also said to have been smuggled out of the women's camp in Birkenau. Such bravery deserved so much more, but Andrew could only hope that this Carter reporter would know how best to use this material without betraying the source. He hoped he would use it to get the world at large to stop and acknowledge what was going on and the stop it, something the Holy See were not prepared to do. He typed the message and sent it by diplomatic carrier through to an American contact within the Vatican Press service, Observatore Romano and awaited a response.

Adam had made his mind up that he'd have to do something, if only for the memory of Isaac Tauber, he would have to take a stand. He had planned to go back to America to see if he could get any political support for his quest to highlight the genocide of the Jews. Adam knew he was in trouble, he was walking a tightrope. In the old days before the war he was so sure of himself, so independent and clever but now he wasn't so sure, everybody was reading but no one was listening. He'd tried every avenue to try and get someone to corroborate his findings, he pursued every scrap of information coming from Germany. He all but camped outside the buildings where the daily press reports were distributed and searched for any sign that some sort of action had been taken in Poland. His bitter reflections only deepened as he immersed himself in his thoughts as he made the short trek back to his apartment every evening. The people of the occupied lands were holding on through the lengthening madness of Nazi persecution in the knowledge that somebody, anybody would eventually come to help them, and they had a basis for hope. Hadn't they? Did they not deserve to cling to something, any glimmer that somebody cared enough to do something, bomb the camps, at least the masses would be out of their misery, Adam's chagrin and disappointment became a personal torture.

Henry Mollayan had convinced Rudolf Hess that the answer to his life's ambition lay in Rosslyn. He had told his senior officer at SOE that he was working on a disinformation plan against a senior member of Hitler's inner circle, he asked for the resources and complete operating freedom should he manage to entice his target to take the bait. Mollayan himself had been present on the last three occasions when information had been fed to the quarry by no less a peer that the Duke himself! Churchill had been informed of Mollayan's plan and had given it tacit approval on the condition that if Hess did take the bait and come to England there would be no possibility of any negotiation or treaty making. Mollayan had fed the story that Hess wished to broker a deal with England that would allow a peace between them and a common purpose in fighting the Russians. He stressed that the subterfuge that had been used had placed a lot of his network in great danger and he insisted on a top level secrecy clearing on all communication on the operation.

On 18 May, Hess called Rosenberg to his office

'My dear Albert, I am about to fulfill our destiny. I leave at midnight tomorrow night intend to parachute into Scotland where I will be met by a representative of the Duke of Windsor, he will take me to a location in Rosslyn where I will gain access to a church, a church that holds the answer to the secret of the Essene'

Rosenberg was ashen

'You are the deputy to the Fuehrer, you cannot go anywhere!

'Fool' shouted Hess ' you of all people Albert, know the power of the Yahweh. We have no access to the Englander, we do not know the fourth man, the Jew bitch has told us all we know and our attempts to entice the Englander out has come to nothing'.

Hess didn't know that Mollayan had suppressed every message that Hess had sent regarding Maria Tannenbaum, he didn't believe for a minute that she was alive and more importantly, he needed Adam Carter for his own reasons.

Rosenberg continued

'Der Fuehrer, what does he think of your plan?'

'He doesn't know, but when I return triumphantly, we shall have the ultimate weapon, we shall rule the world. Now, Rosenberg, I need you to give this to him when I leave.

Hess handed Rosenberg a letter and said, 'I must leave now, I will contact you to signal my safe arrival, the Duke will arrange a way'. Needless to say Rosenberg, if you should think about telling anybody, you will be signing your own death warrant. The letter explains everything, do as I ask'.

Hess parachuted into Scotland on the night of 10 May, he was spotted and on hitting the ground was set upon by locals and given a beating. A local policeman who arrested him and took him to the village jail saved him. He had landed nearly 100 miles north of his intended destination and insisted on telling everyone who he was and that he wished to speak with the Duke of Windsor.

Mollayan was awakened at 4.04am,

'Sorry for disturbing you Sir, but we've just intercepted a message saying that Rudolf Hess is a traitor to the Reich and is condemned to death'.

Mollayan froze, they could not have discovered his ruse, or could they? The voice continued,

'There is another strange report Sir, we received a call from a Army training barracks in Ballater in Scotland, they say to send some of our chaps up there right away'

'Why?' asked Mollayan

'Well Sir, that's the strange part, they arrested a pilot who parachuted into the region last night, he has been demanding to speak to the Prime Minister, says his name is Hess, Rudolf Hess.

Mollayan jumped up ' No one is to speak to him until I arrive, is that clear?

'Yes Sir' replied the voice

'Now' said Mollayan ' Has he been searched yet?'

'Yes Sir', he was unarmed and carrying some papers….

'Good' said Mollayan 'Is there a doctor up there?'

Again the voice confirmed that the village doctor was available. Mollayan issued instructions for the prisoner to have a complete body search, the doctor was to pay particular attention to his mouth and teeth and his other body cavities. He explained that he did no want the German to take poison, they usually secreted a cyanide capsule in a false cavity in their mouth and at the first hint of discovery, and they bit into it…

'Put him in a restraint if you have to, on no account is he to be left alone, I'll be up there as soon as possible and remember he talks to no one.'

Mollayan got out of bed, got dressed and arranged for a flight to take him to Ballater immediately. He couldn't and wouldn't believe that he had tempted Rudolf Hess, the architect of the German Reich to follow the Yahweh until he saw him with his own eyes.

He was not disappointed, seven hours later he was sitting in front of Deputy Reichfeurhrer Rudolf Hess in person.

Mollayan walked into the room and the man opposite him glowered making no attempt to hide his disdain

'Who are you?' spat Hess 'I demand to see Churchill, I am here on a mission of critical importance to the future of Europe, as we know it'. I protest this humiliation, I am not to be treated like some common criminal, Do you know who I am and who I represent!

Mollayan ignored him; his eyes showed almost boredom

'My name is unimportant at the moment' said Mollayan 'I want you to tell me what you are doing here in Scotland?

Hess replied 'I will only speak to Churchill, I am here at the invitation of the Duke of Windsor, you have no right to barge in here and question me like this, I demand.......

Mollayan's nostrils flared ' Stop now foolish man, I know why you are here and I can tell you to your face. 'You will not succeed'. I want you just to recognise what comes out of the end of this muzzle, you will do exactly as I say or you will die!'

Beads of perspiration popped out on Rudolf Hess's upper lip, to refuse to acknowledge this man would be to miss the opportunity of discovering what he knew but if he did recognise this stranger, he would risk showing his hand and the cover story that he had worked so hard to put in place would be ruined. His mind raced as he considered his position

'Who was this man? Hess asked himself

How did he know about the reason for his flight?

Had he been betrayed in Germany?

Did the British know about Yahweh?

'Who are you? Hess asked.

Mollayan's eyes were as cold as slivers of broken glass and they seemed to draw blood from Hess's protests

'You will remain silent until you are questioned, if you speak another word I shall have you removed and I can promise you that it will be a long time before you speak with anyone again!'

'You will tell me what you know about Yahweh'. I will permit you the rest of the evening to reflect on your predicament and when I return in the morning you will co-operate fully with my investigation.'

'Who are you?' whimpered Hess

'I am the reason you will not succeed' and at that Mollayan turned and marched to the door of the room, he opened it and spoke to the guard.

'The doctor has seen the prisoner?

'Yes Sir' barked the guard

'Bring him some food and place a guard on this door; no-one is to communicate with him until I return in the morning, is that clear?'

'Yes Sir' barked the guard a second time

Mollayan left the room without even a second glance at the dishevelled man sitting in the chair, the man who 24 hours earlier was the second most important man in the Third Reich, now he was prisoner no 3345536 and no –one least of all his cohorts in Germany knew where he was.

Mollayan was pleased, he had delivered his birthright, and he had protected Yahweh from its most vile threat and in doing so had captured the most dangerous Nazi of them all.

Rosenberg sat in his office, it had been confirmed that Hess had flown to England by Luftwaffe control. Himmler and Bormann were damning him as a traitor and condemning him to death when the war was won. The Fuehrer was perplexed and restless, he could not comprehend why Hess had left his side, He had sent for Rosenberg and asked him of Hess's intention, finally flying into a rage of mammoth proportions and swearing death upon his mentor. Rosenberg had cowered at the ferocity of the attack, he knew he was finished as well; he was too closely allied to Hess and would never be trusted by either Goering or Himmler. He lifted a drink and re read the letter on the desk again

Mein Fuehrer

My honour is loyalty and this is why I must embark on this mission, if I am successful, the Reich will proclaim us as 'supermen', founders of the 1000 year Reich. The power that we seek is greater than any man and will ensure our destiny long after you and I have gone. I must seek the power because I fear that you folly by attacking the Slavs and Untermensch in the East. We had a plan you know the plan, your course of action is betraying the plan and all that we stand to achieve. You are not of the Thule, you do not understand. When I return you will see the power and the glory of the creator.

Rudolf Hess

09 May 1941

Rosenberg scrunched the letter up and threw the last communiqué of Rudolf Hess on the fire and then proceeded to burn all of the files that had been collated by Hess on the 'five'. He resisted throwing the cloth of Netzer on the fire, instead wrapping it around the 'guider' and stuffing it in the back of his personal safe. Rosenberg returned to his desk, opened a drawer and took out a bottle out; he poured a drink and sat back, contemplating his options as to what he had to do to ease this nightmare away from him. This was an omen; the tide was starting to turn

On the 20th of May 1941, Hitler made his move, he attacked Russia.

He attacked Russia.

Adam burst through the front door of the apartment, his arms full of reports and papers that he'd taken from the archives of the Globe in London; he'd planned to sit that evening and research his next report that was to go back to the states. He'd had word that his work was now been syndicated by 13 papers and radio were using his diary report as content for their main news delivery. Adam was feeling happy with himself as He'd be able to talk to Megan this evening as well. He pushed the front door, it appeared to be sticking and when he finally got in, he saw, lying on the floor, a manila envelope with his name on it in a hand writing he didn't recognise. It read

Mr. A Carter
26 Harberton Mews
Kensington
London
England

Adam put his bundle and lifted the envelope; he tested the weight and felt the envelope. His curiosity finally got the better him and he walked over to his desk, rummaged about for the letter opener and slit the package along its top and spilled the contents out onto the desk.

He lifted the handwritten note first

Dear Mr. Carter

You do not know who I am but that is unimportant at the moment, should you wish to verify my identity, you should call this number. I have sent you something that I think may interest you and your readers, all I ask are that you publish it in its entirety.

I can assure you that this is not a trick and what is contained in the report is a true report of a bona fide eye -witness.

I trust you will know what to do with this

Adam looked at the envelope and recognised the diplomatic seal of the Vatican. He lifted the report and began to read it, as he read he felt a nauseous wave overpower him, he fought against it until he reached the second page, he succumbed to his stomach and rushed to the door and heaved the contents of his lunch onto the top step. He still had the page in his hand containing the words

It was then that I noticed the four large chimneys away towards the back of the camp. I stayed in my place for over two hours and by my calculations there were 300 or so going in every

20 minutes or so. As I watched more closely. I noticed three people on the top of the flat roof of the sanitation centre, they were dropping something into the building, and it must have been what killed the people because they were all wearing gas masks.

Before I left I witnessed two large hills of bones some two stories high.

He went back inside and lifted the second report; he flicked through the pages until he looked down at the bottom of the last page. Adam Carter saw a name and fell back in to his chair, removed to a street corner in Berlin and a face peering through the back window of a black sedan .... Maria.

Adam said the words but he didn't believe them, he thought it was a trap that had been set to attract him back to Germany. He had no one that he could talk too and was prepared to ignore the message purporting to come from Maria until he'd done some checking, it was too much of a coincidence and it could be a hoax. Adam reread the report then locked it away in his safe in the apartment. He went back to his study and was reaching for a bottle of scotch when the telephone rang

Mollayan, on hearing that Adam had traveled back to England had made arrangements there and then for him to be watched by his people from the moment he got off the plane. He'd read with growing concern at the profile that he was beginning to create for himself and knew it was only a matter of time before the lodge would be one to him.

Adam picked up the telephone, a glass of scotch in his hand

'Hello'

'They must not succeed' whispered the voice

'Who is this? demanded Adam, the whiskey turning to ice in his veins.

'I will send someone for you tonight' said the voice

'Who is t........

'No questions now, Isaac would want you to do this '

'Where' said Adam

'Stay where you are, a driver will pick you up in 1 hour's time'

The phone line went dead.

Adam reeled at the mention of Isaac's name and was still trying to make sense of what was going on when his doorbell sounded.

Adam was sitting in a windowless room, he had arrived an hour earlier and had been taken in the car by a man who introduced himself as 'Fred', and for the remainder of the drive volunteered little or no information. Adam tried to see where he was going but to no avail, eventually the car turned into a guarded lane way, two sentries manned a sentry box and barrier, both were heavily armed, there was also a machine gun nest set back from the road and camouflaged. The car pulled up in front of a fairly non-descript building, Adam got out and was ushered to the room he was now in.

The door opened and an older man walked in, he was about 55, Adam guessed, 6.2 tall, well built with graying hair which was brushed back from his face. He smiled and put his hand out .....

'Welcome to Cheltenham, Mr. Carter, My name is Henry Mollayan

'Call me Adam, everyone else does'

Mollayan smiled, '

'Would you like a drink? Something to eat perhaps?

'Why have you brought me here?'

'All in good time, I trust you had a pleasant trip' said Mollayan

'Yes' said Adam 'You mentioned a friend of mine, what do you know about him?

Mollayan made a mental note and continued 'aaaaaah Isaac Tauber?

Adam flared 'Look I want to know what's going on?

'Very well' said Mollayan 'They must not succeed' what does that mean to you?

Adam fed Mollayan the line about meeting Isaac and helping him flee and the words were words that Isaac had repeated to him when they were talking about Hitler and the Nazis, he said Isaac had some idea about a treasure or something...

Mollayan smiled and nodded his head, damn; this boy was good, very good indeed. There wasn't even a flicker as he relayed the story, that what it was a story. Mollayan decided to see if he could shake him a little.

'I see your father was in the forces, he served in Palestine for a time?

'That is correct' said Adam

'He was murdered?

'Yes' said Adam 'He was shot in 1912, we never did discover the reason why and no one was ever caught.

'Strange' said Mollayan 'I took the liberty of looking up his file at regimental GHQ, seems he was involved in an investigation of his own when he was in Palestine, another death in suspicious circumstances'

Adam stared hard at Mollayan 'Why the interest in my father? asked Adam

Mollayan backed off 'It must have been hard for you at the time?

'Yes it was' said Adam 'I apologise for my tone, I'm a little tired after the journey'

'Perfectly understandable' mused Mollayan 'I'll arrange dinner. I promise you all will become clear then.

Adam rose and followed Mollayan to the door; he turned and spoke 'How do you know Isaac?

'I knew his niece' replied Mollayan nochantly

'And who might that be? asked Adam

'A girl I used to know, a girl called Maria.

Adam paused at the door, his mind racing, Maria! This was going to be more difficult than he thought…

'We'll have to see what we can do then' said Mollayan 'They mustn't be allowed to succeed'

Adam followed Mollayan in silence, unaware of the whereabouts of Maria, not sure if she was alive or dead.

Had either Henry Mollayan or Adam Carter, given their particular interest in what was happening, wanted first hand information of what life in the camps was like, they could have availed of the testimony of Maria Tannenbaum, who had been in four different camps from October 1938. On the 13 December 1941, she'd been put on a train from Munich and 15 hours later has been whipped out of an enclosed car and taken to stand in front of a white coated SS officer in a place called Belzec for something called 'selection'. She was instructed to go to the right and joined a line of pretty girls; the vast majority of the transported Jews including all of the children had gone off to the left….

'Where are they taking them? asked the new girl

'Have you no smell? One of the girls who were cutting hair spoke in whispered tones.

'They're going up there; she pointed towards a large black funnel of smoke pouring out into the blue sky.

Maria Tannenbaum had arrived in Belzec. She had her first report of information she had collected from various sources and edited, smuggled out three weeks later.

The Construction of the Balzac Extermination Camp

Balzac, a small town in the southeast of the district of Lublin, close to the border of the district of Lvov and on the Lublin-Zamosc-Rawa Ruska-Lvov railroad line, was selected as the locality for the first extermination camp. The area specified for the camp was a railroad siding half a kilometre from the Belzec railroad station.

The Pole Stanislaw Kozaka (A friend of Maria's) described the beginning of its construction:

In October of the year 1941 three SS-men came to Belzec and demanded 20 men for the work from the municipal administration. The local council chose 20 workers from among the inhabitants of Belzec, and I was one of them. The Germans selected the terrain to the southeast of the railroad station, which adjoined a siding. The railway line to Lvov runs along this sidetrack. We began to work on November 1, 1941, with the construction of huts on the plot adjoining the siding. One of the huts, which stood right next to the siding, was 150 feet. Iong and about 75 feet. wide. The second hut, which was roughly the same measurement. was intended for the Jews who went to the baths. Next to this hut we built a third hut, which wasmuch smaller. This hut was divided into three sections by wooden walls, so that each section was 12 feet. wide and 24 or so feet.long. These sections were6 feet. high. The interior walls of these huts were built such that we nailed the boards to them, filling in the empty space with sand. Inside the hut the walls were covered with cardboard; in addition the floors and the walls, to a height of 4 feet. [were covered] with sheet-zinc. A 3m.avenue, fenced in with barbed wire, which was 3 m. high, led from the first to the second of the above-mentioned huts. A part of this fence, facing the siding and beyond it was covered with pines and firs that had been specially felled, in order to conceal the siding. From the second hut a covered passage, ca. 6 feet. wide, 6 feet. high and roughly 100 feet. long, led to the third hut. By way of this passage one reached the passage of the third hut, from which three doors led to its three sections. Each section of this hut had a door on its northern side, these doors, like the doors to the passage, were closely fitted with rubber. All the doors in this hut opened toward the outside.

The doors were very strongly built of three-inch thick planks and were secured against pressure from inside by a wooden bolt that was pushed inside two iron hooks specially fitted for this purpose. In each of the three sections of this hut water pipes were fixed at a height of 10 cm. from the floor. In addition, on the Western Wall of each section of this hut water pipes branched off at an angle to a height of about three feet. from the floor, ending in an opening directed toward the middle of the hut. The elbow-pipes were connected to pipes, which ran along the walls and under the floor... 70 "blacks' have dug the trench" that is to say, by former Soviet soldiers who worked with the Germans. It was 18 to 20 feet deep m. deep, 60 feet. wide and 150 feet. long. This was the first ditch in which the Jews, killed in the extermination camp, were buried. The "blacks" dug this ditch in six weeks, at the time when we built the huts. This ditch was later continued as far as the middle of the northern border. That was already at a time when we no longer worked on building the huts. The first hut that I mentioned was at a distance of approximately 60 feet. from the siding and about 350 feet. from the southern border. At that time when we Poles were building the huts, the "blacks" put up the fence around the extermination camp; it consisted of posts with closely spaced barbed wire. After we had built the three huts described above, the Germans dismissed us Poles from work on December 22, 1941

Report No 2 ... Testimony of Jan Kolka... to Maria Tannenbaum.

In the second half of December, Christian Wirth was appointed Camp Commandant of Belzec, with Josef Oberhauser as his adjutant. SS-Scharfu"hrer Erich Fuchs reported on Wirth's arrival in Belzec:

One day in the winter of 1941, Wirth put together a transport. I was selected along with eight to ten others and transferred to Belzec in three motorcars... Upon our arrival in Belzec we met Friedel Schwarz and two other SS-men whose names I do not remember. They served as guards during the building of a hut that we were to fit out as a gas chamber. I heard Wirth say that in Belzec "all Jews were to be bumped off." For this purpose the huts were fitted out as gas chambers. Men then installed shower nozzles in the gas chambers. The nozzles were not connected to a water pipe because they were only meant to serve as camouflage for the gas chambers. The Jews who were to be gassed were untruthfully informed that they were to be bathed and disinfected. Wirth developed his own ideas on the basis of the experience he had gained in the "Euthanasia" program. Thus, in Belzec he decided to supply the fixed gas chamber with gas produced by the internal-combustion engine of a motorcar. Wirth rejected Cyanide B. The gas was produced by private firms and its extensive use in Belzec might have aroused suspicion and led to problems of supply. He therefore preferred a system of extermination based on ordinary, universally available gasoline and diesel fuel.

Her reports were smuggled out of the camp and were in the hands of the Vatican, it formed part of a corroborating report that had been submitted by Count Malvezzi. The Count had been worked for the Instituto per la Riconstruzione Industriale that controlled most of the banking system and investment procedure in Italy. Mussolini had founded it in 1931 and the Count had been invited by Hans Frank to come to Poland in early 1940 to see for himself how the Reich were using labor to assist with the war effort. The Count was appalled at the treatment meted out by the Germans and protested vehemently to Frank who ignored his protestations and claimed

'Soon I will have the pleasure of informing the ReichFuehrer that the Greater German Protectorate is now 'Judenfrei'. When we came here there were over 3 million of them, now there are less than 300,000'.

'Surely you have not sent all of them to the east? questioned Malvezzi. 'Where are they?

'Poof, up in smoke' laughed Frank as he pointed at the map 'All that is left are in Warsaw and very soon they will be no more either'. 'Have a drink dear Count, we have some delicious new entertainment coming in tonight, a pair of twins from Hungary that I am led to believe do amazing things'...

The Count excused himself and went to his room where he wept like a child. He then decided to inform the Pope of the happenings and set about establishing a network of contacts and diplomatic processes to make sure that the testimony reached the Holy Father.

Andrew Lassiter hadn't slept in nearly two days; in fact he hadn't left the library in two days. Cardinal Santini had gone to Castelgandolfo with the Holy Father and Bernard was visiting a sick relative. Andrew had been plundering through the various manuscripts and books to try and determine the Essene story. He'd been staggered at the complicity of the church in the cover up of what seemed to be a very plausible rendition of fact. He wondered as to the possibility of the role of the Magdalene, he was staggered at the devotion of the Templars and their Cathar brothers in arms. The inquisition and the reasons for it beggared belief and he was sitting now staring at a painting by Poissin called 'The Shepherdess' and wondering what it had to do with the mystery, what he was about to find out threatened to push him over the edge…

He had stumbled on it by mistake, he'd been trying to find location evidence within the Languedoc region of France of Templar sites and on one of the old maps, and he noticed a more recent marker 'Rennes Le Chateau' and a name 'Abbe Saunier'.

Andrew began to cross reference the place and the name and discovered a report that had dealt with the suspension of a priest called 'Saunier' whose parish was Rennes Le Chateau.

It transpired that this poor priest, overnight became incredibly wealthy and spent lavish amounts of money on the parish, he commissioned and constructed a uniquely shaped library close to the village and money was no object. Evidence had been gathered that suggested that Saunier had discovered a great secret, so great that the church was frightened enough to move against him. It didn't specify in the report what the secret was but it used the presence of the painting and statues of the devil in the church as evidence of some sort of heretical practice.

Andrew read on,

Saunier had dedicated his church to Mary of Magdalene, the woman who washed the feet of the Nazarene with her hair. Andrew had heard all of the old conspiracy theories and rumours that she was in some way special to the Nazarene, he like all the other church bred, learned academia, and dismissed such stories as unfounded rubbish.

In front of him he was reading an account of how it was alleged that Mary of Magdalene had escaped to France after the crucifixion, he agreed that was plausible given that the Languedoc was predominantly Jewish at the time. He'd heard all of the stories about the SAN GREAL, the alleged Holy Grail carrying the blood of Christ and how it had everlasting life qualities. He gave no credence to such stories; his church however at the time were totally pre occupied with them and given the lengths, to which the medieval church had gone to stamp out dissent, this was hardly surprising. He was about to turn the page when he noticed a misspelling at the bottom of the page and a strange notation...

Andrew caught his breath, he looked, mesmerised, at the words SANG REAL. This had to be a mistake, but it wasn't. The notes cross-referenced to Rennes Le Chateau and someone by the name of Jacques De Mollay, the last leader of the Templars.

Andrew went back over to his inquisition notes and found the record of de Mollay, he'd been arrested, tried and crucified as a heretical leader of the Templars at the prompting of the then King of France who was trying to find the source of the Templar wealth.

Andrew was perspiring, he knew what SAN GREAL meant and how it could be dismissed as a 'Grail' fantasy. He also knew what SANG REAL meant and if it were true, then Mary Magdalene didn't carry the cup of Christ from the Holy Land, she carried the seed of Christ, his child, his bloodline into

France where they lived and began a family dynasty that the Templars had sworn to protect and the secret of which, Abbe Saunier uncovered.

Andrew couldn't take it in; the sheer scale of the implications would destroy the church and have immense implications for all that considered the church as their rock of faith. It was then that the sheer immensity of his discovery hit him, sitting there on his own in the Library of the Sacred Congregation for the Propagation of the Faith in the seat of global Roman Catholicism in the Vatican, he began to remember his father's words 'They must not succeed'

Mollayan excused himself and Adam followed a soldier as he led him into a furnished room where he waited only a matter of minutes before he was joined once more by Mollayan.

'I trust you are hungry? Asked Mollayan

'Yes', said Adam

Now then, You want to know who I am and what I know. 'asked Mollayan 'Before I commence, can I just check on your recollection of Isaac Tauber's words?

Adam reiterated the story that he'd told earlier, he noticed that Mollayan was looking at him but didn't appear to be taking in what he was saying, and it was as if he was preoccupied with something else. As Adam began to relay the contact with Isaac, Mollayan put his finger up to his lip and motioned Adam to be quiet; he then turned on a tape recorder that was sitting on his desk. The tape spooled and Adam heard a voice that he thought he recognised.

'In order for us to fulfill our destiny, we must be ruthless, as strong as Krupp steel. We will have to engage Zion like no other race has ever contemplated. Our solitary aim is the extinction of the race; we must not contemplate anything other than sending them to final damnation.'

There followed a rustling of papers and some muffled conversation, Adam strained to hear what was being said

‘We have, in Adolf Hitler, the perfect front for our plan, he will galvanise the thinking of the people into achieving our objectives within the country. Once we have taken power, he will be instructed as to the actions he must take. I will assume the role of his deputy and ensure that he fulfills our destiny.

A round of applause was followed by another voice questioning….

‘Are you sure that our plan will produce the desired results?

Adam listened as the tape spooled on…. There was a hissing and then the first voice spoke again

‘We will succeed where others have failed, we will deliver the creator to his people, the people of the Thule. In order to do this we will have to eradicate the people that have persecuted him, there can be no mercy’

‘That’s Rudolf Hess! exclaimed Adam

‘Yes’ said Mollayan ‘ He’s talking about genocide of the Jews as the price to be paid for delivering the creator, do you know what he is talking about?

Adam stared hard at Mollayan, his mind a turmoil

Mollayan continued

‘What do you know of the Thule?

‘Are you aware of this creator?

‘What did Isaac tell you about the messages?

Adam started to respond but Mollayan cut across him ‘Remember Adam, they must not succeed’

Adam eyes blazed.

‘Maybe you should tell me who you are and what you want from me?’ I am saying nothing until I get some answers’

‘Aah’ said Mollayan ‘Stubbornness will only result in the deaths of innocents including your friend Maria’

Adam stood up 'my friend Maria?

Mollayan motioned him to sit down

'There are some things I must tell you' Your friend Maria is in Belzec, a concentration camp

Adam, white-faced went to speak but Mollayan put his finger to his lip to silence him.

Mollayan continued....

'You did not tell me that your father and her father were in the same regiment in Palestine'

'You did not tell me that she gave you something to keep in Berlin, You did not tell me that you came to Britain in the company of another Jew. You did not tell me that you possess information that the Nazis would kill a race for'. Do not dare to sit and deny any of what I have said to you, it is true, I know it is true because you are Adam Carter and by your birth you have sworn to protect the 'One'. They must not succeed!'

Adam was incapable of doing anything other than to stare at Mollayan.

'Who are you? he mumbled as Mollayan, regaining his composure, returned to his seat.

Sapieha in Krakow had stopped sending messages to Rome. Andrew had urged Santini to make contact with Sapieha and ask him to recommence the testimony that he was receiving from the camp at Belzec. Andrew was at the stage where 'Maria' had become a personal crusade for him, he needed her testimony to allow him to make his case to the Holy Father.

Privately, he was relieved to focus on 'Maria' his other studies were becoming more and more complex and more and more 'heretical'. What Andrew did not know that was when Sapieha received the request from Santini, he had stuffed it hastily into the stove saying

'If I give publicity to this and it is found in my house, the head of every Pole would not be enough for the reprisals that

Gaulieter Hans Frank would order... it's not just the Jews.... Here they are killing us all!'

Santini relayed Sapieha's message back to Andrew, they were sitting in the Apostolic Palace and Andrew was listening as Santini told him of the conversation.

'Another brother is in Krakow, he is presently on his way to join us here. His name is Fr. Rossi and he has been working on our 'network' since 1936. I want you to meet him and debrief him on the situation in Krakow'.

Andrew's torment was heightened by the fact that all of the research that he had been doing, suggested that there was a link, however tenuous between the activity of the Nazis and the terror that rained down on the protectors of the Yahweh in earlier times. Nazi practices pointed at various occult beliefs dating back to the time of the Templars. He'd uncovered incontrovertible evidence from Sauniere's papers that the Templars used the five-pointed star 'the pentangle' as a hidden method of communication in the Languedoc. He'd found evidence of explorations carried out by a little known German archeologist called Rahn in the early 1930s. The five-pointed Star had featured heavily in Poissin's painting and Andrew thought it was a code enabler of some kind but he wasn't sure. He suspected that the Nazis had uncovered part of the story and were just as eager to uncover the secret as he'd become in protecting it. If the SANG REAL proved to be true, then the owners of the truth would have the world at their mercy, what was the world without faith?

He was convinced that the Templars were committed to the protection of something, be it the bloodline of the Magdalene and that this practice had been continued across the centuries by an organisation called the 'Priory of Zion'. He hypothesized that the Nazis were seeking these secrets for some reason and were prepared to commit every calumny to achieve their aim. He was unsure as to his father's role in the mystery but was convinced that he was involved in the protection of whatever this Yahweh was. He committed himself to trying to find out more about this mysterious 'Priory of Zion'.

Andrew met Fr. Rossi later that evening and was surprised to discover that the priest was not much older than he was. He introduced himself and they retired to a private room to talk. Fr. Rossi told Andrew of the horrors of Krakow, he described it as 'an apocalyptic spectacle'. The words stunned Andrew, it was if he was in a parallel and his own discoveries were heightening his awareness of seeing all unfolding before his eyes. Rossi continued

'I wish you to hear these words, the Cardinal must be told and the Holy Father must be compelled to act before this madness consumes all that we exist for'

Rossi's eyes were filled with tears and his shoulders started to shake as he recited what he had seen, bestiality of an inhuman kind where nothing was sacred and death was a welcome respite.

'I went to Monsignor Sapieha and begged him on my knees to do something, anything to try and help and this is what he said to me'

Rossi went to his pocket and removed a letter written by Sapieha.

'We cannot help these people; we must not say so for fear of shortening lives. We are living through the tragedy of these unfortunate people and none of us are in a position to help them anymore... There's no difference you see, they have taken away our freedom but at least we have our lives and with life there is the hope of seeing the end of our cavalry'

Andrew never felt rage like it, he could feel his pulse, and his head was throbbing as his hands clenched the side of the table ... he forced himself to read on

'There is no comparison to this circle of hell and distinctions make no sense'

Rossi watched as Andrew started to shake his head back and forward and pray softly into himself. He stopped and looked at Rossi and then said

'I checked the dossier of the Cardinal today when Maglione was out of the office'

Maglione was another of the Cardinal's private secretaries and had proved to be quite a boorish and distasteful man, Andrew did not like him.

'I can tell you that the Cardinal is not aware of the scale of this madness'

'But' said Rossi 'I have sent every report directly to his office'

Andrew opened a folder and removed a page.

'A report by Count Malvezzi on action taken against Jews in Poland'

It was a cover page and written in long hand was a response

'The Holy See has received news of severe treatment of Jews but cannot check the accuracy of these reports'

Maglione signed it

Rossi shouted...

'Auschwitz is 40 miles from Krakow, when the wind blows you can smell the death, what is it that these people want?'

Look at this report that I have brought with me from 'Maria'. You are aware of her; you know she is in Belzec?

Andrew began to read

At the end of February 1942 the installations for mass extermination were completed.

The first two or three transports, each consisting of four to six freight cars fully loaded with a hundred or more Jews, were used for trial killings in order to test the capacity and efficiency of the gas chambers and the technique of the extermination process. The

tests lasted several days. The last group to be killed consisted of the Jewish prisoners who had taken part in building the camp.

Bottled carbon monoxide is used for these experiments. However, a short while later the gassings were carried out with carbon monoxide from the exhaust fumes of a motorcar engine. The engine from an armoured vehicle ("250 h.p.") was installed in a shed outside the gas chamber, whence the gas was piped into the gas chamber. Wirth continued to experiment in his search for the most effective method of handling the transports of Jews, from their arrival at the camp to their extermination and the subsequent removal of the corpses. Everything is arranged in such a way that the victims remain unaware of their impending doom. The intention is to convey to them the impression that they have arrived at a work or transit camp from which they would be sent on to another camp. In addition, everything is to proceed at top speed so that the victims have no chance to grasp what was going on. Their reactions were to be paralyzed to prevent escape attempts or acts of resistance. The speedy process increases the camp's extermination capacity. In this way, several transports are received and liquidated on one and the same day. The entire camp covers a relatively small, flat, rectangular area. Its southern side measures 265 m., the other sides 275 m. It is surrounded by a high wire fence, with barbed wire attached at the top and camouflaged with branches. Young trees are painted along the fence so that no one is able to look into the camp from the outside. There are three watchtowers in the corners, two of them on the eastern perimeter and the third on the south-western one. There is an additional watchtower in the centre of the camp, near the gas chambers.

A railroad track some 500 m. in length led from the Belzec railroad station into the camp through the gate on its northern side. The southern and eastern boundaries are lined with conifers. Belzec is divided into two areas. Camp I, in the northwest, is the reception and administrative sector; Camp II, in the eastern section, is the extermination sector. The reception sector comprises the railroad ramp, which has room for twenty freight cars, and two huts for the arrivals -- one for undressing and the other for storing clothes and baggage. Camp II, the extermination sector, comprises the gas chambers and the mass graves that are located in the eastern and north-eastern part.

Trees surround the gas chambers and a camouflage net has been spread over their roof to prevent observation from the air. There are also two huts in this sector for the Jewish prisoners working here: one serves as their living quarters, the other as the kitchen. Camp II is completely separated from the other sector by a strictly guarded gate. A low path, 2 m. wide and 50-70m. Iong, known as the "tube," fenced in on both sides with barbed wire and partly partitioned off by a wooden fence, connects the hut in Camp I where the arrivals undressed with the gas chambers in Camp II. The living quarters of the SS-men are at a distance of ca. 500m. From the camp, near the Belzec railroad station. All the SS-men are employed in the camp administration. Each SS- man has his specific job and some of them are assigned more than one task. From time to time there is an exchange in the spheres of responsibility.

SS-Oberscharfu"hrer Gottfried Schwarz is the Deputy Camp Commandant, SS-Oberscharfu"hrer Niemann is in charge of the extermination sector of Camp II, and SS-Oberscharfu"hrer Josef Oberhauser, Wirth's adjutant, holds responsibility for the construction of the camp. SS-Oberscharfu"hrer Lorenz Hackenholt, together with two Ukrainians working under him, is responsible for the operation of the gas chambers.

The Ukrainian unit numbers 60-80 men, divided into two groups. The Ukrainians serve as security guards inside the camp, at the entrance gate, and on the four watch towers; they also carry out several patrols. Some of them assist in operating the gas chambers. Before the arrival of a transport, the Ukrainians are deployed as guards around the ramp, at the hut for undressing and along the "tube," as near the gas chambers. During the experimental killings they have to remove the corpses from the gas chambers and bury them. Jewish prisoners known as SonderKommandos do this work now.

After a long painful silence in which Andrew felt his stomach churn incessantly, he addressed Rossi

'I will make sure that the Cardinal is told of your discoveries, now, what can you tell me of the girl 'Maria' asked Andrew.

'I don't know very much about her, I receive the messages from one of the Polish 'Kapo's'. He met her in the camp brothel; she hadn't been used by the Germans and was kept as an entertainer because of her piano playing abilities. She is from Berlin, a German Jew, her name is Maria Tannenbaum, and I think she was a reporter or writer before the war'.

'Why do you think she was a reporter?' asked Andrew

'All of her testimonies were in shorthand and she used a series of what I can only guess were code words to ensure the validity of her evidence'. She always ended her testimonies with the same four words'

Andrew's heart was pierced as he mouthed what Rossi said...

'They must not succeed'

Rossi was startled 'You knew those words! How did you know those words!

Andrew sat motionless in the chair, his fate was destined by those words and he knew it.

'What did you say the girl's name was?

'Maria Tannenbaum', now will you please tell me what is going on? We think she has been moved to Birkenau.

Andrew straightened up and composed himself,

'It is important that you find out where she is, Father Rossi, in time I will explain all but first of all, I need you to do me a service'

Rossi gave Andrew a puzzled look...

'What service would that be?'

Andrew smiled a sad smile at Father Rossi...

'I wish for you to hear my confession'

Chapter 15

Henry Mollayan poured two drinks

'What I am about to tell you can never leave this room or be repeated to another soul, do I make myself clear?'

Adam nodded and listened incredulously as Mollayan told him his life story to the day he left America. Mollayan left nothing out and when he had finished he said

'I am a bloodline descendant of Jacques de Mollay and a member of an organisation called 'The Priory of Zion' I have sworn to protect the Yahweh with my life and will take whatever steps are necessary to do that. Your father was also a member, Reid, Johannsen and Lassiter were of course compelled to join as a result of their discovery in Palestine'.

Adam stopped him 'What of Maria's 'father'? Why was he killed?

'Maria's father was a Jew who refused to believe the evidence that was laid down in front of him, as I said we will do everything to protect, we had no choice.

'And my father? Did he threaten you as well? Tears welled up in Adam's eyes.

'Your father was one of the most committed men in our organisation, he was killed by people who wanted the information he possessed for their own ends'

'Who were these people? asked Adam

'Freemasons who had discovered missing 'degrees' at a church in Rosslyn, you know it?

'Yes' said Adam 'My father took me there some times'

'Mollayan continued 'there was a fundamental schism in Freemasonry in the late 17 century when the English nobility tried to take over the organisation. Up until then the 'Priory of Zion' had cultivated the oath in order to pay reverence to the 'creator' or what you would call Yahweh. When the schism took place, we created fictitious lodges and worked within this typically English set up to protect Yahweh... Somehow, they discovered the find that your father had made and he was murdered not because he'd made the find but because he had risen to quite a senior rank within their organisation... They felt he had betrayed their perverted philosophy on the happenings in the Temple all that time ago'

'So Isaac was right wasn't he? said Adam 'The Nazarene, Jesus Christ was a messenger, a mortal, he died and was buried, there was no resurrection was there?

Mollayan nodded his head 'The Nazarene was an Essene child, his mother was an Essene. His preaching was correct to a point but his use of ABA or 'father' should not have been taken so literally. His brother James was the true leader of the Essene at the time, he was the chosen one. It was decided that Jesus would 'missionary' the message in an attempt to allow James to protect the truth from Rome'.

'But' said Adam 'this means that all that has gone before is wrong'. The Magdalene, The Templar's, the Inquisition all of it happened to protect this 'Yahweh'.

Mollayan continued ' Saul championed our cause, he was told what to do and he did it. Rome eventually assumed ownership of his brand of so called 'Christianity' leaving the remainder of the Essene in peace to protect. They escaped to France and established a dynasty that exists to this day through us.

'Protect' said Adam 'protect what?'

'His coming' revealed Mollayan 'his coming'.

For the next three hours Mollayan took Adam through all the missing pieces, he told him about the Freemasons and how he had protected him in London 9 years earlier. He told him about the plans of the Nazis and how close they had come to capturing the clues discovered by Adam's father. He explained all about the Thule and how he had tricked Hess to Scotland

'You convinced Rudolf Hess to fly to Scotland that was YOU!

Mollayan outlined the Thule plan and smiled as Adam inadvertently said 'No! , They must not succeed! Adam also realised what he'd said.

'One thing, is my family safe?

'Yes' said Mollayan ' as we speak, they are protected.

'O.K then, my father, how is he involved?' said Adam ' The clues, I mean'.

'Your father discovered information leading to the whereabouts of the Holy Sepulchre, in it are the articles of Yahweh, the incontrovertible proof of the power. It must stay protected until the time is right and the signs appear. Your friend, Tauber knew this and had already translated some of the Cyrillic' How many pieces do you have? Where are they?

Adam hesitated ' How do I know all that you say is right?

Mollayan smiled ' Tell me about the mark on the side of your father's chest?

'How did you know ......

Mollayan opened his jacket and shirt ' Was it like this one?

Adam nodded, he looked ruefully at Mollayan and said

'We have to go back to London'.

Mollayan told Adam to retire for the evening, he would make the necessary arrangements for their journey the next day. Adam confirmed that he had three pieces of the Cyrillic, the one's belonging to his father, Reid's and Tannenbaum's. Mollayan suspected that the Nazis had come into possession of the piece owned by Johannson, why else would Hess have fallen for his ruse? More importantly, how was he able to recognise the ' will not succeed' or the mark of the Essene. No, Mollayan was sure that Hess had at least one piece. That left one piece unaccounted for. The last he heard of Lassiter was of him going off into the Australian Outback to farm sheep, he was confident the secret would stay safe, without all of the pieces the Cyrillic was useless. Had he had known just how close he was to the closing of the circle, he would not have slept as well as he did that evening.

Mollayan retired and reflected on Adam, his demeanour and his personality. He wondered as to whether Adam would have the necessary qualities to be assimilated into the 'Priory'. Surely he realised that in possessing the Cyrillic information, he was going to be faced with a stark choice, devote his life to the protection of the one or face being 'accidented'.

Mollayan knew that he, himself, was in danger, his position of trust within the falsehood of Freemasonry could be in jeopardy if they discovered who he had sequestered in his headquarters. He resolved to assist Adam so long as he had control of the Cyrillic.

Adam could not sleep, he didn't trust Mollayan for one moment but he was in no position to do anything at the moment. He wasn't really that sure what he could do. He knew Maria had been alive, was she still alive? Hr didn't know who this priest was but he was sure that the priest represented the only other link to the Yahweh that he had. He would go with Mollayan to London, he needed his protection, he'd agree to provide Mollayan with copies of the Cyrillic, he intended to give him Isaac's research notes and the copies, he wasn't going to divulge any of the translations and the 'guiders' and daggers were staying with him. He resolved to tell Mollayan about the message from the Vatican in the morning.

Adam reasoned that if Mollayan had Hess at his disposal, it may be possible to glean information that would lead him to Maria. Mollayan had already told him that he would get

Adam a commission in the Press Corps following Montgomery's Army if and when the invasion of Europe took places. All Adam could do was ensuring his own safety and try and make contact with the priest in Rome.

Try as he might however, Adam struggled with the very reasoning behind all of this. He was being asked to accept that the fundamentals of Christianity were all one massive cover up perpetuated by a few 'believers' in order to protect a deity that was yet to return! They had done their job so well that future believers had been put to the sword as blasphemers and occultists by the very church on whose foundation was based on their untruths. The hypothesis that Isaac had painstakingly researched and demonstrated in their time together had now been given independent corroboration by one of the people supposedly sworn to protect the Yahweh.

His father had died protecting it. And yet there were so many unanswered questions, so many articles based on faith... Adam stopped and said the word out loud 'Faith'.

What was it that compelled the masses to believe or have faith, desire, need, some form of opium that helped in times of trouble. Was faith a convenience for things that could not be explained rationally, an article of faith measured a person's commitment to the opium of the belief. Dynasty's were built and fell on that very issue. How far would protectors of a faith go to ensure that it was upheld. Adam began to comprehend Isaac's questioning all those years ago, his hypothesis and 'what if' scenarios now dawned on Adam in a new light. No Resurrection meant that the Nazarene was not the Son of God, therefore the claims of the Christian world to their one true God was based on a contrived falsehood.

Adam shivered involuntarily as he considered all that he had learned, whatever the truth was, he had the where with all to try and unravel this mystery yet he was chained to the protecting of ... what? A restless Adam eventually fell into a fitful sleep plagued by thoughts of confusion and dread.

Bright sunlight pierced the crevasses in the wall of the wooden hut, the hut where Maria Tannenbaum was surviving in. Her day had routine, she was awakened by the Kapo's at 6.30am and marched out for roll call, and the half hour before rising was spent 'managing' the sick, supporting them to roll call. One of the tricks that the girls used was to prick their fingers and smear the blood on the faces of the ill, rubbing it in and hoping that it would be enough to allow them to live another day. The morning was always the worst, the trains started to arrive at 9.00am, a bewildered, starving humanity were vomited out of cattle cars and beaten to the tunes of a chamber orchestra playing at the camp gates.

Maria was part of the ruse and she hated herself for it, she watched as the people came of the trains, mothers making useless attempts to protect their children, fathers anxiously, almost beseechingly looking for some way to protect. Their very soul had been destroyed and any semblance of identity had been desecrated by their arrival. Maria ached as she watched the faces of the children in the line and the shouts 'Juden Raus'. They were marched off to 'shower'. The people who were taken to the body of the camp had something, they had lived for another day.

Maria's diary was hidden in the toilet block, toilet was a misnomer, it was an open trench that was serviced by a continual flow of water, and some of the inmates had made the mistake of tracing the water source and drinking it, only to die of typhus. It was a particularly sadistic game that the camp guards played, they were always in competition, and how many Jews could you kill with one bullet? How many Jew babies' skulls could you crush? . One of the officers had a particular predilection for selecting a young girl or woman from the arriving train. He would take her to his quarters and have some of the inmates made her 'pretty'.

Maria had been told that these girls assumed an air of importance because of their beauty, some of them castigated the inmates and laughed at their misfortune. The inmates said nothing, their eyes were dead, and they knew what would happen as it happened every time the Officer made a selection. They prepared a meal at the house and the Officer would seduce the girl, he would promise her life and a quality within the camp. She was special, he would seduce her fears to the point where he would listen to her requests for her family to be given an easy time. The meal would finish and the officer would drink, they would then go to bed and the Officer would command his woman to dance, the music was a nauseating precursor to the finality of the girl's fate.

They would go to bed and the Officer would force himself upon her, as his sexual excitement built, he would caress her face and neck and stroke her shoulders until he felt himself coming. As he began the final process of satisfaction, he proceeded to strangle his victim in the throes of passion and watch as her eyes bulged from their sockets whilst he felt himself leak into her. After satisfying his lust, he invariably fell asleep, the girl lay where she landed until the next morning when the house girl was told to 'clean the room' . The final act of depravity was completed when all of the names that the victim had given him were selected for 'special' treatment and were garrotted with piano wire and hung in public view of the inmates.

Maria carefully recorded all of the happenings that she was aware of, the testimonies of the people that surrounded her. She had managed to stay alive by being indifferent and selfish to the point of cruelty. She hated herself for being so callous but she was driven by a survival will and she comforted herself that she had managed to send messages to the outside telling of the horror. She lived from day to day with the comfort that somewhere, somebody knew and that it was only a matter of time before the madness would stop and they would be rescued.

Andrew went back to the library, he needed to understand the 'Priory of Zion' and who they were. He had assumed that the 'guider' that was in his father's package was in some way connected to the source of the mystery. He deduced that the pentangle was made up of five points, there were five people involved in the find, and each would have a 'guider' that when constructed would act as a finding mechanism for what? He was reading the Sauniere files again, looking for anything that would allow him to follow a course of reasoning, any reasoning, the more he read, the more confused he became. He needed direction, a clue, anything that would put him on the path.

Father Rossi hadn't spoken to him since he had made his confession, Andrew wasn't really that surprised, he'd told him about his discovery and afterwards had posed the question as to why the Nazis were perpetrating such evil against the Jews. Rossi referred to the ' God's chosen people' quotation and the fact that the Jews had been responsible for the crucifixion of the Saviour. Was this the final instalment of God's anger at the treatment that they had given to his son? The Jews had been pilloried for centuries in every European country, forced into ghetto's and slaughtered in anti Semitic pogroms which could only be described as culling.

'What are you trying to say? asked a pained Andrew

Could it be our God allowing this to happen? Rossi replied ' You are a troubled soul at the moment, Andrew. I won't break your confidence but I really do think that you should talk to the Cardinal about your misgivings'

'And what do I say? ' By the way, your eminence, did you know that our church is built on a falsehood of such mammoth proportions that to unveil it would probably begin the process of destruction prophesized in the Book of Revelations'. Did you also know that for the last two centuries we have been guilty of perpetrating the most heinous crimes against sections of humanity, crimes on a par with what the Nazis are committing at the moment '

'Andrew, Stop it! You do not know what you say! I will not allow you to destroy yourself this way! God is love, he will find a way! pleaded Rossi.

Who's God? whispered Andrew, Who is God?

The candle flickered incessantly. Andrew had put up the blackout curtains much earlier because of the fear of bombing raids by the Luftwaffe. The Cardinal had been right about Mussolini's stomach for a fight. As the allies invaded Sicily, Hitler moved very quickly to occupy Italy. Of course the occupation brought the SS and the Geheime Statzpolizi as well. Andrew was able to witness first hand the actions of the 'einsatzgruppen' brigades who swept in behind the Wehrmacht forces and rounded up all of the Jews and herded them onto trains for 'resettlement' in the East. He was appalled at the Holy Father's silence and had aligned himself to a faction who was doing their best to save the Jewish children. He found it distasteful however, that the priests were insisting on teaching catholic doctrine and baptizing the children as they were spirited away from their not so fortunate parents.

As he sat in the semi darkness, he pondered the mystery of Yahweh. He was looking for a clue and the Priory of Zion was the key. He had ascertained that Sauniere's trial by the then Pope focussed on the source of his wealth and the devotion that he had to the Magdalene. As Andrew read he began to consider the Sang Real option, the establishment of a bloodline of the Nazarene as a result of the seed being carried inside the Magdalene. This would suggest that the Essene tradition was brought back to life, what if the Priory of Zion was in fact the bloodline?

That still did not explain the Yahweh... It was then that Andrew stopped, Of course! How could he have been so blind... The entity or whatever it was had to have a presence, some sort of manifestation that would underpin its existence. Andrew began to consider his options. He started with the fundamentals of his own faith, those parts of his belief that were mysteries of faith and as such were the foundation of the faith. He thought about the Virgin birth, the resurrection of Jesus, the consecration of the Mass and all the other ponderables brought about by his faith.

He began to think about the promises of the faith, devotion to the son of Man ‘ and on the last day you will be raised from the dead’. Andrew paused again and thought.... What would be raised from the dead? ‘ The souls of all those... The soul!

The soul was the ultimate mystery, the non-physical entity that every living person had, the map of life, the holder of the faith, the evidence of existence and ultimate salvation. Yahweh is the soul of souls and the Holy Sepulchre held its secret! It was too fantastic to contemplate and yet it all fitted. Andrew scribbled down the following

1. *What or who did the Essene worship and ultimately protect?*
2. *How is salvation administered to the vessel?*
3. *A soul of souls 'I will make man in my image'*
4. *A bloodline that was responsible for the creation of man?*
5. *A hidden, protected sect that enjoyed unrivalled 'godlike' status*
6. *Untold riches and mystery*
7. *Brutal extermination and resistance of the Roman church*
8. *The book of Revelations.*

Andrew was sweating profusely now, he felt that he was at last forming a plausible hypothesis and could start to discount his theory through knowledge. He was so engrossed in his work that he failed to hear the door opening at the back of the room and he turned with a start to find Giovanni Santini, his Cardinal standing behind him.

'Good evening, Andrew, I trust you are well?

'Eminence, I didn't expect to see you here'

'Yes, I wanted to speak to you about something...

Andrew stopped and waited for the Cardinal to speak

'You've been spending quite a bit of time in the library recently, Father Rossi has expressed some concern that you are working too hard'

The Cardinal walked over to the desk and began to scour the material on it, he picked up the questions that Andrew had written and read them. He turned and looked at Andrew

'There is an evil among us and its soul belongs in hell, it has been sent here to deceive us but we know it all too well'. The cardinal's eyes were fierce and his lips were pursed as he continued ' Andrew, it pains me that you are working so hard and are obviously unwell, I think a little rest and recuperation is required, you will leave in the morning for Perugia. The brothers there will see to all of your needs, both physical and spiritual'.

'But Eminence isn't Perugia a retreat monastery? asked Andrew.

'That is so' replied Santini

'Why are you doing this, Eminence? You know there is nothing the matter with me, I am being removed because of the work I am doing?

'What work would that be, Andrew?

Andrew stopped and looked at the Cardinal who appeared calm and composed; he watched as the Cardinal lifted the telephone and called for the sergeant of the Swiss Guard to come to him. Five minutes later there was a knock on the door and the sergeant at arms entered the room

'Your Eminence'

'Sergeant, Father Lassiter is going on retreat, I would be obliged if you would assist him in his preparations'

Andrew sat in the chair, panic stricken, coldness passed over him as he watched the sergeant collect all off his papers. The Cardinal sat impassively across from Andrew. Andrew spoke

'Eminence, there are things we must discuss, I have been in your service for a number of years now and you have never shown displeasure with me. You seem aggrieved at me for some reason and are telling me that I am tired and unwell'. I am entitled to know the basis of your decision'. I do not wish to leave but it would appear that you are giving me no choice.'

'Its for the best, Andrew, you need a rest, the decision is final and you will leave in the morning'

'How long will I be away? asked Andrew

'You will be sent for once we've had the doctor give you a clean bill of health.

'I would like to take some private belongings with me'

'But of course, said the Cardinal 'The sergeant will assist you'

Santini proffered his hand and Andrew went down on one knee and kissed his ring, the cardinal moved towards the door and then stopped and beckoned to the sergeant at arms.

'Sergeant, may I have a word?

The sergeant went over to the Cardinal and together they walked outside to the corridor where the Cardinal issued brief instructions to the Sergeant.

'Make sure that Father Lassiter goes straight to his room and do not allow him to leave your sight, you will bring all that he packs in his cases to the guardhouse where I will search them. Father Lassiter has been working on some, let us say, 'delicate' matters of state and I want to be sure he gets complete rest. When he is finished packing, you are to make arrangements to have the motor pool have a car ready to take him to Father Agnelli's house, is that clear?'

The sergeant looked at the Cardinal

'Eminence, is Father Lassiter not to go to Perugia?

'Father Lassiter is to go to Father Agnelli at Monte Cassino.

Andrew was accompanied to his room by the sergeant at arms. He went into the room and began to pack. He was relieved that he had not left any evidence of his work in his room. He could not believe that Father Rossi would break the confidence of the confessional that meant that the Cardinal either knew what Andrew was looking for or had been instructed to remove him because of the questions he was asking and the research he was accessing from the library. All he could do was to concur with the wishes of the cardinal, he was obviously out of the loop with regard to information about 'Maria' and he could not imagine being able to continue his work in Perugia.

He went over to the telephone to place a person to person call. He had no doubt that the call would be monitored at the listening post but he hoped that he would be able to get a message to the only other person in the world that he knew could help. Adam Carter.

Andrew knew that it was a long shot but he couldn't see any other option.

At that very moment Adam Carter was on his way to London. He and Mollayan had traveled down separately and were scheduled to meet in the West End at the Pastoria Hotel that was just off Leicester Square. Mollayan had allocated Adam a car and driver; the driver hadn't spoken one word the whole way to the city. He dropped Adam off at the top of the Strand. Adam got out of the car and headed towards Leicester Square, he was amazed at the damage that he had seen. London was a city under siege from the air, there were ballast balloons everywhere, anti aircraft batteries were right next to huge spotlights and all of the important buildings were sandbagged above door height. As he walked he was unaware of the man who had stepped out of the shadows of the Admiralty Arch and was following him up the East Side of Trafalgar Square. Mollayan had sat and listened that morning as Adam told him of the package that he had received from the Vatican; his only comment was when he asked who had signed the letter

'Lassiter' said Adam

Mollayan's lips moved imperceptibly, Adam swore he seen a shadow of fear in his eyes and waited for a response

Mollayan grasping the chair spoke very clearly

'I believe that the message you received is authentic, I also believe that we must contact this man as soon as is possible. We'll make arrangements when we reach London'.

Adam arrived at the hotel to find Mollayan waiting for him. They exchanged pleasantries and Mollayan then went on to explain that he had managed to arrange a posting to the Press Corps for him, he said it would be the safest way for him to travel to Rome when the time was right. Mollayan continued ‘there is already considerable dissent in the Italian rank and file and it will only be a matter of time before Hitler assumes control and occupies Italy, Greece and the Balkans’. The SS are already in Rome.

‘What will happen then?’ asked Adam

Mollayan replied ‘I would speculate now that Montgomery has thrown Rommel out of Africa and we joined with Patton to invade Italy, it’ll only be a matter of time.

‘But that could take years’ said Adam

‘There is nothing more we can do at the moment and anyway there are more pressing matters here at the moment, like your safety. This is what we must do!’

Adam listened and when Mollayan had finished speaking, he said

‘I still need a few answers to some questions; if we can do it here then I would feel better about my situation. As for Rome, it has something to do with the Yahweh doesn’t it?’

‘I am afraid so and I will try and help you in any way that I can’ replied Mollayan

Adam then proceeded to describe the Yahweh as he understood it to Mollayan. He started with his father’s role, put in place everything that he had learned from Isaac and relayed back to Mollayan what he had told him. Mollayan didn’t interrupt and when Adam had finished, he looked quizzingly at Mollayan

‘Am I close?’

‘I’m impressed at your comprehension of what must be a very difficult philosophy for you to accept’ said Mollayan.

‘I have some questions for you’ said Adam

‘I’ll help where I can’ said Mollayan

Adam asked Mollayan why his father and the other men didn’t simply keep their find secret and put the ‘guiders’ together and seek out the Holy Sepulchre themselves.

'Because', said Mollayan 'There was one amongst them who belonged to us. When the Cyrillic was discovered, he knew immediately what it was and was able to convince the other four that they should split the 'treasure' with a view to looking for it later. That gave him the necessary time to inform the Priory and put in place the safety option.

'You mean, kill Tannenbaum and coerce the rest to a life of protection' retorted Adam.

'They were all handsomely compensated' said Mollayan 'The jeweled dagger itself is worth a considerable amount of money'. We also ensured that they received a substantial 'loyalty' payment'.

'So' mused Adam 'Who was the 'one of you'?

Mollayan replied immediately 'Your Father'.

'How, why?' asked Adam 'My father had nothing to do with anyone to do with you people

'That is correct' said Mollayan 'but your mother was the daughter of one of our bloodline, your father assumed her role when he married her'.

It was Adam's turn to be taken by surprise, no!! he was in shock; he remembered Isaac telling him about the first conversation that Maria had had with him, she said 'Yahweh is here' or something to that effect.

Mollayan was sympathetic when he next spoke

'I'm sorry but you had to work this out for yourself. I will help you find this priest because he may have information that is of use to us. You will have to accept the mantle that has been placed upon you, at a later date you will be indicted into the Priory, for now we must ensure your and its safety'. You may not have noticed earlier, I've had one of our people follow you from when you left the car, he'll stay with you for the duration of your time here. You need to assist me in determining what the Nazi's have discovered, I'm due to question Hess again to-morrow, and I'd like to be able to see if I can get him to divulge his sources.

Adam nodded his head, his mind was still whirling from his 'discovery' but he felt strangely at ease and purposeful.

'I need to telephone Megan and let her know that I am all right, and then we'll eat. I suppose I am right to assume that they are being watched or should I say 'protected'. You have to tell me more about this 'Priory' as well, I don't remember Isaac speaking to me about it ....

'I'm not surprised said Mollayan, few people know of us' You'd better sit down' said Mollayan 'this could take a while ....

Mollayan began by picking up the where Isaac had left off 'You're friend was a very learned man and he had discovered things that I would have thought had been safely buried

Can you recall what he last told you?

Adam replied 'He told me about the inquisitions and the 96 articles that Martin Luther had promoted which caused the schism in the church'

'Very good' said Mollayan 'Luther in many ways was responsible for a lot of free thinking which was published widely. Two lesser-known tracts were published in 1615 and became known as the *Rosicrucian Manifesto's.* The publications announced a new age of enlightenment and hermetic liberation in which certain universal secrets would be unlocked and made known.

'Isaac talked about this' said Adam 'something about a brotherhood that dated back as far as the early Egyptians'

'Very good! exclaimed Mollayan warming to the subject.

'The brotherhood of the Rosy Cross' Mollayan continued 'was headed up by a man called Simon Zealotes who was a lifelong confederate of the Magdalene. The gospel writer John Mark was also a member of the brotherhood and was the disciple that looked after Mary, the mother of the Nazarene. Some bibles added the word home to the text that described his calling but this was erroneous. John had in fact become the personal assistant of Mary.

John, because of his closeness to the Nazarene's family was aware of the truth behind the marriage at Cana. There was no doubting that the Nazarene had come from a kingly dynasty but his wife Mary of the Magdalene was also of royal descent and worthy of carrying the *sang real* ....'

'The what' said Adam?

'The Cup of Christ 'the Holy Grail' said Mollayan, berating himself that he did not unveil the absolute truth, the time was not yet right.

'The Rosicrucians were the direct descendents of the personal; assistants of both royal families, they undertook to serve and protect the house of the Holy with their lives if that is what it took. They have evolved over the centuries and have protected the *sangreal* against all calumny and danger. Today they, I should say we are known as the *Priory of Zion.*'

'But' remonstrated Adam 'you said they were freemasons!'

Mollayan put his hand up, 'I warned you not to confuse your comprehension of Freemasonry with the truth ....'

'Yes, Yes' said Adam 'You mean the original Temple Masons, I remember'.

Mollayan grinned, this boy was worthy of his protection after all.

Adam smiled as well 'Don't forget, I'm a journalist, I remember interesting things'.

'Yes', said Mollayan 'we have to consider your son and heir don't we?'

Mollayan excused himself and went up to his room, he made two telephone calls, one to his SOE office to confirm arrangements to interview Hess once he had the information from Adam and a second call to another Priory member

'It is safe and he knows about the legacy of his birth, I told him about his mother.'

'Very well' answered the voice 'It is imperative that you find out what Hess knew, I have no doubt that the allies will win this madness, but I fear that any discovery of our secret would endanger the welfare of our way.'

'I speak to him tomorrow; I'll talk to Adam again tonight. They will not succeed'.

After dinner, Adam and Mollayan retired to a lounge area. Mollayan poured two brandies and as the first air raid sirens of the night started to sound, they got up and moved to a secure location in the adjoining building. Adam was very relaxed and began to talk, he asked Mollayan about the Abbe Saunier and Rennes le Chateau.

Adam wanted to know how he fitted into the mystery. Mollayan told him of Saunier's discovery and subsequent arrangement that he made with the Priory of Zion. A Holy court of enquiry in the Vatican tried him because of his 'situation'. He refused to comment and went to his grave with the secret intact. Adam asked Mollayan what the secret was

'Saunier discovered the key to the gate' said Mollayan 'He discovered that the Magdalene escaped from Palestine with the holiest of secrets, the blood of the Nazarene. The Templars, the Cathars and we, the Priory of Zion have sworn to protect the reason why the Magdalene left in the first place'

'The Yahweh' said Adam

'That's right' said Mollayan 'Don't be fooled into thinking that the Roman church do not know of our secret, down through the centuries that have committed all sorts of heinous crimes to suppress or control the Yahweh'

'I don't understand' said Adam 'If the Priory want to protect the Yahweh and the Church wants to ensure that it stays buried, why all the killing?

Mollayan sighed

'The fundamental principle of faith in the Catholic church is based on the facts contained in the synoptic gospels which were written by Matthew, Mark Luke and John. These had been written primarily based on the testimony of Paul although some would claim that Luke's gospel was written soon after the Nazarene died. The Roman church effectively claimed the Nazarene as their Saviour and consumed his ministry into those three years that he preached across the Holy Land. They ignored the Essene culture and claimed that Mary was indeed impregnated by God through the Angel Gabriel. The relegated the role played by the Baptist and the Magdalene and did not acknowledge the presence of James, the brother of Jesus as a person of importance. They have preached the 'second coming' doctrine for the last two millennia and ruthlessly challenged anybody who had sought to question their doctrine. Just think what would happen if the world's 500 million Catholic believers knew what we knew'?

'So you're telling me that there hasn't been a coming, what has to happen is yet to happen? said Adam.

'Nobody knows what is going to happen, that is the fundamental issue, the Catholics, the Jews, The Moslems, the Hindus, they all have their particular slant on what is coming, the truth is... No one actually knows. We know only what we protect' We know the truth about the Nazarene, we know Paul was one of us, we know that there is a Holy Sepulchre hidden and protected. We know that you are chosen and there are another 4 offspring that are linked to the Cyrillic. As for me, I am a direct line descendant of one of the eight families that discovered the truth under the Temple in Jerusalem during the Crusades and subsequently formed the Knights Templar, sworn to protect the truth. We have been able to do that for all this time and we have survived all the crisis that time threw at us. Nothing however has come close to the madness that attacks us at the moment'.

'You mean the Nazis' said Adam

'I mean, the Thule' said Mollayan, they discovered the Essene by accident and whilst they have not been able to decipher the importance of their discovery, they have used Talmudic scrolls and archeological discoveries to underpin their theories of purity and Aryanism. I am convinced that they have gained access to your discovery, why else would Hess have taken the bait that was set to come to Scotland'.

'I don't understand' said Adam ' Hess came to Scotland on the premise of discovering the Yahweh?

'No' said Mollayan 'But the church at Rosslyn does divulge some interesting clues that we've used in the past to throw these intrepid discovery seekers off the scent.'

'Such as?'

'The fundamental principals of freemasonry, for one have been shaped as a result of, let us say, disclosures planted at Rosslyn.

How do you know all of this? said Adam

'Because, my friend, I am a member of the 35 degree within Freemasonry in this country, there are only three of us and as a result of my intervention, you weren't murdered back in 1938 .

'What!!'

'Oh yes ' continued Mollayan

'I thought I'd explained all of that to you, the Freemasons pose as big a threat to your safety as the Nazis do. Thankfully I have been able to protect your presence here and will continue to do so. Now, we'll meet here in the morning, bring what you have with you, we'll then decide on our next course of action. By the way, my people in Rome tried to make contact with your priest friend, it appears that he has vanished, I'm expecting another call tonight with an update, I'll be able to tell you more then..'

'But ' stammered Adam

'You cannot do anything about it, rest, make your arrangements and we'll proceed accordingly'.

Mollayan got up, put on his coat and left the room. The air raid was over and he headed round to the War rooms where Churchill had based all of the strategic command structures and where the Cabinet met. He checked into the SOE office, filed his calls and then deciphered the messages that had come in from his operatives, he'd been particularly interested in gleaning the mood of the German High command. One of his most trusted operatives was an Abhewr operative who was attached to Admiral Canaris's staff. He also had a girl who was the sister of a French resistance fighter working as a maid in the household of Albert Speer.

As he siphoned through the messages, his Rome contact flashed a notice, Mollayan took out the decipher book and began to read the message ....

'Priest moved forcibly from Rome stop Has been sent to Monte Cassino stop Our friend in Vatican very concerned stop when questioned about move stop something like will not succeed stop awaiting instructions stop.

Mollayan had his worst fears confirmed, the name Lassiter had not been a coincidence!

Who was this priest, what had he discovered? Mollayan reached for the call book and called the BBC to post the following message on the World service that night

... Greetings to our paternal friends in Rome, we are taking a walk in the sun and would like some company, say some kind words for our safe return and give our regards to our missing friend, we'd like to write but cannot remember his father's name. The rain in the South is going to be heavy ...

He knew he would have to wait another 24 hours at least before he got his answer .... Who was that priest?

Chapter 16

Adam meanwhile, had been to the special storage facility that the bank had established at the onset of the war. It was located in a concrete basement in a large house in Chelsea. He'd accessed his box and copied the writings down, Mollayan, he decided could see these along with Isaac's Tauber's writings, he had arranged for a photographer to take a photograph of one of the 'guiders' for him as well. He left the bank, telephoned Megan and assured her that both he and she were safe, sent love to the children and then returned to the Hotel, had a late dinner and retired to bed where he slept soundly.

Francisco Munari listened to the BBC broadcast and noted the message, when he had finished he went upstairs into the attic where his father, Guiseppe, was monitoring troop movements that were moving across the Appian Way.

'London need the name of the Priest, will you speak to the padre? said Francisco

'I will' replied his father.

'We need to find out why he has gone to Monte Cassino that's a closed monastery is it not?

Francisco's father nodded his head and said

'That's not all that's happening there either, we have reports of SS in the village, there were three SS divisions went through earlier, a murderous looking bunch they were too. Someone called Dirlewanger, Oskar Dirlewanger and they've been recalled from the Russian Front commands them. They seem to be on some sort of rest because they have been billeted with the Italian forces in the barracks in the village, you don't think there is any other reason for then being there do you?'

It would appear that our Italian army is losing the stomach for the fight, Il Duce is convincing no one anymore.' I don't know why SS are in the village but God help anybody going up against them'.

Guiseppe got up, put on his jacket and flat cap and went back down the stairs, out the back door to his bicycle; he pushed it out of the back gate, got on it and cycled over to The Irish College. He worked there as a Janitor, had done for 30 years and had come to know the personalities that inhabited the college. He'd been friendly with Sister Dolores for a long time; she was his conduit messenger to Mollayan's contact within the Vatican. The nun who was in her 70s, shuffled up to the water font, wet her hand and blessed herself. She turned around and saw Guiseppe who beckoned for her to sit down. They exchanged pleasantries and then Guiseppe asked her the identity of the priest who had been removed ....

'His name is Father Andrew Lassiter; he is the Personal Secretary to Giovanni Batista Santini and worked up until a few days ago at the Sacred Congregation for the Propagation of the Faith. He was very popular but recently he seemed to become very withdrawn. He was friends with a Priest from Poland, a Father Rossi.

'Rossi? enquired Guiseppe

'The very same' said sister Dolores 'You know his father, I believe he still mends the shoes of the faithful.'

'That he does' said Guiseppe, making a mental note to speak to his old friend and see if he could get talking to his son.

All of what he had discovered was relayed to London. Mollayan read through the script until he came to the name of the priest .... Lassiter! Sweat broke on his head as he considered the implications of his discovery .... the missing piece of the Cyrillic had been compromised and its owner was on the way to Monte Cassino.

He quickly sent instructions to Italy asking Francisco and his father to find out all they could about him, friends, associates, anything no matter how insignificant had to be reported to him. He summonsed Adam immediately and told him of his 'discovery'.

'I think the priest is the missing link! said Mollayan, It's incredible but I think he may be the son of Nicholas Lassiter.

Guiseppe met with his old friend the next day and enquired after his son. Antonio Rossi said that his son had been doing work in the East and seemed troubled from he returned. He was with him yesterday and asked him what was troubling him

'It's nothing papa, don't worry, I've just been working too hard'.

Antonio looked at his son, he could see dark circles around his eyes and he had lost a considerable amount of weight.

Guiseppe Munari was asking after your welfare, you know, Francisco's father ...'

'Ah, yes' said the priest

'He would like to be remembered in your prayers, he said that he'd been talking to that nice priest you'd introduced me too, what was his name? yes, that's right Father Lassiter wasn't it?

Father Rossi paled at the mention of Andrew's name and his father knew that something was wrong, especially when his son snapped at him when he continued to ask of his welfare.

'Father Lassiter has been sent away on some work for the Holy Father, I do not know where he has gone or when he will return and it would be better for you if you didn't concern yourself with such matters'

Antonio was telling this to Guiseppe when the sirens came on, both men looked up in surprise, this increased to amazement as in broad daylight they were able to see the pilot of a Focke Wulfe zoom across the piazza above them

'The Germans?

In Rome?

Guiseppe left Antonio standing and rushed home where he found Francisco busily decoding a message he had received from Mollayan

'Did you see the plane? panted his father

Francisco nodded his head and said 'The SS are billeting into the village up near Castelgandolfo, it'll only be a matter of time before they are in the city in numbers.

'I must tell Mollayan immediately '

'Why the rush?' questioned his father

'Because I found out from our Sergeant friend in the Swiss Guards that that is where they sent the priest that Mollayan is enquiring after. Father Lassiter was sent to Monte Cassino two weeks ago and no one has heard from him since.'

Mollayan received the message whilst he was at his head quarters, he'd met earlier that afternoon with Adam and they had agreed on a plan of action to try and reach Lassiter. He recorded his own findings in his personal diary and locked it away again in the safe. He'd told Adam of the combination in case anything was to happen to him.

He rang through to the outside office; He needed to find out where they had gone as he was sure that the Vatican certainly wouldn't be able to suppress that information. He put through a call to the War office and was assured that the information that he'd requested would be on his desk as soon as possible. He then telephoned Adam at the Pastoria to give him the news and was told by the desk that Mr. Carter had gone out but would return shortly.

Mollayan checked his watch, he was due at a meeting at 7.30 that he couldn't miss, he called for his driver to come to the front of the building and he left with the intention of going back down to the country immediately. As he was leaving the office the telephone sounded, Mollayan lifted the receiver and said

'Mollayan'

'Go immediately to see Hess, he wishes to speak with you'

One hour later, Mollayan was sitting opposite Rudolf Hess. He was dressed in a British Army uniform that had all of its markings removed and he looked tired.

'If I give you what you ask, what will I receive in return? 'questioned Hess

'You are hardly in a position to bargain with me, tell me what you know and I will consider its worth' responded Mollayan wondering to himself why after nearly 18 months in captivity, Hess wanted to speak now

For a brief moment the old arrogance and anger flared in the eyes of the deputy Fuhrer. It was momentary because he had long come to terms with the fact that the man in front of him had effectively tricked him out of Germany on the promise of him discovering the secret to the holiest of holy, the secret of the soul that he understood to be Yahweh. He also realised that with the information that he'd collected, he was in absolute danger of being 'silenced' permanently. He had heard all of the reports of his alleged treachery from Germany; his jailers had taken great pleasure in tormenting him with Lord Ha Ha's speeches from Germany which accused him of betrayal of the highest order.

He squirmed as he heard first Rosenberg and then Himmler castigate his actions and denounce him as a lackey and traitor.

'I will tell you about Thule, I will tell you about our discoveries, I will tell you about the Cyrillic and what we know about it. I can tell you what happened to Johannson. In return I want an assurance that I will not be executed. Those are my terms and they are not negotiable'. If you are who you say you are, then what I have to tell you will be invaluable in your quest, you cannot afford for me to divulge it to anybody, my price for my secrecy is my life.'

Mollayan studied Hess for a moment. He realised that he was serious about his life, had he not been, he would have consumed the poison secreted in a false cavity in his mouth and found by the doctor up in Scotland. Mollayan also knew that the Russians and the Americans had requested access to Hess; the British had so far not succumbed to the requests. He knew that for the duration of the war at least Hess was safe, primarily because the War Office couldn't comprehend his act of folly and had agreed that Mollayan be his case officer, they would support any action Mollayan deemed necessary in the short term.

He decided there and then that he would grant immunity to Hess until such times as the outcome of the war was known as long as he was of the understanding that Mollayan could only protect him as long as he had a use.

'I am a soldier of the Reich' said Hess 'and will never betray the Fatherland'

'I don't care about your Fatherland' retorted Mollayan 'I have much more important work to do. Tell me what the Thule knows about he who is to be protected'.

Hess smiled ruefully at Mollayan

'I would like some cigarettes, some coffee, a change of uniform and a private cell'

'Do not try my patience' said Mollayan

'If you wish to be told about your boy Carter, the Jew, Tauber and the discoveries that we made by reading and understanding the 'tanach' ....

Mollayan stopped him mid sentence and got up, walked over to the door and snapped out an order for cigarettes and coffee to be brought to the prisoner. He instructed the Captain of the guard to telephone the Pastoria and advise Mr. Carter that he would see him first thing in the morning.

Hess lit a cigarette and leaned back, looking at Mollayan intently, he knew that he had to convince this man of his worth as he seemed to be instrumental in determining what his future was

'As a result of research carried out in late 1928, we ....

'Who are we?' asked Mollayan

'The Thule' responded Hess

'Continue' said Mollayan

'We realised that it was within our power to take control of post war Germany if we were able to harness the unrest that existed at the time and put it to good use. Our signs told us that we were the chosen people of the Great Defender and that we were direct descendants of the lost people of Atlantis, other people referred to us as a mystical 'lost tribe of Israel'.

'We, of course totally rejected any link between German and Jew but we could not afford to discount the theory of the lost tribe. We set up a research department to investigate the Tanach or what you would call, the Old Testament'.

'Who headed up this department? asked Mollayan

'It was originally under the command of Alfred Rosenberg but as it became obvious that we were destined to create the 1000 year Reich, we appointed a non Thule member called Adolf Eichmann to complete the research. We discovered that the Jews who observe only recognise the Old Testament and discount the Brith Hadasha, commonly known as the New Testament. We deduced that the vast majority of Jews didn't believe in the Jesus, Son of God tale anymore than we did. We decided that any information to be had would come from the Old Testament. We discovered reams of prophetic theology, most of which we were able to adapt and use as speech material for Adolf Hitler.

‘Wait a minute! said Mollayan ‘Are you saying that Hitler is not Thule?

‘Hitler was a spy who was turned by us and created into what he has become, he is starting to believe in his own infallibility. It was never our intention for him to be our supreme leader, we created a monster in allowing him to take control and when he launched ‘blitzreig’ against the Poles and was successful we decided to let him have his moment of glory. The mistake we made was in allowing Himmler to raise his SS morons as a rival to the Wehrmacht, without the SS there would be no Himmler, no Heydrich and no Muller. We subscribed to the founding of the pure Aryan blood and we wanted the creation of the master race, we didn’t realise what was happening until it was too late. Himmler, with his Holy grail claptrap and knights of the round table had convinced Hitler of the SS loyalty and Aryan pureness, we decided to let him fall on his own sword once we had found what we were looking for’.

‘Why didn’t you stop him before he started butchering people?

‘Our goal was bigger, it was decided that Hitler would begin to strengthen the army and warmonger, we would be free to continue on our quest of discovery.

‘Discovery of what? hissed Mollayan already beginning to feel his stomach contract in anticipation of the answer. Hess pursed his lips and grinned at Mollayan

‘Do not assume me to be a complete fool, we wanted the very thing you are sworn to protect, the great discovery, the Holy Sepulchre, the missing link, we wanted the Yahweh.

Mollayan was shaken to the core at the mention of the word……. they knew!! He told himself to calm down and listen with increasing incredulity as Hess told of the research center and the deliberation of the Great Lie. Of course Hess didn’t know that Saul had constructed the New Testament in an attempt to throw inquisitors off the scent but the very fact that Hess had been able to ascertain that the truth could be found in the Tanach was frightening.

He invited Hess to continue and was shocked to silence at how lucky Adam had been.

Thankfully they did not know how important he was but when Hess repeated the Cyrillic translation as told to him by Matteus Netzer, the son of Erich Johannsen. Mollayan excused himself from the room. He went to the toilet as waves of nausea overcame him and he retched violently. He returned 15 minutes later to hear Hess refer to Hitler as the destroyer of the Jews. Why should they worry, the removal of the Jews cleared the way for the Thule to claim ownership of the lost tribe status.

Again Mollayan had trouble hiding his distaste

'You are telling me that the persecution of the Jews is all to do with the 'Lost Tribe'

'But of course' said Hess 'what will it matter what is written in their fairy story testaments if they are all dead'.

'But there are almost six million Jews on the face of Europe alone, surely you are not going to try and remove them all? Mollayan was by now ashen faced.

'And what do you think the 'Final Solution' intends to do' grinned Hess ' The 1000 year Reich will exterminate Judaism without mercy wherever we find them, we will then eradicate the power of that weak fool in Rome and the new Religion of the Thule will rule the world. We will find the Yahweh and control it, we will be invincible!!

Mollayan could feel his temper rising again as he looked at the demonic glint in Hess's eyes.

He stood up, withdrew his hand gun and pointed it at Hess's head; he cocked the gun and fired .... Hess screamed and fell to his knees, as the bullet grazed his scalp...

'I should kill you where you lie' said Mollayan

'We had an agreement' screamed Hess 'You promised!

He winced again as Mollayan fired another shot, by now there was banging on the door as the Captain of the Guard was trying to get into the room. Hess was lying on the floor and Mollayan went over and jammed the barrel of the Webley revolver into the side of his temple

'Please, don't shoot me 'whimpered Hess

He'd wet himself and was screaming for help. Mollayan kicked out at him

'Think well of this conversation, it will be your last for a very long time, I can guarantee you that. You are an abomination to God and man and you will suffer the consequences of your folly. We will have no need to speak again'

Mollayan left the room and immediately telephoned London. Three hours later a doctor appeared at Hess's cell, he was restrained and injected with a new drug that the Doctor had perfected. He was strapped to a stretcher and taken to a location known to only three people. By the time the Doctor was finished with him, Rudolf Hess would have difficulty remembering his name let alone any of his past life.

Mollayan filed his report with his recommendation that Hess be 'altered'. It was accepted on the basis of Mollayan's assertion as to the existence of a Final Solution against the Jews. Mollayan wasn't surprised at this, he felt desperately for the plight of the Jews and he tried to do all he could, they were not however his first priority now that he had gleaned all that Hess knew, they must not succeed, and with his and Adam Carter's efforts they would not.

Adam had missed Mollayan but was buoyed by the news that they would meet the next day.

He had been busy with Isaac Tauber's work and had realised that Isaac, even though he was a Jew had accepted that they were not the chosen race, he believed in the Essene and he believed in the *sangreal* as well. He also mentioned that he thought the truth of the matter had been cleverly concealed in the book of Revelations in the bible. He too had seen references to this Tanach and Brith Hadasha.

Adam was stunned to see Isaac's conclusions on this; he was saying that the whole of the New Testament was a smokescreen to protect the Yahweh by Paul, the real truth lay in hints in some of his letters and the book of Revelations.

Adam read on and began to link the prophecies of Nostradamus back to the Book of Revelations, as he read he cross checked Isaac's notes and the whole myriad of counter story and hidden message began to unravel. Adam gasped as he realised the Book of Revelations was indeed that. A Revelation!

It had nothing to do about the Nazarene returning. No, Revelations cross referenced with the Tanach told a totally different story, one of unbelievable love and devotion to a people who were not aware of their destiny and who were doing everything in their power to destroy it before it happened.

He began to see the subtle difference between claiming to be a follower of a faith and being a true believer, the difference between an Essene and an ordinary Jew or Roman or whatever was simple. The Jews and Romans and all the rest paid lip service to a faith, genuine followers embraced it from the heart and lived in the shadow living their lives in the image of the great one. It was like he'd been hit by a thunderbolt, suddenly it was so simple, embrace the Yahweh and it becomes a part of you, believe in its power and assume its power and protection. Tears rolled down Adam's face as he thought of his Father who had died for his faith. His blind faith in something he'd inherited through the love of a woman and something that his son now realised was worth dying for.

Adam composed himself and carried on reading until he fell asleep. He was woken by the night attendant and went back to his room where he slept soundly in anticipation of his meeting with Mollayan the next day.

They met at 10.00 the next morning; Mollayan confirmed the message from the Munari's that the priest was indeed the son of Nicholas Lassiter. He also told Adam of his discovery that Matteus Netzer was the son of Erich Johannson and an SS man. Adam told him not to worry as he'd pieced together the Cyrillic and with Isaac's help had ascertained that they had the bulk of the message in their control. Adam went on to say however that it was vital that they reached the priest quickly.

'Ah' mused Mollayan 'that may pose a serious problem, my sources tell me that he was sent to Monte Cassino…

'Monte Cassino!' exclaimed Adam. 'Where is that?'

'Its ok, we know where it is and we are having it watched but we cannot move because the SS have been billeted in the village and there is information that would suggest that Hitler is running out of patience with Mussolini. Mussolini has been deposed and the Germans will fight the Americans and the British in Italy. As we speak, Italian garrisons are being surrounded and taken over by Waffen SS'.

Just at that the door opened and a sergeant saluted and handed a note to Mollayan who opened it and read the contents. He slumped back down into his seat and removed his glasses

'This is bad'

'What does it say?' asked Adam

'My sources tell me that a priest was arrested yesterday by the SS in a small village north of Cassino trying to assist what turned out to be Jewish children get food. They were caught and my sources say that all were put into the back of a truck and taken off to a holding camp He goes on to say that trains have been going in and out around the clock, they been seen leaving full of people and returning empty. They think Lassiter was put on a train heading east

'No, no, no, no' shouted Adam.

Chapter 17

Andrew had only been at Monte Cassino for three days and had spoken to nobody other than Father Agnelli who had asked him three or four questions and given him an assurance that he would be looked after

'Where am I?' asked Andrew

'You are safe with us here in Monte Cassino'

'No, No, said Andrew 'there has been a dreadful mistake! I was to go to Perugia'

Andrew was about to launch into an explanation and a request to speak to Santini until the predicament he had been placed in slowly began to dawn upon him. Father Agnelli was standing with his back to the door, a large metal ring with a series of keys where attached to his robe

Is this not an enclosed order? Asked Andrew

'The cardinal advised me of your condition' soothed Agnelli

'Plenty of rest and recuperation and solitary reflection, we have prepared for your coming'

At that Agnelli walked out of the room and closed and locked the door behind him.

Andrew had been placed in a small cell like room, it contained an old bed and there was a place for him to pray as well as a table and a chair. A crucifix hung on the wall above the bed and there was a small window that allowed a slither of light into the void.

He sat down on the bed and tried to collect his thoughts, he knew that he had been too obvious but he could not believe that Rossi had betrayed his confession, No, there had to be something else, Santini would not have acted arbitrarily, that wasn't his style. Andrew began to piece together his actions, could it have been Bernard?

Then it came to him, the day that he sent the package off to Carter, he'd been criminally careless in the way that he had accessed the original file, why several of the nuns had seen him go into the room with nothing and leave with a file. Even the cleaners knew that the *Camerlengo* had to authorise every document moved from the library and whilst Andrew would be well known and no one would have dared challenge him, a few well appointed questions would tell anybody of his strange behaviour on the day in question. How he had demanded access to the newspaper-cutting file and laboriously copied everything that some reporter called Adam Carter had ever written. Why he'd even been stupid enough to try and bypass the official communication process for using a diplomatic bag. All in all, Andrew berated himself; he hadn't exactly made it hard for somebody to find out what he was at.

Santini was no fool, he knew of the *papa's* decision on the plight of the Jews and whilst he may not have agreed, the *papa* had spoken and no one was going to betray the decision he had made. Sitting in his cell Andrew came to the only conclusion that he could reach, he would escape from the monastery at the first opportunity and work out what he was going to do once he'd got out…

He didn't have to wait long for his chance, he'd noticed a cart going into the garden area every third day, and it had a large tarpaulin stretching over a frame. He watched as it sauntered in and out without so much as a by your leave, save for the driver, a very old man to bless himself as he went through the front porch.

Three weeks after arriving in Cassino, Andrew was permitted access to an enclosed garden which was adjacent to the main garden area, he simply waited at the bottom of the wall until he heard the cart going past, and he scaled the wall and lay in the thick covering of ivy that covered the top of the wall. He couldn't believe his luck as the cart returned it was filled with hay!

Andrew simply threw himself off the top of the wall and landed in the midst of the hay. He quickly burrowed into the body of the hay and waited. There wasn't a sound as the cart ambled back out through the porch and across the bridge. Andrew, buoyed by his good fortune, never once stopped to think about how easily he had absconded from Cassino.

Santini was sitting at his desk when the telephone rang; he lifted the receiver and said

'Si'

'Father Agnelli, Excellency, Father Lassiter has absconded as you thought he would, what should I do?'

'Do? Said Santini ' Do? You will do absolutely nothing, Father Agnelli. Father Lassiter was never there, do I make myself clear'.

Santini replaced the handset and lifted the jeweled encrusted crucifix that he wore around his neck and kissed it lightly. He pursed his lips and then lifted the receiver again and spoke quietly into the mouthpiece, he replaced the handset and walked quickly to his desk and opened a locked drawer with a key that he had attached to his waist. He removed the file containing all of the 'Maria' reports and the Cardinal Sapheia correspondence and methodically, sheet by sheet, he tore them into little pieces before placing them in a bin. When he had finished, he lifted the bin and walked across to the hearth of the fireplace and emptied the contents of the bin onto a fire that greedily consumed them.

He returned to the desk and pressed an intercom

'Ask Father Rossi to come and see me now'

Rossi walked across the marbled floor and entered the ante- chamber and sat down. He still marveled at the magnificence of the Vatican and the rooms and corridors that held so much history and secrets of the church. In his mind he imagined the great happenings and crisis that were resolved, the articles of faith, the papal bulls, all emanated from the room that he was sitting outside...

'You can go in now, his eminence is expecting you'

Rossi got up, walked across to the door, which he knocked, he opened the door to be greeted by the Cardinal. He was taken by the simplicity of the room, a large desk, three chairs and a lounge seat, his eyes drank the beauty of the montage that unfolded as he walked across the vast area towards the desk.

'Come in Father, we have much to discuss' said Santini

Father Rossi took the pro offered hand of the cardinal and glazed his lips on the top of the ring, he retreated to the seat and waited for the Cardinal to speak

'Andrew has settled in very well' said the Cardinal ' We will remember him in our prayers'

'Si; mumbled Rossi

'You must not blame yourself, he was overworked and seemed completely preoccupied about something, you don't know what it was that was bothering him so much?

Rossi gazed at his Cardinal, looking for a clue in his face, some help, a sign that he knew what was going on, truth of Andrew's predicament. There was nothing, the eyes of the Cardinal bored into Rossi's face.

Santini spoke 'I will make sure you are kept informed of Father's Lassiter's progress It has also been decided that you will remain here in Rome with us, you will not be returning to the East.

'But the conduit... The reports' stammered Rossi

'We will make the necessary arrangements' you are to report to the Camerlengo, he will instruct you to your new duties'

Montini rose from behind the desk and guided Rossi to the door

'If by chance, you should hear from Andrew, you will of course tell me' said Santini

'Eminence, I do not understand, how would I he....Rossi tried to keep a sense of calm in his voice but only succeeded in stuttering

Santini raised his hand, 'Father Lassiter has something that is troubling him and he may need to share his burden, you are his friend, I wish to help him, if by any chance he tries to contact you, I must know so as to allow me to do all I can to help him, Is that clear'

'Si' stammered Rossi and watched as Santini turned on his heel, reentered the room and closed the door hard behind him.

Rossi walked out of the building and crossed the piazza; he wandered aimlessly for some time, torn between the instruction that he had received and the message that he had carried in his soutane. He sat down heavily and removed the message, opened and reread it for what seemed like the hundredth time

This is a message to the Polish Parliament in exile in London.

In January the Germans began to liquidate the Krakow ghetto. A few German dozen Germans were thereby killed. Several hundred Jews were killed on the spot... after three days the Aktion was halted. Six thousand were taken away to the Umschlagplatz. The liquidation is occurring throughout Poland. In mid February they are to liquidate the Warsaw ghetto. Alert the whole world. Appeal to the Pope for official intervention and to the Allies to declare German war prisoners as hostages. We suffer terribly. The surviving 200,000 await annihilation. Only you can save us. The responsibility with regard to history will rest on you

The message was accompanied by a report that had been passed on to a curate on the outskirts of Warsaw by one of Rossi's confidants.

'There is no terrain in the ghetto left to fight on, the intense heat of the conflagration has turned even the pavements into a sticky mass of tar. The flames have consumed all of our food and the wells that we dug so laboriously have been filled with rubble. All around us, the roar of the fire, the sound of falling walls, the roar of the guns, outside it is Spring but in here a holocaust reigns. Why have we been forsaken so! In the name of any God, help us please, they are burning our children in front of our eyes'

Rossi stared at the last line and then stood up quickly as if he had been awakened suddenly. He pushed the letter back into his soutane and strode purposely off towards the Delegatura facilities that had been set up within the building that housed the Vatican radio, he knew what he was going to do.

He followed the instruction to the letter, sent the message to London and even though it went against everything that he had ever been taught, he'd already decided on his course of action. The day that Andrew had been removed from the Vatican, he had gone to the library where he's got a message that simply said

'Their will has been done, they must not succeed'.

He paled as he struggled to comprehend the reality of the message.

Andrew had foretold him what would happen to him and had left instructions that all of his research including the sealed package was to be forwarded to London to an address that was written on the package, an address that Andrew had agreed with Rossi in the event of anything happening to him. Rossi walked into the library and went to the pre arranged place he found all of Andrew's notes, he didn't have to open them, he knew what was in them.

He left the Vatican and went to his father's house, to complete the next part of his task.

'I want to talk to Francisco Munari, it is important!

His father said nothing, he rose off the chair put on his coat and beckoned his son to follow him. They were soon in the loft of the Munari house.

Francisco Munari asked the Priest what he wanted

'I understand you may be able to help me, I must get this package to a man in London.'

'What makes you think I can help you, priest? snarled Munari

Guiseppe's voice snapped

'You will not speak to him like that, I spoke to his father after you made your request, I have known his father for 30 years and he will never betray us'

Francisco looked at his father and then smiled

'I apologise Father', of course I will do what you ask'

Later that same night, a Lysander 2-seater airplane landed in a field high near the city. Torches had lighted the runway, the pilot landed the plane, taxied to the end of the field and waited as a man ran from cover, climbed into the cockpit and strapped himself in. The plane took off and landed in a strip in Sicily where the man transferred to another plane. They reached the coast of England as dawn was breaking and at 1.00 that afternoon Francisco Munari was standing in the office of Henry Mollayan. He handed over the package, went to eat and then was taken to a barracks where he was debriefed and allowed to get some sleep.

Adam could not contain his excitement, not only did they have Andrew's legacy, they were in possession of all of Maria's transcripts and the Vatican reports from Krakow as well as Rossi's full report and the testimony from inside the ghetto. They also had all of Andrew's research which when read with Isaac's notes confirmed the scale of the cover up and lengths to which the Roman church had gone to suppress the Yahweh.

Mollayan watched as Adam devoured the information, his awakening complete.

'What do we do now?

Mollayan went over to his desk and sat down.

'We must assume that both Maria and Andrew are or will be dead. Both of them are probably in the camps and we now know that the Nazis plan to exterminate the Jews. We don't know where Netzer is but he could not know the significance of his legacy. I think that we should construct the message and the map and determine the location of the Holy Sepulchre. If we discover that it is in danger, we must take steps to remove it...

'How are we going to do that? , There are only the two of us'

'Ah, my impetuous friend, you forget there were eight knights in the caves under the temple, their ancestors have sworn to do their utmost to protect the Yahweh. They do not know anything other than their responsibility and are only activated by the Master of the Priory of Zion, he is the one who by birthright is the sole protector of the Yahweh.

'And where, may I ask do we find such a man? asked Adam with sarcasm in his voice.

'That is what I mean by impetuousness Adam, you've already met him.'

Mollayan smiled at Adam and the penny dropped, Adam felt stupid and went to apologise

'There is no need' said Mollayan ' You will learn as you go along'.

Adam and Mollayan had settled down to begin the task of assembling the myriad of information that they had collected. Mollayan was aghast at how much Isaac Tauber had guessed, he was after all a Jew and was very uncomplimentary to the Nazarene in his writings. What Isaac had to say was tame compared to the first glaring discovery that Andrew Lassiter had uncovered. He'd found two manuscripts in the Vatican Library that suggested that the Nazarene be in fact the bastard son of a man of Egyptian descent. Both of the manuscripts contained evidence of this and seemed to have been edited by hands unknown, whole sections of the text had been removed. What was staggering was that the assertion of bastardy remained in the text, all that had been removed had been the supposed identity of the father, and a man called Ben Pandira.

Andrew then started to ask questions as to the origin of the name and came up with a loose Egyptian translation Pa-ntr-ra. Mollayan could only imagine his astonishment when he discovered it to be a title of the Egyptian sun-god, Ra. Mollayan knew that the Nazarene had spent time in Egypt as a youngster, having supposedly fled from Herod but was incredulous that Lassiter's assertions could be held up to scrutiny although...

He didn't realise how close Andrew had come to uncovering the truth, had the young priest had possession of the document that Adam was now reading aloud from, Mollayan guessed that Lassiter would have deduced the Essene bloodline. It would only have been a matter of time before he worked out the SANG REAL and realised that the Nazarene did not ascend directly into heaven as claimed by the scriptures.

Mollayan spoke aloud

'Had Andrew heard any of that stuff you are reciting, he'd have known the full story'

'What do you mean? asked Adam

'Isaac Tauber discovered the origins of the Yahweh in the secret teaching of Moses who was a Nazarene along with Judah, Samson and the prophet Samuel. They believed in a mystical being that transcended the belief of the ordinary Jews. Their followers rejected all prophets after Moses and rejected the first five books of the bible, the Christian Church claimed that Moses had written these!

What do you think happened these people? Mollayan mused.

Adam responded...

'The descendants of the Essene, by any chance?

Mollayan smiled

'Very good Adam, when the Nazarene was crucified, he was called 'Jesus the Nazarene'

(The title Jesus of Nazareth is a mistranslation of the term). All of his family was associated with this group. John the Baptist was a member as was the brother of Jesus as well. They all believed and worshipped this mystical deity....'

'The Yahweh? asked Adam

'What else? retorted Mollayan.

For the next three days, the two of them painstakingly plotted the parallels of both codes of existence. Mollayan was able to fill Adam in on all of the Templar history and their unswerving loyalty to the cult of James, the brother of Jesus and the living resurrection as practised by members of the Jerusalem church. Adam read with increasing horror of the hatred during the Crusades, through the Inquisition and right up to the discovery by Abbe Saunier of the Sang Real in France all those years ago.

Mollayan told him that it was Saunier who along with some other notaries, namely Poissin the painter had assisted the Priory of Zion who were remnants of the eight Templar families and aligned with the remaining Rosicrucians had sworn a death allegiance to the absolute secrecy of the Yahweh until it was time for the Yahweh to unveil its true glory.

Mollayan followed the false trail propagated as the truth by the Roman Church, Saul had indeed done his job well. He had succeeded in hiding the deeply antagonistic ideology preached by the Nazarene during his ministry. His followers would have known about and basked in the joy of the 'revealed knowledge' as he did, the secret knowledge of the Divine Realm. The rise of Christian Orthodox religion had all but eradicated the presence of the followers of the 'knowledge'.

Mollayan stopped Adam and showed him to the place in Andrew's writings.

'Our priest friend would have been very troubled when he read all of this stuff' said Adam

'I'm afraid that it's a bit too much to take in' he continued. 'I found reference in Isaac's work to writings by Plato in something called 'Timaeus' where he refers to a deity called the 'Demuirge', he describes him as the creator of the world, the builder of the material universe but an entity distinct from and inferior to the supreme God'

'Show me that! Mollayan reached across for the document

Adam passed the document and watched as Mollayan eyes became wider. Mollayan, himself could not believe what he was reading, an old Jew and a young Priest had effectively 'timelined' the origin of the Yahweh.

Of course Mollayan never doubted the existence of proof, here he had it staring him in the face. An eerie chill passed over him, he had the proof that thousands of years of abuse and calumny had sought to either destroy or gain for their own end. All the pieces of the jigsaw started to fall into place as Mollayan began to gather his thoughts. Adam sat bemused as Mollayan began taking out loud.

'So that is why Saul was regarded as a renegade by most of the disciples and the Nazarene's family, all of his real testimony was supposed to have been destroyed when Jerusalem was sacked in 70AD'. Mollayan knew different now, they'd been suppressed and hidden away by those of the faithful who wished to exalt Paul and promote his conception of the Nazarene as God!'

Mollayan began to chuckle to himself, Paul's true testimony was denigrated in favour of the letters and rubbish that he preached after his 'encounter' on the road to

Damascus, the Christians had done his job for him! Sudde. however Mollayan stopped reading and looked over at Adam...

'What do you think that it was that my ancestors found under the Temple at the time of the Crusades?

'The Holy Grail, Treasure.... I don't really know...

'Proof' exhorted Mollayan ' They found incontrovertible proof of the existence of the Yahweh through the discovery of the writings of Paul and the Magdalene and were able to gather the treasure of the Essene in their quest to continue the job of secret worship and protection of the Yahweh.... The one who is greater than the creator!'

'What does this mean for us? said Adam

'It means that your map will point us in the direction of the truth, I will swear on my life that the Holy Sepulchre contains the truth, the absolute truth as told to and recorded by Paul!!

The two of them cleared away the debris and placed the pieces of the Cyrillic on the table and with the help of Isaac's translation were able to read the message....

'I shall be the Father and he shall be my son, he is the branch of my forefather who shall arise to rule in Zion at the end of time'

Adam and Mollayan read the passage into themselves. It was as if history was opening a door to them that had never been previously entered. They knew that an Essene priest had written the Cyrillic and that Adam's father had found it near the Dead Sea at a place called Qumran. They proceeded to turn the pieces over and align them, they could not understand the markings on what appeared to be a primitive map. Adam spoke first ....

'Isaac makes reference in his notes to something called the 'seven trials of truth' what do you think that is?

'I've no idea lied Mollayan, but I suspect we'll find out if we decide to follow the destiny of the Holy Sepulchre'.

'What about the Nazis, do you think they know any of this?

Mollayan smiled ruefully

'I don't think they will bother us at the moment, I should have told you earlier but I had to be sure that you were capable of accepting the mantle of responsibility that has been thrust upon you'

'What do you mean?

'I mean that you are 'protected'. I have already taken steps to silence Rudolf Hess, he will no longer be a threat, and furthermore I am not alone in this quest. We have Priory members in places you wouldn't imagine. I can tell you for example that there was a meeting yesterday in Berlin that effectively curtailed the activities of the Thule.

What? How? said Adam

'I am not the only Prior who enjoys trust, you can be thankful to my counterpart in Berlin for removing the threat of the Thule. We should also know what they knew within the next few days'

Mollayan then went on to explain the family connection of his counterpart in Berlin who like Mollayan could trace his lineage back to the founding of the Templar and had worked tirelessly under intense pressure to undermine the work of the Thule. Once Rudolf Hess had been removed it was only a matter of time 'Who is this person? asked Adam

'His name is Canaris, he is an Admiral and heads up the Abwehr, the German Secret Service'.

'But he is a German, we are at War with them!

'We are at war with the Nazis, it is unfortunate that we are on different sides but you must understand that each of us have sworn our lives to the protection of a greater goal no matter what the circumstances '

'But if 'we' win the war, he will be captured and tried as a criminal, how can you let that happen?

Mollayan sighed ....

'Adam, we cannot dictate who or what we are. We have been at war for four years now, soon it will be 1944. I have no doubt that Admiral Canaris has done all in his power to assist his 'Fatherland'. There is however circumstances where even nationhood is superseded. Canaris, like me is sworn to protect and whilst we fight on opposite sides, when it comes to the Yahweh, we are brothers'.

'I understand' said Adam ' it just takes a bit of getting used to, that's all'. Let's get back to the message, what do you think it means?

'Lets break it down into pieces and try and understand it in the context of Andrew and Isaac's writings'

'Come and look at this said Adam, I've found some more references to Saul or Paul in Isaac's notes. I think this may be of interest'

'What is it? Asked Mollayan

'It's a reference to an Essene scroll called the 'Habbakuk Pesher' where reference is made to a power struggle between James and Paul. In it James refers to Paul as a 'spouter of lies' for preaching a false doctrine to the Gentiles. It would appear that Paul's interpretation of the Nazarene was not very popular with the Essene.

'I'm not surprised to hear that' said Mollayan,' especially when you consider that Paul was essentially preaching that the Nazarene was indeed the Son of God. James and the Essene knew that he wasn't but they had not been enlightened in the way that Paul had been enlightened. You see James and Paul essentially believed in the same doctrine but it was necessary for Paul to ostracise himself from the Essene in order to get credence with the Gentiles for his preaching. Furthermore, Paul had embarked upon his wanderings by then, his letters would have already been common knowledge to many thousands of people.

'That being the case, he seems to have exceeded his brief' said Adam. 'It says here that Paul totally believed in the relevance of the historical Son of God theory and claimed that he was basing his teaching on the spirit meditated revelation vouchsafed to him on the road to Damascus'

'Of course' said Mollayan 'that is where he would have been influenced by the Yahweh for the first time. He had no choice other than to do what he was commanded, he couldn't allow the Essene to be infiltrated by followers who believed that the Nazarene was the 'Son of God'. What better way then, than to proclaim him as a God to all men. The Essene would never tolerate Gentiles in their midst. Paul in creating the schism had protected the truth.

'O.K' said Adam ' what now?

Mollayan was deep in thought, he got up and walked over to the map on the wall and studied the area around the Dead Sea at the place called Qumran.

'I think we should determine the whereabouts of the Holy Sepulchre if we can from the clues that we have. If we can find it, we will know whether it is in danger or not, if we don't then it will remain safe within its secret place. Either way I don't feel that we have any choice.

Adam responded

'I think I've found our starting place' said Adam, holding a handwritten page in his hand. 'Its part of the priests testimony, he talks about the soul, here let me read it to you'

The soul is the ultimate mystery, the non- physical entity that every living person has, the map of life, the holder of the faith, the evidence of existence and ultimate salvation. Yahweh is the soul of souls and the Holy Sepulchre holds its secret'

Adam then called Mollayan over to where he was sitting,

'He's made out a list of questions, what do you think?

1. *What or who did the Essene worship and ultimately protect?*
2. *How is salvation administered to the vessel?*
3. *A soul of souls 'I will make man in my image'*
4. *A bloodline that was responsible for the creation of man?*
5. *A hidden, protected sect that enjoyed unrivalled 'godlike' status*
6. *Untold riches and mystery*
7. *Brutal extermination and resistance of the Roman church*
8. *The book of Revelations.*

Mollayan studied the list for a few minutes and then announced

'We must pray that this man survives'

Adam and Mollayan lapsed into silence, their thoughts on a priest who had become part of them through his writings, a man who they were helpless to assist, a man who was one of them ....

Chapter 18

He refused to divulge his identity to anyone, he knew he couldn't rely on assistance from the Vatican, they'd told him that he was going to Perugia, he'd ended up in Monte Casino. It had been his own fault for removing his collar once he'd left the hay cart. He tried to disguise the fact that he was a priest before he entered into the village as he didn't want to have to answer any awkward questions. He had neither money nor food but he knew that if he was able to get back into Rome, he could get help.

He knelt down beside a stream and washed and drank the cool water, he didn't even see the man as he stepped out from behind hedgerows and strike him hard on the side of the head.

When he woke he'd found himself in the company of two families that were hiding in a hay barn. He came to his senses slowly.......

'Where am I' mumbled Andrew.

He struggled to get up from where he was lying but a heavy foot was placed in his chest, forcing him back down again.

'Who are you? demanded the voice

'I am a pre..., I am a worker from the monastery at Monte Cassino, when I saw the Germans in the village I got scared, I am from Australia, they might think I am British' stammered Andrew.

'Let him up' said a woman's voice ' Give him something to eat'

Andrew gnawed hungrily at a piece of black bread whilst looking around the cave.

The woman spoke again

'We are Jews'

'We were ordered to report to the square for re-settlement, all of our families had been taken down yesterday. The Nazis called in their network of informers, they must have bled them for information during the night because we were all well hidden. The priest in the village had taken all of the children into the church and we'd gone into the hills. By dawn, a swift merciless sweep had found all of the children and the rabbi and the rest of the older folk'.

The woman started to shudder, ' They marched them unceremoniously to the cemetery and shot them all. It didn't matter, men women children, all were shot then they doused their bodies and set them on fire, look, you can still see the smoke'.

Andrew went to the front of the cave and looked down on the village. He could hear the sirens screaming in hideous harmony to the wailing of the women in the cave and watched as the SS scored every house in the village and shot anyone they found. He stayed at the front of the cave for quite a long time and was joined by the woman who had spoken to him when he regained consciousness

'What will you do?' she asked

'I'll go down into the village and see if I can find any food' said Andrew

'You can't go down there ' hissed the woman 'it's not safe.

Andrew stood up and moved into the cave

'Don't worry about me, I will be alright'

'Listen to me' said the woman' my son knows a path through the mountain to the next village, stay with us and we will go over there tomorrow' she pleaded

Andrew pondered his situation. He was the only young man in the group and he didn't know where he was, if there was a chapel in the next village, he might be able to contact someone although at this stage he knew that Santini would have been informed of his absence and would in Andrew's mind have people out looking for him.

'Alright' said Andrew ' we'll go over the mountain to the next village in the morning, now let's get back into the cave and get some rest'

Andrew and the woman went back into the cave and lay down to sleep.

He rose early the next morning, some of the people were already awake and had drunk what water was left from the night before.

'Let us go now' said the woman and motioned to the small boy to lead the way

'Show us the way Luca ' she said

The boy went out of the front of the cave and had not walked 10 meters when a guttural cry shouted

'Hande Hoch' , 'Juden Raus'

'Ni Juden' screamed the woman as she ran forward to grab the small boy 'Ni Juden!!!!!

'Raus Raus' .... Followed by the cocking of several machine pistols

Andrew ushered the rest of the people out of the cave and they were taken down into the Village Square. Andrew was shocked to the core at what he saw, there were dead bodies everywhere, lying on the ground, hanging from trees, some of the corpses had been burned to a crisp...

What looked like an officer sauntered out of a burned out house, a cigarette dangling from his lips and a slavish smile etched on his face

'Anyone speak Inglesi' he sneered

Andrew watched as a truck reversed from a side street onto one side of the square whilst at the same time he noticed three different points on the other side of the square where soldiers were manning machine guns

'I do' stammered Andrew struggling to hold his voice with some sort of calm

'and who are you?

'I am the priest of the village' stammered Andrew

'A priest huh? said the officer ' well priest, I have a task for you

At that two of the soldiers began to separate the women and the children who started to scream. The first one lifted one of the children and snapped his neck like a twig and as the child's mother ran forward, the sergeant drew his service revolver and drilled a neat hole in the front of her head. Andrew rushed over as a pool of blood spread on the ground beneath the slain woman. All he could hear was the guffaw of the sergeant as the sun caught the glint of the skulls in his jacket lapels

'We are here because the stinking Italians are no better than you Jews, he spat viciously

'Now priest I suggest you pray to your God as to what you should do next'

The rest of the older men had been herded into one of the houses, the soldier lifted a heavy crossbar and locked them in. Suddenly came the sound of breaking glass as 4 other SS men lobbed grenades through the windows, the house exploded in a ball of flame as the sergeant grinned across at the women

'Take them and do with them what you want, he leered at his men as he walked across and grabbed the woman who had spoken to Andrew, he put one hand around her neck and shoved his other hand between her legs, she stiffened and then shouted and spat in the face of the sergeant

'Gut' he exclaimed 'a mare with spirit, I will surely enjoy fucking you ....

'Wait' said Andrew 'These are innocent people ....

The sergeant stopped and put his hand up ' Men' he exclaimed 'we have a martyr in our midst, Gunther, bring me the rope!

Andrew was held by two men and stripped to the waist, a length of rope was tied to each of his wrists and he was pulled into a 'crucifix' like position before each of the ends of the ropes were tied to the backs of two motorcycles,

'We'll have a bit of fun before the fucking begins, right priest, nearer to your god you'll be

The two motorcycles started and revved their engines and took the slack of the rope, one of the women fainted and the others huddled around her, their faces white with fear, no one daring to speak.

Andrew felt the pressure of the rope on his arms as the sergeant dropped his hands and the bikes moved forward. Andrew grimaced and then screamed as he felt his shoulder dislocating. The bikes stopped.

'Your God suffered did he not? sneered the sergeant, perhaps you would like a drink?

As Andrew stood in the square, the sergeant walked across to him and opening his fly, relieved himself against Andrew. He then spat in his face and was about to drop his hand again when a shout came from behind him.

A tall, well dressed man was striding across the square having climbed out of a half track that had entered the square on the only side that hadn't been blocked by the soldiers. He was dressed in black but he did not have the same markings on his collar.

'Who is in charge here? he whispered.

The sergeant took a step back 'I am, he said 'Who wants to know?

My name is Major Gernstein, perhaps you have heard of me?

The sergeant face paled, 'fuck! Of all the officers to come walking into his square at this time, it had to be Gernstein. Everybody knew him by reputation as a fearless soldier who fought with Prussian values and was oblivious to the politics of the SS or anyone else for that matter. He fought hard and sometimes to the last man and stories abounded of his bravery and how he treated anyone who did not uphold his strict code of waging war.

'Have you Dirlewanger scum forgotten how to report to a senior officer?' he sneered.

'Sergeant Willi Shultz reporting Herr Major, I beg to report that there is nothing to report.

'No? mused the major, 'We'll see about that'

The soldier who led the men that had thrown the grenades into the building came running across the square

'Save some of those bitches for usssssss

'Bring that man to me'

The two soldiers that were with the Major grabbed the man and pushed him in front of the Major

'Report!'

'We followed our orders and the buildings has been destroyed Herr major'

One of the women wailed and the Major stopped and walked over to where Andrew was standing

'Who are you? asked the Major

Andrew winced as he spoke 'I am a prisoner, we all are, I hope you are proud of your men, they just locked 30 old men in that house over there and blew the house up. He shot that woman '. Andrew moved his head in the direction of the sergeant.

The major sauntered back across to where the sergeant was standing. It had started to rain and two of the other men guarding the women mouthed to each other, 'this is it' he's for the high jump, I always said the way he treats women is fucking disgraceful'

The Major had sent a Luetnant across to check on the house, he returned accompanied by a small boy who was shaking with fear

'Tell the Major what you saw ' cooed the Luetnant

The boy recited in broken English how he'd watched as his grandfather was put into the house and then the soldiers laughed as they threw the grenades in.

'They were trying to escape' stammered the sergeant thinking what the fuck all the fuss was over a few dead prisoners, obviously this Gernstein had never been on the Russian Front, there he would have seen real killing.

Gernstein walked across towards the dead woman

He straightened up and beckoned to the sergeant

'Perhaps you would be so kind as to show me the point of entry of the bullet'

The indignant sergeant slowly turned crimson. All this absurd amount of fuss over a dead bitch with a bullet between the eyes, hell did these people live in a fool's paradise.

'The point of entry' insisted Gernstein ' just as a matter of interest'

The sergeant pointed to the forehead of the woman and the neat hole that had been drilled by the bullet

Behind Gernstein stood his ordnance officer with a sub machine gun under his arm, behind him stood two military policemen or 'headhunters' their silvery crescent shaped regalia glittering in the sunlight. One of the women had come over to Andrew and untied his hands, he fell to the ground.

Gernstein instructed two of the women to help him before turning back to the sergeant

'Now where were we?' he mused ' Ah yes, How did this prisoner die?'

'She was shot trying to escape' the sergeant grunted

'and the child?

'He fell'

Most of the men that had been standing around the sergeant started to move away from him

'This woman was shot from the front at close range, perhaps I should ask the priest what happened.

The sergeant glanced towards Andrew

'We've been fighting for 5 weeks to get to here, we were having some fun ....

'Fun? whispered the Major 'Fun?

Andrew spoke up

'The soldier is a disgrace to his uniform, he murdered the mother and child in cold blood'

At once there was a cacophony of sound from the assembled women. Andrew noticed a frosty sparkle appear in Gernstein's cold Prussian eyes. His aide stamped forward like a hungry rhinoceros and pushed the sergeant towards the 'headhunters'

'Special Field Order 19/5' said the aide

The military police dragged the sergeant around the corner and for a minute there was silence until two shots rang out. One of the policemen returned and snapped a salute to Gernstein

'Sentence has been carried out sir!

'Very Well' mouthed Gernstein ' Round up these men and escort these people down to the station'

'But' said Andrew 'they are innocent people, they've done nothing, why must they go?

They are Jews and they will be resettled' snapped Gernstein 'You are free to go, priest'

'I will stay with them' said Andrew

Gernstein looked at Andrew for a moment then turned on his heel

'As you wish, priest, take them all to the station now!

Gernstein walked back towards the half track, opened the door, got in and tipped his driver who sped out of the square as quickly as he came in.

Andrew winced with pain and one of the women came over to him, 'I am a nurse, let me see if I can help you.

The nurse expertly worked her fingers along the line of Andrew's shoulder and finally placed one hand on the front of his shoulder and at the same time flattening the heel of her other hand against the flat of his shoulder at the back. She called over to one of the women to bring a piece of wood over to her.

'Put this in your mouth' she commanded 'this will hurt'

Just as Andrew clenched his teeth into the wood, the nurse pushed hard from the front and used her other hand to hold him steady. There was a loud crack and the blood drained from Andrew's face as the pain cracked through every nerve ending in his body.

The nurse removed her head scarf and fashioned a sling

'It will be sore for a day or two but I think I have managed to get it back into place' she said

Andrew thanked her and turned to walk towards the rest of the people who had now been formed into two columns and were being escorted into trucks.

'Where do you think we are going' said an old woman

'I don't know' answered another 'but at least we are still alive.

The trucks drove for most of the morning and on into the afternoon until they reached what appeared to be a freight yard on the edge of a large town.

As they were herded into a makeshift compound, Andrew noticed that most of the soldiers wore the black uniform of the men that he had seen in the square. As he was looking around the camp Andrew walked over towards him, he spied a soldier with a torn uniform lying on the ground. The soldier was moaning, Andrew looked around to see if he could see the woman who had helped him, he spotted her and waved for her to come over to help.

Just as she began to pull away the dirty bandage, the soldier moaned loudly. Andrew grasped his hand are started to whisper in his ear

'She is a nurse my son, she will help you, Where did you come from?

Another soldier joined them, he was older and he spoke to Andrew in a low voice.

'We had been retreating for three days when the SS arrived, at first they were O.K and

we thought that they were there to help us, then we discovered that the Duce had been disposed and that Badoglio had taken over the government. Once this rumour went out, the SS moved against us, they shot all of our officers and disarmed us before force marching us to this place, we've been here for 48 hours without food and drink'

Had Andrew known just exactly what was going on at that moment, he would not have given much thought as to his future. Mussolini had been disposed by his own council two months earlier and it was rumoured that Italy had signed an armistice with the allies who were already fighting their way up the country from Sicily. Hitler had formed a new Army Group B under the control of Erwin Rommel and had sealed the all of the alpine passes between Italy and the rest of the Reich. The commander of the third Panzergrenadier Division was already in Rome with explicit orders from Hitler to take out the city including the Vatican.

General Jodl had asked the Fuehrer about Rome and Hitler had responded

'I'll go right into the Vatican. Do you think the Vatican embarrasses me? We'll take that over right away, their entire diplomatic corps are in there, that rabble, we'll get that bunch of swine out of there, later on we can make our apologies. As for the Jews, send them to the home we have prepared for them!'

The assembled group of generals glanced furtively at each other, as Hitler continued with absolute clarity to give orders as to how his generals were to assimilate Italy into the Reich. He finished by ordering General Kesselring to come up with a plan to rescue the Duce.

The troops who were manning the station yard were part of an advance party that had been put together by Himmler to accompany the regular army and round up as many Jews and undesirables as they could lay their hands on. The village that had been attacked by the Germans had been effectively decimated by Dirlewanger's troops, if you could call them that. The general order was that they were not supposed to operate on their own but the Wehrmacht commander had sent them up the road to the village to secure the road. The company had taken it upon themselves to practice their particular brand of 'soldiering' especially when they discovered that there were Jews in the village. When Andrew reached the yard, he noticed a large sign written in chalk, it read 'Umschagplatz'.

Andrew stayed with the injured soldier for the next couple of hours and talked with him and his friend. The nurse had managed to patch him up and the crowd had settled down in the hope that they would get something to drink or eat. One of the older men had come to Andrew to see if he would ask for food. Andrew has looked around to see if he could spot the officer that had been in the village square earlier that day. Andrew saw the officer walking into the compound and stood up, immediately drawing attention to himself. One of the SS soldiers ran across and hit him hard on the chest pushing him to the ground. The soldier cocked his machine pistol and shouted at Andrew

'Stay where you are Jew, You'll be moving soon enough!

An ancient locomotive grunted slowly into the station dragging behind it a creaking row of wagons. Immediately there was a lot of activity, three groups of soldiers, some with dogs uncoupled three of the wagons and reversed them into a siding. The rest of the wagons were pulled open and the soldiers started to whip the people at the front of the yard into the empty wagons. By the time Andrew reached the front he could see that as many people as possible were being crammed into the wagon. Most of the children were crying and the men and women had their hands stretched out of the slits in the tops of the doors shouting for water.

'Where are we going?' they wailed

They got their answer three days later.

It was dark when they arrived, Andrew had fallen into a fitful sleep on the train, troubled by visions and dreams of damnation. For two days he had watched as the humanity in the wagon had degenerated into a seething mass of hopelessness. He watched helplessly as the weaker men were pushed away from the air vents and slowly sank to their knees, he saw women begging the men, offering themselves to the stronger ones if only they'd lift their children up and let them breathe. On the second day, one of the women had been caught feeding her child with a loaf that she had secreted in her clothing by another woman, a fight ensued and the woman with the loaf was killed by the other woman with her bare hands, her child was in a pretty bad way as well. There had also been several people who had collapsed and were very sick, Andrew counted over 90 people in the wagon and they'd had no food or water and there was no sanitation in the wagon. When the train slowed and then shuddered to a halt, all of the people started to shout and scream for the doors to be open. What met Andrew's eyes can only be described in Dante's Inferno. There were soldiers and dogs everywhere, kicking and pulling the people out of the wagons. Two or three of the younger men had tried to run and had been slaughtered before they got five yards away from the wagon, the rest of the people were being pushed towards three or four channels. At the top of which sat men with white coats and beyond them a large set of gates with a watchtower on either side and a sign said which in Andrew's pigeon German said something about something about hard work and freedom under a name 'Flossenburg'.

In those first couple of hours, Andrew witnessed all that Rossi had told him about and more, he saw the selection procedure, he smelled the pungent sweetness in the air and saw the smoke billowing from the crematoria on the far side of the camp. The dogs strained at the leash, one guard allowed his dog to savage an old Jew, Andrew watched on helplessly as the dog tore at the throat o the old man.

He passed through 'selection' and entered into the main camp where he began to understand the feeling of being forsaken, his torment exacerbated by the knowledge that his Holy Father, the Vatican knew that this was happening in these places but had chosen to do

Nothing.

On the second night that Andrew was in the camp two men approached him. One of the men was old and emaciated, the other seemed stronger but seemed oblivious to what was going on around him and was being guided by the older man.

The old man shuffled up beside Andrew

'You are the priest they talk about, you came in two days ago'

Andrew blinked convulsively and stammered

'Do I know you?

'No' said the old man 'but I wish to speak with you about some things, we'll go inside into the hut'

The hut was silent, some of the inmates were lying in a stupor of tiredness and pain in their bunks, the Kapo wasn't at his usual; spot near the stove, he was probably over near the women's camp, screwing some women in return for some bread or word on how a son or husband was doing. Andrew ushered the two men over to his place in a bunk near the door. Inside the barracks over 1500 prisoners were often crammed in. Barracks were heated with only one small stove at the end of the building. The Latrines were located outside the barracks and each one serviced close to 4000 inmates. On many occasions men and women were directed to use the same latrines. Thankfully those that were in the hut appeared to be sleeping and the work details had yet to return to the huts. Andrew ducked into his space and the old man sat down beside him whilst his son stood facing them and staring into space.

'You're new so you're strong, you'll get closer to the stove as we die' he glanced down the hut, 'My name is Mordacai Melamed and this is my son Emanuel.

Andrew took the hand of the old man and then proffered his hand to the old man's son only for the younger man to ignore the gesture and continue to stare blankly at the partly covered window.

Andrew went to speak and the old man held up a tired arm to stop

'We will be dead soon' he said 'and there is much I have to tell you this evening'

'Dead?' whispered Andrew, ' you mustn't think like that, you are alive, you will get through'

The old man raised his hand.

'What age do you think I am?

Andrew looked at the old man, he had little or no hair, what was left were like dank clumps on a parchment like skull. His face had several sores on it and when he opened his mouth, there was only blackness. His nose was very obviously broken and he was stooped over. His hands were knarled and twisted and he was very thin.

'You have had a hard life' said Andrew' I am sure you are in the autumn of your life'

'Far from it said the old man, I am 51 years of age and my son here is 24'

Andrew was conscious of hearing his own sharp intake of breath, the old man continued

'Emanuel and I arrived here in December 1942. Shortly afterwards, the Germans marched our entire labour team, 200 still relatively healthy and robust men, into a nearby forest. The air was freezing, and snow covered the ground. In the distance we saw and smelt the clouds of smoke emanating from the crematoria, but were still unaware of the terrible truth behind those malodorous clouds. An SS officer, Otto Moll, ordered us to enter a straw-roofed hut in the forest, full of naked bodies. "We saw a mass of naked corpses, men, women and children. We were horror-stricken into an eerie unnatural silence. It took us two days to recover a semblance of normality."

That was our first day as Sonderkommandos at the camp, which housed the death factory that consumed our people. I was lucky in that they found out that I was a skilled carpenter and they needed skilled tradesmen to work in the Seimens factory. But my son, my beautiful son has been reduced to this state because he was a SonderKommando. I was able to bribe the Kapo to allow him to come back into the camp. They knew it didn't matter, he would die soon, he is a 'musselman' and he will not survive the role call and he will be taken off to the 'showers', I will go with him.

'But the showers' stammered Andrew

'You don't understand' said the old man 'when we came here in 1942, I had my wife, my two sons and two daughters. My elders on had his wife and their two young children. My wife's mother and father were also on the train and when we eventually got inside the camp, I found another three members of my family on my own father's side. I never saw any of the women again; I have since found out that they were all killed on the night that they arrived. There is only me and my so left and when roll call comes tomorrow, I will go with him because I'm tired and these last few nights my Janet has been calling me.'

Andrew put his head into his hands and started to tremble. The old man put his hand on his head and said

'You are strong and if you keep your head down, you might get out of here. We have all heard rumours and we know that the allies are in Italy. That is where you came from, yes?

Andrew lifted his head and looked at the man through watering eyes.

What do you want of me Mordacai?'

'You do know that you are in the Flossenburg camp?

Andrew nodded

I have been collecting a testimony for the time that I have been here, it is vital that when this is all over, somebody tells the world what happened to us in these places. Don't worry, the testimony is hidden in a safe place, it is not in the camp, I will tell you where it is, you must promise me that if you survive you will do what you have to do to make sure that the world knows. I have told three people that I will trust with my life and I have told you because you are a priest and I am told that you will listen to my plea and honour my wish.

'You have a record of here? said Andrew

'Here' said the old man reaching beneath his coat 'look at this' He handed Andrew three pages of long hand, on the first page was a roughly drawn map and Andrew quickly read what was on the paper

'Flossenburg has 93 sub camps and external kommandos. Of these satellite camps, 47 are for the male prisoners and 27 hold the female prisoners. The prisoners confined to these sub camps are workers of all creeds and country who have been supplied to labour in any of the various labour projects. Of these 93 smaller camps, Hersbruck, Leitmeritz, Muelsen, Obertraubling, and Saal are considered the worst. This is where the Jews are.

Following is a list of Flossenburg's many sub camps:

Altenhammer Obertraubling

Ansbach Pilsen

Chemnitz Plattling

Eisenberg Poschetzau

Falkenau Rathen

Graslitz Rathmanndorf

Hersbruck Rabstein

Holyson Rochlitz

Janovice Saal

Krondorf Schlackenwerth

Leitmeritz St. Georgenthal

Meissen Venusberg

Andrew turned over to the second page, scrawled on the top of it was one word

'Sonderkommando'

'What does this mean? Asked Andrew

Mordacai took his son's hand in his own as he spoke

'Read the pages'

Andrew began to read

The Sonderkommandos have better physical conditions than other inmates. They have

Decent food, they sleep on straw mattresses and wear normal clothing. Despite this seemingly rosy picture, the selection process regarding the Sonderkommando teams was every bit as frightening and horrifying as that which determined which new arrivals would be sent to the gas chambers. One of the selected was so horrified that he felt he could not continue working there, so he took a piece of glass and cut his throat hoping in death to free himself from that fate. No Sonderkommandos survive, since they are usually sent to the gas chambers after a few months on the job. I pray that one of these souls live to tell their tale and to ensure this particular chapter of horror not is forgotten and an insight into the daily operation of the assembly lines of genocide is gained

On my son's first day as a Sonderkommando he met an acquaintance, Shlomo Kirschenbaum, who was the Kapo in charge of the Sonderkommando team. He told Kirschenbaum that he did not think he could survive doing that work, and was contemplating suicide. "Kirschenbaum told him that he to felt the same way when he was sent to the Sonderkommando, but was able to adapt. He said that he too, would be able to adapt. He gave him two stiff drinks. He fell asleep, and after waking the next day he felt differently about it, and did not kill himself.

The Nazis deliberately sent Jews to work as Sonderkommandos; the Germans' typical sadistic streak found amusement in a system in which the victim suffered the utmost degradation prior to ending up in a cloud of foul-smelling smoke. The Sonderkommandos were divided into several groups, each with a specific specialized function. Some greet the new arrivals, telling them that they going to be disinfected and showered prior to being sent to labour teams. We are obliged to lie, telling the soon-to-be-murdered prisoners that after the delousing process they would be assigned to labour teams and reunited with their families. These are the only Sonderkommandos to have contact with the victims while they were still alive. Other teams process the corpses after the gas chambers, extracting gold teeth, and removing clothes and valuables before taking them to the crematoria for final disposal. Emanuel is barely 22 and already he looks as old as I am. He went through the selection procedure when I was removed to the factory; they of course knew he was my son because the Kapo told them so. He worked in Crematorium number two, in the room where the prisoners were ordered to strip. When I asked him whether he ever considered telling the prisoners they would soon be killed, he replied,

"What is the point? They are totally defenceless. What is the point of frightening them for no good reason?"

His friend, Yaakov Gabai, died during the selection procedure because he refused to lift the bodies; one of the SS men walked over and shot him through the back of the neck. My son is one of the last loads of "Musselmen" (long-term inmates reduced to starved walking corpses) who is still living in the camp.

On the 13th of October two of his cousins were among 400 Musselmen processed that day. He told me that he told them the truth, and told them where to be in the gas chamber so they would die immediately without suffering.

The Gas Chambers

The SS carries out the actual gassings. The Sonderkommandos then enter the chambers afterwards, remove the bodies, process them and transport them to the crematorium. Then the remains are ground to dust and mixed with the ashes. When too much ash mounted, the Sonderkommandos, under the watchful eyes of the SS, would take the bodies up to the granite quarry and spread it over the vastness of the pit. The SS made it very clear to the men that Sonderkommandos are dependent on continued shipments of Jews for their lives. Any slowing down of operations due to lack of victims meant they were in danger of being eliminated

The Sonderkommandos know that the Germans do not intend to leave any witnesses to their crimes, and periodically Sonderkommando teams are killed by being gassed themselves. I am sure that the entire Jewish nation will be eradicated before these madmen stop. Two months ago I learned that the Germans intended gassing them. There was talk of a revolt but nothing came of it, I went to the Kapo and asked if Emanuel would be able to join me, the Kapo was a strange man, his team had suffered no suicides (the Ss punished the Kapo if there were any suicides by killing members of his family) when I asked him why this was, he replied

"Our ability to adapt is almost infinite. We function like soulless robots; it is the only way to remain sane under such conditions. The only way to survive is to cease being human. The Sonderkommandos reached the stage where they could eat and drink among the corpses, totally indifferent, utterly detached from r emotions. I can only assume that they close themselves down with all energies and thoughts concentrating solely on getting through another day, to the elimination of any other thoughts. The human mind is capable of minimizing and neutralizing its emotional elements in order to facilitate physical survival in extremely stressful situations. I notice that the camp inmates hold Sonderkommandos in suspicion, regarding them as the cousins of collaborators, who choose that work to escape death. I know that they do not, this is not the case, blind fate places all of them including my son in the Sonderkommando, they have no control of destiny in that hell hole whatsoever. Nothing will change the fact however those in the camps themselves the Sonderkommandos are regarded as unclean, almost as lepers. I commit these words with my life. The SS forced my son and his friends to become Sonderkommandos; the fact that they were forced to do monstrous work does not change the fact that they are victims, not monsters.

Andrew gave the pages back to Mordacai who looked him in the eye and asked him if he would help

'You don't even know my name' said Andrew

'I have known so many names and now they are all gone and soon I will be gone as well' said Mordacai 'Tens of thousands of people are being murdered every day in the extermination camps'

Andrew raised his hand to stop him, to assure him he would help; how could he not, he'd read a hundred pages like the pages he had just read over the last two years. How could he tell this man and his son that his pope knew what was going on, the Allies knew what was going on and had done so for the last three years yet chose to do nothing. He recalled the conversations that he had with Santini, his answer burned into his brain

'I've heard this talk, but I don't believe it. Germany is a civilized country, The Germans are not capable of doing these things that are claimed – it is a lie.'

Andrew, sitting in one of the very camps that were in fact doing all and more knew that he would do whatever it took to survive.

'Tell me what I need to do' said Andrew

The old man sat back on the bunk as if in a stupor. 'I believe in the final nobility of man and I know you will not turn your back on us. Before I give you the details it is important that you do not tell anyone of this conversation unless you feel that you must pass the legacy that I have burdened you with on to someone else that you feel is capable of bearing this mantle'.

'I understand' said Andrew

'Very well' said Mordacai' I will leave this with you to read, when you have read it, you must dispose of it immediately, I suggest that you eat the paper. Don't worry, it is a copy of one of the entries but it will give you an overview of the whole camp and what goes on in it, I want you to become a survivor and the less attention that you bring to yourself the better. You are young and once they find out that you are not a Jew, you will be moved into one of the foreigner work camps, Flossenburg is a hard labour camp and you'll most likely be sent to the Messerschmit complex to work.'

'They can tell I am not a Jew?'

'They make selections every week and take some inmates to Dachau for special experiments, they are usually Slavs or Jews that go, but they use the exercise a second chance to weed out those that have escaped the first selection off the transport'.

Mordacai stood up and grasped Andrew's hand, there were tears in his eyes as he said

'If you see me in the compound, ignore me, you cannot speak, with me, nor I you. We will not speak again, it will be too dangerous. No - one else will know that we have spoken and the papers that I speak off will only be safe if they are allowed to remain in hiding. At the back of the officer's mess there is a single grave, go to it if and when the allies come and you will see it. It is the grave of one of the children of the camp doctor who is buried there. I was part of a detail that was commanded to take down stone from the quarry to the gravesite. If you find the grave and look back towards the officers mess you will see that we have laid a path of stone bedded into the earth, under the fourth and fifth stones of that path, I have buried most of my testimony'

'But how did you manage to do such a thing? Asked Andrew

'I was the carpenter on the site and it was easy for me to secrete the papers in a wrapping and drop them into the holes in the ground and cover them before the stones were laid. I was the kapo in charge of the work detail. It was easy to attract the attention of the guards because we were very close to the woman's camp and the guards were always looking to see if they could spot any new girls who they could get to use in the camp brothel'

Andrew watched through forlorn eyes as Mordacai stood up and shuffled towards the door, Emanuel holding onto his arm. He opened the door and winced as a draft of wind rushed up the camp. This brought a moan of protest from those Jews who were down at the stove. He stopped at door and turned, his eyes said goodbye and then the door slammed closed.

Andrew retreated into the back of the bunk space and placing his back against the wall so as to allow what light was possible to illuminate the folded wrap that he now carefully opened. It was a single page of paper covered in a handwritten scrawl. Andrew began to read.

On May 3, 1938, Flossenburg was established in this beautiful area of forested mountains. It is said that Herman Himmler himself chose this ironically beautiful spot. The camp is situated near the German cities of Bayreuth and Weiden; Flossenburg was originally established to house political prisoners but became a death camp in 1941,

The prisoners at Flossenburg were meant to be worked to death, and a great many of our people died from the brutal treatment. Flossenburg's location is mostly likely chosen due to its remoteness and its proximity to both a granite quarry and a railroad. Mining in the quarries is especially difficult and dangerous. The workers are forced to run up steps carrying loads of heavy rock or dragging the heavy granite stones behind them. Many of these labourers have collapsed and died from exhaustion or silicosis, a lung disease caused by inhaling crystalline dust. Despite these difficulties, the quarries at Flossenburg are producing 1,200 cubic meters of stone a month.

The prisoners at Flossenburg and its surrounding camps are also forced to work in various factories producing arms for the German forces. In 1942 and 1943, more and more of us Jews and Slavs are being forced to help produce materials for the war effort.

The prisoners are spread throughout the areas surrounding Flossenburg in order to work in factories run by such companies as Siemens, Osram, Junkers, and the Auto Union Co. The majority of the workers from Flossenburg, however, work in the factories of the Messerschmitt Company. In 1942, the Messerschmitt Company had 800 workers, and by 1944 the number of workers had risen to 5,000. We worked 11-hour shifts producing fuselages and wings for various models of warplanes. Flossenburg's method of loaning out slave labour is quite profitable for the camp. We have heard stories of the SS at, Flossenburg billing the Messerschmitt company over 3.3 million Reichmarks.

A large number of the work squads are employed by various German organizations. The SS, the German railway, various police departments, and city administrations and businesses also use the labour of the Flossenburg prisoners. Since the prisoners in concentration camps were used as slave labour for economic functions, the camps fell under the direction of the Ministry of Economics in 1941.In addition to death by hanging, phenol injection, malnutrition and firing squads, Flossenburg KZ also had a working gas chamber. This "shower room" was their pride and joy in fact Hans Vogel, the camp commandant stated to the Kapo of the Sonderkommandos that Hitler and Himmler considered the Flossenburg gas chamber to be the most aesthetic and efficient in the KZ consortium of gas chambers that many of Germany's prize engineers and furnace makers had built. In the barracks at Flossenburg KZ. 12 and 13 year old Jewish and Slav children were used as prostitutes. These young girls were selected to service Ukrainian guards and certain Kapos. Activity in these barracks is heavy and girls frequently wind up in gas chambers or are brutally murdered by their clients.

Andrew Lassiter held his head between his legs. He retched and his guts screamed with pain. He'd had no food and bile spewed out onto the floor.

He was reading a page that detailed all that he already knew and he was here to see it.

'My God! What have I done?' he cried in anguish 'I am a Judas! I am a Judas!

The puke and the tears and the pain and the knowledge crashed against him like a tidal wave and he staggered blindly towards the stove. He lifted the page and crumpled it in his hand and then remembering what Mordacai had said; he pushed his way to the front and threw the page in the fire, staying there until it burned into nothing. He staggered back to his space, oblivious of the eyes of the Jews that were on him and collapsed in a state of near delirium

'Oh my God, why have you forsaken me? How has man sank to such depths of depravity. I am in hell along with all these other lost souls and we are degraded to the point of hopelessness'.

Chapter 19

It was late at night when the fifth man arrived at the house, he was ushered in to a dimly lit room where four other men were already gathered.

'I'm sorry I'm late' said the man

'No matter, Speer' said Rosenberg 'You of course know Dr. Faltermayer and Professor Emmerich, may I introduce you to Obergruppenfurher Gert Strupper.

After exchanging platitudes and settling down with a drink, Rosenberg called the meeting to order

'Gentlemen, it is my considered opinion that the we are losing the will to win this war'

He allowed the statement to hang for a moment and closely observed the faces of the assembled before continuing,

'I have put together a plan that will hopefully allow us to salvage our mission and continue to wage war against the 'untermensch' in the East'. We must also be resolute in our plans for the Final Solution to our Jewish problem. Professor Emmerich has some interesting ideas concerning that issue. What is clear however is that none of these plans can bear fruit unless we rid ourselves of the Fuhrer!

Speer jumped up from his chair, his face quivering with anger

'I'll have you shot for that' he said vehemently 'I'm sick and tired of your double talk and subterfuge, I was a fool to listen to you, and I should have spoken to the Fuehrer long ago!

Rosenberg remained calm as Speer realised that he was the only one on his feet protesting.

The other men sat on in their chairs awaiting Rosenberg to speak again.

'I want you to listen to what I have to say very carefully.

An eerie silence permeated the room

'Our glory and destiny is anchored in the belief that we are capable of producing a higher civilisation, a super race if you like. To achieve our aim, we must be prepared to ruthlessly crush the existing inferior civilisations. We must purge all those who stand in our way, which means we must eradicate all traces of their existence, take the Jews for example, they have been responsible for all of our ailments and will continue to be a scourge on the world. We are doing the new order a favour and in years to come we will be congratulated and held up as a master race for the hard decisions and actions we are taking now.

Rosenberg stopped and took a sip from his drink, Speer noticed that sweat was glistening on his brow and his left hand was twitching violently.

Rosenberg continued

'We cannot allow anyone, and I mean anyone from keeping the German people from reaching their goal'. We can no longer tolerate apologists who already are wringing their hands in the face of the discovery of some of the decisions we have had to take for the greater good of the Reich.'

Strupper jumped to his feet and pointed his finger at Rosenberg. It was the first show of temper Alfred Rosenberg had ever seen from him and he was clearly startled into silence

'Damn you!' said Strupper 'I am a Prussian officer and I have fought for the glory of the Fatherland. I am neither a fool nor a coward and I will not listen to this drivel in the face of the disaster that we are facing. I have been here from the start and I want to know now what you are talking about, what is all this 'Final Solution' talk your refer too? Have we got the new weapons or not?

Rosenberg's eyes bulged in disbelief at his ignorance

'Where are my weapons?' bellowed Strupper 'Give me them and we will turn defeat into victory and give us the time to negotiate a peace. We will join the Allies and fight the Red hordes and take revenge for Stalingrad. This time we'll make the streets of Moscow run red with their blood!

Rosenberg mopped his brow and smiled weakly, he thought he'd better enlighten Strupper about the Final Solution and the inescapable implicitity of his culpability as a member of the Thule. He began to speak in clipped tones

'Our Final Solution is becoming too much for our illustrious leader. For a number of years now, Frau Von Exner has been cooking his meals for him, as you know she was one of our Rumanian's acolytes'.

Every one winced at the thought of the Rumanian that Rosenberg was referring to, his name was Antonescu and all in the room had call to dislike him immensely. Rosenberg continued

'Frau von Exner met and fell in love with one of Heinrich's SS elite and 'Heini' insisted on the ancestry test being completed on her. His department made detailed discreet enquires and it was discovered that one of Frau Exner's great-grandmothers had been Jewish'.

There was a palpable heat in the room as each of the men searched the faces of each other for tell tale signs of betrayal or awareness that they knew what was going on.

'Our Fuhrer is beside himself with grief that he is to lose such a fine cook and confidant, he is distraught. He's been forced to get rid of her and in doing so he has also had to sign orders stripping high ranking officials who were relatives of Frau Exner of their rank'

'So' said Speer 'he is doing what he should do'

'He is not!' thundered Rosenberg. 'She and all the rest of her family should have been eradicated immediately, it is this weakness which has us in the position we are in today. We are being attacked about our finality in settling the Jew problem. That fat fool, Goring has all but surrendered the skies to the allies and I am now informed that no less a luminary than Himmler has expressed concern about our activities in the east. Because of him and his weakness we were forced to close down on the Final Solution process in our camps'.

At that Rosenberg handed each of the men a buff coloured folder marked 'TOP SECRET' and asked them to open and read the contents.

'I have read this report' said Rosenberg 'I feel it is important that you digest the information contained therein as it will help in your understanding of the task that lies ahead'

Speer and the rest of them opened their folders and began to read

From: SS-Gruppenfu"hrer Muller, Chief of the Gestapo

TO: Acktion Group East Commander

7 March 1943

I have received direct communication from the Reichmarshal ordering me to remove all traces of our activity with regard to the Aktions against the Jews. All corpses must be exhumed immediately and incinerated without leaving any traces. I hereby give you my full authority to take whatever action you deem necessary to complete this task. This is to be classed as a state secret and you will not discuss this with anyone. The codename for the process is 'Sonderaktion 1005'. Furthermore you will refrain from any written correspondence and have executive and summary police powers to assist you in your task. You will take charge of two Einsatzgruppen and report only to me with your progress.

Destroy this message when you read it

MULLER.

Strupper flicked to the first page and proceeded with the summary.

Upon his appointment, Blobel, together with a small staff of three or four men, initiated experiments involving the incineration of corpses. The place chosen for them was Kulmhof. For this purpose the ditches were opened and the corpses burnt by means of incendiary bombs, but this led to big fires in the surrounding forests. Subsequently an attempt was made to burn the corpses together with wood on open fires. This method came to be adopted in all the camps of Operation Reinhard. The corpses were carried to the open fires straight from the gas chambers. At the same time, the existing mass graves were opened and those buried there were also incinerated

This operation has been extended to Sobibor.

In Belzec, the incineration of corpses began in November 1942, toward the end of the mass murder under the control of SS-Scharfu"hrer Heinrich Gley who began the general exhumation and burning of corpses; it may have taken from November 1942 to March 1943. The incinerations went on day and night, without interruption, initially at one, then at two sites. At one of the sites it was possible to incinerate about 2,000 corpses within 24 hours. Approximately four weeks after the start of the incineration operation, the second site was set up. Thus, on an average, a total of 300,000 corpses were burnt at one site within about five months and 240,000 at the second one during 4 months. These are obviously estimates of averages. It would probably be correct to put the sum total at 500,000 corpses...

Strupper, his face a deathly pale, kept his eyes riveted to the page as terrifying thoughts ran through his head.

In Treblinka a start was made in the spring of 1943, on Himmler's personal command after he had visited the camp. The vacated ditch area was levelled and sown with lupines! SS-Oberscharfu"hrer Heinrich Matthes, who was responsible for the

extermination sector in Treblinka, has forwarded this report to GHSA

SS-Oberscharfu"hrer Heinrich Matthes. Exhumation Process and Disposal March 1943

'An SS-Oberscharfu"hrer Floss arrived with us, he had served in another camp. He controlled the construction of the installation for burning the corpses. The incineration was carried out by placing railroad rails on blocks of concrete. The corpses were then piled up on these rails. Brushwood was placed under the rails. The wood was drenched with gasoline. Not only the newly obtained corpses were burnt in this way, but also those exhumed from the ditches. The burning of corpses proceeded day and night. When the fire had died down, whole skeletons or single bones remained behind on the grating. Mounds of ash had accumulated underneath it. A different prisoner commando, the "Ashes Gang," had to sweep up the ashes, place the remaining bones on thin metal sheets, pound them with round wooden dowels, and then shake them through a narrow-mesh metal sieve; whatever remained in the sieve was crushed once more. Bones not burnt and which could not easily be split were again thrown into the fire. The camp leadership was faced with the problem of how to get rid of the huge heaps of ash and bone fragments. Experiments at mixing the ashes with dust and sand, in an effort to conceal them, proved unsuccessful. Finally it was decided to pour the ash and bone fragments back into the empty ditches and to cover them with a thick layer of sand and garbage. Alternate layers of ash and sand were poured into the ditches. The top layer consisted of 2 m. of earth.

Strupper kept his head down and fell back into a slump in his chair; the pages of the report slipped from his limp hand and fell to the floor

Rosenberg was standing behind the desk looking out of the window. He knew that at least two of the men in the room would have had no idea of the information in the report and he secretly throbbed with excitement that here they were for the first time witnessing the glory of what he Alfred

Rosenberg had contributed to. Finally, he concluded, Speer and Strupper would see his vision and realise that he alone was capable of leading the Thule to the glory of the 1000-year Reich.

Strupper reared up his head defiantly broke the silence

'I want no part of this! He exclaimed 'You are a maniac! We have the opportunity to soften the blow, negotiate with the allies and what do you want to do? Restart genocide?

Rosenberg sat impassively behind his desk, examining his nails

'Mein Gott don't you see that we are guilty of mass murder! An ashen faced Strupper jumped to his feet and moved towards Rosenberg

'Read the report' blazed Rosenberg 'we have taken the necessary steps to cover our actions until it is safe to do so again.

'Shut up Alfred! We are no better than lepers picking at our sores, we scratch like dogs to cover dung piles, Do you realise what we have done, mien got! The Jews have wept for 2000 years about their Promised Land, what makes you think they or the rest of the World will ever let us forget that we have carried out this abomination! Believe me when I tell you this Rosenberg, the punishment will balance the crime and we will go down in history, not as a master race but as eternal pariahs who have blighted the very being of mankind! We will not be allowed to serve our punishment; we pass our sentences to our children as offspring's of a brotherhood of butchery and inhumanity!

Rosenberg took out his service pistol and shot him between the eyes.

'Read on' he commanded top the others. Speer and the others, numb at what they had witnessed, continued to turn the pages

The Liquidation of the Camps

On November 10, 1944, Kruger, the Supreme SS- and Police Chief of the General Government decreed the places where the Jews and their families were to remain in the ghettos and camps. The continued operation of the three special extermination camps is therefore no longer required as all of those Jews sent to them had been exterminated The Jewish prisoners have been taken from Belzec to Sobibor where they were killed.

.

The report ended with a letter from Otto Globocnik who had been appointed Supreme SS- and Police Chief of Istria, in the region of Trieste. Wirth, Stangl, and the majority of the German personnel from the extermination camps had been transferred there together with him

I concluded Operation Reinhard which I had conducted in the General Goverment and have liquidated all camps. A few SS-men and Ukrainians remained in the extermination camps. In Treblinka even a group of Jewish prisoners was left behind in order to dismantle the huts, fences, and other camp installations. After completion of this work, on November 17, 1943, the last group of Jewish prisoners was shot in Treblinka. The terrain of the former extermination camps was ploughed up, trees were planted, and peaceful-looking farmsteads constructed. A number of Ukrainians from the camp commandos settled there. No traces whatsoever remain.. Written records have been extensively destroyed as you commanded

O.G

Speer threw the report on the table, stood up and leaned against the wall

'What do you propose to do, Rosenberg?

Rosenberg started to speak but Speer stopped him

'We are losing the war in the East, The Allies control our airspace, all of what you said is true but this, this 'Final solution' is why we will all fall'

Rosenberg pushed out his chest

'Faltermayer' he commanded ' we will have the weapons that will reclaim the air as we need them, yes?

Faltermayer was a quietly spoken scientist who had realised as far back as 1932 that he had two choices. One was to throw his lot in with the Nazis who he had found had been very persuasive or run the risk of them finding out that his family bloodline was interspersed by Jews on his mother's side. He decided to volunteer his scientific skills in the hope that the fledgling party would be glad that such an eminent scientist publicly supported them, thus Faltermayer hoped, ensuring that they would not look too closely at his background. It took Rosenberg exactly three weeks to confront him with his ancestry and he'd being doing what he was told to do by Rosenberg ever since. On his instruction, Faltermayer joined the party as a researcher and two years later, he was seconded to a rocket testing facility were he met several other scientist who were working on a rocket combustion system that they finally perfected in June 1942. That was when Alfred Rosenberg had instructed him to suppress his progress reports and ensure that there were 'two' different sets of research analysis results. He was now sitting in a room that in his opinion was full of madmen preparing to assist in making sure that the Fourth Reich as Rosenberg called it actually became a reality. He'd long stopped believing that anyone would ever believe him if he told them that he was 'only following orders'.

'As you are aware' said Faltermayer, not daring to look at Speer 'we've been ready for two years

Speer shouted

'What!

'Faltermayer stuttered 'we were ordered to report our progress directly to Herr Rosenberg and' he trailed off

'Rosenberg' demanded Speer 'what is going on! Are you telling me that we have the weapon now?

Rosenberg straightened his jacket and opened the liquor cabinet, poured himself a drink and then spoke in measured tones

'The little corporal has had his chance, we need the new weapons to carry on the fight and establish the 1000 year Reich. Count Von Stauffenberg has already made an attempt on the Feurher's life and failed' sneered Rosenberg, 'we will not be so careless. Dr. Faltermayer assures me that the plan that he has concocted if administered correctly will kill everyone'.

'Everyone? mused Emmerich

Faltermayer stood up and stepping over the body of Strupper began to speak

'We will turn the bunker into one of the shower room s in the camp, we'll drop a canister of Zyklon C into the air conditioning, and all will die a painless death within minutes of inhalation'.

'You have not explained why! shouted Speer.

'The Fuhrer promised to deliver the two new weapons within days, I presumed that is why you had summonsed me, you had discovered the Thule key and we were going to determine how to use it' Your plan is insanity'.

'Insanity! raged Rosenberg 'I'll tell you insanity!! We worked for twelve years to put him where he was and he had destroyed all of our work in five. We. You, Speer, agreed to our Master plan. Had that been followed, we'd have had a mandate from the entire world to carry out the Final Solution and we would have colonised Britain leaving America no alternative but to become our ally against the Red threat.

'You knew that the Deputy Fuehrer had signed agreements with the Duke of Windsor and the American Ambassador, Joseph P. Kennedy. You also knew that we were never intended to attack Russia until all of Europe had been annexed. Goring along with Goebbels and Himmler convinced the Feurher of his 'invincibility'. Thankfully in Bormann, we have someone who is loyal to us and does all in his power to assist. Now we have gathered here this evening to decide the timing of our attack and to also ensure that we are successful'

'What about the key? asked Speer 'we can do nothing unless we are able to harness its power'

'The key as you call it will come into our possession soon, at this moment our people are bearing down on its whereabouts, once we control it, we will rule the world. 'I have taken steps to keep a link alive, she is now in Buchenwald. No one will question our blood right when we possess the Holiest of Holy. The world will once again bow its knee and swear loyalty to us. Hitler has caused too many problems; he is not Thule and does not understand the destiny. We have already taken steps to integrate our brothers after the war into an organisation called ODESSA. This organisation will promote the true goal of the Thule and will ensure that our legacy remains long after we are gone'

The other two men sat mesmerised at the power of Rosenberg's oratory. They were all Thule members and were completely aware of the destiny of their belief. Speer eventually succumbed to their argument. He asked Rosenberg who was behind ODESSA.

Rosenberg replied

'I have found someone who will do exactly as I command. I met him in Spain when I was attached to the headquarters staff of General Franco. He was a black shirt with a particular taste in subterfuge and blackmail so I had him seconded to the SS Hermann Goring. He has been attached to them for the last five years until recently when I ordered him to begin cultivating his contacts with his Catholic Priest friends in the Vatican. He is an excellent organiser and has already secured safe routes for when the time comes for us to leave.

'Leave?' said Speer

'It may be necessary for us to go away for a while if the war ends on Hitler's death we will need time for negotiations to take place, he will arrange it

'What is his name? asked Emmerich

'His name' replied Rosenberg 'is Licio Gelli'.

Little did they realise that at that very minute, the transcripts of their conversation was been placed on the desk of Admiral Canaris, head of the Abhewr, the German Secret Service.

Chapter 20

In September of 1944 Wilhelm Kertel and Alfred Jodl attended a meeting at Hitler's headquarters in East Prussia.

Hitler was in good form; he smiled when Jodl walked into the command room.

'Kommen sie Alfred' I have good news for you' said Hitler disarmingly ' We will strike a blow that the allies will never recover from!'

Jodl attempted a smile; it was more of a grimace as he stood awaiting his 'good news'

Hitler presented Jodl with the task of coming up with a strategic plan for a major offensive on the Western front.

Hitler spoke to the assembled generals

'I want this offensive to be to be somewhere between the Aachan area and the southern Luxembourg-France boundary. There are only one armoured and four U.S. infantry divisions at this location' is this not correct Jodl?

'Absolutely Mein Fuehrer' snapped Jodl

'Dietrich's Sixth Panzer-Armee will set out twenty miles southeast of Aachan. Mauteuffel's Fifthe PanzerPrum will launch from Schee Eifel plateau. Bramdemburger's Seventh Armee will launch itself from the south close to the Siegfried Line. The Sixth and Fifth armies will drive to Antwerp, with the Seventh and other units protecting the flank'.

Hitler planned to launch the offensive between November 20 and November 30. He was confident the Allies would not be able to react in time to stop the offensive. His plan was dependent upon speed and accuracy. The speed would be provided via the terrain and the woods would provide the cover. Also key to the plan was the weather. Hitler was hoping the attack would occur during weather that would prevent the Allied Air forces from being effective.

Jodl returned with his plan on the 9th October

'This plan had five possible avenues of attack' said Jodl, 'with the northernmost coming from the area near Dusseldorf for thirty-one divisions with one-third of these consisting of armoured infantry. The estimation for fuel called for between four and five millions of gallons along with fifty trainloads of ammunition.

'I have code named this plan, Wacht am Rhein and my strategy is to drive on Antwerp while encircling the Allied armies west of the Meuse River'.

Hitler looked over the papers for some considerable time, eventually he raised his head and looked directly at Jodl

'Wunderbar, Jodl, Wunderbar'

Hitler thought the name of the plan would confuse the Allies into believing it was a defensive operation. The Ardennes was selected as the location for the offensive because the area provided enough cover for a massive build-up of troops and because it was the location where in 1940 Hitler had initiated a surprise attack on France. Hitler believed that by retaking Antwerp the Allies would become irritated with each other and would lead to disputes between the members of the Allies. He believed the bond between the Allies was unstable and could easily be diminished. In doing so Hitler would be able to buy some much-needed time to work on secret weapons and build up troops.

During the months between October and November the Watch am Rhine was renamed Autumn Mist. Hitler changed the name after several of his military commanders tried to convince him to change the plans. The commanders in charge of the offensive, von Runstedt who was his commander of the west, Field Marshall Model, his tactical commander, Josef "Sepp" Dietrich, the leader of the Sixth Panzer Army, and Hoss von Manteuffel, the commander of Fifth Panzer Unit, all of them were sceptical about Hitler's plan. They felt that taking Antwerp was something that just could not be accomplished by the German army at the time. Field Marshall Model said what the others were thinking

"This plan hasn't got a damned leg to stand on".

Hitler was presented with a new smaller plan which changed the objective to only launching a small attack to weaken the Allied forces in the area rather than launching an all out attack to re-take Antwerp. His general's pleaded with him to change the plans but Hitler refused.

Hitler had become unstable. He would not listen to his advising commanders. Von Stauffenberg's assassination attempt had caused him to trust almost no one. Hitler's plan to retake Antwerp was irrational in that the Germans would have no air support and the supplies that they would need were lacking on the ground. Despite all of this, Hitler demanded that they forge ahead.

'I did not wait in 1939, I did not wait in 1940, we will convince the allies to join us and then, we shall see what I will do to the 'untermensch' from the east'.

At 5:30 A.M. on December 6, 1944 eight German armoured divisions and thirteen German infantry divisions launched an all out attack on five divisions of the United States 1st Army. At least 657, light, medium, and heavy guns and howitzers and 340 multiple-rocket launchers were fired on American positions. Between the 5th and 6th Panzer armies, they equalled eleven divisions, broke into the Ardennes through the Loshein Gap against the American divisions protecting the region. The 6th Panzer Army then headed North while the

Fifth Panzer Army went south. Sixth Panzer army attacked the two southern divisions of U. S. V Corps at Elsborn Ridge.

At the same time the 5th Panzer Army was attacking the U. S. VIII Corps some 100 miles to the south. This corps was one of the greenest in Europe at the time and the Germans exploited their lack of experience. They were quickly surrounded and there were mass surrenders.

Manteuffel's Fifth Panzer Army, initially acting as the centre had the mission of crossing the Meuse to the south of the Sixth, but because the river angled away to the southwest might be expected to cross a few hours later than its armored partner on the right. Once across the Meuse, Manteuffel had the mission of preventing an Allied counterattack against Dietrich's left and rear by holding the line Antwerp-BrusselsNamur-Dinant. The left wing of the counteroffensive, composed of infantry and mechanised divisions belonging to Brandenberger's Seventh Army, had orders to push to the Meuse, unwinding a cordon of infantry and artillery facing south and south-west, thereafter anchoring the southern German flank on the angle formed by the Semois and the Meuse. Also, the Fuehrer had expressed the wish that the first segment of the Seventh Army cordon be pushed as far south as Luxembourg City if possible.

Dietrich's Sixth Panzer Army, selected to make the main effort, had a distinct political complexion. Its armoured divisions all belonged to the Waffen SS. Its commander was an old party member, and when regular Wehrmacht officers were assigned to help in the attack preparations they were transferred to the SS rolls.

Josef "Sepp" Dietrich had the appropriate political qualifications to ensure Hitler's trust but, on his military record, hardly those meriting command of the main striking force in the great counteroffensive. By profession a butcher, Dietrich had learned something of the soldier's trade in World War I, rising to the rank of sergeant, a rank which attached to him perpetually in the minds of the aristocratic members of the German General Staff. He had accompanied Hitler on the march to the Feldherrnhalle in 1923 and by 1940 had risen to command the Adolf Hitler Division, raised from Hitler's bodyguard regiment, in the western campaign.

After gaining considerable reputation in Russia, Dietrich was brought to the west in 1944 and there commanded a corps in the great tank battles at Caen. He managed to hang onto his reputation during the subsequent retreats and finally was selected personally by Hitler to command the Sixth Panzer Army. Uncouth, despised by most of the higher officer class, and with no great intelligence, Dietrich had a deserved reputation for bravery and was known as a tenacious and driving division and corps commander. Whether he could command an army remained to be proven.

Jodl despised Dietrich

'The man is not a Prussian officer; he is an oaf, a man of no bearing or substance. I would not permit him to command in my army'.

Von Runstedt replied

'What do you intend to do?

'What can I do? Replied Jodl 'He has been with the Fuerhur from the start, I can do nothing, but I tell you, he will be accountable to me, I will settle for no less!

Von Runstedt was staring at the map

'Where is he now?

'He is attacking along the Monschau to Krewinkel corridor' said Jodl

Dietrich's staff had selected five roads to carry the westward advance, the armour being assigned priority rights on the four southernmost. Actually it was expected that the 1st SS and 12th SS Panzer Divisions would use only one road each. These two routes ran through the 99th Infantry Division sector.

The Meuse had to be reached by the evening of the third day, and crossings to be secured by the fourth.

Three roads were of primary importance in and east of the division area. In the north a main paved road led from Hofen through the Monschau Forest, and then divided as it emerged on the eastern edge.

A second road ran laterally behind the division center and right wing, leaving the Hofen road at the tiny village of Wahlerscheid, continuing south through the twin hamlets of Rocherath and Krinkelt, then intersecting a main eastwest road at Bullingen. This paved highway entered the division zone from the east at Losheimergraben and ran west to Malmedy by way of Bullingen and Butgenbach. As a result, despite the poverty of roads inside the forest belt where the forward positions of the 99th Division lay, the division sector could be entered.

Matteus Netzer had come a long way from his days in the SD, he'd worked in the camps after Heydrich, his mentor, had been assassinated in Prague, Netzer's legacy to his master was to visit his wrath on a small village called Lidice before serving in Buchenwald and Dauchau, he'd still be there other than the need for true blood in the Waffen SS where he was now in command of his own Tiger Tank at last, as far as he was concerned, the objective was clear, his battalion headed up the spearhead in the race to the Muese River and he ordered his men to simply drive over the top of anything that got in his way. He was headed to Baugnez where he been told to report to SS Brigadenfurhur Peipen for new orders.

The initial attack started on the16 December, as Deitrich moved to achieve his objectives of the five roads.

Of the five westward roads assigned the SS Panzer Corps the two above were most important. The main road to Bullingen and Malmedy would be called "C" on the German maps; the secondary road would be named "D." These two roads had been selected as routes for the main armored columns, first for the panzer elements of the I SS Panzer

Corps, then to carry the tank groups of the II SS Panzer Corps composing the second wave of the Sixth Panzer Army's attack. The 277th Volks Grenadier Division, aligned opposite the American 393d Infantry, had a mission that would turn its attack north of the axis selected for the armored advance. Nonetheless, success or failure by the 277th would determine the extent to which the tank routes might be menaced by American intervention from the north.

In the first hours of the advance, then, the 3d Parachute Division would be striking against the 14th Cavalry Group in the Krewinkel-Berterath area. But the final objective of the 3d Parachute attack was ten miles to the northwest, the line Schoppen-Eibertingen on route D.

The first thunderclap of the massed German guns and Werfers was heard by outposts of the 394th Infantry as "outgoing mail," fire from friendly guns, but in a matter of minutes the entire regimental area was aware that something most unusual had occurred. Intelligence reports had located only two horse-drawn artillery pieces opposite one of the American line battalions; after a bombardment of an hour and five minutes the battalion executive officer reported,

'They sure worked those horses to death'.

But until the German infantry were actually sighted moving through the trees, the American reaction to the searchlights and exploding shells was that the enemy simply was feinting in answer to the 2d and 99th attack up north. In common with the rest of the 99th the line troops of the 394th had profited by the earlier quiet on this front to improve their positions by log roofing; so casualties during the early morning barrage were few.

On this part of the forest front the enemy line of departure was inside the woods. The problem, then, was to get the attack rolling through the undergrowth, American barbed wire, and mine fields immediately to the German front. The heavy mist hanging low in the forest enhanced the groping nature of the attack.

In mid afternoon the 12th SS Panzer Division, waiting for the infantry to open the road to the International Highway, apparently loaned a few tanks to carry the fusiliers into the attack The last great German offensive of the War had begun, the Ardennes offensive, Autumn Mist, or what came to be known as 'The Battle of the Bulge'.

When the second day of the battle came to a close, it had become apparent that the German columns advancing in the central sector were aiming at the road system leading to Bastogne. Delayed reports from the 28th Division indicated that an enemy breakthrough was imminent. The 9th Armored Division commander already had sent CCR south to Oberwampach, behind the 28th Division center, when US General Middleton ordered the combat command to set up two strong roadblocks on the main paved road to Bastogne without delay.

In midmorning the troops peering out from the ridge where the northern roadblock had been set up saw figures in field gray entering a patch of woods to the east on the Clerf road, the first indication that the enemy had broken through the Clerf defenses. These Germans belonged to the Reconnaissance Battalion of Lauchert's 2d Panzer Division, whose infantry elements at the moment were eradicating the last American defenders in Clerf. Lauchert's two tank battalions, unaffected by the small arms fire sweeping the Clerf streets were close behind the armored cars and half-tracks of the advance guard.

Luettwitz' XLVII Panzer Corps was coming within striking distance of Bastogne by the evening of 18 December. The 2d Panzer Division, particularly, had picked up speed on the north wing after the surprising delay at Clerf. Luettwitz' mission remained as originally planned, that is, to cross the Meuse in the Namur sector, and the capture of Bastogne remained incidental-although none the less important-to this goal.

Matteus Netzer's tank group had led the assault on enemy positions for Bastogne, there was nothing between him and the Muese. The killings at Malmedy never even crossed his mind as he took up position at the front of Lauchert's spearhead.

The first indication of the nearing assault was a storm of Werfer and artillery shells. Then came the German tanks borrowed from the 2d Panzer Division, ramming forward from the north and east. In the confused action which followed the American tankers conducted themselves so well that Lauchert later reported a "counterattack" from Longvilly against the 2d Panzer flank. But the Shermans and the American light tanks were not only outnumbered but outgunned by the Panthers and the 88's of a flak battalion. The foregone conclusion was reached a little before 1400 when the last of the light tanks, all that remained, were destroyed by their crews who found it impossible to maneuver into the clear. The armored infantry were forced to abandon their half-tracks. The same thing happened to the three tank destroyers. At least eight panzers had been destroyed in the melee, but Longvilly was taken. The ground that was made by the quick thinking Lauchert was all for nothing as the attack floundered on a combination of poor weather, poor supplies and greater American strength.

The German High Command were declaring to the people at home that that this operation was intended to re-establish the military prestige of the Third Reich, carry its people through the gruelling sixth winter of war, and win a favourable bargaining position for a suitable and acceptable peace. In late December German propagandists claimed that the object of the Ardennes offensive had been to cripple the attack capabilities of the Allied armies and chew up their divisions east of the Meuse. Model, and Rundstedt, accepted this as a reasonable tactical objective in the operations from Christmas onward.

The attainment of this goal, to chew up allied divisions and dull the cutting edge of the American armies, was achieved in only limited fashion. The attack of twenty-nine German divisions and brigades destroyed one American infantry division as a unit, badly crippled two infantry divisions, and cut one armoured combat command to pieces.

The American war correspondent, Drew Middleton, most closely approximated the truth when, in the first days of the Ardennes battle, he characterized the offensive as "the Indian summer" of German military might. He'd been feeding the story of the battle back to Adam in London and Adam was writing up his findings in a day by day 'war diary from the front' and sending it out on the wires. Even his old paper had started to syndicate it from him.

Adam had made another two attempts to join Drew in the War theatre but Mollayan had prevented him from being assigned, this was a source of considerable anger for Adam.

'Dammit Henry. I can't sit here until all is over; I'm a reporter for God's sake. You must allow me to go!'

Mollayan had heard it all before and did not even lift his head in response

'You have a greater responsibility Adam; you'll go when I say it is safe to go'.

Adam left the room, slamming the door behind him.

When, on 14 December, Hitler told his generals that German industry had been preparing for the Ardennes offensive for months, he meant this quite literally. Of the total production of armoured fighting vehicles which came out of German assembly plants in November and December 1944, the Western Front received 2,277 while only 919 went to the East. As late as 5 January 1945 all the German armies on the Eastern Front possessed only two thirds the numbers of panzers employed in the Ardennes. Equally important, of course, was Hitler's decision on 20 November to shift the Luftwaffe fighter strength to the Western Front. This diversion of materiel to the west was accompanied by a reallocation of military manpower. On 1 December 1944, the total number of combat effectives under OB WEST command was 416,713, and one month later 1,322,561 effectives were carried on the OB WEST rosters

Rundstedt personally addressed himself to the Fuehrer on 22 December with a plea that the Ardennes offensive be brought to a halt in order to reinforce the Eastern Front

Guderian, directly charged with operations against the Russians, used the occasion of official visits on Christmas Eve and New Year's Day to petition Hitler for the movement of troops from the west to the east.

At the end of December, in the Ardennes headquarters, Guderian telephoned the Fucrhur

"Everybody looks with dismay to the east where the big Russian offensive is about to begin any day." I must have tanks, planes but most of all, I must have men!

Hitler stubbornly refused to accede to all these requests, even after the Allied counterattack on 3 January began to collapse the German salient. Inexplicably he waited until 8 January to start the Sixth Panzer Army moving for the east.

This was only four days before the commencement of the Russian winter offensive.

Canaris himself had summonsed Rosenberg to Berlin for what he described as a 'long talk'. He dispatched two of his Abhewr operatives to accompany him.

'Why have I been brought here like this?' demanded Rosenberg

Admiral Canaris never even lifted his head

'Sit down' he commanded

Rosenberg sat down and was about to launch into another tirade when Canaris brought his hand swiftly down on his desk

'Enough! As you sit, I could have you shot as a traitor, I could hand you over to the SS. Do you know what they did with the co conspirators of the Stauffenberg plot?

I'll tell you, they were strung up with piano wire in public and then beheaded and incinerated. Now, do I have your attention?' snarled Canaris.

Rosenberg sat in a state of perplexed confusion and visibly wilted as Canaris spelled out the fates of his co-conspirators.

'I have a firsthand account of how you shot a General of the Wehrmacht, which is murder! Furthermore Professor Emmerich and Faltermayer have been attached to the Fuehrer's personal staff in the Fuerherbunker as liaison officers'. Speer is elsewhere in this building helping us with our enquiries.

Rosenberg knew now that the Thule had been compromised and that he was exposed and at the mercy of Canaris

'What do you want me to do?' said Rosenberg

'You will go back to your desk in Berlin as if nothing has happened; you will not make contact with any of your co conspirators on any account. You will bring me any artifacts belonging to you or the traitor Hess and you will in no way continue this foolish search for this mystical weapon that does not exist'

'But you do not underst….

'Silence' hissed Canaris 'these are my terms, sign this letter and get out of my sight!

Rosenberg bent down and scribbled his signature on what was effectively his death warrant; he threw the pen down and walked to the door, opened it and walked out into the corridor. He sat down for a minute to compose himself and think about his situation when another armed detail marched around the corner, in the middle of the detachment was the figure of Albert Speer, no doubt about to receive the same fate as Rosenberg.

Inside the office, Canaris breathed a sigh of relief. He went to his wall safe and took out a diary with a black cover and an ornate design on the front. Into it he placed the letters of both Rosenberg and Speer.

Chapter 21

It was dawn in the camp. Gray fingers of light groped across the retreating blackness of the retreating night and the first whisper of the wind whistled its arrival through the slats of the hut where Maria was lying.

For days now, Maria had noticed that the camp guards were becoming increasingly restless. They'd stepped up the selections in the last five months and there were now less than 2000 people in the camp, describing them as people is a misnomer, Maria corrected herself, 2000 souls in the camp. She'd been in Buchenwald since being driven overland from Birkenau at the head of a death march. There had been rumours some time ago about an uprising in Warsaw and when Maria tried to discover what had happened, she didn't have long to wait. That had been the last 'selection' she witnessed in Birkenau before her move.

She had been summoned to the gates on this particular evening with the rest of the musicians and ordered to set up and make ready for their performance.

A small locomotive stood ready in the railroad station to transport the first section of freight cars into the camp. Everything had been planned and prepared in advance. The train consisted of 60 closed freight cars fully loaded with people: young ones, old ones, men and women, children and babies. The car doors were locked from the outside and the air holes covered with barbed wire. On the running boards on both sides and on the roof about a dozen SS-soldiers stood or lay with machine guns at the ready. It was hot and m the people in the freight cars were deadly exhausted.

As the train came nearer it seemed as if an evil spirit haa taken hold of the waiting SS-men. They drew their pistols, returned them to their holsters, pulled them out again, as if they wanted to shoot and kill. They approached the freight cars and tried to reduce the noise and the weeping; but then they screamed at the Jews and cursed them, all the while urging the railroad workers to hurry: "Quick, faster!" After that they returned to the camp in order to receive the deportees. As the train approached the gates, the engine blew a prolonged whistle that was the signal for the Ukrainians to man their position in the reception sector and on the roofs of the buildings. It was also the signal for Maria and her musicians to begin to play. One group of SS-men and Ukrainians took up positions on the station platform. As soon as the train was moving along the tracks inside the camp, the gates behind it were closed. The deportees were taken out of the freight cars and conducted through a gate to a fenced-in square inside the camp. At the gate they were separated: men to the right, women and children to the left. A large placard announced in Polish and German:

Attention Warsaw Jews! You are in a transit camp from which the transport will continue to labour camps. To prevent epidemics, clothing as well as pieces of baggage is to be handed over for disinfection. Gold, money, foreign currency, and jewellery are to be deposited at the "Cash Office" against a receipt. They will be returned later on presentation of the receipt. For physical cleanliness, all arrivals must have a bath before travelling on'.

The undressing procedure and the manner in which the victims were led to the gas chambers was the same as ever yet it never got any easier for the musicians who knew where the victims were going but daren't show emotion lest they suffer the same fate. .

The cars were full of corpses. The bodies were partly decomposed by chlorine. The stench in the cars made those still alive, choke. Waiting SS and Ukrainians beat them and shot at them... On the way to the gas chambers Germans with dogs stood along the fence on both sides. The dogs had been trained to attack people; they bit the men's genitals and the women's breasts, ripping off pieces of flesh. The Germans hit the people with whips and iron bars to spur them on so that they pressed forward into the "showers" as quickly as possible. The screams of the women could be heard far away, even in the other parts of the camp. The Germans drove the running victims on with shouts of: "Faster, faster, the water will get cold; others still have to go under the showers!" To escape from the blows, the victims ran to the gas chambers as quickly as they could, the stronger ones pushing the weaker aside. At the entrance to the gas chambers stood the two Ukrainians, Ivan Demaniuk and Nikolai, one of them armed with an iron bar, the other with a sword. Since the chambers were overcrowded and the victims held on to one another, they all stood upright and were like one single block of flesh. Breakdowns and interruptions occurred in the operation of the gas chambers. If such mishaps occurred when the victims were already inside the gas chambers, they were left standing there until the engines had been repaired.

And all the while Maria and her orchestra of pathetic souls played merry tunes and wore painted smiles.

They all heard the rumours that the Russians or the Americans w were coming. She'd known about the camps in the East being evacuated, some of the inmates had ended up with her in Buchenwald. The German activity had definitely changed and it certainly looked as if there was something wrong. They had heard the boom of guns in the distance for some time now and as another Christmas, 1944 passed, Maria detected a definite change in the attitude of the Kapos. She been in the medical bloc for ten days, she had originally been sent in to help the doctor but had contracted some sort of virus and found herself locked in with the sick people at night.

The doctor, a French Jew, had been kept alive purely for his skills and he had been kindly towards Maria, he was able to convince the Kapo that he needed her in the bloc on an almost regular basis. He stressed that the ward now had several cases of Typhus and he wouldn't want to run the risk of her spreading the disease.

She'd been lying awake waiting for the Appell call when she thought she heard the boom of a gun. She jumped up and ran to the door... the guards were nowhere to be seen. She went over to the cot and woke her two friends.

'Quick, get up, there is something wrong' urged Maria

'What is it?

'The kapo has gone, there is nobody outside and they haven't sounded Appell yet' said Maria. The doctor rushed into the room

'They've gone' he gasped 'we're the only ones that are left'.

They went to the door, down the steps and onto the open ground in front of the huts, several other bunches of women had come outside when they heard it again, the boom of a gun. Things started to happen very quickly then. First of all the gates to the men's camp opened and the men came across. The older children were running through the huts shouting

'They've gone, they've gone. There's no one here!

Maria was shaken to the core, 'Gone', 'where' flashed through her mind as she walked across to the place where she played in the Orchestra. The train ramp was empty, the watch towers were empty. She heard a shout and when she turned, four of the inmates had caught one of the female kapos hiding in one of the hut. They dragged her out by the hair and started screaming

'She murdered our babies! Kill her, Kill her!

By the time Maria got across to the place, the woman was an unrecognisable bloody mess on the ground; it was if she'd been savaged by wild dogs. The men had started to move around the camp calling out the names of their loved ones or walking in a daze. Maria began to shake and then wail as she realised that the Germans had gone, they were free!

What Maria didn't know was that a decision had been taken the previous evening to evacuate the camp. The kapos and Blockaltesters hadn't even bothered with evening appell, it was if they were in total shock as the dawning of the decision riveted into their brains. The torturers had finally reached the end of their reign and the inmates knew it. The SS then arrived and whipped everyone into 'zu funct' columns of five, they'd abandoned the sick in the blocs without food, but not before they'd ferreted out several inmates who they thought were trying to hide and promptly hung them up on piano wire to die, burning their bodies so as to leave no evidence. Maria had slept through most of this as the women had been moved early in the morning, several hours after the men had left. Maria stood in the middle of the compound, her eyes scanning the perimeter, her ears pricked for any noise that spelled danger she heard a noise behind her and turned to see a young boy of about 12 standing in front of her. He was painfully thin and had sores on his body, she went over and asked him his name but he would not answer, instead he put his hand in her hand and refused to let go.

Maria called out to a man who was running past…

'What is happening?

'We have survived! The guards are gone, the Americans are coming, we saw the jeeps in the men's camp just before dawn, and we are free. Come with me, someone said that there is a lorry over at the guardhouse, we are going to drive it out of here.'

Maria and the boy followed the man across to the guardhouse where several other inmates had managed to start a truck, Maria could see several bodies on the ground, and at least she thought they were bodies. One of the men, Jacob, was sitting behind the wheel of the truck, his shirt was covered in blood and he had a whip and a gun

'We tore at them with our bare hands ' he said ' they couldn't stop us and screamed for mercy when we got them' We have to escape, get food. I am from Silesia but I know the area, we will try and reach the partisans in the forest or try and get back to Munich.'

Maria climbed into the truck with the boy, the truck started and they headed straight out of the main gates. They passed the crematorium, two of them had been damaged but were still standing. The buildings that held all of the camp records were blazing, a small bonfire was raging outside as the mountain of meticulous reports flashed up in the air in flames in a vain attempt to scream the truths that the fire was consuming. There were no SS anywhere as the lorry crashed through the gates of Arbeit Macht Frei for the last time.

Chapter 22

Andrew had wakened early, he hadn't been able to sleep that previous evening, the numbing cold had knawed at his very soul and he had lain awake for most of the night contemplating the forsaken state that he found himself in. He tried on several occasions to find the old man and his son but had failed miserably, all of the inmates in the striped suits looked the same to him. He watched the treatment meted out to those inmates with the star on their uniform, he'd seen how their camp number had been burned into their arms and how they'd been brutally treated by, in many cases their own people. Andrew had been lucky, he's been classified a political prisoner and had a red stripe put on the front of his jacket.

He'd listened the previous day as the Kapo and the Blockalster had spewed out their hate filled instruction to the newcomers in sneering tones

'You are here because you deserve to be here; whilst you are here you will do exactly as we tell you. You have not been brought here to relax, you have been brought here to work and work is what you shall do. Prisoners who do their work should have no cause for concern, they will be left alone. Woe betide any of you who show the slightest insolence or resistance to orders, we do not tolerate any infractions of the rules'

Andrew couldn't believe what he was seeing let alone hearing, he couldn't comprehend how man could do what these men were doing to their fellow man. The tirade continued

'Break the rules and you will suffer the standard *funfundzwanzig auf arsch*, 25 lashes across your bare arsh my sweeties. If we catch you at sabotage, you will hang. The first lesson you must learn is one of respect.

'When you hear the word Aufstehen, you will react without a moment's delay. If you are late to any appell call you will be punished. When you are told to Antreten, you will fall into line and you will waste no time in doing so. You will not flinch nor look right or left, you will be statues until you are told to move. When you hear the words Mutzen ab, you will smartly remove your hat and slap your hand against your thigh, Mutzen Auf, you will put your hat back on your head.

'Lose your shoes and you will march barefoot, lose any other part of your uniform and you will be punished.'

On and on it went, hour after hour, day after day. Andrew quickly learned that the slightest infraction of the rules meant possible death. He'd witnessed two occasions when in both cases prisoners had been slow to react, one of them had be drowned in a vat of soup because a passing SS officer had seen him spill a little of it onto the ground. The second man had been walking across the main parade ground when a shot rang out and he fell down dead. Apparently the camp commandant liked to practice his shooting and often sighted his rifle from the balcony of his house, sniping at anyone who happened to stumble across his crosshairs. It was said that he'd killed nearly 200 prisoners in this way.

Despite all of this lunacy, the camp was still flooded with rumours of advances by the allies. On one of the days, everyone in the camp had been startled by a low flying plane bearing the single white star of America on its wing tips. The guards were becoming more and more barbarous and the damned smell never went away. If anything the crematoria were working harder that ever. People were dying quickly and the bestial competition between the Kapos and the Lithuanians continued. Andrew had noticed that some new people had arrived in the camp and when he eventually managed to question one of them, he discovered that the camps in the East had been evacuated, the man, a small, pathetically thin man from Paris had explained to him that nearly 5000 prisoners had been gathered together and force marched from Auschwitz, if anyone fell behind, the SS shot them on the spot. When they arrived in Mauthausen, there were only 1900 of them left. Andrew then learned of a German pastor; a man called Bonnhoffer who had supposedly been sent there because he'd been involved in the plot to kill Hitler. Andrew was astounded, a plot to kill Hitler, could it be true? The little Frenchman was still talking

'Tell me about this place, what have you learned?' he persisted 'Can we escape?'

Andrew stared at the little man, was he mad?

'Listen to me' said Andrew gripping the little man by the lapels of his jacket 'listen and just maybe you'll stay alive'

Andrew proceeded to describe the confines of the camp

'The entrance to the SS headquarters is located on the northwest side of the camp. At the entrance stand wide gates that lead into the two-story stone administration building in the SS section of the camp. To the left and right inside the gate, there are rows of wooden barracks, which house the camp guards. When on duty the higher-ranking SS men spend the night there, but they usually dwell in the handsome wooden villas located on the south-western slope of the village. Also located in the outer region of the camp, are the workshops, offices, and storage rooms for the prisoners' possessions that have been confiscated earlier upon arrival. The commandant's office is also located here, and directly in front of that is the area called the mustering place. This large open area, measuring 120 by 40 meters, is where we face roll call multiple times each day. The whole camp is surrounded by an electric fence'.

Andrew could feel beads of perspiration breaking on his forehead as he concentrated on the words he had read in the testimony whilst at the same time relaying his own knowledge of what he had seen. He continued

'The prison camp and outer SS area is surrounded during the day by a long chain of guards. A double fence encloses the prison camp as well as the special camp for the Russians. The inner fence consists of thickly interwoven barbed wire, while the smooth upper strands of the outer fence are electrified. We discovered this because two of the musclemen tried to climb over it, the guards didn't even shoot at them, and they just watched their bodies fry on the wire.' Andrew grimaced at the memory of it.

'Both day and night, six large watchtowers armed with guards with heavy machine guns and hand grenades patrol the area of the prisoners. There are also 12 small sentry towers that contain guards with light machine guns and also four massive bunkers. So put all ideas of escape out of your head'.

'How long have you been here? he asked Andrew

'Not long 'replied Andrew 'but long enough to know that an escape attempt is futile,

What barrack are you in?

'14' replied the Frenchman

You must watch the Kapo in there, he is a German convict and is vicious'.

'Thanks for the advice' said then Frenchman before melting away into the new arrivals.

The world outside the camps was changing by the day unbeknown to either Maria or Andrew. Hitler and his generals had committed all of his forces to a mighty offensive in the West. Hitler himself had established headquarters at Ziengenberg near Frankfurt and had plotted the Ardennes offensive himself. Buoyed by initial gains and the overrunning of several American positions, until notably in the town of Bastogne, the Americans under the command of General

McAuliffe held ground long enough for relief from General Patton's Third Army to reach them, effectively ending the German onslaught. They had lost some 120,000 soldiers, 600 tanks and assault guns and the Luftwaffe had all but been wiped out, suffering nearly 1600 losses in the air. The situation was exacerbated immensely when on the 12 January 1945, Marshall Konev's Russian army group broke out of its bridge head at Baranov and together with Zukov's forces crossed the Vistula and headed for Silesia at speed. Fifteen days later Zukov's forces were 100 miles from Berlin.

The night of April 15 seemed endless to the 1.3 million veteran soldiers of the Red Army waiting along the rivers Oder and Neisse in eastern Germany. They were poised for the great assault on Berlin-the "final hour of vengeance, " as Marshal Georgy K. Zhukov called it. It was the chance to pay back the hated Germans for the rape of the Russian homeland, for Keiv and Stalingrad, for the deaths of loved ones and friends.

A slogan scrawled on one of the waiting tanks read "50 kilometres to the lair of the fascist beast." Victory was close enough to taste. In a command bunker overlooking the Kustrin bridgehead at the centre of the Oder line, Zhukov and his aides sipped strong, hot tea as they watched the crawling hands of the clock. Farther south, along the Neisse, where Marshal Ivan S. Konev was in command, the waiting was equally tense. Before dawn on the 16th, the onslaught began. Along the Oder signal flares burst high over the river; instantly the thundering flashes of thousands upon thousands of heavy guns split the foggy darkness. For more than half an hour the cannonade continued; then the Russians hurled themselves into the attack.

On the Neisse, the crossing proceeded under a dense smoke screen. The Germans were waiting in strength. Anticipating the bombardment, the German commander on the Oder, General Gotthard Heinrici, during the night had pulled his men out of front - line positions to Seelow Heights, a formidable crescent of bluffs set back several miles from the river's west bank. "When one of his officers protested the withdrawal, Heinrici responded: "You don't put your head under a trip hammer, do you? You pull it back in time." Now, with the Russians floundering across the marshy terrain below the highlands, he hit them with everything he had. As the attack became mired in the mud, Zhukov angrily ordered his two tank armies into action ahead of schedule to force the issue by sheer weight of arms-but he succeeded only in creating a gigantic traffic jam. By the end of the first and the second day, his hammer blow at Germany's heart was still bogged down in the Oder swamps.

Hitler had now taken up residence in the Chancellery in Berlin where he summonsed Jodl to discover his views on the pending situation. Ribbentrop and Guderian had been denounced as traitors because they had clamoured for an armistice to be signed with the allies in the hope that all could then turn to meet the Bolshevik 'threat'. They sat there clinging to the belief that they'd receive a communiqué from the Allies asking for their help in defeating the Russians. The following weeks and months convinced them that it would never happen as the allies smashed into Germany on all sides and an ever decreasing band of soldiers retreated into a last defence of Berlin.

On April 20 American Armies reached Nuremberg and Zukov was on the outskirts of Berlin.

Mayer, the camp commandant of Flossenberg shouted from the office

'We have been ordered to evacuate the camp! The allies have broken through and could be here at any moment, shoot those not fit to walk!'

He continued to shovel papers onto the burning fire; all of the scrupulously maintained records of genocide were now going the same way as the souls they referred to, up a chimney.

He'd ordered his troops to take the rest of the Jews across to Dachau. The prisoners of Flossenburg were facing their final trials. More than 15,000 men and women were forced to leave the camp behind in a Death March. As the fire burned, Reinhard Mayer began to take off his uniform. He removed the black jacket with the grinning skulls of death and took off his shirt and tie; he pulled at his britches and threw his patent leather riding boots out of the window. He pulled on the uniform of a Wehrmacht soldier, a tank Grenadier.

It was torn and there were bloodstains on the arm, Mayer wasn't that worried how he looked, he knew that if he was picked up he was facing summary execution. He'd already managed to move some of the gold that he had stolen to a safe location and the two Lorries loaded with the stolen artifacts had left the camp three weeks previous under the command of his sergeant. He knew that they were headed for some caves up near Lake Como. He hoped to pass himself off as a common soldier and get lost in the general melee.

Three days later, an advance battalion of US Cavalry liberated Flossenburg. They entered the camp and were greeted with the overpowering smell of death, bodies were piled in mountains of death, and those inmates that survived sat on the ground staring at the sky. When the soldiers went into the camp, they were appalled at what they found, the crematoria were supposed to have been blown up but the fuses had failed. They found rooms filled with human hair, one with spectacles. Shoes, Clothes. They had liberated a 'death factory'. On the third day, medical people arrived along with two press teams who started photographing everybody. The camp had been searched from top to bottom, they'd found nine guards hiding in the forest surrounding fields, they were taken back to the camp and shot after being made to dig their own graves. Given the evidence that confronted them, it was not surprising that the soldiers should have assumed that the bodies found in the mortuary, on the floor of the gas chamber, and next to the old crematorium had been victims of the gas chamber.

The crematorium was a long low brick structure with a tall smokestack from which smoke poured day and night. The gas chamber was 20 feet square and has 18 nozzles across the ceiling that looked like shower outlets. Most if not all of the dead found in these areas perished through starvation, exposure, sickness, mistreatment, and execution by means other than poison gas.

Outside, there was still a plentiful supply of cans with something called Zyclon-B on the ground

The cans bore the name of the manufacturer, A.E.G. FARBEN INDUSTRIE

To the outside of the gas chamber door were attached forms for keeping records:

Gasheit, time of gassing. Zu, Close. . . Uhr, Time...

Auf, Finish. . . Uhr, Time. . .

Below that was the sign of a skull with two cross bones and a warning:

Vorsicht, Careful. . . G A S

Lebensgefahr, Danger to Life

Nicht Offenen, Do Not Open

On the fourth day, Captain William Prenter was manning the office that had been set up to try and gather information on who was in charge and to try and assemble some logic to the madness that they found themselves in. The officers couldn't venture out into the camp for fear of disease, many of the inmates were in the death throes of dysentery and there had been a serious cholera outbreak. He had ordered that no inmates were to be taken for questioning until the medical people had cleared them. Captain Prenter had just received the numbers of those who had died through the night and was about to call his headquarters when the door knocked

'Come in'

The sergeant at arms entered the room and went over to the desk

‘There is an inmate who would like to speak to you urgently sir.’

‘Has he cleared medical? asked the captain

‘Yes sir, he’s in fair health considering what he has been through’

‘Very well Sergeant, send him in, do you know his name?

‘Yes sir, his name is Andrew Lassiter and he claims to be a Catholic chaplain.’

Andrew Lassiter was shown into the office of Captain Prenter.

‘Sit down’ invited the Captain ‘what can I do for you?

‘My name is Andrew Lassiter and I am a Catholic Priest, I have been an inmate in this camp for 7 months and I wish to make contact with my superiors and report my whereabouts. I have also documented the happenings in this camp and I want to discuss them with you’

How did you end up here? asked Prenter

Andrew relayed his story from the time of his arrest in the village to his arrival in the camp; he stopped and then looked at the Captain

‘The war? Is it over?

‘As good as’ said the Captain, ‘we were told that the Russians attacked Berlin this morning, we are hearing unconfirmed reports that Hitler and Goebbels are in Berlin in the Bunker. All of our military police are searching for Himmler and Muller. There is some sporadic fighting going on in Berlin and in the Black Forest, other than that; we seem to be in complete control.

Andrew Lassiter shuddered and then started to cry, tears cascaded down his cheeks and he sobbed uncontrollably.

After he had gathered himself, Andrew was asked if he could assist Captain Prenter in his investigations.

'We have only been able to find four camp guards in the whole place; we have them in custody although I don't know how long we can keep them from the Jews. We've already had to shoot above the heads of inmates who rushed the stockade in an attempt to get at them'. There were only 2000 prisoners in the camp. We got reports that some of our advance parties had discovered a lot of bodies up on the road towards Namering along highway N-14 toward the Czech border. Had we not stopped the inmates, they'd have torn this place to shreds'.

'You can hardly blame them' said Andrew 'Have you any idea what the Nazis have perpetrated on these people!

'We have a holding pen down in the town, if you are feeling up to it; I'd like you to accompany me to see if you can recognise anyone'.

'I will do all in my power to bring these animals to justice' raged Andrew

It still hadn't sunk in that he was free, he sat back in the chair and looked around the room, Andrew spied the telephone sitting on the side of the desk

'Can I make a call on that? asked Andrew

'Yes of course, go through to the Operator and he will patch you through'

'Could you do it for me, please? asked Andrew

'Very well, said the Captain 'Who do you wish me to call'

'Person to Person to the Vatican in Rome, I wish to speak to a Father Philip Rossi.

William Prenter stared at Andrew Lassiter in disbelief 'That's a faraway call… father'

Andrew started to shudder again at the mention of the word 'Father' he'd grown used to 130995 and responded accordingly.

Prenter paused 'let me see what I can do'

Father Rossi had just returned from Mass and was about to go to his office when he was called to the reception area at the Secretariat building

'Father Rossi, there is a person to person call to you from Germany, a Captain Prenter wishes to speak with you'

Rossi paused

'I know no-one of that name' as he walked across to the desk, he was handed the receiver 'Hello'

'Si'

'Is that Father Rossi? Father Philip Rossi

'Si'

'My name is Captain William Prenter; I am currently in charge of investigations at Flossenberg concentration camp in Germany. I have with me, someone who would like to speak with you......

Prenter handed the receiver to Andrew who cleared his throat and spoke faintly

'Father Rossi?

'Who is this, I cannot hear you'

'Is it safe?

Father Rossi froze where he stood, sweat broke out on his forehead and he started to stumble forward, he gripped the phone and shouted

WHO IS THIS?

Andrew's eyes welled up again as he spoke into the receiver

'Philip, it's me, Andrew ... is it safe?

'Yes Yes! shouted Rossi 'Where, how ....

The line clicked dead in his hand. He felt himself falling and when he came around, the receptionist was mopping his forehead with water

'You fainted, Father. Are you all right?

'He is alive, Praise be, He is Alive!'

Chapter 23

'But the war is nearly over, surely there is no threat from the Nazis now? said Adam.

Mollayan snorted.

'We have protected the Yahweh for nearly a century; the Nazis were the latest in a long line of gold diggers and trouble makers looking for the secret. You seem to have conveniently forgotten about the Catholic Church and the Freemasons. Just because the war is over, that does not make you safe, on the contrary. We will take our time. You can return to your family for a while, you'll be safer in America and I'll send for you when we are ready to move'.

The past two years had passed Adam by in a maelstrom of unfulfilled ambition and frustration. He had failed to convince Mollayan to allow him to travel with the press corps to Rome after it was liberated. He'd watched as D Day came and went as he kicked his heels in a safe house in London, working with Mollayan on the origins of the Yahweh and fitting in the testimony that they'd received from Rome. Mollayan was now attached to the SOE department at the War Cabinet and even when he left on some of his clandestine meetings, he always ensured that Adam was practically kept locked under constant observation

Part of Adam was angry yet he knew that he could do nothing at the moment. There was too much still to understand and Mollayan was right, Adam could be protected much easier in America than in London. He was about to concur when the thought of Maria and then Andrew came into his mind.

'I will do as you say on one condition'

Mollayan looked up....

'And what would that be?

'I will do as you say but only after I have satisfied myself as to the fate of Maria and the Priest. If there is any chance that they are alive or need our help, then I stay'.

Mollayan could see that there was no point in trying to sway him on this

'Very well' he said 'There has been a 'displacement agency' set up. I will try and find out what I can'.

There were bodies everywhere, lying on the road, in the fields, in the rivers, the stench was unbearable and there were flies swarming in thick clouds of black, the noise they made as nauseating as the stench. The lorry had traveled about 25 miles before it ran out of petrol and the group had split up, some of the men wanted to try and reach the forest and join the partisans. The rest of the inmates decided to start walking as best they could towards the border. They could only manage a couple of miles at a time and spent the rest of the time foraging for berries and water. Maria had managed to find a large coat, she'd taken it from a dead soldier, she also found a scarf. She sat on the ground and her new friend, the boy from the camp lay sleeping in her lap. Every now and again he would cry out in his sleep but other than those noises he had yet to speak a word.

Maria knew that she would have to leave the group, there were too many of them and they were too conspicuous in the countryside. She had seen no evidence of any soldiers on the ground yet but she thought that the planes flying overhead were American because they didn't attack them. It was dusk when the boy woke and Maria told him that she was leaving, he held on to her and as she got up to go, he jumped up.

'Tttake me! The boy mumbled as a single tear rolled down his cheek.

Maria hugged him and then led him by the hand from the shed they were staying in, out onto the road. They hurried away from the shed and walked for about two hours until they came across a ruined church. Maria was tired and decided to rest up for the evening. She went over to the entrance and stepped inside. There was little of the roof remaining and there were shell holes in two of the walls. As she moved along she spotted water in a font.

She cupped her hands and tasted it, letting it go into her mouth and then submersing her face into it. She then called to the boy and bade him to do the same. She had her back to the altar and was looking for something to lie on when she heard a noise

'Who is there?

Maria spun around and looked for an escape, the boy stood rigid, as if suspended in time; the voice was coming from the front of the church. They moved towards the door

'Wait, don't go, I won't hurt you, look.....'

Maria stood and watched an old man come from behind the altar, he was limping and was only able to walk with the aid of a stick. As he got closer, Maria could see that he was no threat to them

'Who are you? she said.

'My name is Andrei, I was going to try and reach Krakow to try and find my son, he'd been taken there by the Germans to work in one of their factories. Two days ago three soldiers came into the church, I hid in the sacristy and I overheard them saying that the Russians were in Krakow and the war was lost. The soldiers stayed the night and when they left the next morning; their uniforms were lying on the seats over there.

'Show me' commanded Maria

The old man shuffled over to the seat and pulled over a black jacket, he was handing it to Maria when the boy rushed forward, snapped the uniform from the old man's hand and started to tear and pull at it; he stood on it until it began to tear. Maria and the old man watched as the boy savagely destroyed the coat. When he was finished he sat down on the floor and began to cry, a whimper at first but as they watched, he sobbed and shook to the point of convulsion. The old man knelt down and took him in his arms. Maria was crying as well, the old man said

'Stay here this evening, I have some bread and I found some wine in the cellar. I have lit a fire behind the altar and you can rest tonight'.

What is your name?

'My name? Maria stared at the old man; she had not been asked her name in six years of being in various prisons and camps. She looked blankly and again started to cry, a wail of despair and torture, she couldn't get the words to form

'MMMMyyy nnnname iiiissss MMMaria, Mmaria TTTTTannenbaum.

Maria couldn't know that orders existed to keep her alive all that time; Rosenberg had concluded that he never knew when he might need her.

Prenter spent hours talking to Andrew Lassiter.

Andrew told him all that he could remember whilst Prenter showed him photographs of people and Nazis that they were looking for. Andrew looked through the photographs and stopped at one

'Who is this? he asked pointing to a photograph

'We believe him to be Admiral Canaris, head of the Abhwer'

'He's dead' said Andrew flatly.

'How can you be sure? said Prenter.

'What date is it? asked Andrew

'Today is the 24 of April' said Prenter

'It was about three weeks ago ...

'We were all summonsed to the front parade ground by Mayer, he was the Camp Commandant. We watched as ten men were paraded in front of us. They were ordered to strip and were flogged in front of us. One of the men had been in Flossenburg from 1939. His name was Johann Esler and he told me that he had tried to execute Hitler in 1939. I also watched them flog a pastor, his name was Bonhoeffer, they threatened to crucify him unless he rejected his God. He refused to do so and was beaten without mercy and carried to a gallows where they hung him with piano wire and allowed his body to stay there for four days. On that day, the man in the picture was murdered as well along with another officer; he must have been high ranking because Mayer tore red epaulettes from his jacket and struck him in the face with his whip. As these murders were going on, the Camp was emptying at a fast rate. The huts were also filled with bodies as the guards went on what could only be described as blood frenzy, they had a problem, there were still too many of us to kill. I was lucky because an old man showed me where to go and hide if there ever was trouble like this'.

'Where is the old man now? Asked Prenter

Andrew stared over towards the still smoking crematoria building

'He's gone' he shuddered

Given the circumstances and the threat that Canaris, now dead, was to his plans, all things considered Albert Rosenberg was a reasonably happy man. He realised a long time ago that the war was lost and that he would have to flee the country. The millions and millions of currency that he'd stashed over the past six years plus the art work and the gold bullion that had been systematically looted from every country in Europe would ensure that he would not have any trouble. Always the manipulator, he'd set a train of events in place that would completely rip the heart out of the old movement whilst protecting the remnants of the Thule at the same time. He'd discovered that Himmler was secretly meeting with Count Bernadotte, a Swedish diplomat, to engineer surrender to Eisenhower in the West. Roosevelt was dead and Rosenberg rightly guessed that Eisenhower would have 'de facto' power in Europe. Goering had all but committed suicide because he had reacted to the prompting of Rosenberg and activated a testament document written by Hitler in 1941 that declared that in the event of anything happening to Hitler, Goering was nominated to accede him to power. Goering sent a message into the chancellery bunker in Berlin

'My Fuehrer

In view of your decision to remain in the fortress of Berlin, do you agree that I take over at once the total leadership of the Reich, with full freedom of action at home and abroad as your deputy in accordance with your decree of June 29 1941? If no reply is received by 10 o'clock tonight, I shall take it for granted that you have lost your freedom of action and shall consider the conditions of the decree to be fulfilled, and shall act in the best interests of our people. You know what I felt for you at this gravest hour of my life. Words fail me to express myself. May God protect you, and speed you quickly here in spite of all.

Your Loyal

Hermann Goering

Speer was in the bunker when the message was relayed to Hitler. He immediately called Rosenberg

'Goering has been stripped of his office, is to be arrested and shot as a traitor. He is no longer a party member and has been declared an enemy of the Reich by the Fuehrer' said Speer. 'Furthermore, forget any plans you had to introduce gas into the bunker, they've built a 12 foot fortified chimney over the ventilation shaft, the SS will shoot anyone who goes within ten meters of it'

'No matter' said Rosenberg 'this is going better than even I could have imagined'. In a few hours time the Fuerhur will learn of Heine's treachery as well. Now do what you have to do, say your goodbyes and get out of there as fast as you can. I've heard reports that the Russians are in The Tiergarten. You would not want to be in the bunker when they arrive'

Speer's hand gripped the telephone

'The Fuerhur and Dr. Goebbels have decided to remain in the bunker to the last. The Fuehrer is to be married this evening to Fraulein Braun...

'Gut' said Rosenberg 'A noble death, should serve our cause well in the coming times'

'What cause?' hissed Speer

'My dear Speer' replied Rosenberg ' this defeat is but a setback, we will regroup and gather our strength and then we will be reborn, believe me when I tell you, the Fourth Reich will not make the same mistakes as the Third one has. We will forge alliances with the Americans and then we'll see how strong the 'untermensch' from the East really are. We will be strong as Krupp steel, we shall ... Speer, Speer, shouted Rosenberg Speer,

Do you hear me Speer, we shall be great, I, Alfred Rosenberg have seen it in the stars, we will possess the Yahweh and the world will bend at our knees, Sppeeer!

Albert Speer stared at the handset that he had placed on the table, no lessons learned, all the killing, the sacrifice, for what?

He stepped back out of the room and headed back along the corridor, he had one last thing to do. He knocked the door and a voice called out

'Enter'

Speer opened the door and walked inside, the man sitting behind the desk looked up and then said

'The Fuerhur is making plans for the relief of the city; he is not to be disturbed'

'It is you I wish to speak to' as he sat down at the desk of Martin Bormann.

Chapter 24

Prenter hadn't allowed Andrew to go outside the confines of the camp as there were hundreds of corpses piled at the entrance of the camp, each of them were dressed in the camp uniform and had a bullet hole in the back of their head.

Prenter sat silently as he listened to Andrew's tale. The telephone rang and he picked it up

'It is a call for you'

'Hello'

'Is that Andrew Lassiter? Father Andrew Lassiter?'

'Yes'

'My name is Mulroney; I'm a chaplain with General Patton's staff. I received a call this morning from the Apostolic Nuncio in Rome asking me to make contact with you and offer you whatever service I could'.

'Who did you speak to?' asked Andrew

'A Father Rossi, he asked me to give you a message.'

'Yes' said Andrew

'He told that they did not succeed and me to tell you that the package was received. He said that he would try and arrange safe conduct for you to return to Rome'. In the meantime I am to assist you in any way that I can '.

'That is very kind of you' said Andrew 'please bring me a soutane and if possible I would like to say a Mass'

'I will see you this evening' said Mulroney 'God be with you'

Andrew reflected on those words 'God be with you' his God had certainly not been with him ... Or had he? After all Andrew has survived where others had died. He knew that he was not ready to return to Rome. He wanted to help Captain Prenter and do what he could for the survivors in the camp, and then he had to discover the whereabouts of 'Maria' he owed it to her to see if she survived. He also had to speak to the journalist; he very much knew that his journey was not at the end yet. He turned to face the Captain.

'How can I help you?'

'I would like you to accompany me down to the holding camp. We have nearly 13.000 Germans, Nazis in the camp and we have no way of checking who or what they are.

Our Military Police and working in tandem with the Americans and the French, it would appear that the Russians are doing their own thing. If you feel strong enough, I would like to take you for a little drive around the camp'

'Very well' said Andrew, 'I take it you are doing your best for my fellow inmates....

'The Jews?'

'My fellow inmates!' said Andrew 'I expect to be treated no differently; secondly you said that you have a displacement list system. Can you check if someone is alive or has survived?'

'Do you know her name and the camp she was in?' said Prenter

'Her name is Maria Tannenbaum and she was in Birkenau and Belzec

Prenter went very quiet.

'Auschwitz/ Birkenau was one of the 'death camps', we know it has been liberated by the Russians but we have no way of checking if anyone survived, I'm sorry. I suppose we could post the name and see if the Red Cross picks up on it. I presume she is a friend of yours?

'She is indeed' said Andrew 'I've never met her but I'll know her when I meet her, she is my friend, a very brave friend!'

Early the next morning, Prenter and Andrew set out for the holding camp. Andrew didn't really know what to expect. Prenter had provided him with a uniform and a cap. As they approached the camp, he shivered involuntarily as he saw the gun towers and the searchlights. An M.P opened the main gate and they were joined in the back of the jeep by another M.P

Meyer and his corporal had been arrested shortly after they left Flossenburg, they'd been picked up by a patrol of US paratroopers who after they had pushed them around a bit, herded them into an old barn and went through the assembled men.

Any of the men who showed any evidence of SS or Concentration Camp membership were taken outside and didn't return. At one point Mayer turned to see one of the camp cooks looking at him, he thought he was about to be recognised but the cook obviously decided it was better to say nothing. The men were split up the next morning and Mayer and the corporal were in the main holding camp in the town. They were fearful that they been taken so close to the camp but their disguises had worked so far ....

The klaxon sounded and all of the prisoners shuffled out onto the parade ground. They formed into squares and Mayer took up position at the back of the square containing all those below the rank of corporal. He'd been careful not to respond to any of the language tricks that the investigators were trying and so far had stuck to his story that his name was Willi Greim and he was from a little village called Leckwitz on the western bank of the Elbe. They'd tried the 'show me your papers' ruse but he was too smart for that. He'd watched SS men getting caught as they lay in their rag disguises and when asked for their papers, produced nearly new documents with all the correct stamps, an impossibility at this stage of the war. All he had to do was stick to his story and stay out of sight.

The party of officers walked up and down the lines, it was the same officers who had questioned him twice already but he didn't recognise the new man who was moving in and out of the squares.

Andrew was tired, very tired. The magnitude of the last few days was starting to take its toll on him. He just wanted to get this over with and get back to his billet. As he walked, he glanced across the row of sullen men staring at him; he stopped and then strode forward and touched a man about three rows back from the front. The man lifted his head and panic flooded his eyes

'This man was in charge of the kapos of the Sonderkommando detail, I saw him shoot 8 children in the head as their mother's watched on.'

'Nein nein!' exclaimed the man 'You are wrong!'

Captain Prenter nodded at the M.P who went forward and pulled the man out, he told him to take off his coat and he caught his left arm and ripped at the sleeve of his shirt....

'He's one of them, Sir!' exclaimed the M.P 'he's got the blood group and number on the inside.'

The man was dragged away and the ranks closed again. Andrew saw that there were only two more 'squares 'in front of him. He walked purposely up and down the lines looking at each of the men. He spotted the commandant's corporal almost immediately and called for the M.P to check him out.

Mayer watched all of this with an impending sense of panic, he'd prayed to a God that he had long forsaken that this 'stranger' would not spot him. He, at the same time tried to remember the man's face but it was useless, so effectively had he run his camp, one dead Jew was the same as another, so what if there was some brutality, they were only Jews!

Andrew passed Mayer by without giving him a second glance, as he passed Mayer exhaled and started to cough violently, so much so that Andrew went back to see if he was choking. Andrew reached Mayer and asked him

'Are you all right?

'JA'

Andrew was rooted to the spot. That voice, he would never forget that voice. The guttural command, the arrogance of the snap. Andrew thought he was going to fall; Prenter was following him and went over to Andrew.

'You are tired; you've done enough for one day......come

But Andrew wouldn't move, he couldn't move. He whispered to Prenter

'Have that man take his cap off and stand up straight.

Prenter ordered the man to do as Andrew asked, immediately he asked this, he could see a look of steely determination in the man's eyes. He stood erect and looked directly at his accuser. Andrew stared at him for what seemed like an eternity, he knew immediately who was standing in front of him, he couldn't comprehend the savagery and arrogance that still remained in his eyes.

Captain Prenter spoke

'Do you know this man, Andrew?' who is he?

Andrew took a deep breath and steadied himself before speaking

'The man before you is not who he says he is. You have in front of you StardartenFuerhrer Reinhard Meyer, up until recently, the camp commandant of Flossenberg Concentration Camp.

Andrew walked forward to him

'May you God forgive you for what you have done'

Mayer replied

'I followed my orders like all good officers should do' snapped Mayer back in clipped tones

The two M.P's moved in to take him from the square. As they reached him Andrew noticed that Mayer eyes had narrowed and he appeared to be grinding his teeth. Prenter saw it too and shouted

'Quickly, restrain him; get his mouth open, he is taking poison!!

Mayer fell to the ground and as the cyanide hit his nervous system, he started to vomit and convulse on the ground. By the time the medical orderlies had arrived Reinhard Mayer was dead.

Andrew went back to the billet and rested, later that evening he said his first Mass and he also said Kaddish for the survivors that were with him. He once again was a priest and he decided to stay at the camp for as long as he could be of assistance and in the hope of hearing something about Maria.

Mollayan rushed over to Adam's room, he knocked hard on the door

'Adam, it's me, let me in.

He waited a few minutes, the door opened and a very disheveled looking Adam Carter asked

'What's wrong?'

Mollayan pushed passed him

'There is no time to lose. Andrew Lassiter is in a displaced persons camp near Flossenberg. He survived! We have to reach him and find out about him. We cannot allow him to go back to Rome with the information he has'

Adam stood against the door, his brain muddled, trying to rub the sleep out of his eyes spoke

'Rome? What's that got to do with it?

Mollayan by this stage was throwing Adam's clothes into a bag

‘Rome, you fool, will want to know about him! Who sent him to Monte Cassino in the first place because he was asking too many questions? How was he able to contact you? How did he manage to send you his package? How did he end up in Flossenberg? For all we know, he may already have been ordered back to the very place he was sent from?

‘And?’ said Adam

‘And’ said Mollayan exasperatingly ‘he knows about you, he tells them, they know about you, if they know who you are, they’ll know what you are and more importantly what you possess! We must reach him before they do!

‘O.K, I understand, here, here, give me that’.

Adam took the case and finished putting the clothes into it. Mollayan’s driver was waiting for them at the door; he’d managed to hitch a lift with a team of investigators that were flying out to start questioning the SS people that had been captured. Two hours later, they were airborne across France. A military strip had been set up about 20 miles from Flossenberg and by mid afternoon they were standing in Captain Prenter’s office. Mollayan had been able to pull rank through the SOE and had instructed Adam that he was to act as his assistant and do nothing to bring attention to himself, listen to Mollayan and follow his lead in any discussion.

‘I want to speak with one of the inmates from the camp, His name is Andrew Lassiter’.

‘On who’s authority, may I ask?’ said Prenter

‘I am a Colonel in the SOE and I am here on direct secondment from Montgomery’ said Mollayan.

Prenter lifted the telephone and asked for Andrew to be brought up to the office. Whilst they were waiting, Prenter made small talk with Mollayan about London

‘I haven’t been home in 18 months. I have a wife and new baby. They live with my parents in Kent’.

‘That’s nice’ said Mollayan ‘I’m sure you are looking forward to getting home’

‘Very much so’ said Prenter. We’ll stay there for a while before we go back to America.

The door rapped and Adam and Mollayan turned as Andrew Mollayan walked into the room. They were shocked at his appearance, he was painfully thin, his face was very haggard and there were two black areas under his eyes. He didn’t walk, it was more of a shuffle but there was a resolution in his eyes that showed determination and resolve. He locked eyes with Adam and held the stare

‘You wanted to see me? Said Andrew addressing Prenter

‘Sit down, Andrew, these two men wish to speak to you, they are.....

Mollayan interceded ‘We’ll take it from here Captain, if you don’t mind. What we have to say is classified. I’m sure you understand. You don’t mind if we use your office, do you?

Prenter blustered and looked embarrassed, he glanced at Andrew and then cleared his throat.

‘Of course, take whatever time you like, I’ll be outside if you require anything’.

‘You’re very kind’ said Mollayan.

Prenter pushed back from the desk, stood up and lifted his cap that he put on and straightened it and marched towards the door. When it was closed, Mollayan turned and looked at Andrew before he spoke

‘Father Lassiter, thanks to your efforts, they did not succeed!’

Andrew looked blankly at both of them

‘My apologies, Father. My name is Henry Mollayan and this is Adam Carter’

Andrew’s eyed widened and he stammered

‘What! How? Where did you come from?’ said Andrew.

'Relax' said Adam 'He'll explain all to you as we talk, you are the first part of our mission, there is someone we need to find.

'Maria' said Andrew.

It was Adam and Mollayan's turn to be amazed at his words.

'It would appear that you have us at an advantage, Father! Please explain how you know about Maria, we will fill in all of the other pieces of the story. When you have that knowledge you will have a very difficult decision to make.'

'I know' said Andrew.

Andrew begun by explaining his father's legacy and all of the research that he had done in the library of the Vatican. He explained how Adam was brought to his attention and also how the Holy See were made aware of the Final Solution as early as 1941, primarily from testimony smuggled out of Auschwitz / Birkenau by a girl called Maria. She had managed to convince one of the Polish workers that she was a catholic and that he had to take her writings to someone in Krakow who would know what to do. My friend, Philip Rossi acted as a conduit between Krakow and Rome, they knew and they did nothing!!'

Mollayan and Adam remained quiet as Adam continued to speak

'Cardinal Santini took an interest in my work, I think he guessed what I was searching for, or rather had found'

'What do you mean 'found?' said Adam and Mollayan simultaneously.

'The Holy See already knows when the Yahweh will return

'WWHHHAAAat!!

'In 1917, three children in Fatima professed to a visitation. They said that they were bathed in a blue light and were told three secrets. Two of the secrets have come to pass, one was to do with the War and the second referred to something coming from the East. It was the third secret that proved to be the most significant, so significant that the only person who is allowed to read it is the Holy Father himself.'

The rumour is that the secret tells of the end of the world, my research indicates something different. It was easy for the church to claim a 'Mary' visitation, the children were nearly illiterate and easily convinced to retire to a life of Holy Orders or divine devotion to Our Lady'

'That is why you were sent away?' asked Adam

'I was told I was going to rest in Perugia, someone slipped me something and when I awoke, I found myself in a war zone, I escaped from the monastery and then met up with some Jews, the rest you can guess. I was captured, helping some Jewish children and ended up in Flossenberg. I have survived and all I want to do I'd find Maria if I can. Once I find out what happened to her, then I will decide what to do

'We decide' stated Adam, giving Mollayan a look of steely resolve. Outnumbered, he shrugged his shoulders and replied

'Let us bring Andrew up to speed with what we know and then we will see what we can find out about Maria' for the meantime I think Andrew should stay with us and we can decide what to do. I will clear it so as to give Andrew special witness protection,

Agreed?'

'Agreed' said both of them

Chapter 25

Maria and the boy, his name, they thought was Samuel, and the old Pole, Andrei, traveled together for three nights. They hid up during the day, afraid that they would be picked up and taken back to a camp. They had fallen in with a bigger convoy of refugees on the second day but had split from them when the column came under attack. They had no chance of getting food in a convoy either but a woman had told them that there was a Red Cross camp had been set up in a village some 10 miles away and that they should try and make their way to it. Andrei reached his old farm and insisted that they stay with him for one last day. He was able to get some food and they had their first hot meal in how long? Maria had already decided that she was going to try and make it across Germany.

That evening, Maria went and settled Samuel, he always had difficulty getting over to sleep and shouted a lot. Maria usually let him sleep beside her, both for warmth and comfort. He still had not spoken and did not leave Maria's side. He hadn't shown any emotion since the incident in the church and Andrei was very worried that he was still in a state of deep shock and that if he didn't receive some help soon, he would be permanently affected. He stopped, and ridiculed himself, how many where there that would be permanently affected by the madness of the last years? He decided that all he could do was to make them as comfortable as he could and pray for them as they continued their journey.

Samuel had fallen asleep in Maria's arms. Andrei had fixed up a fire and as they lay in front of it, Maria fought off the urge to sleep. She had to decide what to do, where to go and she realised that the only person that could help her, the only person who knew her and her secret was Isaac Tauber. She began to think about Isaac and the young journalist who shared her secret. She wondered about the Cyrillic and what had become of it. Was it safe? These thought flooded through her head until she was given temporary respite by the unset of sleep.

She was dreaming. In her dream she was bathed in a fabulous blue warmth, she could hear the most wondrous voices singing and as she floated along, she felt a peace she'd never experienced. Her mother stepped out and embraced her, she saw her two fathers, the brothers Tannenbaum. They were standing together, smiling at her.

A voice spoke 'Maria, Maria, you have served me well'.

She looked up to where the voice was coming from but could see nothing, the voice continued, 'you are alive and I am safe and soon there will be someone to keep you safe. You must do as he says and not question your heart. Soon you will understand, I have sent you a sign to help you understand'. She felt something touch the inside of her arm and then she floated off into a peaceful, deep sleep.

She woke early the next morning with a start and it took her a few moments to get her bearings. Andrei had gathered up whatever bits and pieces of food that he could scavenge to give to them. It was time to leave and Andrei had told them about a neighbour who was prepared to take them down towards the Red Cross camp. He said that the city was under the control of the Americans but that refugees were allowed to travel once they proved their country of origin. Andrei warned Maria that Jews were still being killed and in her state she would have to take extreme care. He begged her to stay with him and rest up but she said that she had to return to her home. They hugged each other and left with tears in their eyes.

They lay on the back of a trailer that was filled with refugees and was heading for the border. Maria started to tell Samuel about the dream she had the night before. She recalled the warmth and seeing her mother; she remembered a voice telling her something but couldn't remember what. It didn't matter because Samuel liked the story, he smiled for the first time since they'd met and his smile made Maria smile. They had survived and Maria could tell the world the truth.

They arrived in a small village in the early afternoon and Maria decided to walk the rest of the way. They had been walking for only ten minutes when she spotted a jeep with a Red Cross on the side of it. She rushed over and banged on the side of the jeep. The back doors opened and a soldier shouted

'Who's there?

Maria went around and asked him where they were. He explained that they were in Military district No 1 and that they had an hour to get to where they were going before curfew. When Maria told him that they had nowhere to go, he asked them where they'd come from

'Birkenau' stated Maria, and lately Buchenwald, we hid ourselves when the camp was evacuated and we've lived in the forest since,

The soldier gaped at Maria and said

'What did you say?'

Maria said it again

'Birkenau'

'You and the boy?'

Maria answered

'His name is Samuel, he and I are from Birkenau.

'You'd better come with me!' said the soldier

They both got into the back of the jeep and drove for about 30 minutes, when the jeep stopped and Maria and Samuel got out, they found themselves in a village of tents. They were taken to one of the largest tents where they joined a line of people waiting to be fed. Maria sat with Samuel at her side for nearly an hour, the line had hardly moved and she was becoming more and more angry. Just at that moment, a side flap opened and a number of officers stepped in. Maria marched across and said

'Who's is in charge here?

A sergeant moved to direct her away from the group but one of the officers stopped and called out

'Sergeant let her through!

Maria brushed past him and spoke

'We are all survivors who have spent the last six years been whipped into lines and queues by the Nazis, we have escaped and have come here for help. The last thing we want is for you to do the same thing!'

Upon hearing her voice, some of the men came over beside her. Three of the soldiers rushed forward with rifles to hold them back

'See what I mean' said Maria 'We are no threat to you, we are here because you say you can help us, if you cannot, we'll be on our way. We just want to go home'.

The rest of the men nodded their accent. The Colonel put his hands up to speak

'There are so many people here, we must try to keep order....

'That's what the Nazis did, you're just doing what they did!'

The colonel dismissed the men and walked across to talk to Maria directly

'I will see what I can do, what is your name?'

'My name is Maria Tannenbaum and I am from Berlin. This is my friend, Samuel and he stays with me'.

The Colonel snapped out an order

'Take this woman and her young friend over to the Officers tent and see if we can't hurry this damned mess up'.

Maria and Samuel were taken over to another large tent. There was a large map of Europe on a stand and a series of skull and crossbones pasted on different locations. Maria sat down in front of an officer who said

'You've been in Birkenau?

'Yes' said Maria, as well as Belzec and Buchenwald

'You are the first survivor that we've spoken too from that camp, it seems that it was the worst of all.

We had heard that there had been no survivors at all. We have spoken to people from Belsen and Buchenwald and Flosenburg and Dachau but we haven't spoken to any Auschwitz or Birkenau survivors. So far we have found evidence of 23 camps'

Maria was numb, the scale and magnitude of the slaughter overwhelmed her; she sat quietly for a few minutes until the officer spoke

'I need to ask you some questions about the camp that you were in, when I am finished, I will post your details on our lists so as to assist you in meeting up with anyone who knows you'

'There are lists?' said Maria.

'Oh yes, we've started to compile lists of those people who come to us'

'But the Russians?' stammered Maria

'We are liaison officers attached to a special department, all the officers here speak German and English, we have a limited amount of time because we are operating in the American zone. We operate under the flag of the Red Cross and have a limited time here. We'll probably have to move on in three or four days, just as soon as we can arrange transport. There is still heavy fighting in and around Berlin …

'What is the date? Asked Maria

24 April 19 and 45 am' replied the officer

Maria glanced over at Samuel and wondered whether any of his family had survived. She decided that their best chance of getting back to familiar surrounding lay with the Red Cross. Maria turned and spoke to the officer

'How do we get home?

'We have started to repair the rail network and are running special repatriation trains every other day. "We can only go to parts of France and Germany, it is still not safe to travel as there are groups of fanatical Nazis called 'werewolves' who refuse to surrender and continue to attack vulnerable targets but as I have said we have surrounded Berlin, won't be long now'

'Can we get on the next train going into Germany? said Maria

'Where are you from?

'Munich' Maria lied

'I will see what I can do, I have to ask you some questions however.

The officer asked Maria to tell her about the camp. She told her about the orchestra, the killings, the camp guards, the Kapo's. She repeated the story about the Camp Commandant…

'We've captured him! exclaimed the officer

Maria went on to tell him about the experiments and the Sonderkommando, those Jews used to clear out the crematoria after the incineration of the bodies. He asked her about Samuel, she said that he had been in the camp but that he was too traumatised to speak and had remained by her side from she met him. She then told him about their journey to the camp.

'We may need to talk to you again, we have captured some of the perpetrators and there will be trials. I'll need a written statement from you'

Maria told her about the messages that she had sent out in the early days and the records that she had secreted on her. The officer excused himself and went to the telephone

'Did you say there was a special investigation group set up to collate evidence of what was going on in the camps prior to our 'discovery'

'Yes' said the voice on the other end, 'it's being headed up as a war crimes investigation by some big wig from SOE, hold on a minute, yes, that's right, His name is Mollayan and he is currently seconded to Patton's Fifth Army. They liberated Flossenberg, I think.

I need to speak to this man' said Maria, I have vital information that will help him'

Maria didn't know nor care whether this man existed or not, if he could help her get home sooner, she would do anything to quicken up her journey.

'I'll try and reach him for you, we have orders to pass on any information from people who were in the so called Greater Government area camps'.

The telephone rang in Prenter's office, it was picked up by the Sergeant

Colonel Mollayan please?

'He not here, can I take a message? said the sergeant

'Tell him that I have someone here that he should speak to, she claims to have sent information out on the camps as early as 1941. I have her here in Military District 1 American Zone at the moment at Red Cross Headquarters. She is a German Jew, says her name is Maria, Maria Tannenbaum. She says she'd been in different camps including Birkenau from 1941. Your people may want to speak to her.'

'I'll leave him a note' said the sergeant and rang off.

Maria remained at the desk with Samuel until the officer returned. When he sat down again, he said that there may be some people that might want to talk to her. She and Samuel would be sheltered until clearance came through and then they would be free to continue on their journey.

'Why can't we leave now? asked Maria angrily 'We've suffered enough!

'We are not keeping you against your will, Miss, You are free to go. You should however know that we think you can help us capture some of the people who committed these crimes against you. A special investigation team has been set up and I have already contacted them. If you chose to stay, I will make sure that your stay is comfortable. A shower, some hot food and a bed for the night. It's better that what you can expect on the road'

Maria glanced over at Samuel and nodded

'Alright, we will stay for 2 days and then you'll put us on a train to Germany.

'Very well' said the officer 'I need to register you, Do you have a camp number?

Samuel gripped his left forearm with his right hand

'It's O.K' said Maria ' look, I'll read mine off before I do yours'

She pushed the sleeve of the jacket up to her elbow and touched the blue numbers on her arm. They had faded from the last time she had looked and she had difficulty reading the numbers. She wondered why it had faded and was about to start reading as a strange sensation passed over her. It was very calming and lasted for as long as she touched the numbers. She read them out to the officer and did the same for Samuel. When this was finished, they were taken over to a hostel that had been commandeered as a reception centre. Samuel refused to leave her side so they shared a room. Samuel retreated to the bathroom, Maria sat down on the bed and gathered her thoughts. She wondered who wanted to see her and whether the information that was referred was what she had sent out with the kapo all those years ago. There was a sudden noise and she turned towards the sound and found herself staring at herself in a mirror. She looked hard at the image looking at her, she didn't know who it was.

She didn't recognise her own image, her hair was lank, what teeth she had left were discoloured. There were open sores on parts of her body and her eyes were sunken into her head. . She brushed away a tear as she got up and turned the mirror face down.

Mollayan and Adam had settled Andrew and came back into the office. They thanked Prenter for the use of his room. They had decided to retire themselves and were about to leave, they'd reached the door when Prenter called out

'Sir, there's a telephone message from you. Someone from a Red Cross detail was on looking for you, something about evidence some girl had'

'What?'

'The sergeant took a call…

Mollayan ran back and snapped the message out of Prenter's hand, he quickly scanned it and then let out a shout!

'Its her!'

'Maria?' said Adam

'Maria' said Mollayan 'is in a Red Cross station in the American No 1 Zone! I'll telephone and make sure she stays there, go you across and tell Andrew. We'll then make arrangements about getting to her.

Mollayan telephoned the Red Cross HQ and was put through to the investigating officer.

'You have a field station somewhere near the border yes?

'We do' Who is this? asked the officer.

'My name in Henry Mollayan and I'm attached to Patton's fifth Army, I'm a special investigator into War crimes and it is essential that you put a girl who is in that camp under absolute protective custody, do I make myself clear'

The officer grimaced, another do gooder.

'What is her name?

'Maria Tannenbaum, I want you to secure her and confirm with me as soon as you have done so. 'On no account is she to leave your care, do what you have to do to keep her there, tell her that a friend of her is coming to see her. Tell her Adam is coming and it is safe'. Do you understand!

'Yes Sir'

Later that evening, Maria's door knocked, she got up to answer it. It was the officer from the Registration.

'I have a message for you, a friend of yours is coming to see you, he says his name is Adam ....

At the mention of his name, Maria staggered against the door, the officer moved to catch her but was too late, she fainted and hit the floor hard. When she came round she was lying on the bed and was conscious of her brow being cooled

'Adam, Adam is that you?'

She opened her eyes to see Samuel peering at her, stroking her hair and he'd been crying.

'It's all right' said Maria 'there is someone coming to help us, they'll be here soon'

The officer had stayed in the room and once he'd seen that she wasn't hurt, he repeated the message to her. He told her that he'd received orders to ensure that she was made as comfortable as possible. He'd arranged for one of the doctors to visit her. At the moment, the door rapped and the officer answered it, it was the doctor. The door opened wide and he stepped inside, at that moment Samuel threw himself at the doctor and began screaming and shouting

'Nein, Nein, leave us alone!

The doctor was knocked back and fell to the floor, his bag spilled its contents and as Samuel continued to shout and kick at him, the other officer removed his pistol and cracked Samuel over the head once and he collapsed in a pile. Maria was screaming at the officer.

'You've killed him, oh my God, you've killed him' screamed Maria.

The doctor moved across and felt for a pulse

'He's alright, he'll have a hell of a sore head when he wakes up though'

Maria raged

'Have you people no sense, can't you see he's just a child!

The officer and the doctor stood as Maria got up of the bed and came down and cradled Samuel's head in her lap. As she was lifting him, the doctor noticed a mark on his back. He instructed the officer to lift him up onto the bed, face down. He cut Samuel's shirt open and gasped in horror at what he found, the child's back was a mass of scars and burns, some were open and oozing, others had scabbed and there were older ones that had formed into ugly red welts across his back. The doctor spoke

'Fill a basin with some tepid water and you'll find some saline in my bag, this child has been tortured'.

The doctor prepared a syringe and injected Samuel, Maria, who stood, mesmerised at what she was seeing, stammered

'What could have caused that?

The doctor continued to work at Samuel, bathing and dressing his wounds.

'What camp were you in?

'Birkenau' replied Maria 'Samuel came across from Auschwitz when the fence came down'

'I may be wrong 'said the doctor ' but I'd guess that this little fellow suffered at the hands of the 'Angel'

'The 'Angel?' asked Maria

'Yes' said the doctor 'We have reason to believe that there were a series of experiments carried out in Auschwitz on people of all ages. We've already uncovered evidence of gross, unbelievable practice against inmates. I think young Samuel was one of his patients'

'Who would do a thing like this?' whispered Maria

'The Angel of Auschwitz' said the doctor 'Mengele, Dr. Josef Mengele.

The doctor went on 'from what we can gather, he arrived in 1942 armed with a theory that it was possible to breed Aryan pedigrees in the same way that one would breed dogs. He carried out horrendous experiments on twins, cripples and old people as well as along with a cohort called Professor Karl Clauberg, perpetrated mass sterilization on thousands of women'.

'Wait a minute! exclaimed Maria 'I remember him! . I'd been in the camp about three months when we were summoned to play in the orchestra one morning. We were taken over to where the Gypsies were barracked, they had their own separate camp barracks because there was a suspected typhoid epidemic.

That morning whilst we played, all of them were dragged out of the barracks, Yes, I remember now, he was there, I'll never forget his face. He was wearing a white coat and white gloves and he smiled as he issued the orders!'

'We were told by one of the guards that against their names in the official camp register were written the letters 'SB' *Sonderbehandlung*, (Special treatment)

The doctor had stopped treating Samuel

'You saw Mengele? , You know what he looks like?

'I will never forget, that is my reason for being alive, to survive, to scream to the world and swear vengeance on all those who committed these atrocities'

Maria began to shake and swayed again, the doctor helped her sit down

'You need your rest, I'll look after Samuel, Has anyone checked you yet?'

'No' said Maria 'just look after Samuel, given what he has been through, it's hardly surprising that he attacked you'

'Yes' said the doctor 'for him, a white coat meant excruciating pain for him, I'll not wear it again when I come to see him.

Before he left, the doctor gave both of them a heavy sedative and instructed that no one was to be admitted to see them without his express permission. He was told about the orders issued by Mollayan and said

'When Colonel Mollayan arrives, send him to my office, I will want to talk with him first.

Mollayan and Adam had left Flossenburg the previous evening, Mollayan was travelling as a 'Special Investigator, War Crimes' and had managed to get accreditation and clearance for Adam on the strength of his SOE contacts. They'd decided to travel together and had told Andrew that he wasn't fit to travel. They'd explained that they had found Maria and were going to bring her back with them.

Mollayan explained to Andrew that it was vital that he did not talk to anyone else from the church, if Mollayan was right, then the church would know the danger of Andrew meeting Maria. He was sure that they didn't know that Maria had been found, it was bad enough that Andrew had nearly single handedly discovered their complicity in Yahweh. For Andrew to be able to produce live evidence that the Vatican knew about the Death Camps as far back as 1941 through Maria's testimony would be simply too much for them to take.

When all of this was put to Andrew, he nodded saying

'That part of my life is over; I do not wish to be a part of 'them' any longer'

Adam gasped

'But Andrew, you were a private secretary to the person who is probably going to be the next Pope!'

Andrew retorted

'I was a priest first who wanted to serve my God, I now know that in order to serve MY God, I must do different things, starting with doing what I can for Maria.

Adam and Mollayan nodded to each other

'We'll leave you alone, you are here under my command, speak to Prenter if you need anything, we'll return in four or five days from now.'

'Very well' said Andrew

Mollayan and Adam traversed Berlin and in doing so learned that the Chancellery had been breached and that according to the Russians, both Hitler and Goebbels was dead.

Chapter26

Twenty four hours earlier, Giovanni Santini held a personal audience with Father Philip Rossi

'Father Rossi, I have great news for you!

'Si? Eminence' replied Rossi

'Andrew Lassiter is alive! We have reports that he was liberated from a camp in Germany some days ago. We are trying to ascertain his whereabouts in order that we may bring him home to the mother church.'

'That is indeed wonderful news, Eminence'

'You seem perturbed about Andrew' said Santini 'Is there anything you wish to share with me?

Rossi had agonised about this moment for a long time, he could and would not betray his confessional obligation to Andrew but he carried the pain and anguish of what Andrew had told him like a wound. He looked at the Cardinal

'Why was Father Lassiter sent from us?

Santini's eyes narrowed, Rossi knew something but what? He composed himself,

'He was sent to Perugia to rest as he had been under severe pressure of work'

'But, your Eminence, You told me at the time that Father Lassiter was at Monte Cassino

The cardinal flared

'I do not recall telling you this ...

It was out before he realised what he said, Rossi stared at the Cardinal, he'd lied, Andrew was correct! The Cardinal quickly regained his composure and spoke to Rossi

'Andrew was not a well man. It was decided to give him some help and the Holy Father himself remembered him in his prayers. He had been handling, let us say, 'delicate matters of state' which proved to be a bigger burden than we thought. It was decided to help him but there was administrative mix up and a mistake was made. By the time we realised what had happened, Andrew had left Monte Cassino and we didn't know where he was'

Rossi struggled to hide his contempt, he didn't believe the Cardinal for one minute and realised that Andrew had been right. He resolved to all that he could to protect Andrew starting with telling Santini absolutely nothing!

'I know that the two of you were close, you are his confessor are you not?' said Santini, ' Have you heard from him at all?

'No' said Rossi 'He has been uppermost in my prayers as well and I pray for his safe return'

The Cardinal knew that he was being lied to.

'You will of course tell me if he contacts you?

'Of course Your Eminence, it will be by the grace of God' said Rossi.

Rossi knelt and kissed the ring on the Cardinal's left hand and left the room leaving the Cardinal alone with his thoughts. On his instructions all of Andrew's work had been sequestered to him and the library was now only accessible with written permission. Most of the 'contentious' material had been removed. The Cardinal still could not understand why Andrew had embarked on his 'discovery', what triggered him to dig so deep. Of course Santini had heard all the rumours of the Third Secret, he ignored them, he'd see for himself one day, he told himself.

The missing piece of Santini 's jigsaw was knowledge of the Cyrillic, had he have known that Andrew possessed incontrovertible evidence of Yahweh, he'd have never let him near the Vatican let alone trust him with 'secrets'. If he knew that in four or five days hence that Andrew was going to be reunited by one of his nemesis's, the author of the Auschwitz proof, the Cardinal would not have rested at all.

He called his personal secretary to his room

'Father Rossi has expressed a wish to return to Pastoral duties, he has served us well through these troubled times, can we find him a flock somewhere?

'In Italy, Eminence?' enquired the Secretary

Santini pondered the question

'No, said the Cardinal 'I think we should reward Father Rossi with some missionary work. See what is available in Africa, no on second thoughts, contact my good friend in Buenos Aires and see if he could use the talents of a vibrant priest in his missionary.

'Very well Your Eminence' said the secretary retreating and wondering what calumny Father Rossi had committed to be sent there.

It was drizzling rain, a gray overcast sky darkened the pathetic conditions that Mollayan and Adam found when they arrived at the Red Cross centre. They were taken to the command room where the doctor's request was relayed to them. Mollayan agreed and the doctor was summoned to the Command room.

'Good evening Doctor, I believe you wanted to speak to me about Maria Tannenbaum'

'Colonel Mollayan, I presume?' said the doctor.

Mollayan nodded and invited the doctor to sit down. He introduced Adam as his assistant and then spoke directly

'You said that you needed to speak with me...

'Yes' said the doctor ' Maria and Samuel have both suffered extensively at the hands of the Nazis and I want to make sure that they get every chance of recovery and without further trauma. Secondly, the doctor paused 'Is there something wrong?

'Who is this Samuel that you speak of?' asked Mollayan

The doctor explained how Maria had arrived at the camp and what had happened when he went to treat them and the aftermath

'Samuel was tortured in Auschwitz, probably by Mengele himself, I haven't had a chance to examine Maria but I would guess that as well as her poor physical condition, she is probably suffering as well from any number of maladies'

'When can we see them?' said Mollayan

'I have them sedated at the moment, you can see her when she is wakened and I've had a chance to examine her, you must do nothing to upset her and she will not be able to cope with being moved for a day or two'. There is something else, as far as I am aware; she is the only person so far that we have been able to ascertain that can recognise 'The Angel'. I would very much like to see that bastard brought to book!'

'By the Angel, you mean Mengele? Don't worry, we'll catch him. I'm sorry Doctor, I should have shown you my papers. I am with the War Crimes Investigative Tribunal, if Maria can tell us about Mengele as well as all the other things she knows, she will prove to be an invaluable witness. My associate Mr. Carter knew Maria personally before the war and is a close personal friend of hers.

'She'll need all of her friends and more 'said the doctor nodding at Adam 'Just be very gentle with her'.

'You can count on it' said Adam.

Maria was awake when the doctor returned

'How do you feel now?

'A little better' said Maria 'how is Samuel?

'He is poorly' I will do my best' said the doctor continuing

'Your friends have arrived, I will give you a quick examination and then I will fetch them.

Don't worry about Samuel, he is heavily sedated and won't waken for another 12 hours at least'.

The doctor examined Maria and left after helping to prop her up in the bed. She lay there with all sorts of thoughts flooding her mind, how would he react when he saw her? What had happened to Isaac? How was it safe? The door knocked and she stretched over and put the light off

'Come in' she said

Mollayan and Adam entered the room; it took them a moment or two for their eyes to become accustomed to the darkness in the room.

'Maria?' said Adam 'It's me Adam, Adam Carter.

They heard a sharp intake of breath and then Maria spoke

'Is Isaac with you?

'No' said Adam 'the man that is with me is our friend, he has helped me to find you and it is because of him that we are safe.

'Is it safe?

'Yes' murmured Adam 'Thanks to you it is.

'And Isaac?

'I'm sorry Maria, Isaac died some years ago, it was just after we'd escaped from Germany he died of a heart attack...'

Adam stopped because he heard Maria crying quietly. He went over to the side of the bed and stood beside it, he took her hand in his and said

'You're safe Maria, I will take you away from here, you'll get better and you'll get your life back'

What could he say, whatever came out was so inadequate, hell, he couldn't even begin to comprehend the mental and physical torture that this girl had suffered, he felt so helpless.

Maria spoke

'Why didn't they come? I told them what was happening, why didn't they come? Did they not believe me?' sobbed Maria

Mollayan spoke for the first time with a gentleness that took Adam by surprise.

'They didn't come because you were Jews, they entered into an agreement with the devil and they closed their eyes and ears to your suffering. In time I will explain everything to you. It is enough now for you to know that you are safe, we will protect you and your friend Samuel as well'

'Samuel!' panted Maria

'Don't worry' said Adam 'he's sleeping and has been treated, he'll be with us all of the time.

Maria fell back in the bed

'I would like to talk to you alone' she said to Adam.

Adam nodded over to Mollayan who immediately got up and left the room. He spoke to Maria

'He is our friend and ally and we have much to thank him for'

Maria reached over and turned on the light, Adam gasped as he looked at the bed, he was talking to her but he didn't recognise what was lying in the bed as Maria

'Oh my God, Maria, what have they done to you?'

They were both crying now, Adam was ashamed of himself, he thought he had been burdened up until that point with Yahweh. He looked at what was once a lively vivacious girl now reduced to what could only be described as an iated waif. He put his hand to her face and stroked the side of her head.

'I'm so sorry Maria' I should never have left you there, I should have went back, I should have done something.

Adam was now openly sobbing, for Maria, for Isaac, for Andrew. He wept openly and bitterly as he looked at Maria. She was upset as well and for her sake Adam tried to control his emotions, he eventually managed to talk to her.

'Don't say anything, we'll take you and Samuel with us when we leave. Mollayan is making arrangements for us to go to somewhere in Germany where you can rest up and we can decide what to do next'

'But you said Yahweh was safe!

'It is, It is, don't worry' said Adam 'There are things that we must do to make sure that it stays safe, that' all.

'Very well' said Maria 'I would like to rest now'

'Of course' said Adam 'call if you need anything'

Adam got up and headed for the door, as he opened it Maria spoke

'You haven't changed much' she said Thank you for finding me.

He started crying again as he closed the door. Mollayan was waiting in the corridor

'Whatever it takes! Until the ends of the earth, those bastards must be caught!' raged Adam

'They will, don't worry' soothed Mollayan 'you'd better sit down, I have some more news'

'What?' said Adam

'I've spoken with the doctor, Maria rescued Samuel in the camp, he is 13 years old, has been tortured and is deeply traumatised.'

'He comes with us'

'But we have nowhere to take him, we are still in danger from other sources 'said Mollayan

'Go in and look at that girl! See for yourself what they did to her! He comes with us!' shouted Adam.

Mollayan put his hands up

'Calm down, O.K, he can stay with us until we decide what we are going to do. There's something else you should know, at this stage the doctor cannot be sure but he thinks Maria has contracted T.B

'NO!' said Adam

'He doesn't know how badly she is affected but he did say that if we don't get her into proper surroundings with proper care, she'll not recover.

'What do you mean by 'not recover' said Adam

'I mean that she may die! We must move and move fast!' said Mollayan

Chapter 27

The passports had been delivered along with military papers clearing the four men for travel to Rimini. The local curate of Bad Weisee had delivered them. He headed up out of the town until he reached the turn off for the lake road. He was stopped about 330 yards down the path. One of the men stepped out and put a gun to his back

'It's me, Father Dorchan', cried the priest

'Gut' said the man 'Have you got them?

'They came this morning in a Vatican seal' he said

The leader spoke

'Priest, you have done well, we must tell our friends in the Vatican about your help'

One of the men walked across and blindfolded the priest

'I'm sorry, this is for your own good, if you don't know where we are hiding, you won't be able to tell.'

The man took the priest back through the forest but turned sharply before the road, they walked on for another few minutes, the priest thought he heard water running. It was the last thing he'd remember as the man removed the blind fold and pushed him over the edge his body hit a precipice on the way down, he was dead as he splattered into the water.

'It is done' said the man on his return

'Gut' said the leader 'it is time for us to assume our new identities'

It took them 20 minutes to change into the garb that the priest had left them, they'd already had their SS numbers and blood groups burned off by the leader. As they left the bunker, they left their identities behind them and moved off, heavily disguised as four Dominican Priests on their way to the Vatican and then on to Rimini. They had changed their appearance so much that no one would have recognised them from their SS pictures. Three of the men, GruppenFuerhrer Albert Mainz, StardartenFuerhrer Ernst Brunner and Oberleutnant Matteus Netzer had all served along with the Deaths Head brigade in various camps, they had sworn to protect the man that took them this far, the man that guaranteed their safety, his name was ... Mengele, Dr. Josef Mengele.

At that very moment Alfred Rosenberg was also making good his escape. He'd been kept informed by both Bormann and Speer as to the goings on in the Bunker and had accepted the death of the Fuerhur with a shrug of his shoulders. He knew that Doenitz had been appointed supreme commander, he didn't really care, his new alliance Gelli, had made his travel arrangements and he was hiding in an apartment awaiting his escort.

Minutes were like hours as far as Andrew was concerned, he'd spoken to Prenter on two occasions to ask if there was any news and declined a further four opportunities to say Mass or participate in any services with the Padre. He stayed in his room, he took his meals in his rooms and reflected on his decision. At night he had vivid dreams about his father, it always started by him imagining that he was bathed in a blue light, when this happened, he knew that his father would talk to him and he relaxed. The first time it happened, his father apologised for the legacy and said he would do all in his power to be with him. His father visited him three times after that and each time he told him things about the future. Andrew couldn't make sense of some of the things that he had been told but that in itself didn't surprise him given the circumstances that he found himself in. He was grateful to his father and any comfort that he got came from the thoughts he had. He was, however at a loss as to why he had the sensation of a blue light in his head when he awoke.

He thought about Rossi and wondered as to whether he should try and contact him. He decided that there was no point, Rossi would try and talk him out of his decision to renege on his vow. No, he would make sure Maria was safe and then do what Mollayan wanted him to do. After that he would return to Australia and do what his father did.

He would bury the Yahweh like his father had done before him and survive, safe in the knowledge that he knew the truth. As he waited for news, he thought about his sister in Australia and he thought about Maria. He tried to imagine her pain, her hardship. He'd been in the camps; he'd seen with his own eyes what the Nazis had done on the Jews. He trembled with anger every time he recalled the memo in the file 'The Holy See cannot corroborate these reports without independent evidence' or words to that effect. Somehow, someday, the world would know the truth; he owed it to the countless dead because of the silence of the Holy See.

On the third day he received a telephone call from Adam who told him that Maria was unwell and she had to be moved quickly away from the camp. The hope was that they could arrange passage on a train that had a hospital compartment. Mollayan had decided that he and Maria and a boy named Samuel would go to the South of France, Mollayan had relatives there who would look after them. It was agreed that Mollayan would return to Flossenberg and collect Andrew and everybody would meet up in France.

'Where?' asked Andrew

'A little village called Rennes le Chateau' Mollayan said you'd know it well?

Andrew chuckled down the line

'Tell my new friend that I like his sense of humour. I know of Rennes le Chateau, I'll tell you all about it someday Adam.'

'We will meet up in 4 days time. Mollayan has already left to collect you. We are leaving to-morrow on a hospital train for Bad Weisee and from there we'll travel across to France'

'Have you told Maria about me? Asked Andrew

'No' said Adam 'she is unwell and has had enough shocks for the time being. Meeting you in France will be time enough. I'll prepare her for that meeting as we are travelling'.

'I'll see you soon, take care Adam' said Andrew as the line went dead.

General John Smythe had an easy war, his position within Freemasonry made sure of that.

During the war he served in counter intelligence and co-ordinate the actions of the various resistance groups that harried the Nazi war effort so successfully. His main role was logistical, his department sourced and supplied the drops of ammunition and provisions that were vital and also ensured that the pickup of escaped prisoners of war and allied airmen was planned and executed. Now that the war was over, he'd been seconded to a new War crimes investigation unit.

He transferred to Northern Germany and set up headquarters at Flensburg. The day he arrived, it was discovered that a prisoner, SS General Richard Glueks had killed himself in the hospital. This was a setback because Glueks had been Inspector of the concentration camps since 1940. Smythe was furious and issued an order that all matters of discovery, no matter how trivial had to be reported to him personally.

Over the next few days, his staff began compiling lists of captures, sightings and inter agency requests for identification of suspects. Smythe poured over these lists hoping that he would be able to capture a leading Nazi. He knew of the intention for trials to be convened at the earliest opportunity and knew that Nuremberg had already been selected as the location. Smythe had set up a reporting system and used a sort of clearing-house approach to categorise the information that came through to him. His department was ordered to arrest Admiral Doenitz at the request of the Russians. Doenitz considered himself to be the acting German Chancellor and had set up an interim Government in Flensburg.

Smythe himself went with the arresting party and as they were speaking to Doenitz they heard a commotion in the next room and a single shot. They rushed in to find Admiral von Friedberg. He had been a signatory to three separate instruments of surrender, slumped over his desk, dead from a bullet fired from his own gun.

Doenitz was taken away and Smythe returned to his office and started to work through the list of suspects on his desk. He was reading the lists when a name on the list chilled the very blood in his veins, his temples began to throb and he was conscious of a knowing sensation in the pit of his stomach. He tried to compose himself and pale faced, he lifted the telephone receiver, dialed a number and spoke to his subaltern in the outer office

'When did these lists arrive?

'This morning Sir'

'Right' Smythe commanded 'I wish to speak to a Colonel Mollayan who is based at Flossenberg. I also want to speak to the person who identified Reinhard Mayer, the camp commandant of Flossenberg'

'What is his name, Sir?

'Lassiter, Andrew Lassiter.

Smythe then telephoned London and was able to ascertain that Mollayan had indeed left London with another person and had arrived in Flossenberg. They'd spent three days there and then; acting on information had requested travel papers to Russian occupied territory in Silesia. Smythe hadn't spoken to Henry Mollayan for nearly five months and wondered what he was doing. He tried to reach Mollayan directly over that period but hadn't been able to make contact with him. He put a call through to the Lodge in London and discovered that Mollayan hadn't spoken to anybody there either for the same period.

Smythe wasn't unduly worried about this but there was something that did give him cause for concern, who was this person that was with him? London had told him that Mollayan had requested travel for two people, meant that this person was with him in London, Flossenberg and Silesia? Smythe was also worried about this Lassiter person, coincidence?

Whatever, Smythe would know soon enough, he'd requested the travel documents for Mollayan and his companion to be relayed to him and he'd have Lassiter for questioning as soon as possible. Smythe telephoned Group Headquarters and left a message for Mollayan to contact him directly. He was told that Mollayan had left to return to Flossenberg but that his associate was still with the girl.

'What girl?' asked Smythe

'The girl from Auschwitz, Sir

'What's her name' hissed Smythe

'Tannenbaum, Maria Tannenbaum.

Chapter 28

At that moment Maria Tannenbaum and Samuel and Adam had boarded a train that would take them to a holding centre that had been set up behind the American lines. Mollayan had assured them that he would work out a travel option for them once he had made sure that Andrew was safe.

Smythe was helpless, he had no jurisdiction over the Red Cross and all he could find out was that the final destination of the train was somewhere in Army Group 5. Smythe still didn't know what was going on but if Mollayan had returned to Flossenberg, then the suspicion that he had about Lassiter was correct. What was Mollayan up to? He wouldn't be stupid enough to go after Yahweh on his own, would he?

Smythe telephoned Hemmindale and told him what he had discovered. Hemmindale was much more direct, he told Smythe to find out who was with Mollayan.

'It is imperative that you discover who is with Mollayan' said Hemmindale 'if you don't know who it is and I don't know who it is, then we are in trouble'

'Perhaps it is an Army thing?' mused Smythe

'I don't think that Mollayan's name being mentioned in conjunction with the names Tannenbaum and Lassiter has got anything to do with Army and everything to do with Yahweh!' raged Hemmindale.

'You don't think ... asked Smythe

'I don't know but I'm not prepared to take the risk' said Hemmindale

Smythe's worst fears were confirmed 2 hours later. Mollayan's assistant had traveled under papers that Mollayan had arranged for him. Smythe immediately telephoned Hemmindale

'It's Carter!'

'What did you say? Hemmindale was deathly silent

'Why else would he request papers, Mollayan is travelling with Carter and they've found the Tannenbaum girl and this Lassiter character has to be connected in some way to Nicholas Lassiter. I missed Carter and the girl; they're on a Red Cross train bound for Bad Weisee. Mollayan has returned to Flossenberg'.

'They will all meet up somewhere soon, we have to stop this now!' roared Hemmindale

'I've instructed Flossenberg to get Mollayan to contact me'

'Fool, all you've done is alerted him! Get on to Flossenberg and take care of Lassiter yourself, you have the ultimate sanction.

'Very well' Smythe replied.

Mollayan had been told about the telephone message when he arrived back in Prenter's office. He turned on his heel and sprinted across the compound and into Andrew's bunkhouse. One of the other men said that Andrew had gone for a walk. Mollayan swore and was heading for the door as Andrew returned. Mollayan caught him by the arm and almost frog-marched him out into the compound.

'Where were you?' commanded Mollayan

Andrew held up a soiled package, 'I promised an old man that I would retrieve this'

'Take this overcoat and money and get out of here as quick as you can' panted Mollayan

'What is wrong' said Andrew shoving the package into the pocket of the greatcoat.

'You're in danger, go into the town and stay in the hotel until I come for you'

'But...'

'No questions, do as I say'.

He gave Andrew directions and instructed one of the soldiers to drive him into town. He then went back to Prenter's office and asked to be left alone.

First of all he called to check that Adam and Maria had left for Bad Weisee and that the reception committee that he had prepared for them was ready to spirit them away when they arrived at the holding centre, he then called Smythe in Flensburg.

Smythe's telephone jarred into life

'Yes'

'Call for you Sir, a Colonel Mollayan

'Put him through'

'Henry?' said Smythe

'Good Afternoon, General 'said Mollayan

'You're at Flossenberg?'

'Yes'

'My sources tell me that you have Lassiter with you'

Mollayan stalled just enough for Smythe to confirm that Hemmindale's analysis was right.

'Who?' said Mollayan

'Let's not play games Colonel, We both know what you have done, if you give us what we want, I will promise you a quick death'.

'I'm sorry' said Mollayan 'I cannot do that'.

'Understand this then, I will do all in my power to destroy you and that idolatrous entity that you are protecting'

'So be it' said Mollayan.

Smythe was in the process of contacting Hemmindale when his office door burst open

'Come quickly Sir'

'What is it, man?

'Our people brought in a prisoner called 'Heinrich Hitzinger' he'd described himself as an official of the Geheime Feldpolizei and we arrested him. He's been in Meinstedt for three days...

'And' said Smythe

'And Sir, well that is' the officer hesitated

'What it is, man? 'Spit it out' commanded Smythe

'I think it could be Heinrich Himmler!

Smythe rushed to the door and called for a jeep to be brought to the front immediately

'Where is he?'

'He is in a cell in a camp at Westertimke'

'As fast as you can, come on man drive!

At that moment 'Heinrich Hitzinger' was asking to see the camp commandant. That was a Captain Tom Sylvester and he agreed to the meeting

'What do you want?' asked Sylvester

'I am Heinrich Himmler'

'Really' said Sylvester

'I want to speak with Field Marshall Montgomery'

'I shall advise the authorities' said Sylvester and issued orders for Himmler to be returned to his cell.

By the time Sylvester was back in his office, Smythe was waiting for him

'You have a prisoner here, A 'Heinrich Hitzinger, I want to see him

'You cannot' said the Captain 'I have forwarded him to Luneberg where he is being kept in isolation.

'Let me guess' said Smythe 'He claims to be Heinrich Himmler!'

The Captain stuttered ...

'How did you know?'

'That's why I'm here' exclaimed Smythe

Smythe rushed back to the jeep

'Luneberg!'

Himmler was incarcerated in an apartment building in the Ulzener Strasse that had been cleared for military use. As Smythe was coming through the second checkpoint in the street, Himmler was visited by an army doctor, Captain Wells, who ordered him to strip.

Smythe was bounding up the stairs as Himmler's jacket was searched and a cyanide capsule was discovered.

The doctor told him to put on an unmarked uniform and left the room. He was coming out of his office a couple of hours later when he saw Smythe rushing towards him

'Where is he?' shouted Smythe

'Who' said the Doctor.

'The prisoner you just examined'

'He is in that room' said the Captain pointing...

'Did you find any poison?

'Yes' said the doctor, 'he was carrying...

'Did you check his mouth?' shouted Smythe

'No'

'Who's with him?'

'Colonel Murphy from Monty's Intelligence has just gone in with our Doctor Wells'

Smythe ran down to the room and burst through the door just as Murphy spoke

'Check his dental cavities'

Himmler's eyes narrowed at the sight of Smythe, his chin began to move

Smythe shouted

'Open his mouth! He's got a capsule in his mouth!'

Within a second Himmler was writhing on the floor, Wells had thrown himself down beside Himmler and forced his mouth open and tried to extract what was left of the capsule. Smythe rushed to the door and shouted for someone to bring him a stomach pump. They worked on him for 12 minutes but it was no use, Heinrich Himmler was dead.

Smythe walked back to the office where the Doctor was.

'Make sure he is removed, I want that bastard out of here as quickly as possible '

'We'll need a padre for him and a grave '

'Fuck him' said Smythe 'bury him with the dignity he showed his victims!'

The next day, three sergeants put the body into the back of a truck and took it to the woods outside the town; they dug a grave and threw the corpse into it. One of the sergeants said

'Let this worm go to the worms'

They put a surface of grass on the gravesite and the area was thoroughly evened out so that no sign remained. Smythe, satisfied with the outcome, returned to Flensburg, determined to settle Mollayan with the same efficiency. In his haste however to catch Himmler, he'd forgotten to call Hemmindale and report the conversation. When he eventually did make contact he was told that Henry Mollayan had effectively disappeared along with Andrew Lassiter. Hemmindale had spoken to a 'brother' attached to Montgomery's staff; they'd had the train stopped. There was no sign of Carter or the Tannenbaum woman either. Heinrich Himmler had given them a chance to escape!

The escape had everything to do with luck and nothing to do with planning as far as Mollayan was concerned. Having replaced the receiver with Smythe's words ringing in his ears, Mollayan slumped back in the chair just as Prenter walked back into his office

'Colonel Mollayan'

'Good day Prenter' said Mollayan 'I trust you are well'.

'Yes, thank you Sir' replied Prenter 'I had to go and sign the release papers for the French Jews; they're leaving with the Red Cross today'.

Mollayan responded

'Where are they going? Paris?

'No' said Prenter' they left yesterday, today's convoy is heading South, Grenoble, I think.

Mollayan excused himself again; sped down to the village where he collected Andrew and simply walked over to the Red Cross convoy and cadged a lift! They hopped up into the back of the truck and both of them were only 85 miles from Rennes le Chateau by the time Smythe talked to Hemmindale.

He was worried about Adam and Maria but they'd discussed alternatives in a case of emergency, all Mollayan could hope for was that Adam would be able to recognise and deal with any emergency. Had he have known what was happening on the train, he would not have been able to contain himself. Adam knew that Maria was ill, seriously ill. He didn't realise the significance of her illness until about two hours into the journey when Maria began to cough violently.

Adam held her as she perspired profusely and fought for breath as her body was racked with pain. Samuel sat at the edge of the seat holding her hand whilst Adam mopped her brow with a damp cloth. He went up to get the medical orderly who was travelling on the train

'My friend is sick and she needs help' said Adam

'Are you going to Bad Weisee?' asked the orderly

'Yes' affirmed Adam

The orderly checked Maria and then gave her a jab

'You're right, she should never have left the hospital, said the orderly. 'Her temperature is rising and I'm afraid that the strain that will place on her heart may induce a heart attack'. I am surprised she was allowed to leave the hospital.

'It was too cold for her to stay' said Adam, he didn't want to discuss the fact that the Russians had given the entire camp 48 hours to clear up and head west. The Russians were searching out any Germans in uniform and killing them. There was also talk of whole sale deportation of village population's back into Russia. The rest of the displaced people were on the move, expelled by the Red Army. East Prussia had already been cleared of Germans and there was talk that the Sudeten Germans were being literally evicted in what they stood in as Czech authorities moved their own people in.

'Let me see what I can do' said the orderly

He went away and came back twenty minutes later

'We have to stop before we cross into the Russian Zone, the Americans have a checkpoint just before we reach the Russians. I'm told that a hospital train will be coming through on its way to Paris. It is scheduled to make a stop at Bad Weisee on the way through but it will be seven or eight hours before it gets there. I could try and see if we could get you on the train, at least your friend would have a Doctor to look after her. The train is an official Red Cross train and I'm told that there are some 'camp' people on it.

Adam nodded and thought to himself

'Bad Weisee can wait, she needs a doctor more than a memory at the moment'.

Maria had fallen into a fitful sleep and Samuel stayed awake by her side. Adam closed his eyes and awoke with a start as the orderly shook him to tell him to get up and make ready to switch trains. He helped Maria onto a stretcher and climbed aboard the train that had started to move away slowly. Adam checked Maria and turned to look for Samuel, he wasn't there!

Adam panicked and ran back to the door of the train to see two of the Red Cross people catch Samuel by the shoulders and put him back on the other train. He fought and kicked and Adam could only watch as one of the men produced a syringe and plunged it into Samuel's arm. Samuel fell to the ground and his limp body was carried back onto the train. Adam beat the window in frustration as the orderly closed the door and the train rumbled into the Russian controlled zone.

Adam's train had backed into a siding and came to a halt. An orderly came down the corridor and Adam opened the door and beckoned to him

'How long will we be here?' asked Adam

'As long as the Russians decide, I'm afraid. Last week they made a train wait for nearly 20 hours. They search all of the trains looking for Nazis' he said.

Adam returned to the compartment, Maria was lying in a bunk like bed that stretched the length of the compartment. Apart from a chair against the other wall, the compartment was empty. There were no blinds on the window and Adam was conscious of men moving up and down the platform outside.

'There's been an uprising in Prague' said one of the voices 'they're trying to drive the Germans out before the Russians arrive'.

'No matter' came the reply' the Poles thought tha would do the same in Warsaw and look what happened, I ... telling you, I wouldn't be in a hurry thinking about getting home just yet.

'Whaddya mean?'

'These Russkies, they're not gonna stop until they've taken all they want, I wouldn't be surprised if we end up fighting them as well'.

'You're shittin me, howdya know all this'

Adam peered out of the window to see two G.I's sitting on a bench outside the station masters office

'I'm telling you, it's true. There was a train thru here yesterday with some of our guys on it. They said that they'd been fighting SS in Prague, they were part of some recon outfit, when the russkies arrived, our boys hauled ass back to Bohemia. There's even talk that we're gonna give that all over to the Russkies as well. I'm telling you we'll be fighting them sooner than you think'.

Albert Rosenberg was sitting in a dank cellar in the bottom of a bombed out building in Wilhemstrasse waiting to be guided across the Russian lines by one of his new friends contacts. He was dressed in civilian clothes and had wrapped himself in a greatcoat to try and fend off some of the cold. Sitting there, reminiscing about the previous twelve years brought a grimace to his face, If only Hitler had followed the plan, they'd be at the gates of Moscow with their American allies dividing the spoils of war. He'd been hiding in the bunker for nearly 12 hours now and he was beginning to get a little bit worried. He'd known for some days that Berlin was no longer defensible as the Russians occupied most of the city. All he had to do was make it to the subway at Fredrichstrasse. He'd been told that he would be collected and taken into the British Zone where plans had already been made to spirit him away. The last time he had ventured up to the surface to see what was happening, he'd watched some Hitler Youth scramble across the rubble, they saw him and one of them called to him

'Run for your life, the Fuerhur is dead and the Russians are swarming all over the Potsdamerplatz'

Rosenberg knew that Bormann had a plan to try and negotiate with The Russians. He'd sent General Krebs who spoke fluent Russian to see General Chuikov who was the Soviet commander of the troops fighting in Berlin. Rosenberg also knew that it was doomed to failure. Gelli had told him in a last communiqué that the Russians wanted the unconditional surrender of everyone in the Fuerhurbunker as well as the soldiers that were fighting on the streets. Gelli had also told him that Mussolini and his lover Clara Petacci had been caught by the partisans, shot, stripped and hung in a square in Milan before being cut down to lie in the gutter.

Gelli convinced him that his best chance of getting out off Berlin in one piece lay with the messenger that he would send to get him. Rosenberg had thought he heard a noise and stepped back into the corner, cocking the personal Luger that had been a gift to him from the Fuerhur.

A single beam of light scythed through the darkness.

'Show yourself' hissed the voice

Rosenberg stepped into the light and found himself staring at a young girl, she could not have been much more than 16 years of age, she was dressed in rags, she wore a dirty shawl over her head and her face was gaunt and smeared with dirt. She wasn't wearing any shoes either and her feet were cut and bleeding. Rosenberg shied away from her outstretched hand and cocked the Luger, pointing it at the girl.

'What do you want' said Rosenberg

'Kommen sie' replied the girl

Rosenberg's mind spun. Bormann had told him that the Testament was in force and that by now Doenitz would be issuing the orders. He knew that he could not permit the Russians to capture him, he nervously flicked his tongue across the molar at the back of his mouth in a reassuring movement, aware that if the worst come to the worst, he would cheat the Russians of their prize.

'Kommen sie' urged the girl, 'I know where to take you'

Rosenberg put the luger in his pocket and followed the girl back up onto the street, she walked across to a pile of rubble and pulled out a soiled piece of red material and handed it to Rosenberg

'Wave it at the Russians' she said 'They'll think you are my father

Rosenberg unfolded the material and seen the cheap stencil of the star, he pulled it out and wrapped it around his shoulders. Suddenly there was a horrendous screaming sound and Rosenberg threw himself flat onto the ground soiling his suit and tearing the knees from his trousers

'Stalin Organs' mimed the girl, you'll get use to the sound'.

They hurried along what Rosenberg recognised as the remains of Berliner Allee and turned left towards Virschowstrasse. They passed the Horst Wessel hospital or what was left of it. On Landsbergerstrasse Rosenberg noticed that there were bodies swinging from the lampposts with signs fluttering from their chests

'I am a coward and a traitor to the Reich'

Eventually they made it to a barrier near the Alexanderplatz only to be accosted by three Hitler Youth wearing greatcoats, one of them had picked up one of the glittering plates of the 'headhunter' military police, it hung casually around his neck. Two dead horses lay in the middle of the road, their entrails spilt out onto the ground and scattered around the shallow crater left by the Red army shell that had found them.

Rosenberg stopped to speak to the oldest of the Youth but the girl tugged at his sleeve. As they reached the next corner, there was the sudden sound of rifle fire, it was just a ragged volley of about half a dozen shots, but sounded so near that

Rosenberg stopped in his tracks, frightened that he was moving into a line of fire. The Hitler Youth ran up behind him and one of them started to fire wildly from a smeisser machine pistol that bucked and leapt in his hands as the fire spewed from the barrel. Rosenberg reached over and slapped the youngster in the face and took the gun from him.

He turned around to look for the girl and staggered backwards as he saw her body lying on the ground in front of him, her eyes wide open in a mixture of surprise and shock, her stomach a bloody mess where the bullets had hit her. In a rage Rosenberg turned and emptied the remainder of the machine pistol ammunition into the three Hitler Youth, he didn't stop firing until the gun jammed. He stopped, threw the gun down and flattened himself against the side of the burned out building, wrestling with his wildly beating heart and blinking the sweat away from his eyes.

After a moment he dared look around the corner and saw five or six shapes scrambling over a pile of rubble. They were coming his way!

'Hey you!' one of them shouted

Rosenberg turned.

Don't move!

Rosenberg raised his hands above his head and waited. As they got closer, he could see that their uniforms were green and that there were police badges on their sleeves. Rosenberg knew straight away from his time in the East that these were 'special' police like the police he had used in Warsaw and places like that.

The Wachtmeister ambled over to him.

Where are you going Jew?

The words stung into Rosenberg's brain.

'A Jew? How could they possibly think he was a Jew'

The man spoke again 'Jews are not allowed on the street, step out where I can see you'

Rosenberg stood up, conveniently dropping the red rag that the girl had given him to the ground.

'Check my papers' said Rosenberg offering his party card and identity card.

The Wachtmeister looked at the card and then looked at Rosenberg before snapping out a perfect 'Heil Hitler'.

'I apologise Sir, you cannot be too careful and we have orders to shoot...

'I've seen your handiwork major' said Rosenberg 'where are you going now?

'We've heard that there are still SS fighting over near the Zoo, we were going to try for there and join up. Stay low sir, there are snipers in every building'

Rosenberg followed the men around the corner and away from the lighted areas. He'd gone to the back of the line and there was one soldier behind him. They'd been traversing the Alexanderplatz for nearly an hour when the Major held up his hand.

'We will go on ahead and check that the way is clear, Mauser will stay with you and take you when we signal to him'

Rosenberg nodded and sat down against the wall as Mauser took up the point. The others went across some open ground and the major had just turned to wave to Mauser when a long burst of fire coupled by a series of hand grenade explosions obliterated the area where the major and his men had been standing. Mauser stood up and took a round straight between the eyes from the sniper that had been sitting up in the top window space of the burned out department store.

Rosenberg didn't move at all, he stayed exactly where he was until daylight broke. He was sitting against the wall when two Red Army soldiers came from behind him. Intending to take a leak, they'd propped their guns against the wall and were undoing their flies as Rosenberg stirred from his sleep. They rushed over, hauled him to his feet and slapped him about before emptying his pockets and stealing his watch. They also found the Luger that thankfully was bereft of bullets in his pocket. Just as they were about to force him against the wall, their sergeant came across to them. He'd heard the rumpus and thought that they'd found some fresh German girls for fun. When he reached the men, he strode across, slapped the two men in the face and took Rosenberg's watch from one of them.

He then cast his eye over the disheveled man who stood in front of him.

'Take him with you; the officers can question him back at base.'

It took the Russian NKVD exactly 20 minutes to discover just who they had in captivity and more importantly, the first thing they did was to remove the capsule of cyanide that was secreted in the mouth of a now unconscious Alfred Rosenberg.

Chapter29

Maria slept for quite a while in a restless sort of way and when she woke up and didn't see Samuel she began to panic, this brought on another bout of severe coughing and the Doctor had to ease her again.

Adam had no idea what had happened to Mollayan but they'd agreed that in the event of a separation, Mollayan had been very specific as to the actions that Adam had to take. He'd told Adam

'If anything happens that prevents either of us from meeting up in Bad Weisee, you are to make your way as best you can to either Munich or Innsbruck. You are to go to either of these two addresses that you must memorise and stay there until I contact you. If you do not hear from me for five days after Bad Weisee, you must presume that I am dead or incapable of helping you. In that case you must protect as best you can. Hopefully this will not happen but we cannot afford the risk.'

Adam had agreed at the time and despite his initial panic at losing Samuel, knew that when he reached Munich, Mollayan would know what to do ... he hoped.

Once Mollayan had settled Andrew in one of the houses in the village, he set about arranging a transfer for Adam and Maria. First of all, he contacted his superiors in the SOE in London and told them that he had two material witnesses secured for the prosecution in the event of forthcoming trials. He learned that several high ranking Nazis including Goring and Jodl had been arrested. He also learned that Alfred Rosenberg had been captured by the Russians and had been handed over to the Americans on the assurance that should there be trials, the Russians would be given the opportunity to be represented in the Judicial process.

He was told about General Smythe's activity and the death of Himmler. When he heard this, he realised that he had been lucky and suspected that Adam and Maria and Samuel would have got away as well. He got clearance from London to hold his witnesses in his own custody. London didn't want the Americans or the French getting access to them until they had been de-briefed by British Intelligence.

His bosses in London would not have been happy had they known where Mollayan was.

They thought he was still based in Flossenberg. He used this to his advantage. His plan was simple.

If Adam and Maria arrived in Bad Weisee he would get London to issue a hands-off warning to Smythe. Mollayan would simply turn up with an ambulance, claim protective custody and drive them away. He could of course call on the remaining members of the Priory but he was reasonably sure he would be able to handle it himself. They'd be in France before anyone would know and since he would have to sign for the two of them as prisoners, no one would know where they were. The fact that there were millions of displaced people wandering all across Europe would in itself prevent any resources being allocated to find a reporter and a camp survivor.

The second thing that he done was to make contact with both 'safe' houses, Frau Verheyden had been a Priory member for years and had kept people in her house in Munich for years. Herr Johann Kessel was a Priory member as well and was one of the few people who remembered Mollayan from his earliest days.

He called Innsbruck and left the necessary code word, he then rang Munich where the telephone was answered on the first ring

'They must not succeed' said Mollayan

'They will never succeed' a voice answered

'Good day Madame Verheyden, I trust you are well?'

'I am thank you. And you?'

'Ca va' answered Mollayan and then started to say 'when the fields are ripe with corn and...

'I don't understand' countered Madame Verheyden 'your package is already here, they arrived yesterday.

Mollayan stopped, something had happened!

'May I speak? Said Mollayan

There was a pause and then Adam came on the telephone

'Henry, we had to get off the train. Maria is desperately sick, I lost Samuel. We've no money; we can't stay here. Maria needs a doctor....

'Slow down' said Mollayan 'Start at the beginning'

Adam relayed the whole story to Mollayan. He told him how he had fallen asleep the previous evening.

'When I woke, the train still hadn't moved and light was streaming through the window. I stood up and took off my jacket and tried to fashion a curtain by pinning it across the window. Maria was in a deep almost coma like sleep, her breathing was very shallow and her chest hardly lifting at all. I left the compartment and walked down the corridor until I stumbled across a doctor moving up the train towards me'.

The doctor accompanied me back to the compartment where thankfully Maria was still sleeping. The doctor checked her pulse and checked her vital signs.

'I cannot let her travel on this train; she will die if she does. I will get her into the army hospital in Munich; it's not far from here'. We don't know how long the Russians will make the train wait here.

He arranged transport to the hospital as quickly as possible and I went with Maria in a field ambulance. Thankfully she slept through the journey. The Americans are treating her. I could do no more for her so I came out and tried to make contact with you, had no luck and tried the number that you made me write down' said Adam wearily. 'There is something else you should know...

'Yes? Replied Mollayan

'We lost the boy' sighed Adam 'he never made it off the first train that we were on'

'Does Maria know?' asked Mollayan

'Thankfully not but when she wakes I'll have to be there'

When he had finished, there was a silence as Mollayan consumed the information he had heard. It was not good.

'Adam let me speak to Frau Verheyden'

Frau Verheyden returned the receiver to Adam and Mollayan spoke

'You did the right thing going to see Frau Verheyden' said Mollayan 'What I am about to say will be hard for you to take but believe me, it is for the best. I want you to leave tonight....

'I won't do it' shouted Adam

'Listen to me' said Mollayan. 'My cover within freemasonry has been blown, it will take them less than a day to figure out what has happened. I can protect you in Rennes; I can't protect you in Munich! Maria will die if you move her, Madame Verheyden's son is a doctor, she will nurse Maria to health and we will monitor her progress and move her when she is fit. I need you here with Andrew, and me, remember we have to protect the Yahweh from both the church and the freemasons!

Adam murmured something about trust and then said

'Very well' I'll leave within the hour'

Adam tiptoed into Maria's room in the hospital, she was awake

'Is that you, Adam?' whispered Maria

'Yes' said Adam

'Where is Samuel?' asked Maria

Adam was silent, wrestling with his conscience until eventually he spoke

'Samuel went on to Berlin alone' said Adam.

Maria was silent for a minute and then started to cry softly, Adam went over and put his arms around her and held her, saying 'He'll be all right, he's a strong kid!

Maria looked into Adam's eyes and said

'You're leaving, aren't you?'

'Yes' said Adam 'for a while, Mollayan thinks we're in danger if we stay together

'Frau Verheyden is one of us and her son is a doctor; he'll look after you until I return

You need to rest, get well and regain your strength. I will return for you when it is safe'.

'You have to get better for Andrew, he is so much looking forward to meeting you'.

Maria sighed and said

'Take care for me and hurry back'

Adam got up and went out of the room, he was very upset and it took him a few minutes to compose himself. He went down to where Frau Verheyden was sitting, she had come with him to the hospital, she looked up and said 'Fear not young man, we'll take care of her and get her better. You have to protect us and make sure they do not succeed'. I will take her to my home and will nurse her to health, my son works here, he will arrange it.

Adam smiled at the old woman, he had not encountered devotion like this ever

'I'll do my best, you can be sure of that'

With that Adam took his leave and following Mollayan's instructions began his long journey to Rennes le Chateau.

First of all he changed into civilian clothes at the hospital, taking his uniform and throwing it in one of the many bins that were at the back of the hospital store. He had received a travel pass from the doctor and Frau Verheyden's son had provided some money and a train ticket to Paris. Adam arrived in Paris the next day and by cadging lifts and using what limited trains that there were, he managed to get across into the Languedoc and finally to the village of Rennes le chateau. The journey had taken five days and Mollayan and Andrew greeted a very tired Adam.

He assured them that Maria was all right, he relayed his escape story and the loss of Samuel to both men. Andrew had a lot of questions that he wanted to ask about Maria but Mollayan said

'It's late and you both need rest, we have a very busy couple of days ahead of us. Tomorrow we will assemble the map and put Andrew's information into what we know. Go on, get to bed now' said Mollayan.

'Goodnight' was the simultaneous reply and all three men retired, unsure of what the tomorrow would bring.

Smythe and Hemmindale were in constant contact

'We've lost them again' said Smythe

'Don't worry' said Hemmindale 'Mollayan is still under Army Jurisdiction and will have to surface soon, when he does we'll be ready. We'll wipe out the whole sorry lot of them and put an end to this idolatry once and for all.'

'Shouldn't we follow them and see where they lead us or rather what they lead us to?' asked Smythe.

'We'll cross that bridge when they resurface, that will be a decision for the inner sanctum'

'Very well' said Smythe 'so we wait?

'Not for long' said Hemmindale 'not for long'

Chapter 30

Giovanni Santini had reached the same conclusion after hearing that Andrew Lassiter had 'vanished' from Flossenberg. His enquiries had brought to light the interference of that infernal Priory of Zion organisation. He reasoned that if they were protecting Andrew then there was more to young Lassiter than met the eye.

He had spoken to some of the Germans that the Holy See had assisted in 'relocation' and he was able to glean information that confirmed his original suspicion. He was correct to think that Andrew Lassiter had prior knowledge of the Holy Sepulchre and Santini had put him in a position whereby he knew all or as much as he needed to know about the great lie. Santini had no option, Lassiter would have to be silenced in some way but the more pressing problem of finding him was uppermost in Santini's mind. Santini had always known that the Nazi's had been predominantly anti-Christian in their ideology. Sitting now in his private rooms, surrounded by the opulence that a prince in the church could command, he ruminated as to whether their ideology was so criminal? They persecuted the Jews, so what? The Jews crucified the saviour, the German crucify the Jews. What really concerned him was that there had been no reporting of the discovery of Martin Bormann. This was not good as Bormann had access to information that would be 'embarrassing' for the church. Santini had no objection to giving Bormann assistance so long as he was able to control the assistance, not knowing where Bormann was did not augur well. Santini pushed it to the back of his mind, he knew of someone who for a fee would find Bormann quickly if need be.

Batista winced as he recalled reading the circular the Bormann had produced as far back as 1941

'Only the Reich government and by its direction the party have a right to leadership of the people. The possibility of church influence must be totally removed. Not until this has happened does the state leadership have influence on the individual citizens. Not until then are the people and the Reich secure in their existence'

Batista thought that Rosenberg had been the most dangerous enemy of the Holy See because of his determination to uncover the lie and rid the Reich of Christianity once and for all. Batista knew even when witnessing the signing of the concordat in 1933 that the Nazis would never uphold its contents. Batista had all of the copies of the reports that were sent to Ribbentrop detailing some of the crimes that were committed against the church. Needless to say, they had never received a reply to any of them. Secondly the practice of saving Jews by insisting that they convert to Catholicism had not produced the results that were anticipated and many of the so called 'converts' would renounce their faith now that the war was over. Of course it was beneficial to assist some of the more influential people to escape; the Vatican had long had an arrangement whereby certain assistances could be gained in return for...

Batista decided against his better judgment that a waiting game was probably the safest thing to do at the moment, sooner or later young Lassiter would show himself and when he did, Batista would be ready.

Andrew hadn't slept well, he had another vision of his father talking to him, the blue light was almost consuming and he heard his father say

'They must not succeed'

Andrew woke with a start to find Adam at his side

'You were dreaming' said Adam

Andrew had sat up in the bed and rubbed his eyes before speaking

'Can we do this thing that is being asked of us?'

'We have no choice said Adam 'I must do it for my family and...

Andrew interjected

'I must do it for my father.

Adam spoke

'Mollayan will help us, don't worry. We'll succeed and Maria will be safe as well, I'm sure of it'.

A rueful laugh escaped from Andrew

'What's so funny?' asked Adam

'I nearly said 'Praise be to God' a bit hollow, given the circumstances, don't you think?

Adam chuckled and said

'I made the same mistake as well, you're maybe not that far out, maybe we've just got the name wrong!

They got up early the next morning and began to piece together the information that they had amassed. Andrew was absolutely staggered when he read Isaac's testimony and had he not have been able to part corroborate what Isaac was saying could not in his wildest dreams have imagined the scale and immensity of their 'discovery'. For a long time Andrew was very quiet and at one point actually left the room and went outside. Adam went to follow him but was told to remain by Mollayan

'He, like you, must deal with this in his own way'

Mollayan eventually got up and went outside where he found Andrew sitting on the side of a fountain. He went over and put his hand on his shoulder. Andrew looked at him through glazed eyes

'You know what the worst thing is? For years I prayed that Jesus Christ would come into the life of my Father and that he would see the error of his ways. I couldn't understand his antipathy towards the church. Now I realise that he was right and I was wrong.'

'That's not true' said Mollayan 'you were like Thomas in the Christian bible, you are and would remain a doubter because you would not know about Yahweh. You must remember that the only people who dictate history are the winners. We of the Priory stem from eight families who, a long time ago, made a discovery that forced them to change their lives. We are doing the same.'

'But the lies, the church, the people, free speech. All of these are fundamental to why we exist, you're asking me to accept that 500 million people are living a lie?' said Andrew

'And are happy in their oblivion' countered Mollayan 'One day the truth will be told and it will not matter because the time will have come. Do you see why we must protect, we protect because we know the truth!! The church would have us castigated as harlots and zealots in order to discredit us, remember Andrew, the victors have always dictated History and the church have lived in their gospel for so long that any challenge against doctrine is a challenge against God himself.

'What about these other people, the Freemasons?' asked Andrew

'That is more sinister' answered Mollayan 'they have created a pseudo religion that would be an affront to your senses. It is a secret underhand, scheming, manipulative organisation that is full of its own sense of righteousness and is a sickening hybrid of the origins of the happening in the Temple. Narrow-minded aristocrats who wield their power with sickening results control it. They wish to consume and control the knowledge of Yahweh and use it as a justification for their own interpretation of the timeline of the Temple'

Andrew was watching Mollayan as his shoulders visibly sagged. The stress of the past few weeks were beginning to tell on him.

'You must rest Henry' said Andrew 'I know what my responsibility is, I will do what is necessary.

They both rejoined Adam who turned and exclaimed

'I think I know where the Holy Sepulchre is!

Adam had been pouring over the assembled Cyrillic and the map that Mollayan had provided on which the markings of Adam's father's dig were shown. As he traced a path from the one site that was present on both maps, he noticed that there were a series of markings on the Cyrillic map that identically matched the wording on the other side of the Cyrillic. Adam held the Cyrillic up to the light and seen a shape overlaid into the map, a shape that he recognised! It was a 'guider' shape and Adam surmised that if the 'guiders' were placed on the map, they would show the location of the Sepulchre.

They only had one 'guider' with them so Adam began the task of placing and marking the location of each guide point. When he had finished, he held the Cyrillic up to the light again and as the sun blazed through the window and hit the map, the guide marks that he had made formed a rough circle around a spot on the map, a place called Sulamein. It appeared to be on the other side of the hill as marked on the Cyrillic. He checked his father's Map and whilst he could find no reference to 'Sulamein' he deduced that the sepulchre was hidden at the reference point on his father's map!

Mollayan examined Adam's work and studied both maps before finally exclaiming

'I think you are right!

Andrew butted in

'So is it safe?' he asked

'One of us will have to go and find out' said Mollayan 'it'll have to be me'

'Why?' they asked

'Adam will have to return to America soon, his pretence for being away is wearing thin and because of the threat from Smythe and Hemmindale, we cannot stay together much longer. You, Andrew have to make up your mind as to your future actions. If the church find you they will find away to make sure you do not speak about your discovery.

'They'll know that you know about Maria's evidence and the fact that they did nothing and won't tolerate any inference that they were negligent. Furthermore one of you will have to look after Maria and keep in contact with Madame Verheyden. That leaves me as the one to go and see. If the sepulchre is in danger, there are Priory members who will help me. It's best that you do not know who they are, your job is to ensure that no one succeeds in discovering what we know' said Mollayan

'You've told me that Megan and the kids are safe' said Adam

'They are'

'Then as long as I can telephone them. I'm in no hurry to return and I'm still sending copy back to the States'. Adam retorted

'Adam, you are one of the five, there are only three of you. The church doesn't know that Maria has survived and don't know you. Mollayan continued

'They will know about Andrew but so long as he stays quiet they will not do anything to compromise him. The freemasons know about me now and through Smythe will have worked out that Maria has survived and that the name Lassiter might be a connection. You have to be protected as much as the Yahweh itself. If any of our enemies captured you, we would be able to protect neither.' Isaac knew that, I know it and the sooner ......

'But what about Maria and Andrew?' asked Adam

‘They don’t matter as much as you do’?

‘Why not’ said Adam indignantly

Mollayan was beginning to get angry with Adam

‘Because you’ve got a son and heir and are responsible for passing on the mantle as it should have been passed onto you!

‘That means nothing!’ raged Adam, ‘Maria could have a child!!’

‘No she can’t ‘thundered Mollayan ‘Samuel wasn’t the only one that Mengele experimented on! Satisfied now??

Mollayan was ashen faced and struggled to compose himself. Andrew couldn’t believe what he had just heard and Adam was standing in a state of complete incomprehension at what he had just heard. It seemed like an eternity before anyone spoke and then Mollayan said

‘Have you had a chance to interpret the Cyrillic yet? Andrew’

Adam went over and put his hand on Mollayan’s shoulder

‘I’m sorry, Henry, I didn’t know.’

‘I should have told you but you have enough to contend with at the moment and you must remain focused’ replied Mollayan.

Andrew spoke up

‘You asked me about a translation, I think we are better with an interpretation of sorts. Let’s all examine the Cyrillic and apply what we now know.

‘I shall be the father and he shall be my son. He is the branch of my forefather who shall arise with the interpreter of the law to rule in Zion at the end of time’

Andrew continued

‘I’ve broken the Cyrillic into segments for the same reason it was done in the beginning.’

Adam and Mollayan glanced at each other, they'd been pretty frank with Andrew but they hadn't told him everything. He knew about some of Isaac's work, not it all and Mollayan had volunteered no information about his thoughts on what the Holy Sepulchre contained.

'I shall be the father and he shall be my son...

'I think this refers to the Yahweh assuming the pastoral role as a father whilst at the same time suggesting that the Father and Son is part of a trilogy. If you consider Catholic doctrine, you'll find a 'Holy Trinity' God the father, God the son and God the Holy Spirit. I think that the church is in some way playing lip service to the notion of a 'third entity' in that the Holy Spirit has always been viewed as a gift from God. I think that Yahweh is the overall Spirit and the Father/Son link are creations of convenience for the Spirit or form that the Yahweh chooses to represent itself'.

He is the branch of my forefather

'I think that this suggests that the Father/son image isn't the first 'God' like entity that has existed. It could well be that the reference to the forefather applies in some way to an earlier creation of man that was maybe exterminated as a result of one of the nature driven Ice Ages or whatever. We cannot be sure but I would hazard a guess that Yahweh decided to have a second or even third go at creating a life form and realised that an entity of control through worship would be an integral part of creation'

Who shall arise with the interpreter of the law...

'If you follow my logic then the interpreter of the law is the person/s who buried the

Yahweh in the first place. I get confused here because it is obvious that all of this happened a long time before Jesus had his ministry. I ask myself about your assertion that Saul/Paul preached a false gospel, who told him, how did he know? I also think that anybody who has protected or venerated Yahweh is included within this 'interpreter' category.

Mollayan again glanced over at Adam and then said

'I think we can help you but I would prefer it if you finished your analysis'

'Very well' said Andrew

'Rule in Zion at the end of time'

'This is the bit that really frightened me' said Andrew. In every doctrine that has ever been reached, the inference of the longevity of devotion was always 'until the end of time'. When I read this for the first time I missed the significance of the wording, it was much later when it suddenly dawned on me what was actually being said.

If I'm correct in my analysis then I believe I know the reason why the Yahweh has provoked such widespread acts of bestiality, the latest one being the attempted genocide of the Jews!

Adam never took his eyes from Andrew's face, Mollayan was barely breathing and concentrating on every word that the priest spoke.

'O.K' said Andrew 'I*n Zion* has always been claimed by the Jews as their 'home'. This dates back to their time in Egypt, the exodus led by Moses and the giving of the tablets of stone. Scripture has us believe that they wandered the desert for 40 years until they were finally led to their Zion. For the next 1500 years every empire that coveted their space has ruled them. That's why I think that Zion is not a country. Zion is the name given to this version of our world. I know that's a bit much to take but I think the next bit gives it away. You see, I think that the word 'at' implies that the decision to terminate this latest attempt at creating a world has already been made and *'at the end of time'* has already been pre determined.

Adam spoke first 'Where does all the killing fit in then'

'Simple really' said Andrew 'Their, meaning the Nazis, Freemasons even the Catholic Church, interpretation is based on conjecture and only having part of the story.

Take the Thule for example, they believe they are descendants of a lost race and decide that the Jews have lain claim to their mantle. They believe Zion is Atlantis so what do they do? Wipe out the Jews. The Catholic Church .... Andrew took a breath 'The Roman Catholic Church. A religion developed in Rome by Romans at the end of their military empire. What better way to continue to flourish and control the masses without military muscle?

The Crusades were a perfect example, let the people fight for the cross, no matter how many die, the Roman church is seen as protectors of the Cross and Jesus isn't a Jew anymore, he's a deity and therefore doctrine can be written to prove he came to save who?

The Inquisition ensured that Jesus came on Earth to save only those who subscribed to the doctrine preached by the Roman Church. By the time Luther and the various other 'faith options' came along, it was too late. Look at the final part of the inscription

to rule in Zion at the end of time'

'I believe that this is the notice, no matter what is done to try and prevent or change or control. The Yahweh will rule this world at the end of the time ...... no matter what!!!

Quiet reigned on the gathering, each man locked in contemplation of the magnitude of what was being said.

'You were puzzled with the role of Paul and his message' said Mollayan. 'I didn't realise the significance of it myself at the time but when I heard your Sang Real evidence. I knew that it would only be a matter of time before you worked out that the 'Priory of Zion' were descendants of the Templar Knights who had discovered a truth, so significant it enabled them to assume an almost Godlike status. You, of course would have been correct. The Templar Knights had gone on the Crusade for one reason only, you see, each of those eight families could trace their bloodline back to the time when a certain woman arrived in this very village carrying the Sang Real, the blood of Jesus'.

Andrew slowly began to nod his head

'Jesus was an interpreter' said Andrew

'Jesus was 'the' interpreter! answered Mollayan and his bloodline have protected the giver of the interpretation, the Yahweh since then. The woman, Mary of Magdalene, knew all about Saul/ Paul, she was the vessel that the Yahweh used to reach Paul. She also knew that Paul had been told of the Holy Sepulchre and what it was.

Up until now I was of the opinion that Paul's testimony of what actually happened on the Road to Damascus was under the temple and that the Templar Knights had been sent to protect it. I now know that wasn't the only thing there!

'What else was there? Asked Adam

'I think that the end date, the notice to quit, the end of the world date was also there' said Mollayan. 'I also believe that the secret of Fatima that Andrew has made reference to, tells the same story. Everyone is looking for the knowledge of Yahweh, they cannot comprehend the scale to which their deeds and actions are contributing to the end of their world.

Adam spoke

'Does this mean that the 'interpreters' can be likened to the animals on the Ark. I mean, a time will come when we will be invited to join Yahweh in another life .... an afterlife?

Again there was another long silence until Adam spoke

'I remember a conversation I had with Isaac Tauber and he said something to me that I took with a pinch of salt, I now know what he meant when he said

'Be scared Adam, be very scared indeed'.

At that moment the reality of Andrew's synopsis weighed heavy on all of their minds and although they didn't say it, both Adam and Mollayan knew that Andrew was right in his interpretation of the Cyrillic. All of the evidence and writings suggested the same.

Mollayan stood up and said to Andrew

'What do you think the Holy Sepulchre contains?

'The key to Yahweh, the secret of the soul'

Mollayan nodded his head in agreement.

'There's something else you should know' said Andrew

Mollayan lifted his head

'What is that' they both said simultaneously

'I don't believe that any of us has to go anywhere!'

'But the Holy Sepulchre, the map? said Adam

'Yes' said Andrew ' the Cyrillic map shows a location called '*Sulamein* a place we cannot trace on the other map.'

'That means nothing' said Mollayan 'places change and we need to be sure'.

'I am sure' said Andrew

'How'

'Because we have in our possession the map and the 'guiders' and I think that they are showing us *'Sulamein'* not as a location of a vessel but as the place where Yahweh will return to! I am positive that we hold the key just like all our fathers did. They didn't go looking for a site, they took the pieces of the Cyrillic so that the very thing we want to do wouldn't happen!

They could never have known that we would re assemble the Cyrillic!

'But' said Adam' if you are right, then the only people who know about *'Sulamein'* is the three of us!

Mollayan interjected

'Hold on a minute, go back to the 'where Yahweh will return' bit

Andrew smiled and said

'O.K, Henry, you agree with me with regard to what we think is in the Holy Sepulchre, Yes?

Mollayan nodded his head

'And we both agree that Adam had located *'Sulamein'* on the Cyrillic?

'Where is this going? asked Adam

'I believe that *'Sulamein'* is an interpretation and that the Cyrillic tells us what it is, not where it is. We will never discover where it is, whoever hid it made sure of that. What is important is that we now have incontrovertible proof as to what it is! said Andrew.

'I don't understand' said Adam

'Let me guess' said Mollayan 'If I follow you, you are suggesting that we no longer require the mystery of faith, we have the proof of the Yahweh in our hands!

'Exactly' said Andrew

'Will somebody tell me what you are talking about!' shouted Adam.

Mollayan looked at Andrew and invited him to speak

'Sulamein' if I'm correct means 'soul of man'. The guiders have shown us the proof that there is a 'soul' and that it will be reclaimed by the Yahweh at the end of time!' exclaimed Andrew.' 'Imagine what would happen if the Church or anybody else had that information. Now do you see why they must not succeed?

Adam struggled to comprehend the revelations of the last few hours, he was still reeling about Maria. Now he was been asked to accept that he and his future bloodline were some sort of 'interpreters' of a deity that would come back at a pre-determined time to gather his flock and start again.

'I need some time on my own to get my head around all of this' said Adam

'Of course' said Andrew 'but remember this, there are three of us who know the truth, we must do whatever we have to ensure it stays that way.

Frau Verheyden was in fairly regular communication with Mollayan about the state of Maria's health, she had indeed contracted TB and whilst Frau Verheyden's son had managed to stabilise her condition but she didn't appear to be getting any better and he was afraid that she may have a relapse.

Mollayan discussed the situation with both Andrew and Adam

'In light of Andrew's discovery, I don't really see that anything can be gained from going to look for the site of the Holy Sepulchre' said Adam. I also believe that we must do all in our power to protect and deliver Maria to safety. I must admit that I am still at a loss to understand my own role in protecting the Yahweh'

'I can see the connection between the Templars and the Freemasons and why freemasonry has tried to suppress the knowledge of Yahweh. I also understand why the Catholic Church will do all in its power to suppress the evidence that we have uncovered. I accept that my mother was a descendant of one of the original Templar families and I can understand my father's willingness to assume that mantle of responsibility. I also understand the significance of my father's finding of the Cyrillic, in fact the more I think about it, the more I am of the conclusion that it was no accident. What I fail to understand is this. If the Magdalene took the bloodline of the Nazarene to Rennes le Chateau and established a bloodline to protect the Yahweh and the Templars went on a crusade to reclaim the secrets of Paul's testimony, why not just bury the existence of the Yahweh then?

'Why has there been a continuous blood trail over the centuries when it could all have been secreted away all those years ago and we could have sat back and waited for this 'coming' asked Adam.

Mollayan spoke up

'We have venerated the truth and have been punished to near extinction for our belief, don't you see that we, you, are the interpreters of the truth. You were 'discovered' by Isaac Tauber who had part of the picture but not it all. I've had to expose myself to protect you because as far as we are concerned, you are the only person at the moment who can ensure that the secret of the Yahweh continues to live to the point that when the sign eventually does arrive, it will be acted upon by the 'interpreter' at that time'.

Andrew walked over and put his arm around Adam's shoulders and said

'Our father's played their part in protecting the Yahweh as best they could. You've witnessed the lengths to which these people will go to try and acquire the secret of the Yahweh. Your own father was murdered, protecting the knowledge. You've told me about Captain Reid, what happened his father? Johannsen? How do we know he wasn't murdered as well? Maria's father? My own father was forced to live a life of isolation in the outback of Australia'

Andrew continued

'By all of our actions, we have exposed the Yahweh to its greatest danger in centuries and we must work fast to ensure that there is no possibility of it being exposed'.

'What about the families? The Templars?' asked Adam

Mollayan walked across to the table and sat down, there was a bottle of wine on the table and he poured three glasses. He took a sip from him and then invited Adam to sit down.

'I have tried to give you as full a picture as I can about these matters but even I have been shocked by the revelations of the past few hours. The Priory of Zion believes in the truth of the message relayed to Paul all those centuries ago. That is all they have, they do not possess the facts that you do. They are committed to protecting their faith just as the Church and the Freemasons are committed to protecting their version and in doing so are quite prepared to eradicate any threat or opposition. We are small in number and our people are old. I am the last bloodline descendant of Jacques de Mollay and ...

Andrew held his hand up as if to command silence

'The Jacques de Mollay, last Grand Master of the Templars?

'Yes' said Mollayan.

Andrew walked over to the table and gulped at his wine before beginning to speak

'Have you heard of the Shroud of Turin?'

'Of course' said Mollayan 'the Church have for years suggested that it is the burial shroud of the Nazarene.' They obviously don't choose to accept the truth.

'Which is?' mused Andrew

'The Nazarene was removed from the tomb in the shroud, therefore making it impossible for the Shroud to be the Nazarene.

'You're right' said Andrew 'about them not accepting the truth that is because they choose to. They know it is not their saviour who is represented in the shroud but they decided it was better to have the masses believe it was Jesus than have them actually discover the truth'.

Mollayan sensed that another revelation was coming from Andrew and he steeled himself

'You know the truth, Andrew?

'I know who was in the Shroud of Turin exclaimed Andrew

'Who?'

'None other than your ancestor, the last Grand master of the Templars, Jacques de Mollay! Furthermore the church knew it as well and did all in their power to have it suppressed for fear of creating a medieval deity of worship'. Jacques de Mollay was widely considered by many to be a holy martyr, by some he had been proclaimed as a 'second messiah' who had once again been crucified by Rome. His death was linked to the onset of the 'black death' plague that ravaged Europe and the church were of the belief that if it were discovered that they had a hand in the extinction of the Templars, they ran the risk of being swept away by a new cult. What did they do? They encouraged people to worship the shroud as a relic of the saviour and Templarism went underground.' That's when it came into conflict with the modern day freemasons.'

Mollayan and Adam were speechless, all of their discoveries and knowledge was being put into a historical perspective of such ferocity that to deny the need to protect the Yahweh would be tantamount to a heresy of Armageddon like proportion.

Chapter 31

Adam broke the silence by lifting the bottle of wine and pouring some more drink

'We've agreed that the Holy Sepulchre is safe?

'Yes' the other two replied

'Our immediate goal is to ensure that Maria recovers, after that we must decide on a course of action.

Addressing Andrew, Adam said, 'What would the church do if they knew what we know?

'Do not underestimate the power of Rome' said Andrew 'I suspect that they already have been able to work out who I am. That will put them into a frenzy that will be driven by the fact that I have disappeared!

Mollayan interjected 'The Army Chaplain, I suppose?

'Exactly' said Andrew 'Rome will know I've disappeared with two others, they'll know who with a phone call. If they think we are a threat they will do all that they have to suppress that threat!

'At least the masons know little' said Adam

'I'm afraid that's not true either' said Mollayan as he relayed the conversation that he had with General Smythe two days previously.

'They'll not know where we are but they'll be ready for us when we surface. I cannot be in your company for much longer as my being here puts us all in mortal danger.

Andrew added

'Do not underestimate Rome either, it is not just a church, it is an independent state, in its organisation ; and the worst form of state, an autocracy which will stoop to any level to protect its jurisdiction and dominance. Remember this, knowledge does not always bring wisdom; ignorance never does, yet this is the mantra that has festered in the church for hundreds of years. Ignorance breeds fear and fear in the church is treated as a threat. I, myself have seen what the church is capable of with regard to the suffering of others and I am not proud to have been a part of it.'

Mollayan awoke early the next morning and left the house to communicate with London, he knew that he wouldn't be able to stay in Rennes le Chateau for much longer. Smythe and Hemmindale would go to the Grand Council and seek permission to have him 'sanctioned'. Given the nature and depth of his perceived betrayal, he knew that he would not suffer an easy death if he was caught. He was sure that Adam would be able to return to America and the Priory would ensure that he remained safe. Andrew was a different proposition altogether. Mollayan had never met anyone like Andrew before. He was astounded at his powers of deduction and had no doubt that Andrew could take his place as the principal in the Priory of Zion. He had to be sure that Andrew wanted this, he couldn't bring himself to consider the alternative but the fact was that if Andrew did not undertake allegiance to the protection of Yahweh, then one of Mollayan's last acts would be to ensure he didn't live to damage its safety.

Andrew was consumed with thoughts of a woman he'd never met, a woman who had captivated his thinking through her bravery and brought him on this voyage of discovery. In quiet moments, he found himself contemplating their first meeting, she didn't know who he was and when she found out would probably consider him an apologist for the very people that she'd turned to for help.

The last report that they had received had said that she had to be moved to a warmer climate. Andrew pressed Mollayan to make arrangements to bring her south as quickly as possible.

Mollayan's network of people kept him informed of activity within his group and he used this to communicate with London every day. The day after they arrived in Rennes le Chateau, he had received orders to return to London. There had been a General Election and Churchill had broken off from the Potsdam conference to learn the results. The legacy of Roosevelt was now becoming very apparent in reports that were being sent directly into Mollayan's office. The final conferences, the British-American meeting at Quebec (the Octagon Conference of September 1944) and the British-American-Soviet meeting at Yalta (February 1945) took place in the wake of the successful landings in Normandy.

Important issues were British-American co-operation on developing the atomic bomb, including the question of whether to share this information with the Soviets; how to divide Germany into zones of occupation; and to arrange for Soviet entry into the war against Japan. By the Yalta Conference, political issues had come to the forefront. The Americans went to Yalta determined to obtain Stalin's support for the United Nations. Issues that more vitally concerned the British and the Soviets were establishing boundaries in central and Eastern Europe and setting up governments that would be satisfactory to all of the allies. The most complex discussions centred on Poland. The British had declared war on Germany in order to protect Poland and had hosted a Polish government-in-exile during the war; the Soviets had occupied Poland and installed a Communist government; the Americans wanted to promote democratic governments in Europe and to satisfy the large number of Polish-American voters in their own country.

Mollayan closely monitored the topics he discussed with his Priory partners.

Intelligence reports and diplomatic dispatches traced the efforts by General de Gaulle, whom Churchill continued to dislike and distrust, to control the French Committee of National Liberation and to be recognised as the political representative of the French people. U.S. intelligence also monitored the influence of the French Communists who had built a strong base in the French Resistance.

Political affairs in Italy also commanded attention when Italy unexpectedly surrendered after the invasion of Sicily. Here, as in the occupation of France, the allies strove to establish stability and to advance military operations without allowing the Fascists to stay in power. As usual, Roosevelt until his demise and Churchill approached these objectives differently, supporting the Italian monarchy and America supporting an independent "democratic" leadership. These issues became entangled in drafting the Italian surrender terms. An important topic was the decision to declare Rome an "open city," thus saving it from military destruction.

In Eastern Europe the dominant issue was the fate of Poland. The British supported the "London Poles," the exile government that had fled in the face of the Nazi invasion. During 1943, relations between the London Poles and Moscow deteriorated and when the Red Army moved into Poland in 1944, Stalin set up a puppet government in Lublin, leaving it to the United States to mediate between the two. Special files traced U.S. relations with the London Poles during 1944-45, and other files described Churchill's October 1944 agreement with Stalin to divide political influence in Romania, Greece, Bulgaria, Yugoslavia, and Hungary between Britain and the Soviet Union.

Mollayan had no doubt that a showdown between the super powers was on the cards and the status quo would be seriously affected if any weaknesses materialised on the part of any of the allies. He could not have predicted what was about to happen in the forth coming British General Election. The Conservatives had been defeated and Winston Churchill, its leader, was no longer Prime Minister. Labour assumed power and Clement Atlee returned to Potsdam with the onerous task of making the final decisions on the carving up of Germany. Potsdam ratified the policy of removing all Germans from Poland Czechoslovakia and Hungary. Germany and Austria were divided into Zones of Occupation.

Mollayan was recalled to be briefed before taking charge of the British Zone in Berlin.

'I have to return to London' said Mollayan 'I have orders and I must comply'.

'You can't go back to London! shouted Adam 'You'll be a sitting duck as soon as you get off the plane'

'Don't worry about me; I can take care of myself'. Mollayan turned around and called the two of them into the house. Adam walked in first, followed by Andrew. Mollayan had put the light out and was sitting in the dark.

'A car will arrive at 4.00pm; it will be driven by a man called Blanc. He will take Adam from here down to the coast and across into Spain where arrangements have been made for you to return to Boston. A man who will make him known to you by saying 'I was sent by the father' will contact you. He will be your contact and will ensure your safety in paramount and the information that you possess is kept safe'.

'I'm going nowhere!' raged Adam 'until I know that Maria is safe!

'Maria is dead' said Mollayan 'She died yesterday afternoon'.

A sob escaped from Andrew's throat, Adam rushed across to where he thought Mollayan was, lost his footing and collapsed in a pile on the floor. He got up and turned on the light to find Mollayan sitting in the corner, his back against the wall and his service revolver in his right hand.

'It is time to protect, if I have to shoot you to do that I will' warned Mollayan. 'I'm sorry about Maria, I hoped she'd live but it's over now.'

Mollayan hated himself for the lies he was telling, Adam was his friend and he could see the hurt in his eyes but Mollayan had more important things to worry about. He'd been told that there was going to be repatriation to Israel for European Jews. The news coming from Germany was not good, less than 100,000 Jews had survived and those that had managed to return to their places of origin were being killed as they tried to take repossession of their shops and homes. He'd managed to secure a berth on a hospital ship for Maria. She would travel under a pseudonym and he been assured that one of his people, a high ranking member of the Haganah, a Jewish organisation involved in the repatriation of as many Jews as possible from mainland Europe in advance of the setting up of a free Jewish state, would take care of her.

Adam was in a state of shock, here he was, standing in a room of a place he'd never heard of, being asked to deal with the death of a person who had affected him more than any other person had in his whole life. He couldn't comprehend the callousness of Mollayan and they never spoke to each other for the remainder of his time in the house. The car arrived at 4.00 and he simply walked out of the house and never looked back. Andrew was sitting on the wall outside and Adam went over to him. They looked at each other and then hugged

'They must not succeed' said Andrew

'I know' said Adam, his eyes brimming with tears.

'We'll see each other again' said Andrew

Adam turned and got into the car, he closed the door and sat back in the seat, there was an envelope sitting on the back seat with his name written on it in Mollayan's handwriting. He looked across at the house and saw Mollayan standing at the window, watching the car turn in the yard. Adam didn't acknowledge him as the driver moved through the gears and the car gathered speed. He was alone with his thoughts and didn't lift the envelope until they'd reached the bottom of the valley. He tore at the envelope and two sheets of paper fell out.

Dear Adam

My time is short and there is still so much that I must do. I am deeply sorry for having to lie to you but I trust you will understand my motives after reading this letter. Maria, as we speak is being transferred to a Hospital ship bound for Palestine where she will be looked after by our people. When she is fit and well, you will be told but she must never know that you are alive. You will put each other in danger. I have taken steps to ensure that she is convinced that Yahweh remains safe. She will do as she is told. I have also included details of the Priory contacts that you will need in case you are in danger. As you know, my effectiveness has been eradicated as a result of my unmasking. I have an able replacement in mind but I must be sure of some things from him first. If I am right then he will prove to be a worthy replacement. You are my friend and I know that my demise will not be in vain as you will protect and pass on the knowledge of the Yahweh until the day that we are all reunited in the glory of the Yahweh.

Take Care

Your Friend

Henry Mollayan.

'Stop the car!! , I must go back!!' shouted Adam

The driver didn't respond, Adam hit on the partition and shouted

'Stop the car now'

He tried the doors but they'd been locked from the outside. Adam thrashed about the back seat until eventually the driver spoke.

'You know what you must do; the master knows what he must do. I will make sure you are safe, you make sure we are safe!'

With that, the driver closed the partition and concentrated on the long drive south.

Mollayan walked out of the house and over to where Andrew was sitting

'Are you alright?' asked Mollayan

'No' said Andrew 'she didn't deserve to die after all that she had been through, we should have done more to help her.

'What will you do now' said Mollayan

'What choices do I have?' answered Andrew ruefully. 'I have renounced my vocation to myself; the church will do all in their power to prevent me from telling the truth and are probably looking for me as we speak. I could return home to Australia and lead a purposeless life.'

'There is another choice' said Mollayan

'There is? asked Andrew

'Join me, us in protecting the Yahweh. The bloodline of the Nazarene and the remnants of the eight families and the Priory of Zion have succeeded in protecting the Yahweh for the last 2000 years. Join us in our quest to make ready for HIM when HE returns'

Andrew stared long and hard at Mollayan, struggling to contemplate the magnitude of what he was being offered.

Mollayan continued

'I must warn you that you will face danger every day and your life will not be your own. You will have to take the place of one of our most important men and it will not be easy. If you accept this challenge, you will surrender your previous existence and will assume whatever role you require to protect the Yahweh.' You will have to watch the activity of the Freemasons and the Church as well as looking for the sign that is to come. Your main priority will be to protect Adam and his off spring as they are the 'interpreters' of the message and we believe that that is how the sign will come. What do you think?'

Andrew didn't answer for a while but he knew deep down that the role he was being asked to assume was his destiny, he felt that strange sensation coming over him, the one he experienced when he thought his father was talking to him.

He looked at Mollayan and was aware of a blue light and a voice saying

'You are my son and I am your father and you, like I must do what you have to do to ensure we reunite together when the time comes'

Andrew stood transfixed as a wave of energy passed through him, he closed his eyes and when he opened them, Mollayan was standing in exactly the same place as before but he was smiling and simply said

'Welcome'.

They spent the rest of that evening and most of the next day discussing the ramifications and possible scenarios that could occur as a result of their discovery. Andrew was able to put all of the work that he had done on Rennes le Chateau into context and learned that they were effectively in sanctuary when they were here. Mollayan told Andrew that all of the families within the village had an association with the Priory through the Church of the Magdalene at the top of the village and the work of Abbe Saunier in keeping reverence to her alive.

He told Andrew of the makeup of the eight families and then said that he would have to go into hiding for at least six months in order for the Priory council to be informed and understand the secrets that they protected

'What secrets? Asked Andrew

Mollayan smiled again,

'I'm sure you take great interest in knowing what Paul really believed in! His last testimony, the letter your church never uncovered, the truth of the visitation on the road to Damascus!'

Andrew was stunned

'You have that?

'And more' said Mollayan 'Do you think the Vatican Library is the only Library with valuable artifacts? In the next six months you will learn to see the world in a different light. I envy you really; I don't believe there is anyone who has learned the secrets of the world from the Roman perspective and from the truth!

'What must I do?

'Protect the Yahweh; they must not succeed, ever!

'Who's place am I taking? asked Andrew

'That is not important' replied Mollayan 'oh yes; there is one other thing ....

Andrew lifted his head

'Yes?'

'It's about Maria' said Mollayan

'I understand' said Andrew 'I would have liked to meet her and share our common goal. We'll meet again in HIS glory.'

'She's not dead' said Mollayan 'I had to tell Adam that she had passed away in order to get him to leave this place, he'll know by now that she isn't dead and will be safe. I'm telling you the same. She will be safe and must never know of your existence or presence in her life unless it becomes absolutely vital. Do I make myself clear?

Andrew's heart jumped, Maria Alive!!!

'I understand' said Andrew.

Chapter 32

Giovanni Santini was not a happy man, despite all of his powers of investigation and contact, they had failed to uncover the whereabouts of Father Andrew Lassiter. Santini was becoming increasingly concerned especially when he learned that Lassiter seemed to have been 'spirited' away by a British army officer named Mollayan. His concern turned to panic when he realised who Henry Mollayan was, none other than the Grand Master of the Priory of Zion himself! This was bad, very bad indeed and had forced him into having a meeting with a man he'd never met, had nothing up until then in common with, but who appeared to be the only person who could assist him in his problem.

He had contacted this man through a man named Licio Gelli. He was the same man that Santini had in mind for solving the whereabouts of Martin Bormann, that problem solved itself, as far as Santini was concerned, Bormann never made it out of Berlin.

Santini knew that Gelli was a freemason and had created his own lodge whose members comprised a who's who in Italian politics and business as well, it was rumoured, as the church itself! Gelli had been only too willing to facilitate the request of a man who had proved to be a 'papa bile' that is, a cardinal with an outstanding opportunity to become Pope.

Gelli made a living as a 'facilitator' and blackmailer and was involved in corruption at every level. It was rumoured that he was the person who was responsible for setting up the passport scam that allowed so many Nazis to travel on

Vatican papers through Italy. He was also linked to the disappearance of millions of $ of Jewish gold that had been looted from the dead in the camps. Santini had no direct contact with this man but was left in with no uncertainty as to whom had arranged the meeting that he was about to host.

The door knocked and opened, a tall heavily built man approached the chair where Santini was sitting. The man was about 60 years of age with a ruddy complexion, a shock of white hair that was receding slightly and piercing blue eyes. They did not shake hands, the man sat down, pleasantries were exchanged and the stranger spoke

'You wished to discuss a matter that you consider to be mutually advantageous to both our 'organisations'

Santini winced and struggled to show his disdain for the man in front of him. He had known of Richard Hemmindale for a long time by reputation as the leader of the Grand Lodge of Freemasons in England. He was aware of his background but never envisaged the day that he, a Prince of the Church would have to meet the likes of this man.

'It would appear that we may both have an interest in discovering the whereabouts of some people who may be in a position to, let us say, embarrass us' Santini crossed his hands on his lap and awaited Hemmindale's response.

'Are you asking for my help?' asked Hemmindale, obviously enjoying the discomfort of Santini, despite their common interest.

Santini bristled

'Cheap jibes will not solve our problem, I am willing to look at ways in which we can both resolve a potential problem, what do you suggest?

'We will take care of Mollayan when he surfaces, we know all about his Priory and what they do, we will find him and stop him.

'He has people with him ….. tempted Santini

'I'm surprised you cannot look after your own problems, if the priest is with Mollayan, I suspect that he will suffer the same fate, as for Carter, what will he do? Tell people? They'd laugh at him. When the time is right we will find out what Carter knows and then we will destroy them.

'Them? Asked Santini

'Come, come, Your Eminence. You know who they are just as well as I do. You had your chance to eradicate their falsehood and failed. That is why you are so afraid ... afraid that they may be telling the truth about your precious Nazarene ...

'You will not blaspheme in HIS house' hissed Santini. 'All I ask is that we share information and when the whereabouts of Father Lassiter is discovered, we will deal with him. In return, I will tell you where your Professor Mollayan is'

Hemingdale stopped; surely Santini didn't know where Mollayan was?

'Agreed' said Hemmindale

'Your professor has been summonsed back to London for a de-briefing by his superiors at SOE, he will then take command of the British sector of Berlin in preparation of the next hostility!

'The next what?'

'You hardly think the Russians will want to stop now, do you? I have it on good authority that Colonel Mollayan will head up SOE's Berlin operation and ensure that to the victor comes the spoils...

Santini rose from the chair and walked towards the door at the far side of the room

'The sergeant at arms will show you out' leaving Hemmindale wondering whether he'd just been dismissed.

Santini went back to his private quarters and lifted the telephone

'Si'

'Have him followed, I wish to know where he goes'

Santini replaced the hand piece and sat back in his chair, satisfied with himself, sooner or later Lassiter would be found.

He didn't know how wrong he was, at that moment Andrew Lassiter was preparing to go on a journey that would take him from the clutches of everyone who was seeking to find him.

Mollayan had discussed every eventuality with Andrew and had told him of the Priory and what they did. Andrew for his part was able to fill in the gaps on the Fatima revelations and the rest of the information that the Vatican possessed. Later that evening, Mollayan left the room and returned about an hour later.

'Your travel arrangements have been made, for the next six months you will spend your time on an island of the coast of Spain. Our people will protect you until you have come through your induction. Then and only then will you be empowered to make whatever decisions you deem necessary'

'You still haven't told me whose place I am taking' said Andrew

'That's not important, you'll find out soon enough, get some rest, you have a long couple of days ahead of you.'

With that, Mollayan bade Andrew good night.

As he lay in bed that night, Mollayan weighed up his next move. He would have to contact his mentor and advise him of the choice he had made. His mentor would be responsible for educating Andrew in the ways of the Master just as he had taught Mollayan, His name was Simeon and he lived in splendid isolation in Sao Miguel, one of the islands that made up the Azores. Mollayan was the only person alive who knew of Simeon and what he did. Andrew would leave the following day for Sao Miguel where he would commit himself to the teaching of Simeon and take part in the seven trials of truth that he had to pass to be able to wear the mantle of the protector of the Yahweh.

Andrew also had a restless night, he thought about where he was going with a certain amount of excitement, it must be important, maybe he was going to work alongside Mollayan in protecting Adam and Maria. He wondered who he was replacing in the organisation. Mollayan had told him that he would find out in time but that for now he was to concentrate on the task ahead. All Mollayan has said was that he was to be taken to a special place where he would spend six months in the company of a teacher who would answer his questions and unveil the truth of the Yahweh. His thoughts then turned to Maria. He was delighted that she was alive but saddened at the fact that for now they would not be permitted to see each other. He understood the decision, only he and Adam and Mollayan possessed the full story, only he had access to the secret files stored within the Vatican library. He knew that they would do silence him, he found it impossible to comprehend the depths to which they would go to protect their sanctity on one hand yet wasn't really that surprised, given how they suppressed knowledge of the Final Solution.

Mollayan and Andrew rose early the next morning, ate a light breakfast and then Andrew prepared to leave

'The car will be here soon' said Mollayan 'You know what you must do'

'I do' said Andrew who at the moment was overcome by a strange sense of finality in their parting…

'I won't see you again, will I? asked Andrew

Mollayan looked away and then walked over to Andrew and clenched him by the shoulders

'It is a great burden that is being placed upon your shoulders; you will have to live the rest of your life in servitude to a greater goal with no sense of self. You must be ready to accept this challenge

'The person that I am replacing…… it's you, isn't it' said Andrew

'Yes' murmured Mollayan 'My time has come and but for one last task. It is time for me to make Yahweh safe. By commending my trust to you, I know I am doing this.

'Come with me' pleaded Andrew 'we can do so much together, they will never succeed'

Mollayan hugged Andrew

'I am a liability and through me they would succeed, believe me' said Mollayan

'What will happen to you?' said Andrew

'I still have things to do, you'll understand soon enough. Go now and remember 'They must not succeed' Mollayan embraced Andrew

A car pulled into the yard and two men got out, one of them handed a package to Mollayan and the other took Andrew by the arm and led him to the car. The other man lifted his case and walked back to the car. Mollayan stood in the centre of the yard and the car spun around him, Andrew rolled the window down and shouted

'They will not succeed'

Mollayan smiled and put his hand up to wave as the car sped off through the yard gates.

Hemingdale went over to the desk and lifted the receiver

'It's me, he's made contact' said Smythe

'When?!' said Hemmindale

'He telephoned my office this morning and we spoke, he told me that he had succeeded and that he wanted to come in'

'What do you mean 'succeeded' asked Hemmindale

'That's the amazing bit really, he's claiming that it was necessary for him to have us think he was one of them in order to gain their confidence, he tells me that he has uncovered the identity of their master and wishes to bring him in. I think it is a trick.

‘Of course it’s a trick you fool! Mollayan is the master! We are the ones who have been fooled! Where is Carter and the Priest?

‘I don’t know’ said Smythe ‘but you were right about Mollayan, he has to return to London for orders and then he goes to Berlin.

‘We’ll do it there, if he makes contact again, play along with him and contact me immediately’

Hemingdale replaced the receiver and went over to his desk and sat down. What was Mollayan playing at? Where were the other two or should he say three? Despite all of his attempts at tracing the Tannenbaum girl, the priest or Carter, it was as if they had disappeared off the face of the earth. The only link that was left was Mollayan. As Hemmindale sat there in the darkness of his Judges chambers, he reflected on his conversation with Smythe, he lifted the telephone and spoke down the line relaying the context of his conversation with Smythe

‘You must find out what he knows and neutralise him’ whispered the voice

‘What about the others? Asked Hemmindale

‘They are nothing without him; cut of the head and the snake will die!’

‘Very well’ said Hemmindale.

Mollayan reached the airport later that afternoon and flew back to RAF Northolt in a Blenheim Bomber that was being refitted as a supply plane.

He arrived in London late that night and went straight around to his old offices in Wardour Street. The camp bed was still in his office so he bedded down in preparation of what was to be an eventful next couple of days.

Hemingdale got word the next morning from the Apostolic Nuncio in London that Mollayan had returned. They’d met at a remembrance service for one of Hitler’s German victims,

Deitrich Bonhoeffer. Pathe has also started showing news reels of the British Army liberation of Bergen / Belsen concentration camp making it very difficult for tempers to be held in check. Hemmindale wasn't particularly interested in the sentiments being passed at the ceremony; one dead German was the same as the next. The service had provided excellent cover for him to speak with Santini's emissary, not that it told him anything new about the whereabouts of the priest or Carter but at least they were able to confirm that Mollayan was in London.

'Tell the Cardinal we'll take care of our own, I'll let you know if he knows anything' said Hemmindale who then turned and walked out of St. Paul's cathedral and right into the face of Henry Mollayan

'I thought I'd come and see you before I left for Berlin' said Mollayan

Hemingdale glanced around, he'd come alone to the meeting with the nuncio and his usual backup of protection wasn't with him.

'I've checked' said Mollayan 'you wouldn't expect otherwise now, would you?

Hemingdale sneered 'You will die a painful death for your betrayal'

'We'll see about that' quipped Mollayan 'I'm leaving for Berlin within the hour, I'll be protected and you'll not be able to touch me'. I'm quite prepared to discuss our little problem but I will only deal with you and Smythe. It would be such a shame for you to go back to the council and admit failure'

'I could have you killed where you stand' rasped Hemmindale

'I don't doubt that, wouldn't be very satisfying would it? I'm well aware that your pathetic excuse of an organisation will demand my death in their morbid time-honored way of the temple. I spit on the way you have made claims on the truth. My salvation will be the knowledge that the truth will prevail'

Mollayan turned and walked away, quipping back over his shoulder

'No doubt we'll meet in Berlin. I hear you are one of the Judges for the trials, till then'

Hemingdale searched for his car, when he looked again, Mollayan had melted into the bustling London crowd.

Andrew had arrived at Sao Miguel after a laborious and tiring journey. He landed on a deserted beach and was taken up a steep set of steps where another man met him. The men who accompanied Andrew stopped at his point, nodded at the man and took their leave without saying another word. Andrew turned to face the stranger

'My name is Andr......

The stranger put his hand up to his lip and beckoned Andrew not to speak to him. They set out at a brisk pace and walked for nearly three hours until they reached a clearing in the forest. The man sat down and took the sack from his back; he took out some bread and a bottle of water and shared it with Andrew. It was the first food that Andrew had eaten that day and he ate ravenously.

The man just sat and watched him whilst he ate. Andrew couldn't comprehend why he wouldn't talk and was becoming quite frustrated that all of his attempts at conversation had been unceremoniously rebuffed. He was just about to say something when a voice from behind him caused him to jump with fright

'So you made it' said the voice

'Who's that? Where are you?' said Andrew

The trees parted at the far end of the clearing and an older man stepped out. Older in that Andrew was sure he was at least 70 years of age, but he had never seen such a fit looking man. He had a ramrod straight back, he moved with the lithe grace of a gazelle and when he walked across towards Andrew with his hand outstretched, Andrew was amazed at his grip.

'My name is Simeon'

At that moment Andrew wondered just what was in store for him, he had so many questions that required answers. Andrew started to speak and again was silenced

'We'll sleep here tonight, you'll need your rest' said Simeon 'You have a long day ahead of you tomorrow.' When we reach the place of truth, I will explain everything, until then, consider our silence as a test, if you wish to communicate with either of us, think your words to us without speaking, we are trained to understand'

'Think my words?' Andrew started

'Shhuuuuuuuuuuushhh', said the old man 'all will be revealed in time. You have a lot to learn before you can expect to assume the role that has been chosen for you.

'It is best that you forget all that had gone before and surrender yourself to me, I will be everything to you for as long as it takes and then we will discover if you are indeed the master'.

With that the old man rolled over and went to sleep. Andrew lay on his back and considered the old man's words and came to one conclusion, his life had already changed and now there was no going back. He would submit himself to whatever lay ahead, driven by the knowledge of the faith and trust that had been placed in him. He would not let anyone down.

Smythe and Hemmindale were in constant contact with each other. It had been relatively easy for Smythe to relocate his operation to Berlin. He was still collating information and taking witness statements in preparation for the forthcoming War trials. Mollayan meanwhile had commandeered what was once Plotzensee prison as his centre of operations. He'd assembled a task force that was charged with ensuring that all of the duties and responsibilities of the British Occupying

Forces within the Berlin Zone were enforced. He'd already had three soldiers summarily executed for looting as a warning to others. There had been widespread interest in the Bunker area but that was in the Russian Zone and they refused to allow any of the other occupying forces anywhere near it. No one had seen Hitler's body and the only real evidence that the allies had, was provided by Mollayan's department.

On his second day in Berlin, he had questioned a young boy, he was only 15 but he had fought in the defense of Berlin for the previous five months. Mollayan had learned that Hitler had indeed shot himself, his wife, Eva Braun, had swallowed poison. As the soviets attacked the bunker area, Hitler's body had been taken up into the Chancellery courtyard, doused with petrol and set alight. Mollayan also learned that Joseph Goebbels had arranged for his six children to be given a lethal injection by an SS doctor, and then had himself and his wife shot by the very boy that Mollayan had questioned.

The real concern for the Allies at the time were reports that an 'Iron Curtain' was being created in the east. The Americans had entered Berchtesgaden, Hitler's mountain retreat, and had discovered papers that had been captured from the Russians. These papers referred to the establishing of a Europe dominated 'Rodina' and laid out the plans that the Russians had for assimilating all of the territory that they had overrun and creating a huge Communist infrastructure. When these reports were analysed, the allies were left in no doubt that the Russians planned to reconstruct Europe under their terms.

Hemmindale flew into Berlin on 10 October. He and Smythe had decided that it was too dangerous to move against Mollayan until such times as they were sure he could be removed. All attempts at blackening his name and having him removed from his command had failed. Smythe had tried on several occasions to get into his headquarters at Plotzensee but to no avail. Smythe subsequently discovered that the Americans had established The Supreme Command Allied powers and a subsequent International Military Tribunal had been set up. A young lawyer, Robert Jackson had made the opening statement in the court on the day that Hemmindale took his place

May it please Your Honours,

The privilege of opening the first trial in history for crimes against the peace of the world imposes a grave responsibility. The wrongs, which we seek to condemn and punish, have been so calculated, so malignant and so devastating, that civilisation cannot tolerate their being ignored because it cannot survive their being repeated. That four great nations, flushed with victory and stung with injury stay the hand of vengeance and voluntarily submit their captive enemies to the judgement of the law is one of the most significant tributes that Power ever has paid to Reason.

This tribunal, while it is novel and experimental, is not the product of abstract speculations nor is it created to vindicate legalistic theories. This inquest represents the practical effort of four of the most mighty of nations, with the support of seventeen more, to utilise International Law to meet the greatest menace of our time, this aggressive war. The common sense of mankind demands that law shall not stop with the punishment of petty crimes by little people. It must also reach men who possess themselves of great power and make deliberate and concerted use of it to set in motion evils, which leave no home in the world, untouched.

It is a cause of this magnitude that the United Nations will lay before Your Honours.

In the prisoners' dock sit twenty-odd broken men. Reproached by the humiliation of those they have led almost as bitterly as by the desolation of those they have attacked, their personal capacity for evil is forever past. It is hard now to perceive in these miserable men as captives the power by which as Nazi leaders they once dominated much of the world and terrified most of it. Merely as individuals, their fate is of little consequence to the world.

Mollayan had assembled a great team on the British side but this young lawyer was making a case that was so chilling in its description, silence abounded in the courtroom as the monotone of the speech continued...

What makes this inquest significant is that those prisoners represent sinister influence that will lurk in the world long after their bodies have returned to dust. They are living symbols of racial hatreds, of terrorism and violence, and of the arrogance and cruelty of power. They are symbols of fierce nationalism and militarism, of intrigue and war- making which have embroiled Europe generation after generation, crushing its manhood, destroying its homes, and impoverishing its life. They have so identified themselves with the philosophies they conceived and with the forces they directed that any tenderness to them is a victory and an encouragement to all the evils which are attached to their names.

Civilisation can afford no compromise with the social forces, which would gain renewed strength if we deal ambiguously or indecisively with the men in whom those forces now precariously survive.

What these men stand for we will patiently and temperately disclose. We will give you undeniable proofs of incredible events. The catalogue of crimes will omit nothing that could be conceived by a pathological pride, cruelty, and lust for power. These men created in Germany, under the Fuehrerprinzip, a National Socialist despotism equalled only by the dynasties of the ancient East. They took from the German people all those dignities and freedoms that we hold natural and inalienable rights in every human being. The people were compensated by inflaming and gratifying hatreds toward those who were marked as "scope-goats." Against their opponents, including Jews, Catholics, and free labour the Nazis directed such a campaign of arrogance, brutality, and annihilation as the world has not witnessed since the pre-Christian ages. They excited the German ambition to be a "master race," which of course implies serfdom for others. They led their people on a mad amble for domination. They diverted social energies and resources to the creation of what they thought to be an invincible war machine. They overran their neighbours. To sustain the"master race " in its war making, they enslaved millions of human beings and brought them into Germany, where these hapless creatures. now wander as "displaced persons". At length bestiality and bad faith reached such excess that they aroused the sleeping strength of imperilled civilisation. Its united efforts have ground the German war machine to fragments. But the struggle has left Europe a liberated yet prostrate land where a demoralised society struggles to survive. These are the fruits of the sinister forces that sit with these defendants in the prisoners' dock.

Mollayan looked directly across at all of the defendants as Jackson's words punched through any veneer of self respect that they had left, all of them except Hermann Goering who met Mollayan's eyes and held them for fully 20 seconds before curling back his lip into a sneer and contemptuously closing his eyes. Jackson continued

In justice to the nations and the men associated in this prosecution, I must remind you of certain difficulties, which may leave their mark on this case. Never before in legal history has an effort been made to bring within the scope of a single litigation the developments of a decade, covering a whole Continent, and involving a score of nations, countless individuals, and innumerable events. Despite the magnitude of the task, the world has demanded immediate action. This demand has had to be met, though perhaps at the cost of finished craftsmanship. In my country, established courts, following familiar procedures, applying well thumbed precedents, and dealing with the legal consequences of local and limited events seldom commence a trial within a year of the event in litigation. Yet less than eight months ago today the courtroom in which you sit was an enemy fortress in the hands of German SS troops. Less than eight months ago nearly all our witnesses and documents were in enemy hands.

The law had not been codified, no procedure had been established, no Tribunal was in existence, no usable courthouse stood here, none of the hundreds of tons of official German documents had been examined, no prosecuting staff had been assembled, nearly all the present defendants were at large, and the four prosecuting powers had not yet joined in common cause to try them. I should be the last to deny that the case may well suffer from incomplete researches and quite likely will not be the example of professional work which any of the prosecuting nations would normally wish to sponsor. It is, however, a completely adequate case to the judgement we shall ask you to render, and its full development we shall be obliged to leave to historians.

Before I discuss particulars of evidence, some general considerations, which may affect the credit of this trial in the eyes of the world, should be candidly faced. There is a dramatic disparity between the circumstances of the accusers and of the accused that might discredit our work if we should falter, in even minor matters, in being fair and temperate.

Unfortunately, the nature of these crimes is such that both prosecution and judgement must be by victor nations over vanquished foes. The world-wide scope of the aggressions carried out by these men has left but few real neutrals. Either the victors must judge the vanquished or we must leave the defeated to judge them. After the First World War, we learned the futility of the latter course. The former high station of these defendants, the notoriety of their acts, and the adaptability of their conduct to provoke retaliation make it hard to distinguish between the demand for a just and measured retribution, and the unthinking cry for vengeance which arises from the anguish of war. It is our task, so far as humanly possible, to draw the line between the two. We must never forget that the record on which we judge these defendants today is the record on which history will judge us tomorrow. To pass these defendants a poisoned chalice is to put it to our own lips as well. We must summon such detachment and intellectual integrity to our task that this trial will commend itself to posterity as fulfilling humanity's aspirations to do justice.

At the very outset, let us dispose of the contention that to put these men to trial is to do them an injustice entitling them to some special consideration. These defendants may be hard pressed but they are not ill-used. Let us see what alternative they would have to being tried.

More than a majority of these prisoners surrendered to or were tracked down by forces of the United States. Could they expect us to make American custody a shelter for our enemies against the just wrath of our Allies? Did we spend American lives to capture them only to save them from punishment? Under the principles of the Moscow Declaration, those suspected war criminals that are not to be tried internationally must be turned over to individual governments for trial at the scene of their outrages.

Many less responsible and less culpable American-held prisoners have been and will be turned over to other United Nations for local trial. If these defendants should succeed, for any reason, in escaping the condemnation of this Tribunal, or if they obstruct or abort this trial, those who are American-held prisoners will be delivered up to our continental Allies. For these defendants, however, we have set up an International Tribunal and have undertaken the burden of participating in a complicated effort to give them fair and dispassionate hearings. That is the best known protection to any man with a defence worthy of being heard.

If these men are the first war leaders of a defeated nation to be prosecuted in the name of the law, they are also the first to be given a chance to plead for their lives in the name of the law. Realistically, the Charter of this Tribunal, which gives them a hearing, is also the source of their only hope. It may be that these men of troubled conscience, whose only wish is that the world forgets them, do not regard a trial as a favour. But they do have a fair opportunity to defend themselves a favour which these men, when in power, rarely extended to their fellow countrymen. Despite the fact that public opinion already condemns their acts, we agree that here they must be given a presumption of innocence, and we accept the burden of proving criminal acts and the responsibility of these defendants for their commission.

When I say that we do not ask for convictions unless we prove crime, I do not mean mere technical or incidental transgression of international conventions. We charge guilt on planned and intended conduct that involves moral as well as legal wrong. And we do not mean conduct that is a natural and human, even if illegal, cutting of corners, such as many of us might well have committed had we been in the defendant's positions. It is not because they yielded to the normal frailties of human beings that we accuse them. It is their abnormal and inhuman conduct, which brings them to this bar.

We will not ask you to convict these men on the testimony of their foes. There is no count of the Indictment that cannot be proved by books and records. The Germans were always meticulous record keepers, and these defendants had their share of the Teutonic passion for thoroughness in putting things on paper. Nor were they without vanity. They arranged frequently to be photographed in action. We will show you their own films. You will see their own conduct and hear their own voices as these defendants re-enact for you, from the screen, some of the events in the course of the conspiracy.

We would also make clear that we have no purpose to incriminate the whole German people. We know that the Nazi Party was not put in power by a majority of the German vote. We know it came to power by an evil alliance between the most extreme of the Nazi revolutionists, the most unrestrained of the German reactionaries, and the most aggressive of the German militarists. If the German populace had willingly accepted the Nazi program, no Stormtroopers would have been needed in the early days of the Party and there would have been no need for concentration camps or the Gestapo, both of which institutions were inaugurated as soon as the Nazis gained control of the German state. Only after these lawless innovations proved successful at home were they taken abroad.

The German people should know by now that the people of the United States hold them in no fear, and in no hate. It is true that the Germans have taught us the horrors of modern warfare, but the ruin that lies from the Rhine to the Danube shows that we, like our Allies, have not been dull pupils. If German fortitude and proficiency in war do not awe us, and if we are not persuaded of their political maturity, we do respect their skill in the arts of peace, their technical competence, and the sober, industrious and self- disciplined character of the masses of the German people. In 1933, we saw the German people recovering prestige in the commercial, industrial and artistic world after the set-back of the last war. We beheld their progress neither with envy nor malice. The Nazi regime interrupted this advance. The recoil of the Nazi aggression has left Germany in ruins. The Nazi readiness to pledge the German word without hesitation and to break it without shame has fastened upon German diplomacy a reputation for duplicity that will handicap it for years. Nazi arrogance has made the boast of the "master race" a taunt that will be thrown at Germans the world over for generations. The Nazi nightmare has given the German name a new and sinister significance throughout the world, which will retard Germany a century. The German, no less than the non- German world, has accounts to settle with these defendants.

The fact of the war and the course of the war, which is the central theme of our case, is history. From September 1, 1939, when the German armies crossed the Polish frontiers, until September, 1942, when they met epic resistance at Stalingrad, German arms seemed invincible. Denmark and Norway, The Netherlands and France, Belgium and Luxembourg, the Balkans and Africa, Poland and the Baltic States, and parts of Russia, all had been overrun and conquered by swift, powerful, well-aimed blows. That attack upon the peace of the world is the crime against international society, which brings into international cognisance crimes in its aid and preparation which otherwise, might be only internal concerns. It was aggressive war, which the nations of the world had renounced. It was war in violation of treaties, by which the peace of the world was sought to be safeguarded.

This war did not just happen -- it was planned and prepared for over a long period of time and with no small skill and cunning. The world has perhaps never seen such a concentration and stimulation of the energies of any people as that which enabled Germany twenty years after it was defeated, disarmed, and dismembered to come so near carrying out its plan to dominate Europe. Whatever else we may say of those who were the authors of this war, they did achieve a stupendous work in organization, and our first task is to examine the means by which these defendants and their fellow conspirators prepared and incited Germany to go to war.

In general, our case will disclose these defendants all uniting at some time with the Nazi Party in a plan which they well knew could be accomplished only by an outbreak of war in Europe. Their seizure of the German state, their subjugation of the German people, their terrorism and extermination of dissident elements, their planning and waging of war, their calculated and planned ruthlessness in the conduct of warfare, their deliberate and planned criminality toward conquered peoples, all these are ends for which they acted in concert; and all these are phases of the conspiracy, a conspiracy which reached one goal only to set out for another and more ambitious one. We shall also trace for you the intricate web of organisations, which these men formed and utilised to accomplish these ends. We will show how the entire structure of offices and officials was dedicated to the criminal purposes and committed to use of the criminal methods planned by these defendants and their co- conspirators, many of whom war and suicide have put beyond reach.

It is my purpose to open the case, particularly under Count One of the Indictment, and to deal with the common plan or conspiracy to achieve ends possible only by resort to crimes against peace, war crimes, and crimes against humanity. My emphasis will not be on individual barbarities and perversions, which may have occurred independently of any central plan. One of the dangers ever present is that this trial may be protracted by details of particular wrongs and that we will become lost in a "wilderness of single instances." Nor will I now dwell on the activity of individual defendants except as it may contribute to exposition of the common plan.

The case as presented by the United States will be concerned with the brains and authority back of all the crimes. These defendants were men of a station and rank, which does not soil its own hands with blood. They were men who knew how to use lesser folk as tools. We want to reach the planners and designers, the inciters and leaders without whose evil architecture the world would not have been for so long scourged with the violence and lawlessness, and wracked with the agonies and convulsions, of this terrible war.

Mollayan listened to the young lawyer's impassioned plea in his opening statement as he again cast his eyes across the men who sat in the dock, to see if he could determine some or any kind of remorse or acknowledgement of the scale of the crime that they had helped to perpetuate. There was Goring, at least eighty pounds lighter since his capture, oblivious to the surroundings, Ribbentrop, Jodl, Kaltenbrunner, Streicher, Frank, Frick, Sauckel. Mollayan's focus however was on two men sitting in the back of the dock. He wanted them to know that they had failed and that the Yahweh was safe from them, Neither Alfred Rosenberg nor Albert Speer could look at him directly, it was if they knew that they had lost and he was the man who had beaten them.

Smythe discovered that Mollayan, with his intelligence background was working on two fronts, war criminal investigation and another task that so far Smythe had been unable to discover.

Smythe telephoned Hemmindale on the night that he arrived

'Have you any news?' asked Smythe

Hemingdale rasped down the line

'Nothing, absolutely nothing! It's as if these people have vanished! I've had the whole of the Grand Lodge activate every member; you'd have thought that something would have turned up by now!'

'What about Santini?'

'They're no better; all they've been able to discover is that Carter's wife has left Boston with her children at the end of May'

'Where did they go' asked Smythe

'They don't know, but I guarantee that she has gone to be with her husband '

'Carter's in America?

'Why else would his bitch and brats leave at short notice and effectively disappear?

'I suppose you're right' said Smythe

'Mollayan is laughing at us because we cannot touch him' said Hemmindale 'The sanction is now nearly 4 months old and if we don't succeed in dealing with this matter, we ourselves will come under pressure to 'resign'

Hemingdale knew that Smythe would be aware of the significance of the word 'resign' , failure wasn't something that was tolerated and the chance was never given for those that failed to talk about their failure. The fact remained that Mollayan had been a trusted member of the 33rd degree in Freemasonry, he knew who was who, he knew all of the secrets of the Grand Lodge and unforgivably, he had sworn allegiance to the 'Great Architect'. He had sworn to uphold that belief and work to eradicate all threats including the infamy of the deity referred as the Yahweh. That alone condemned him to a painful death.

Mollayan was in his office when his orderly came in

'Message from one of your contacts, Sir, said his name was Simeon'

'I'll take it now' said Mollayan

'Hello'

'Everything is well' said the voice on the other end of the line' I have received word from Simeon, your candidate is acceptable'

Mollayan sat the phone down and eased back into his chair, he'd poured himself a drink and as he sat back he allowed himself a smirk of satisfaction. He'd been proved right about Andrew and whilst he knew he was living on borrowed time, he at least could relax in the knowledge that his successor was in place. He'd managed to keep one step ahead of Smythe and Hemmindale but he knew that a final confrontation was imminent and that there would only be one winner. He was well enough versed in the rituals of

Freemasonry to know that he would endure the death of the 'spurned apprentice' , that was his fate as a result of his unmasking, if Smythe and Hemmindale failed, others would be sent and continue to be sent until the sanction was imposed.

Smythe and Hemmindale had their honor to uphold and couldn't be seen to fail. Mollayan was of the opinion that if he was able to engineer a situation whereby they two were 'nuetralised' then at least in his demise, he would be removing a huge obstacle from the paths of Andrew, Adam and Maria. All he had to do was be ready for them when they made their move.

Many of the criminals captured by the allies in the immediate months after the end of the war managed to cheat the judge by killing themselves. On October 6 a Doctor Leonardo Conti, one of the German medical doctors attached to the Mengele group killed himself. Another high profile prisoner, Robert Ley who was head of the German Labour front and a committed Anti Semite committed suicide, leaving a note saying that he could no longer bear the shame of his actions. There was talk that the first trial that Hemmindale was to officiate at was that of the former French Prime Minister, Pierre Laval.

He's already tried to kill himself after being indicted, it was felt he would try again so the French executed him on October 15, Vidkun Quisling, the Norwegian, suffered the same fate, shot for the crime of 'criminal collaboration'.

Hemingdale's first trial did cause a bit of a stir and delayed him from meeting up with Smythe until later in November. He'd been rostered to preside over the trial of a Karl Klaus Schilling, a former distinguished professor of Parasitology at the University of Berlin and before the war a member of the Malaria Commission of the League of Nations.

The trial opened with a request from Schilling, who was defending himself that he be allowed time to write up the findings of his medical experiments in the interest he explained 'of medical science'. Even Hemmindale was revolted when it transpired that he had carried out the experiments on human beings and sentenced him to be hanged on the basis of his opening statement, he was taken away and hanged the next day. Smythe meanwhile was supporting the prosecution in the trial of Josef Kramer who was the commandant of Belsen. In cross-examination he asked Kramer as to his feelings as he took part in the gassing of Jewish women and children

'I had no feelings in carrying out these things' he told Smythe 'because I had received an order that is the way I was trained'

Kramer was sentenced and hanged as well. There was no delay in the search for justice.

Mollayan meanwhile was becoming increasingly concerned with the steady flow of information that was coming from the Russian Zone. The Soviet Union was determined not to relinquish its control, not only over the roads and railways and airfields and industries, but over the political alignments and minds of those in whose its armies stood.

He advised his superiors that plans should be drawn up for a full-scale confrontation sooner rather than later with the Russians. He'd sent a report through to the Joint Chiefs of Staff and had been supported by American intelligence sources as well.

Henry Mollayan wasn't the only dissenting voice in Berlin, Captain John Clark of the newly formed OSS didn't much concur with his commander's point of view either. Clark had heard about the report that Mollayan had written and eventually got his hands on a copy of it. He then met with Mollayan at the listening station that the British had erected in the Tiergarden.

John Clark faced Mollayan in the mess room of the depot. The British had set the building up as an advance supply depot, very few knew of its true purpose. Both the Americans and British were sending and receiving reports from the an sector and Mollayan and Clark had agreed to meet in tempt to share operational information and ensure that could work together if the opportunity arose. Most of the stuff that they were getting out at the moment was low level but a recent American foray had been shrouded in mystery as to the whereabouts of the personnel who went across three days ago.

'We still have not been able to make contact with our people' Clark took up the story

'We sent two teams in, three days ago, low level intelligence gathering stuff, mood of the people, presence of the russkies on the street, food stocks etc. One of the teams arrived back on schedule, the other team hasn't appeared'.

'How did they go across?' asked Mollayan

'On foot' said Clark

'This may be a coincidence but we did have a report of a struggle between two men and a woman at the crossing yesterday evening.

'What happened? Clark asked in hushed tones.

'Apparently a Russian patrol arrived and the man and woman were bundled into the back of the jeep'.

We'd sent a man and woman over' said Clark' in civvies, we thought they'd attract less attention, both were fluent in German'.

'I'll check when I get back and send you a copy of the sighting' said Mollayan.

Clark and Mollayan continued to discuss the techniques that the Russians were using, Clark as ked Mollayan about his communications set-up.

'They call me sentinel, said Mollayan, smiling at the nuance

'You think that's bad, laughed Clark, my codename is Crossfire.

Mollayan was dressed as an Intelligence Corps major. His actual rank was colonel but he felt far too conspicuous in that uniform and wanted to put Clark at his ease for the first meeting. If Mollayan thought that he was inconspicuous, he was mistaken. Mollayan was a fit and healthy individual; he had a soldier's stride and his abundant white hair and bright green eyes seemed to shine as he walked into the mess room. Two of the secretaries nudged each other as he entered, when he spoke with his lilting English brogue, he elicited two very welcoming smiles that he himself returned with a wink.

It had taken Mollayan some time to get used to working with the Americans, he could not come to terms with their profligate use of money and hardware and convenience that their money bought. Clark had a full listening team at his disposal and was able to decipher any message that he received at least three times quicker than Mollayan could.

'Do you know who's heading up their operation on the other side?' Asked Clark

'Not yet' said Mollayan 'Perhaps that's something we could work on?

'No need to' grimaced Clark' His name is Zukovski, I met him the other evening at one of the 'get to know you functions' that out General Clay is so fond of having. Problem is He knew I was a Captain in signals and I knew that he weren't no staff liaison officer. We spent the evening making small talk, showing pictures of our wives and making it very clear that each one of us knew what the other one did'.'

'So, did you learn anything? Asked Mollayan

'He was in my patch Sir, General Clay as much as presented our whole command structure to him on a plate, he just smiled and talked about 'fraternal brotherhood' before he left with, get this, a promise to return!

'Don't worry' smoothed Mollayan 'Next time we'll be ready for him. Check the next time your General Clay is having one of his little soirees and get me on the guest list, we'll have to see what our comrade Zukovski is made of'.

'It's a deal' Clark stood to shake Mollayan's hand, warming to this old fashioned Limey immediately.

'Let's meet away from here in future' suggested Mollayan 'Too claustrophobic for my liking'

'Agreed' smiled Clark. 'I'll walk you to your car'

Mollayan didn't have long to wait for his opportunity to meet Zukovski.

He received a coded message that Captain Clark had wanted to meet with him the following evening. They arranged to meet at the ruins of The Kaiser Wilhelm church which wasn't too far from Zoo Station where the Americans had a listening post and series of observation outlooks that spied onto the Unter Den Linden. The Russians had saturated the area and were heavily fortified right up to and including the Brandenburg gate, the solitary American presence had been established earlier and had already attracted the nickname 'checkpoint Charlie'.

It was Hemmindale who took the call

'Mollayan has arranged to meet his counterpart from American Intelligence tomorrow evening, he'll be alone and armed'

'Whereabouts?' asked Hemmindale

'In front of the Kaiser Wilhelm at 7.00pm.' The phone line clicked dead.

Monsignor Maglione replaced the handset, got up from the desk and walked across from the office of the Secretariat to the private quarters of the Cardinal.

'It is done' said Maglione

'Very well' answered Santini.

Chapter 33

General Genady Zukovski jumped from the back of the jeep and marched into the remains of the Reich Chancellery. He was in charge of the second directorate of the NKVD and was responsible for doctrine and internal security as well as counter- intelligence. He made it his business to know who his adversaries were and had already identified Henry Mollayan for who he was on two separate occasions. He wasn't in the slightest bit taken in by Mollayan's mild manners; he'd had him watched and knew that he was dealing with a skilled adversary.

He'd also engineered face to face meetings with Major John Clark, his counterpart in American Intelligence. Zukovski, a battle hardened survivor of Stalingrad had accompanied Marshall Zukov's Red Army through the hell of the Oder swamp and the bloody hand to hand fighting for control of the Seelow heights outside the city. When the Soviet army reached Berlin in late April 1945, and conquered the capital, Moscow refused to permit Western access to the city for more than two months after the final victory.

The Soviet unilateral squeeze of Berlin for a stretch of eight weeks, following the May 7 surrender, established harsh and intractable patterns.

Soviet generals, for example, cognizant of their nation's earlier treatment at the hands of German soldiers, permitted assorted attacks on Berlin's citizens, including murder, rape, and banishment. Secondly, in the name of reparations, the army stripped clean local factories and offices. And thirdly, the Soviets created and controlled a particularly unforgiving city administrative structure.

Coupled with larger Soviet policy objectives, the Red Army's two-month, unilateral occupation of Berlin, crucial as it was in the short-term, was proving even more vital in the long-term.

The fact that the Soviet army won the race to Berlin, and denied Western access to the city until July 4, determined that Berlin was going to be the center of international conflict should East-West relations decline.

Stalin recognized the special importance of the Soviet occupation zone. He viewed the zone as a temporary entity that in time would reunite with the western half. Moreover, he saw the problem of Germany's "democratization" as one of social and economic restructuring.

Stalin therefore felt it necessary to expedite Communist control over the eastern half so as to establish as strong a foothold as possible for that time when the German occupied areas rejoined as one.

On the very day that Hitler committed suicide, April 30, 1945 and a week before final German capitulation, two Soviet planes carried from Moscow to a location just outside of burning Berlin a team of German Communist Party functionaries. Walter Ulbricht led the first group into Berlin with specific directives in hand to establish a new German order. Anton Ackermann headed a second group into the state of Saxony, and Gustav Sobottka directed a third group into the state of Mecklenburg. Like Ulbricht, Ackermann and Sobottka carried Communist Party plans for remoulding their assigned German territories.

The Soviet directive, dated April 5, 1945, charged each group with organizing its: respective population along a pre-determined, uniform course. For the primary purpose of building hatred against Nazism, on the one hand, and cooperation with the Soviets, on the other, the plan ordered

Communist groups to establish in their areas a radio, newspaper, and book publishing house.

In addition, the three groups received instructions to create local governance units consisting of a mayor, an administrative council, and a yet-to-be-determined number of departments. Anti-Nazis were to head each department. The personnel office was to play an especially important role in recruitment and staff development. Underlining just how valuable this function was considered, the document stated:

"The direction of this office should normally be in the hands of a comrade who in the last few years has worked as an anti-fascist functionary outside of Germany'.

Most often, "outside of Germany" meant Moscow.

Under the direction of Ulbricht and the local Soviet commander, Berlin witnessed the creation of its municipal government, the Magistrat, on May 20, 1945. Dr. Arthur Werner, a former city engineer driven from office by the Nazis, directed the city council from the seat of lord mayor. Among 18 branches of administration, the Communist organizers founded agencies for public health, housing and reconstruction, and food acquisition and distribution. German Communist Party members headed half of Berlin's municipal organs. This effectively gave the Russians control of every utility in Berlin.

Mollayan's interpretation of the situation was slightly different, when he arrived in Berlin he found that Russian artillery and tanks finished off what the allied bombers missed.

Almost half of its four million inhabitants were gone. But the city had not gone under.

Immediately after the War, Mollayan discovered that women were set to work, trimming old mortar from the bricks with hammers, *die Trümmerfrauen*, the rubble-women. Other debris was piled up into several mountains, covered and planted with trees. Politically, the Greater Berlin Area of 340 square miles was divided into four sectors, one for each of the Allies.

The eastern part went to the Russians.

The other Allied Powers, France, Britain and the U.S. divided the Western portion of the city among themselves. This arrangement reflected the allied solution for the whole of Germany. Berlin was an island with special status governed by four nations in the sea of the Soviet Zone of Occupation.

The American and British forces that occupied their sector of Berlin on 4 July 1945 found a city that had been virtually destroyed. Germans everywhere were paying the price for the six years of aggressive war unleashed by their government, but none more so than the citizens of Berlin. The streets were filled with rubble: the destruction wrought by Allied bombers over the winter of 1943-44 had been furthered by the relentless advance of the Soviet Army in March and April 1945. Berliners themselves were still reeling from the orgy of pillage, rapine, and murder that had followed the Soviet occupation. Soviet soldiers careened through streets in lend-lease jeeps in search of violence, booty, and liquor. Other Soviet detachments, sent off in pursuit of "reparations," stripped whole industrial districts and sections of the countryside. Kidnappings and sudden, often inexplicable, arrests were regular occurrences.

As a result, Berliners hailed as saviours, the first American soldiers entering Berlin to take over the Western half of the city. Among the first Americans to enter Berlin was a detachment of soldiers and civilians assigned to the Office of Strategic Services, America's newest intelligence agency. Their presence was transitory; most officers expected to be demobilized and were looking forward to seeing their homes and families again. However, the inevitable friction between the Berlin population and the occupying powers further eroded whatever initial enthusiasm Berliners may have had for the Americans. Some of the OSS officers were predicting that maybe they would not get home as quickly as they thought after all.

In contrast, many American military officers felt that they could deal equitably with their Soviet counterparts in Germany and viewed the presence of an independent, American Intelligence organization as symptomatic of the kind of political interference they saw being imposed upon the Soviet military from Moscow.

Equally important, the US Military Governor in Germany, Gen. Lucius D. Clay, was determined to maintain good relations with his Soviet counterpart, Marshal Georgiy K. Zhukov, and discouraged any activities that he thought might be detrimental to good relations with the Soviet Union. Mollayan had met with Clay when he was introduced to Clark and was suitably unimpressed with his point of view as to how the Russians should be viewed

'They have to be seen as a threat' said Mollayan 'we don't know enough about them yet to treat them otherwise'. We have to organise the people here as quickly as we can into some form of political consensus, if we don't the Russians will do it for us'

Clay dismissed him with a curt wave

'Their boy's blood is the same colour as our boy's blood and we all died fighting the one enemy. Now we are together, I'm damned sure we're gonna be friends'.

Unfortunately for General Clay, his words were to come back and haunt him just three days after he passed those remarks and ironically, SSU Berlin's problem of finding a place for itself in the military power structure soon eased considerably because of the actions of the Soviet Union.

Zhukov was recalled early in 1946 and replaced by the hard-line Marshal Vassiliy D. Sokolovskiy. The Soviets subsequently did everything possible to isolate the Allied garrison in Berlin and cut off any access to potential sources of information within the Eastern bloc. American commanders and diplomats in Berlin soon found it necessary to rely on intelligence sources for even the most basic information on Soviet intentions or conditions inside East Germany. Although Clay apparently would have preferred to keep it at arm's length, he found himself increasingly dependent upon his SSU detachment for information

Working closely with the German Communists, the Soviet military command took measures in the late fall of 1945 to suppress political party activities in Berlin. In a document that Mollayan's SOE gave to the American commander in Berlin, the Communists reported the occasion of a meeting between a Russian Captain Ivan Serov and the chairmen of the four established parties in the Soviet Zone. The memo indicated that Serov wanted to "inform the gentlemen about American politics." Anticipating elections in the near future, and clearly reflecting Moscow's nervousness with independent political power, Serov "prohibited" the parties from "influencing" the municipal offices.

This meant that party politics would no longer be tolerated in the workplace. The military government would now determine "all appointments and dismissals." The order was "not to be discussed." And, finally, any violation of the order would result in "severe punishment."

Serov's order, plus additional Soviet military steps, effectively squashed the meagre activities in the East as of November, 1945 that had been sponsored by infiltrating agents from the British SOE and cleared the way for a Communist-Socialist merger. Moreover, commands against specific political conduct not only chilled free expression and restrained political dissent, but such orders also demonstrated the tight zonal control upon which Moscow increasingly insisted. Finally, Serov's message underscored the Russian fear of Western, and especially American, political influence within the Soviet Zone.

With the Christian Democrats and Liberal Democrats now neutralized, the German Communists could turn their full attention to the difficult task of absorbing the Soviet Zone German Social Democrats into a Socialist unity party. In short, the consolidation process continued into 1946 as the result of a December, 1945, meeting between the German communists and the Soviet Zone. The Conference of Sixty, so-called because it brought together thirty representatives from each party, began inauspiciously. Bitter feelings ran especially high among Social Democrats who distrusted recent Communist policy changes and apparent collaboration with the Soviet military. At one point, Otto Grotewohl, a leading Russian sponsored member charged that the Germans remained as "centralist and undemocratic in its party structure as before," and he argued that unification on a local level would make "unification of the German workers' movement impossible'

Despite the fact that Grotewohl's assessment resonated with many Social Democrats, only one individual dissented from a German resolution that organizational work continue toward constructing a Socialist unity party. The vast majority of members reasoned that if they wished to have any influence over the development of policy during the Soviet occupation, and perhaps beyond, working class party unification offered the only real hope. There was no doubting that the Russians controlled what was left of Berlin and were not planning to be content with their spoils in the East of the city.

They'd even managed to, unbeknown to the Allies, circumnavigate and reroute to their own clearing house what was left of the old Berlin telephone exchange and were amazed to discover that the allies were using the link ups without protection. There was a fill monitoring team of GRU and NKVD people charged to listen in on the Allies conversations.

Zukovski learned about the meeting between Mollayan and Clark 20 minutes after it had been set and had immediately asked for and got permission to do a snatch.

His plan was simple. He'd use a detachment of his shock troops to enter the area under the guise of a drunken incursion, find the men, immobilise them and take them back into the Russian sector. Once there they'd be at his mercy and the allies wouldn't dare to raise any questions given their seniority and the roles they fulfilled

Chapter 34

Darkness fell at 5.00 in the city, the streets were long deserted by the time the curfew klaxon sounded. General Smythe was sitting at his desk in a room that was oppressively small, windowless with its sole decoration being a desk and a chair and a naked bulb dangling from the ceiling. The smell of ruptured plumbing permeated the whole of the building. Smythe had emptied the contents of his case out onto the top of the table when the field telephone that had been hooked up in the building jangled into life.

Smythe lifted the receiver

'The trap is set' hissed Hemmindale 'make your arrangements' and the line went dead.

Smythe and Hemmindale had already discussed their plan should Mollayan take the bait of the meeting, the American Clark would be there at 7.00pm and Mollayan wouldn't make it.

Smythe was to take one of his men with him, a sergeant in the paratroopers called Jones. He was a fellow mason and was told that they had a 'brotherhood' matter to take care of.

They agreed that they would capture Mollayan and kill him where he stood, they'd then perform the ritual of the spurned on his body. Once completed, Hemmindale would return to the Judge Advocate's office and Smythe would go back to the Officer's Mess. In preparation for the ceremony Jones had been dispatched to the hospital where he had returned with three scalpels and a serrated blade that was used for cutting away flesh.

Mollayan relayed his instructions to his second in command

'I'm meeting a contact this evening, take the usual precautions'

'Whom do you want as back up, Sir?

'Tell Honeywell to be ready to move if there's any problem' said Mollayan

'One will be enough, sir?

'Yes' said Mollayan and returned to his office.

It was raining hard in Berlin, this made the city all the more depressing and desolate. The Russians had used their 'Stalin Organs' and T34's to great effect and most of the eastern side of the city was in abject ruins. Genady Zukovski had been with the 'Red Banner' shock battalion, a part of General Anatov's Army Group East. He'd joined them just after they crossed the Oder north west of Oppeln, a village less than 150 miles from Berlin. He'd joined the group in order to arrest an artillery officer; the officer had been writing a commentary of what he saw and sending it home. Zukovski went straight the officer's commanding officer

'General Travkin' said Zukovski, showing the General his credentials, 'You will bring Comrade Alexander Solzhenitsyn to me at once'

'He is one of my finest artillery officers, what do you want him for?'

'I am here on the orders of Comrade Stalin himself! Am I to report that you are being obstructive?

Solzhenitsyn was summoned by the General and ordered to hand over his revolver to Zukovski who then stripped him of his badges of rank and of his military decorations and summonsed two NKVD officers to take him away.

'Why are you doing this?' demanded the General

Zukovski replied 'this man has been criticising Comrade Stalin and he accused him of betraying Leninism and doubting his leadership. He questioned our great leader's ability as a commander and spread wicked lies'

Travkin looked helplessly at Solzhenitsyn and then walked over in full view of Zukovski and shook his hand.

Zukovski had Travkin shot three days later for 'political incorrectness in the face of a criminal of the state'. He stayed behind the front line until he reached Berlin. When the Reichstag building fell, Marshall Zhukov himself arrived in Berlin in advance of accepting the German capitulation, the surrender of Berlin. Zukovski learned of the fate of Hitler and immediately sent a detachment of NKVD to the bunker to remove what was left of the bodies of Hitler and whoever else was there. They were taken to a basement of a house in East Berlin and lay there for nearly seven months whilst the Russians decided what to do with them. They were eventually shipped back to Moscow for fear of being found and used as some sort of memorial or shrine.

Zukovski then began to infiltrate all sections of activity within the city, he'd already been told that the Russians did not intend to comply with the four power rile idea that had been mooted at Yalta. His role now was one of counter intelligence and disinformation spreading. He called to his Captain

'Are we ready for this evening's little exercise?

'Da' said the Captain 'I've picked 8 men to do the job'

'Remember, they are no use to me dead! I must have them alive!

Smythe carefully wrapped the scalpels and blade in a red velvet cloth and put in the two pieces of stone and the set of dividers. He'd been careful to wear gloves and had instructed Jones to do the same. The plan was to accost Mollayan as soon as it was safe to do so, Jones had instructions to kill him and they'd bring him to the spot where Hemmindale would be waiting to complete the task.

Hemingdale, meanwhile had already reached the chosen place and was sitting on a bench opposite the grass area that they'd picked out. He brought the two hoods and was already prepared by removing one of his socks.

John Clark called Mollayan's office in a panic, he'd received information from one of the listening posts that their meeting had been compromised. He'd been aware that the Russians had increased their activity on the intelligence-gathering front, he wasn't able to pinpoint the source of the increased activity but the Americans had known for quite some time that the Berlin communications network wasn't safe.

Had he have known that his original coded message had been sent to Mollayan using that method, he have flipped. He wasn't to know when he placed the code priority that a power failure knocked out the battalion's power and the orderly had gone ahead and pushed the code through on the open line. He probably never thought that anyone would ever work out who 'sentinel' and 'crossfire' was. He was about to find out how wrong he was.

He'd intercepted a message from the Chancellery back to Army Group headquarters marked with the NKVD code. It was standard practice to screen any of those codes with the NKVD attachment. He'd been working the wires when he picked up a signal referring to sentinel and crossfire being 'escorted to service.' The orderly immediately put a call through to Clark, who, realising the danger was now desperately trying to reach Mollayan to warn him. He had taken the precaution of surrounding the church on the pretext of an unexploded bomb, if any Russians did turn up they'd be conspicuous and Clark had a snatch squad standing by to arrest and detains them.

By the time Clark reached Mollayan's office, Henry Mollayan had left for the rendezvous.

The young boy darted across the ruined street and entered the park by the East gate. He'd been living in the park with nine other people and they took turns to scavenge for food and whatever other bits they could make use of. The boy had arrived in Berlin in the previous April and had spent the first month sleeping at the Railway station, He been captured twice in SS recruitment drives for 'cannon fodder' but had simply ran away.

He'd been lucky, two other boys that had been with him the last time he was caught had been caught trying to escape and were summarily hung from lamp posts, a piece of card was placed at their feet accusing them of cowardice and refusing to fight the 'untermensh'. It didn't matter that one of them was a Jew, the SS were past caring what you were, so long as you could fire a gun, you were a defender of Berlin.

He'd discovered the sanctuary of the park by meeting up with an older girl who took pity on him after he had got into a fight with another boy who was trying to take food from the girl. She gathered up the potatoes and put them back inside her coat and was about to disappear back into the ruins when she saw the boy standing in the middle of the street, his hand was bleeding from the blow he got from her assailant. She went over and looked at the wound, it was bleeding, she bent down and tore a strip off the bottom of her skirt and wrapped it tightly round his hand and then took her leave. She moved off through the rubble and looked back, the boy was following her, she moved on, he moved on, until eventually they reached the park gate. She stopped and walked back towards him, he didn't move when she walked up to him and lifted his arm

'Come with me' she said 'You'll be safe'

They walked through the park until they reached the underpass, the scouted around the opening until it was clear and then darted up the underpass, half way up it there was a steel door which the girl hit three times with a stone she found on the ground. A head appeared just in front of them as a manhole cover was pushed back. The girl pushed the boy towards the cover and they both dropped down into the dark. As the boy hit the floor, he was set upon by three other boys and dragged over to the open drain.

'Push him in!'

'Who are you?'

The girl screamed

'Leave him alone, he's one of us!

The biggest boy held his hand up

'Where did you find him, Eva?'

'I'd found food over at the market when I was set upon, he stopped them from taking the food'. Look at his arm, he's one of us, Yacov'

Yacov reached over and grabbed at the boy's arm, he saw the tattoo and the camp marking,

'What's your name?

The boy didn't reply, Eva spoke up

'He can't talk, he hasn't spoken a word to me'

Yacov scratched his head,

'He knows the entrance, we'll have to keep him with us'

'We haven't the food to feed ourselves, toss him in the drain'

'No' said Yacov 'He's from the camps, he'll have a use like all the rest of us'

Yacov went over and grabbed the boy

'If you betray us, I will kill you. Do you understand?'

The boy reached into his pocket and took out a large piece of cheese and a half of bread and offered them to Eva.

'See, I told you! He's one of us'

Yacov took him under his wing and showed him their den and the different ways that they could get in and out. The stranger proved most adept at scavenging and eventually won the trust of the rest of the gang. Every time he returned from a 'trip' he managed to gather food and he always brought a little something for Eva.

It was his turn to keep watch at the far end of the tunnel and he spotted the car first, a long black sedan, not unlike the ones that the 'stapo' used. He watched as one man got out and disappeared into the bushes. The car sped off and the man didn't reappear. It was dark and he wondered what the man was doing when he heard another noise, he ducked down out of sight and watched as two jeeps of soldiers pulled up and began to fan out across the park. He was about to raise the alarm but he noticed that the soldiers were going away from the underpass and heading towards the ruins of the old church. The soldiers were throwing drink over themselves and taking swallows out of the bottle and spitting it out on the ground as they went off out of site. Seeing this, the boy moved closer to the bushes to see what was going on. He stayed a fair bit away but with difficulty was able to see the man, he was elderly and was moving with great difficulty.

He seemed to be painting a design of some sort on the grass …

Mollayan told Honeywell to stay well behind him and out of sight, he was only to make himself known if there was any indication of trouble. Mollayan knew that his counterpart would have the same backup. They split up and Mollayan headed towards the park entrance, he'd cut across the park, there'd still be people about and he was armed. Neither of them spotted the car sitting in the side street and when they split up the back door of the car opened and a man got out.

Honeywell dropped back and stood across from the entrance, he had a good field of view to his right and left. He put his hand in his pocket and took out a pack of cigarettes, opened them and removed one that he put in his mouth and lit up. He saw the man coming towards him out of the corner of his eye and tensed, easing his hand down towards the Remington pistol that was in his jacket pocket.

Smythe had driven around to the far side of the park and had parked the car. He'd doubled back and was watching Jones approach Mollayan's back up from the safety of cover just inside the gate. He watched as the match flickered in front of Jones's face and then as Jones appeared to stagger backwards as he caught the falling man. Jones held on to him and part walked part dragged him across the road towards where Smythe was standing,

'Is he dead?' asked Smythe

'Easy' said Jones 'the knife was in him before the match went out, he never made a sound'

'Put him in the bushes, we haven't much time'.

Jones dragged the body into the bushes and then he and Smythe walked quickly down the path that Mollayan had passed along a few minutes earlier.

Sergeant Yuri Blokhin had been with Genady Zukovski since the relief of Stalingrad. Together they had fought their way across the Motherland right to the doors of Berlin where together they had played their part in the final victory. He was honored to be trusted by his leader for such a task, Genady himself had spoken to his men and stressed the importance of taking the two men alive.

Blokhin and his men moved into the square at the front of the church, they'd walked across the park unchallenged and had started to sing their songs and push each other about as they reached the front of the church. The church was in darkness and there was no one at either the front or the side. Genady told him to expect two men at close quarters to each other, the square was empty, save for a man and woman walking away to the far side of the square. Blokhin's men began to look around the perimeter and Blokhin himself went right up to the entrance of the church, he pushed on the door, it was locked and as he walked back down the steps, he realised that something wasn't right, the square was too quiet

Suddenly, there was a roar of engines as four jeeps converged on the church, soldiers jumped out and surrounded Blokhin and his men, one of them made a move for his concealed weapon and was shot in the leg. The Russians, surrounded, raised their hands and began to shout

'Nyet, Nyet' Don't shoot!!

Captain John Clark stood in front of them and in perfect Russian asked

'Who's in charge?'

Blokhin stepped forward and began to recite the story that he'd agreed with Zukovski, when he finished speaking, Clark spoke

'That's a funny story considering none of your men are drunk!

With that he turned on his heel and snapped out an order

'Take them away, we'll see what a few hours in the Guardhouse do for their memories'

Clark posted three men at the church and took another two men with him and headed towards the entrance to the park.

Chapter 35

Hemingdale had finished his work on the design on the ground and was back sitting on the bench. He was oblivious to the movement of the young boy who had now been joined by six or seven other boys who were spread out behind the bushes where he had been working. Yacov made a sound like an owl to signal that he was in place, he didn't know what was going on but he'd trusted his instincts with the new boy so far and he hadn't been let down, he listened to what he had heard and decided to take a look for himself. The eight of them were spread out and watched in morbid fascination as the older man finished what he was doing ....

He'd drawn a circle and what looked like a crude Star of David, the type all of the boys had worn at one time or other during the war. They continued to watch as the man deliberately didn't finish the sign, the design at no time touched the perimeter of the circle. He then placed a piece of stone and a piece of brick outside the circle, beside them he set a loaf of bread, some wine and then produced a piece of red cloth and placed a gold ring of some sort down on the cloth and began to chant

'Our brother has wrought in the difficult and dangerous work of the ancient ruins, he has penetrated into the bowels and betrayed the secrets of the temple' He must be cast out and dishonoured for his betrayal of Yahweh'

Yacov made the sound again to make sure everybody stayed where they were when the man left the site. Yacov watched as he went back down to the bench and cut himself on the arm, he allowed his blood to stain a part of his shirt, he then rolled up one of his trouser legs, Yacov noticed that he wasn't wearing anything on his left foot.

Yacov turned to see a lone figure coming towards the bench, he slowed down to a near standstill as the man on the park bench stood up and called

'You have chosen to defile the Great Architect, you must be cast from the temple and defiled for you deeds'

Hemingdale watched as Jones rushed up and overpowered Mollayan, he searched him and removed a pistol from a holster that was strapped to his chest. He frog marched Mollayan towards Hemmindale who was holding a gun on him. Jones then retreated back the way he came and was passed by Smythe who was carrying a red coloured package.

Hemingdale jammed the gun into Mollayan's ribs and motioned him towards the bushes

'This is indeed a bonus' said Smythe 'You know what you have done and what I must do' said Mollayan 'Tell us what we want to know and I will give you a quick death'

'You will never succeed' said Mollayan 'I will cheat you even in death'

Smythe came up behind him and cracked him on the head with the butt of his pistol. Jones put the barrel of his pistol to the back of Mollayan's head and was about to shoot when Smythe spoke

'Don't kill him, he will not speak and I want him to feel the penalty of his betrayal'.

They worked quickly together, first of all they stripped Mollayan of his clothes and laid him crucifix style in the centre of the pentangle. Smythe unwrapped the red cloth and placed the three scalpels and the serrated knife between the stone and the brick. Mollayan was unconscious. Smythe took off his jacket and put on a long white robe and he and Hemmindale began to walk around the circle. Hemmindale broke the bread and Smythe opened the wine and threw it in

Mollayan's face. They then lifted a scalpel and both men went to the top of the circle...

Suddenly there was an almighty roar of anguish and pain, Yacov whose eyes had been riveted on the scene in front of him, glanced across to see the new boy crash through the bushes and jump at one of the men, clawing at his eyes. The man put his arm up to fend the boy off and dropped the scalpel. Yacov heard the boy screaming

'Der Weiss Angel!! Der Weiss Angel'

On hearing this two of the other boys had clambered through the bushes and were tearing at the other old man who had fallen to the ground, one of them had lifted the scalpel and was slashing wildly at his face, there were spurts of blood splashing onto the ground. The first man was also on the ground and Yacov himself jumped down to help his new friend, by the time he reached him, it was obvious that the new boy had killed the man he'd attacked, Yacov looked down to find him lying on his back, the boy had tore at his eyes and ripped open his throat with his teeth. He was sitting back from the man on the ground with his hand held tightly across his chest and Yacov could see blood seeping through. .

The rest of the boys were now searching through the clothes of the dead men when Eva shouted that there were soldiers coming.

Jones had headed back the way he came when he spotted the soldiers walking in a search formation, they spotted him and called on him to stop, he ignored them and turned back towards where he had left Smythe and Hemmindale.

Yacov watched as the boy inched across and began to untie Mollayan

'Samuel? Is that you Samuel?' said Mollayan

Yacov rushed over

'You know him?'

Mollayan turned towards Yacov and gasped

'His name is Samuel' Mollayan winced in pain and struggled to catch his breath. Yacov knelt down beside him and listened. Mollayan murmured 'he was in Auschwitz and was tortured by the '*Weiss Angel*'

'Who?' asked Yacov

'Josef Mengele.' '*Der Weiss Angel*'

'That is correct' said two of the other boys 'we were there as well'

Samuel was now tugging at the ropes tying Mollayan's legs, Yacov had helped Mollayan to sit up and he could also see that Samuel was badly wounded. He reached across to get Mollayan his trousers when he heard a gun being cocked, he pushed Samuel out of the way as Jones burst through the hedge firing...

Clark heard the shots and rushed to the source, he ran up the bank and at first was not able to take in the sight before him.

To the left there was a body, he walked over and removed the gun from his hand and took the serrated blade from between his shoulder blades. He saw the other two bodies on the ground, he heard a death rattle coming from one of the men lying on the ground.

He sent one of his men over to check on the other body whilst he went to check on the partly clothed man and the boy.

Mollayan was conscious and was aware of Samuel lying across him

'Samuel, can you hear me? Samuel?

Samuel stirred and lifted his head, there were tears streaming down his face and his breathing was laboured, blood was now flowing freely from the wound in his chest and he was losing consciousness fast. Mollayan reached down and gripped his hand.

He heard Clark's voice but it seemed to be coming from afar and was getting weaker and weaker.

He felt Samuel clasp and then relax his grip on his hand

Mollayan closed his eyes, when he opened them he could see Samuel walking in front of him, beckoning him to come on, Mollayan looked again and moved forward, he could have sworn he was surrounded by a pale blue light ...

For now, the Yahweh is safe.

Epilogue

Captain John Clark made the necessary arrangements and cleared up the site. The men who were with him were visited by other men in the days following the event and convinced that they'd be better to forget what they had witnessed.

Hemmindale's body was removed in his office and discovered the next morning as a suicide, a note saying that he could not stand the suffering that he had witnessed in his trials. General Smythe was posted as missing in action, presumed dead and later awarded the George Cross posthumously. Denver Jones body's was unrecognisable after the remainder of Yacov's gang had finished with it, two of Clark's detail buried him in a grave not far from the site. Clark ordered that the whole site be cleared.

The Russian soldiers were held for three days and then exchanged at Checkpoint Charlie for the man and woman that Clark had lost. Clark and Zukovski met for the second time, they would meet again.

Alfred Rosenberg was hanged in Nuremberg prison. Albert Speer was imprisoned for twenty years. Hermann Goring poisoned himself before his date with the hangman.

Giovanni Batista Santini continues to serve Rome, his life will change irrevocably in the future.

Licio Gelli made it to Buenos Aires where he came to the notice of a young priest from Rome. The paths of Philip Rossi and Gelli will cross again.

Adolf Eichmann and Josef Mengele escaped to South America where they hark for the return of the Reich.

Andrew Lassiter continued to train with Simeon in preparation for the task ahead, he would be called sooner that he thought.

Maria Tannebaum is recuperating in a kibbutz in Eretz, Israel and is being looked after by another survivor called Golda Meir.

Henry Mollayan and Samuel were buried side by side near the tomb of the Unknown Soldier in the British sector in the Tiergarten.

Adam Carter went back to his wife and family in Boston and is protected by the Priory.

He will not have long to wait until he is again required to make sure that 'they do not succeed'.